Power of Four
Book One

Run To Earth

SF MAZHAR

Dedicated to my family

Copyright © 2014 SF Mazhar

All rights reserved.

No part of this publication may be reproduced, distributed, or transmitted in any form or by any means, including photocopying, recording, or other electronic or mechanical methods, without the prior written permission of the author.

ISBN-10:149529000X
ISBN-13:9781495290008

Run To Earth - to hunt or chase something to its lair and trap it there.

- English Collins Dictionary

ACKNOWLEDGMENTS

It is true what they say; that a book is never just the hard work of the author. There are so many people I must thank. First and foremost, I would like to say thank you to my family. To my mum, for her endless hours of babysitting. To my dad, for his words of encouragement. To my wonderful husband, for his love and support. To my sisters, for lending me their ears when I had to ramble on and on for hours about plot points and character arcs. And a big thank you to my M&Ms, for putting up with a mummy that was so often distracted on her laptop. A special thank you to Komil and her team at Shine for getting me the cover of my dreams. A big thank you to Ally and Melissa from The Book Specialist, who edited Run To Earth.

1

BIRTHDAY SURPRISES

The heat was stifling, the darkness unforgiving. Still he ran, blindly following the sound of footsteps in front of him. His lungs seared with pain, begging for a respite he couldn't give. Drops of sweat trickled down his back. Some fell from his brow into his eyes but he blinked them away, concentrating only on running – terrified a moment's slip might cost him his guide. The footsteps ahead of him slowed. That's when he saw the faint glow of a red spot illuminated against the black canvas of his surroundings. The mark grew, getting bigger and brighter until its light burst all around him. He came to a stop, gasping and grunting, doubled over with sweaty hands on trembling knees. Looking up, he found an underground cave and his path ahead blocked by a sea of lava.

"This is it."

He turned to the source of the voice, meeting the blazing green eyes of the boy standing before him. The boy was just as out of breath, but he looked far more composed, even with the cut on his forehead trickling blood down the side of his face.

The boy motioned to the fiery lava before them. "Do it."

His heart clenched painfully. "I-I can't," he said.

"Come on," the boy urged. "You have to hurry."

"I don't know *how!*" he cried in panic.

"Aaron." The boy stepped closer. "Focus. You can do this. I know you can."

Aaron shook his head, then dropped it in exhausted defeat. "I can't."

"Aaron?" the boy called again. "Aaron? Aaron?" The voice was changing, becoming higher. "Aaron? Are you up? Aaron?"

Aaron opened his eyes to the familiar sight of his bedroom ceiling. He lay still, blinking as sleep ebbed away from his soft green eyes. Pushing himself up, Aaron rubbed a hand over his face before raking it through his dark hair. Squinting against the morning light, he looked to the door. It was still closed. While his mum kept her word and didn't come in without permission, it didn't mean her presence went unnoticed.

"Aaron!" she snapped from behind the door.

"Yeah," he mumbled. "I'm up, I'm up."

"Your breakfast's getting cold," she said.

Aaron groaned and fell back. He lay still, dwelling on the strange dream. It was the fourth time this week he'd had the same dream. Each time he got a little further, saw a few more seconds, but it still didn't make any sense. It was always the same sequence of events: first the running, then the cave and then the lava. And today his reluctance to do...whatever it was the other boy wanted.

Aaron rubbed at his head, eyes closed as the mental picture of the boy came to him: tall, dark haired, with the most vivid green eyes he had ever seen. The boy he had never met, yet dreamt about several times a week for almost two months now.

At first the dreams had been different – disjointed, random moments with Aaron doing nothing more than just talking with the older, green-eyed stranger. In the dreams though, Aaron seemed to know him. There was a familiarity so strong it left him bewildered at awakening.

"Aaron! Don't make me come in there," his mum called. His door rattled in warning, and creaked open a crack.

"Alright, I'm up," Aaron groaned.

He forced all thoughts about the boy, and his recurring dream, to the back of his mind and climbed out of bed.

***

Aaron had his teeth brushed, face washed and clothes changed all in under ten minutes. Combing his hair with his fingers, Aaron was turning to go downstairs when he heard a familiar sound outside: feet crunching on gravel, and a deep thrum of several voices. He hurried to the window and swung it open. Leaning over, Aaron grinned at the familiar sight. A crowd of kids, backpacks swung across their shoulders, trudged their way to school. He spotted his friends in their midst.

"Alright, Sammy? Rose?" he called.

On the path below, the Mason twins stopped in their tracks and tilted their heads up to meet Aaron's gaze.

"Morning," Sam replied, his brown eyes narrowed against the sharp glare of the sun.

"Your classes not started yet?" Rose asked. She lifted up a hand to check her watch. "It's almost half eight."

"Running late today," Aaron replied.

"Didn't think you'd get late starts," Sam said.

"Home-schooling has its perks," Aaron returned, but his forced smile didn't fool anyone.

"We're all going to the Blaze after school," Rose said. "Think you can manage to come for an hour or two?"

"Going trick or treating?" Aaron asked.

"No time for tricks. It'll be only treats." Rose grinned. "You in?"

Aaron looked behind his shoulder at the door, hiding the look of despair from his friends. He knew he wouldn't be allowed to go. When he turned round, though, he nodded with a tight smile. "I'll try."

"Hey," Rose called, just as Aaron began ducking back inside. "What's the score for tomorrow?"

Aaron paused before shaking his head. "The usual."

"Aww, again?" Rose frowned. "You said your parents promised a party when you turn fourteen."

"No, I said I was going to *ask* for a party," Aaron corrected.

"And did you?" Sam asked.

"Sort of. I got halfway through my speech and saw the vein about to pop in Mum's forehead." Aaron shrugged at the looks of sympathy. "I weighed my options and decided not to push it."

"That sucks." Rose pouted. "I was looking forward to it."

"Sorry," Aaron said. "I'd better go. Mum's waiting."

He waved goodbye, pulled himself inside and closed the window. As he latched it shut, his hand lingered on the clasp. Aaron wondered, not for the first time, why he couldn't be like everyone else and go to school.

***

"You're not concentrating. Pay attention."

Aaron nodded, but the pencil in his hand continued to tap lightly against the open book. Aaron glanced at his mum. At this time of the day she was his tutor, but even her annoyed expression didn't stop his rhythmic beat. After a few more minutes, she'd had enough.

"Alright." She reached across and closed the book, ceasing the tapping at once. "What's up?"

Aaron shrugged. "Nothing."

She tilted her head to the side, sleek blond hair brushing against her shoulder. "Aaron?"

He looked up at her. He knew talking to her was useless – she would give him the same answer she always did – but she was staring intently at him, waiting for a response. So, taking in a breath, Aaron went for it.

"I want to go to school."

As he'd expected, his mum's expression hardened. She closed her eyes and slowly shook her head. "How many times do we have to discuss this?" she asked.

Discuss? We never discuss. You talk, I listen. Aaron was close to saying it out loud, but decided against it.

His mum got up and walked over to the other side of the living room. She reached the side table and poured herself a cup of tea, the silver teaspoon clinking against the china as she stirred lazily. Aaron watched her, wondering how a women as petite and delicate-looking as his mum still managed to terrify him with nothing more than a sharp look.

"I thought you understood by now that you don't need a school," she said. "I'm more than capable of teaching you everything you need to know. Under my instructions, you're completing work far past the level you would be at school."

"It's not that," Aaron mumbled. "School's more than just classes and lessons."

Her blue eyes narrowed and her mouth thinned to a sharp line. "Hmm, yes." She clinked the teaspoon for the last time and placed it on the saucer. "You want to run around with hooligans, spreading graffiti on walls and raiding cars, is that it?" She lifted the cup and took a sip.

Under the table, Aaron's hands curled into fists. "Not everyone's a hooligan," he argued.

"Is that right?" she asked, an elegant eyebrow raised in mockery. "Have you watched the news lately? It seems the youth of today know less about civil conduct and more about breaking heads and looting." She took another sip. "Perhaps you should listen to the stories your dad brings to the dinner table."

"Just 'cause Dad's in the police doesn't mean he knows everything."

"I beg to differ, Aaron." Her voice cooled. "Your dad knows what's best. You should always remember that."

Aaron's gaze dropped to the table. "I just...I wanna hang out with my friends."

"I don't want you mixing with the wrong kind of company," she said, coming to sit at the table again and setting her cup in front of her. "You're a good boy. I want it to stay that way."

Aaron fell quiet, knowing there was no point in arguing. To his parents, it didn't matter if his friends weren't thugs. It didn't matter if Sam and Rose were neighbours and all they were going to do was hang out. Nothing he wanted mattered.

His mum ran a hand over his hair, ruffling it. She smiled warmly before gesturing to his work. With an inward sigh, Aaron opened his book and picked up his pencil again, reading the question she had printed across the top.

A parent organism of unknown genotype is mated in a test cross. Half of the offspring have the same phenotype as the parent. What can be concluded from this result?

Aaron started his answer, his pencil scratching at the paper.

The parent is heterozygous for the trait...

His fingers tapped the table as he wrote, thrumming loudly against the wooden surface. He allowed the hint of a smile to curve his lips at his mum's annoyed sigh.

***

"I'm telling you, she's in a right mood," Aaron said, speaking into the phone held between his ear and shoulder. Going down the steps into his garden, he carried two bags of rubbish to the bins. "Well, I can't ask her now. 'Cause she'd bite my head off, that's why." Aaron let out a frustrated sigh as he awkwardly flipped the bin lid open and dropped one of the bags inside. "Sam, you know what she's like," he said, finally taking the phone in hand and straightening up to relieve the cramp in his neck. "She won't let me. I don't know, maybe she's scared a five year old dressed as a fairy will attack me or something." He dropped the other bag into the bin but stayed where he was. "I wish I could; it sounds like fun." He rolled his eyes at Sam's offered advice. "Yeah, right! Sneaking out under my mum's ever-watchful gaze? I'd have to be freaking Superman!"

"Superman? Really?" a voice asked from behind him.

Aaron turned to find Rebecca Wanton, his fourteen-year-old next-door neighbour, smiling at him from her garden. She began walking over.

"Uh, Sammy? Call you later, yeah?" Aaron pulled the phone away and quickly pocketed it. "Rebecca, hi." Aaron mentally cursed. It had come out loud and way too excited. He wanted to play it cool and calm, but whenever he saw Rebecca Wanton his brain refused to fully function. It had something to do with her twinkling blue eyes and the way her blond hair framed her face.

"Hi, Aaron." Rebecca smiled, coming to stop at the fence that separated their gardens. "You're dressing up as Superman?"

"No, no...I..." Aaron cleared his throat to get rid of the unusually high pitch. "I just...I was talking to Sam...He wanted to meet at the Blaze."

Rebecca's eyes lit up with delight. "Yeah? You coming this year?"

Aaron shook his head. "No, I'm...I'm busy." He gestured to the house behind him. "Family stuff."

Rebecca looked disappointed. "Oh, right."

Aaron nodded in awkward silence. "I...uh...I love your costume," he said. His eyes lingered on the form-fitting black cat outfit, unashamedly showcasing every curve of her lithe body. Pink-faced, he snapped his gaze back up to her face.

"Thanks." She smiled. "I...I better go." She gave Aaron a last warm smile. "I'll...I'll see you around, yeah?"

"Yeah," Aaron muttered, watching her walk to the gate and slip through it. "Hopefully," he added.

He turned and dejectedly walked back to the house. The back door was slightly ajar, and he was about to push it right open when he caught sight of his uncle sitting at the kitchen table with his dad. Both men were already in uniform, owing to their night shift starting after dinner. Their black and white police ensemble showcased the height of their physical fitness. His dad, Christopher Adams, was taller and broader than Aaron's uncle, Michael Williams, but both radiated an aura of power.

Aaron had inherited his father's dark hair and green eyes, but his physique was nowhere like his dad's yet, something Aaron wanted rectified desperately. Just looking at his dad made him straighten up and stand tall with his chest pushed out. Strong and proud, just like his dad.

Seeing his uncle, a smile spread across Aaron's face. With Michael here, Aaron had a fighting chance to go to the Blaze, even if it was only for an hour. Aaron was about to push open the door and step in when he heard his name mentioned.

"...turning fourteen tomorrow," Michael was saying rather solemnly. "Have you thought about talking to him?"

"You know I want to, Mike, but Kate doesn't agree," Chris replied.

Aaron moved, standing against the wall as he listened in to the conversation.

"You're being unreasonable, Kate," Michael warned. "It's not like you can hide this from him forever."

"I don't need your advice." His mum's strict tone cut through the air. "I'm doing what's best for my son."

"By keeping him in the dark?" Michael asked.

Something clanged loudly, as if his mum had slammed something into a steel pot.

"It's been a year!" Kate hissed furiously. "And nothing! He's done *nothing*, not even in the *slightest*."

Aaron pulled a face. How could his mum say that? He had done plenty in the last year. His studies were non-stop. In the last three months alone he had completed seven projects.

"Do you know why?" she continued. "Because we've been keeping him away. Aaron's not reacted because he's not been near anything that might provoke him."

"You can't do that forever," Michael argued. "He is what he is. He *will* react – you can't prevent it." There was a pause before he continued in a quieter voice. "It's not right, Kate. You can't keep him locked up. He didn't ask for this."

"No one asked for this," she replied. Her voice was quiet, but Aaron could hear the underlying anger.

"Aaron's a good boy," Michael said. "He listens to you, does what you ask, but even good boys rebel if you push them too far. The harder you suppress him, the further he'll jump to free himself."

A long, strained pause filled the room, then Aaron heard the metallic clang that proved his mum was mixing something vigorously in a pot.

"I disagree. The longer I can hold him back, the better," she said in a tight and cold voice that suggested the end of discussion. "I can't change who we are, not forever, but I'll take as long as I can."

"Kate—" Chris started.

"No," she cut him off and Aaron could hear the growl in her voice. "Don't. Don't you *dare* tell me it'll be alright. You know damn well it won't!"

They quietened after that. The only sound Aaron could hear was the faint bubbling of whatever it was his mum was cooking, and his own thudding heartbeat.

***

Aaron jolted awake, blinking in the darkness. It took him a moment to realise he was in his bed, drenched in sweat. Had he been dreaming? Possibly. But the dream was escaping his memory, like water from a cupped hand. No matter how hard he tried to grasp it, the dream faded until nothing was left, nothing but a faint suspicion that he had been dreaming about the boy with the vivid green eyes again.

That in itself was no longer unusual, but when Aaron awoke tonight, he knew with sickening certainty that something was different. Something was *wrong*. He felt strange, jittery, with a racing heart but his body was heavy and sore. Every part of him was tender and burning, like he had a fever. His fingertips felt weird, tingly, like they were suffering from pins and needles. He clenched both hands into fists and then opened them again, repeating the action, pumping blood back to his hands. He was always getting pins and needles in his fingers, especially over the last year.

Slowly the ache died away, leaving him feeling tired and weak but no longer sore. He turned to his side, trying to get comfortable, but as tired as he was he found he couldn't sleep. He glanced at the bedside clock and saw the red glare read, *12:15*.

He smiled to himself. It was past midnight. The first of November. He was fourteen. Maybe now he would be treated differently – less as a child and more as a young adult. He scoffed at his own thoughts. His mum would probably still treat him like a child whether he was fourteen or forty. Isn't that what she said? That she would hold him back as long as she could? The strange conversation he had eavesdropped on spun in his mind, failing to make any better sense to him now than it did when he'd heard it. He closed his eyes, breathing out a long slow sigh.

Clink.

Aaron opened his eyes.

Clink.

He sat up in bed and reached over to switch on the light. Squinting in the harsh brightness until his eyes adjusted, he scanned the room but didn't find anything suspicious.

Clink.

He got out of bed. Padding across the room to the window, he looked out to see Rose and Sam throwing pebbles at his window. The glow of the street lamp illuminated their grinning faces. Aaron unlatched the window and pushed it open. Leaning over the sill, he grinned at them, ignoring the night chill that washed over him.

"What are you guys doing?" he asked, careful not to speak too loudly in case it woke up his mum in the next room.

"Getting your lazy ass out of bed," Sam answered with a grin.

"Don't just hang there," Rose scolded, "get down here."

"We're taking you out, celebrating in style," Sam said. "Hurry up, birthday boy."

Aaron grinned. He held up two fingers, gesturing he needed two minutes to get ready. He pulled back and closed the window.

***

Two and a half minutes later, Aaron crept past his parents' room. His dad might have been on a night shift but he was careful not to wake his mum. Aaron sneaked downstairs, across the hall and into the kitchen. Quietly, he pulled the back door open and slipped out. He hurried down the path, grinning at the twins waiting for him.

"You sleep like the freaking dead!" Sam admonished. "We threw enough pebbles to build a mountain."

"Here's a little tip," Rose said. "Charge that thing you pretend is a phone so when we call, you can answer it."

Aaron grinned and ran a hand through his dishevelled hair. "Sorry. How was I supposed to know I'd be getting midnight surprises?"

"You *should* know," Rose replied. "If your parents aren't going to give you a party, then we will."

"A party?" Aaron asked with wide eyes. "At this hour?"

"This is the hour for parties." Sam grinned.

Aaron looked from one twin to the other, his eyebrows raised. "What place is going to be open now that'll let me in?"

"The same place that'll let two sixteen year olds in," Sam replied.

"It's only the Blaze," Rose said. "Halloween party may be over, but the place is still open till three in the morning."

"Which means we've not got all night," Sam said. "Come on." He started walking down the street.

Aaron and Rose walked alongside him. Rose had her long brown hair bunched up on either side of her head. Her soft brown eyes were still marked with remnants of gold glitter.

"Let me guess," Aaron said, looking Rose up and down. "You dressed up as a gold digger again?"

"It's a killer outfit," Rose said. "Makes sense to reuse it."

Aaron turned to Sam. "Did you go as Facebook again?" he asked.

"Please," Rose said, scowling. "Wearing your normal clothes and sticking a book under your arm with the word *FACE* on it doesn't make you Facebook."

Sam gave her a sideways look but didn't argue. "This year it was Twitter," he told Aaron.

"How could you go as..." Aaron paused. "Never mind. I don't wanna know." They walked a few steps before Aaron asked, "So you've had this party planned?"

"We've lived on the same street as you for, like, forever," Rose said. "We had a feeling you'd be having your usual family-only-celebration." She shrugged. "We figured we'd give you a proper party." Then with a sly grin, she added, "And if you look *really* hard, you might see other faces you know."

"Who?" Aaron asked at once.

"You'll see," Sam said. "We might have invited a few extras at the last minute."

"Like?" Aaron asked.

"Like...Becky, for example." Sam grinned

Aaron almost tripped. "You didn't. You...you invited Rebecca?"

"Yep." Rose chuckled. "And you'd better not waste this opportunity."

"What?" Aaron exclaimed. "What does *that* mean?"

"It means you ask her out, idiot," Rose explained.

Aaron threw her a furious look. "Yeah, sure, I'll ask her out. Where will I take her? Oh, that's right, the only place my parents will allow me to go: *my house,* which happens to be right next to hers."

"Nothing wrong with taking a girl to your room, bro." Sam winked.

"Nice." Rose glared and poked her brother in the ribs. She turned back to Aaron, ignoring the sputtering of her twin. "Talk to your mum and dad. I'm sure they'd be okay with you taking Rebecca out."

"Did all that glitter get to your head?" Aaron asked. "You *know* what my parents are like."

"They're not that bad," Rose countered. "You just blow things out of proportion."

"Rose, they *are* that bad; you just don't believe me," said Aaron.

"Come on, mate," Sam said. "I'm sure they would be okay with you taking Becky out. I mean, you're neighbours. They know her."

"You're also my neighbour," Aaron argued. "They know you too, but they don't want me hanging out with you either."

Sam fell quiet, his smile evaporating. His gaze dropped to the ground as they walked in awkward silence.

"What's their problem?" Sam asked, betraying his honest confusion. "Why don't they want you hanging around with me?"

Aaron shrugged, not having an answer.

"I don't think it's us," Rose said. "Your parents are just paranoid. And given your time at Westbridge, you can understand why."

Aaron groaned. "One incident!" He held up a finger to accentuate the point. "*One* small, tiny incident of bullying and they pull me out of school. How does that make sense?"

"It may have been one incident," Rose argued, "but Matthews had it in for you ever since you joined our class."

"That's 'cause Matthews is a prat," Sam added. "He just couldn't take it that you'd been bumped up to his class."

"He wasn't the only one," Aaron grouched. "The majority of Year Three had a problem with me."

"Come on, Aaron," Rose said. "You were the seven year old that got pulled up two classes because he was too smart. You were showing up a bunch of nine year olds in their own classroom. Of course they were going to have a problem with you."

"You say it like it was my fault," Aaron accused.

"It wasn't your fault," Rose agreed, "but nine year olds don't see it that way."

"Plus, you were the smallest in class." Sam said. "It automatically sets off the teasing reaction inbuilt in us humans."

"So how come you both didn't join in?" Aaron asked, this time with a smile. "You guys were in the same class. How come you two became my friends?"

Rose and Sam shared a look, wearing identical grins.

"'Cause we're awesome," Sam answered.

"And you always brought the nicest treats for lunch–"

A screech of tyres interrupted Rose. The smell of burning rubber was the first thing to register to Aaron, before he even saw what was happening. There was a thunderous crash of metal hitting rock, the deafening roar of an engine, then two bright lights blinded all three of them.

A car suddenly came belting towards him and the twins. The driver must have lost control; as the car was half on the pavement and half on the road, swerving this way and that, with Aaron and the twins in its path. There was no time to move out of the way. Instinctively, Aaron threw up both hands to shield his face – a simple act, no matter how ineffective.

What happened next, Aaron could never have anticipated. The ground under their feet trembled, then shook as if in the grips of an earthquake. All three of them fell to the ground, shrieking in panic. The car was coming towards them but before it could run them over, it stopped and tilted forward – the back lifting clear off the ground. For an awful moment, the car was completely vertical, looming threateningly over them. It seemed inevitable that it would fall on top of them, crushing them to death, but instead the bonnet of the car sunk into the ground. An enormous crash shattered the windscreen. Shards of glass flew in every direction, raining down on the terrified teenagers. The car continued to fall deeper into the ground until only half of it was visible.

Aaron's gaze went from the car to the ground and he stared in utter disbelief. The ground had cracked open – *literally* open. A tear zigzagged from the pavement to the middle of the road, splitting the tarmac wide enough to swallow the front half of the car.

Aaron and the twins shakily got to their feet, staring at the sight of the absurd-looking car sticking out of the ground, wedged between the two sides of the road.

Sam staggered forward, approaching the car. "Hello?" he called, his voice trembling. "Are...are you alright?" he asked the unseen driver.

Aaron's legs threatened to buckle under him but he pushed himself forward. He looked into the car, trying to spot the driver, but all he could make out were the back seats of the Honda Civic.

"Oh God," he whispered. "He must be dead."

Sam reached into his pocket, fumbling with his phone. His hands were trembling as he called the emergency services. "I-I need an ambulance," he said. "There's been a-a car accident. Scottvale Street..."

"The...the ground?" Rose whispered, staring in shock. "How is this possible?"

"I don't know," Aaron replied, feeling his stomach clench and his fingers tingle.

"It doesn't make sense." Rose was shaking her head. "How–?"

"AARON!"

The piercing scream made Aaron jump. He looked over and immediately saw who was crying out his name with such terror.

"Mum?" he gasped in surprise.

Kate was running barefoot down the road, still dressed in her nightclothes. She jumped over the gap in the road like it was nothing, and threw her arms around Aaron.

"Oh thank God! Thank God!" she cried. She pulled away, her hands coming to rest on either side of his face. "Are you okay?"

"Yeah, I-I'm fine," Aaron stuttered. "How did you know I was here?"

She didn't answer. She turned to stare at the car, as if noticing it for the first time.

"Oh my God," she whispered. "Oh, Aaron."

Aaron's stomach lurched horribly. It almost sounded as if she was *blaming* him. "Mum?"

Kate grabbed hold of him, her hands shaking badly. "We have to leave," she said, still staring at the car. "Come on."

"Leave?" Aaron asked. "But the ambulance–"

"We don't have time! We have to go – now!" Kate yelled.

She pulled him away from the car and down the street. Aaron tried to protest, but was taken aback at how strong she was. She was dragging him with next to no problem.

"Mum, wait, wait. Sam—" Aaron pulled back, turning to look at the twins.

That's when Kate saw them, standing awkwardly to the side of the road. Her eyes grew impossibly wide, her mouth twisting in anger.

"No!" she roared. "No! No! No!"

Aaron pulled back, a crippling fear rising inside him. He tried to let go of her hand but her grip only tightened. She whirled around to face him. "What were you doing with them?" she spat furiously. "I *told* you not to be around them!"

Aaron couldn't find his voice to answer. Sheer terror stole his ability to speak.

"Mrs Adams, it wasn't Aaron's fault." Rose hesitantly stepped forward. "*We* came to *him*. We—"

Kate held up a hand to silence her. Her gaze went past Rose, upwards into the sky. For a moment, she stood completely still, her mouth open.

A strange chill spread through Aaron. His heart started beating faster. His stomach clenched painfully and that strange tingle pricked at his fingertips again. He turned, following his mum's stare and saw it. High up in the night sky, a strange white mist was gathering, like a wispy white cloud. It started to grow, doubling in size with every passing second, glittering against the night sky.

A heartbeat later, it was moving, coming straight at them.

2

Fleeing

The bruising grip on Aaron's arm pulled him violently forward as his mum broke into a run.

"Come on!" she screamed at Sam and Rose.

They didn't need telling twice. They ran after Kate and Aaron as fast as they could. The eerie white mist raced after them, gaining speed, closing the distance at an alarming rate. Kate raced back to their street but passed her house, heading further down the road.

"Mum, where...where are we going?" Aaron puffed, running so fast he could barely breathe.

His mum didn't answer but kept on running, never letting go of his hand. A car swerved around the corner, heading straight at the mother and son. It stopped with a screech and the door was flung open.

"Kate! Aaron!" Chris cried, running out of his patrol car.

"Dad?" Aaron had never been so relieved to see his father but at the same time he was more confused than ever at his sudden appearance. He was supposed to be at work, doing a night shift. What was he doing back home?

Chris wrapped strong arms around his wife and son. It was only for a moment, though, before he pushed both Kate and Aaron behind him, facing the approaching mist that was thundering down the road straight at him.

"Get in the car. Get out of here. Now!" he instructed.

Kate pulled Aaron, opened the back door of the car and pushed him in. "Samuel, Rosalyn, get in." She turned and it was then she realised that the twins weren't there. "Samuel? Rosalyn?" she cried, searching the dark street. She spotted them, running in the direction of their home. They had reached the gate and were struggling to open it.

"No!" Chris bellowed, catching sight of them too. "Samuel! Rosalyn! Don't go in there!" He shot after them.

"Dad!" Aaron made to get out of the car but his mum stopped him.

"Stay inside," she ordered, slamming the door shut and standing in front of it.

Sam and Rose pushed past the gate and raced towards their home. The mist twisted around and changed direction, pouring into the Masons' front garden, encircling the small house until it was barely visible through the thick, pulsing white fog. The windows smashed and the front door was ripped off its hinges.

Sam and Rose came to a standstill, frozen in terror. Figures materialised out of the mist, strange shapes that solidified into a group of dark-clothed men. They stared straight at Sam and Rose, a strange hunger growing in their expressions. Someone grabbed the twins and pulled them back, with such force that they fell onto the street. Looking up, they found it was Christopher Adams.

"Get in the car – now!" Chris instructed.

Sam and Rose clambered to their feet and ran. Chris turned to face the men, his eyes dark with rage as he met the glares of the twenty men standing before him. One of them, dark-haired with glittering blue eyes, stepped forward with a smirk. He gave a small nod and the swarm of men descended onto Chris.

Sam and Rose reached the police car and Kate quickly opened the door to let them in. Rose got in but Sam faltered. He turned to look back at their house, surrounded by the white fog.

"What's going on?" he asked, breathing heavily. "Who are those-"

"Get in quickly!" Kate pushed him into the car and shut the door. She ran to the driver's side, got in and turned the key in the ignition. The engine roared to life.

"Wait," Sam said. "Wait for my mum and dad."

Kate ignored him. Twisting the driving wheel, she turned the car around.

"Hey!" Sam slammed a hand against the steel mesh separating them from the front seats. "My parents are in there!" he yelled. "We can't leave without them!"

"I'm sorry," Kate replied, her voice thick with tears. "We can't stay. We have to go."

"What?" Sam cried. "No!" He turned and tried opening the door but, being a police car, it could only open from the outside. He slammed a hand against the window. "No! Mum! Dad! No!"

Rose was crying hard. "Please, Mrs Adams," she sobbed. "Get them out.

We can't leave without them. Please!"

Kate didn't say a word. She raced the car down the street.

"Mum, what about Dad?" Aaron asked, his blood running cold at the realisation that they were leaving him also behind. "Mum, no! Stop!"

But Kate didn't stop. She drove past their house, fingers tight-knuckled around the wheel and her gaze stubbornly fixed to the road. Another police car came speeding down the street, almost hitting into them. It swerved and parked haphazardly in the middle of the road. Michael jumped out if it. His eyes met Kate's just for a moment before he raced onto the pavement.

Kate pressed down on the accelerator, speeding away. Aaron turned to the back window to see his uncle Mike run full speed towards the Masons' house. He caught a glimpse of something silver flash in his uncle's hand before the car turned the corner, then the Masons' house, the group attacking his dad, and his uncle disappeared from sight.

***

"Stop the car!" Sam smashed his hand against the mesh. "Stop!"

Kate kept driving.

"Let us out!" Sam screamed in rage, slamming his hand repeatedly against the metal criss-crossing of the back-seat barrier, but the reinforced steel didn't budge. "Let us out! Stop the car! Stop!"

"Mrs Adams, please!" Rose sobbed. "We have to go back. We have to get my mum and dad!"

"I'm sorry," Kate replied, "but we can't go back. It's not safe."

Her words only enraged Sam, making him lean back and kick at the steel mesh with his feet. But Kate continued driving, not even turning around to tell him to stop.

Aaron didn't understand what was happening. Nothing made sense; not what he saw, nor what he felt. It was like it all belonged in a horrifying nightmare. He closed his eyes tightly. Maybe he was dreaming. Maybe this *was* a nightmare. Maybe, in reality, he was still in his bed, and Sam and Rose had never come to see him. He had never crept out of his house and that freak accident had never happened. After all, the ground does *not* just split open of its own accord. Strange white clouds *don't* drop out of the skies and chase you down the street. Men *don't* materialise out of mist and start attacking your dad. It wasn't real. It couldn't be.

Aaron kept his eyes closed, hoping and praying he was dreaming. Maybe he would see that green-eyed boy again. That would prove he was dreaming. Aaron opened his eyes and stared out of the window, but all he saw were darkened houses and deserted streets whipping past him.

Kate continued driving into the dead of the night, until she pulled up outside a small white building with a sign advertising it as *The Pearl Inn, B&B*.

Kate turned off the engine and turned back in her seat to look at the three teenagers. "Wait here, and don't speak a word until we get inside," she warned before opening the door and stepping out.

"Wait! What's going on?" Sam asked, but all he got in response was the slam of the door.

Aaron and the twins watched in mounting confusion as Kate hurried to the building. Sam pulled out his phone from his pocket.

"What are you doing?" Rose asked.

"I'm calling the police!" he spat. When he held up his phone, though, he saw the smashed screen. Sam cursed. He tried pushing the buttons but the screen stayed dark. Sam threw the broken phone at the window and turned to Rose. "Give me your phone."

"I don't have it," Rose said. "Mum took it from me, remember?"

Sam cursed again, running both hands through his hair. He didn't turn to Aaron. He already knew Aaron had left his battery-drained phone at home. The sound of Kate impatiently knocking at the house's door drew their attention.

The door opened and an elderly man appeared, blinking sleep from his eyes. Aaron was not at all surprised at the man's shock as he stared at the woman on his doorstep dressed in only a nightie, barefoot and shivering. His mum was saying something but the grey-haired man shook his head. Aaron watched as his mum turned to gesture to them. The man's gaze darted to them sitting in the car before snapping back to Kate, but he resolutely shook his head. He stepped back, one hand on the door, ready to close it.

What happened next didn't make sense to Aaron, much like the rest of the night so far. His mum reached out and pressed her hand against the man's chest, halting him. Her other hand reached up to rest on his cheek, almost lovingly, with the tips of her fingers touching his temple. The man's expression changed, morphing from shocked to serene. He nodded at her and moved away, gesturing for her to come in. Kate turned, hurrying back to the car. She opened the door, at last freeing them from the back seat of the police car. Sam leapt out enraged – red faced with blazing eyes.

"What's going–!"

But Kate's fierce glare quietened him. "Inside!" she hissed.

Aaron took Rose's hand in one of his and Sam's in the other, and pulled them across the pavement, following his mum into the building and past the now smiling grey-haired man.

***

The room was small with just one bed, a single dresser pushed into the far corner, a chair perched next to the window, and a door leading to a tiny cubicle of an en suite. The first thing Kate did after locking the door was draw the curtains. Sam and Rose were told to sit down so they perched at the very edge of the bed. Aaron sat down in the chair, his gaze following his mother's irregular pacing. She was mumbling something under her breath, eyes closed, hands clutching at her stomach and sometimes at her chest.

"Mrs Adams?" Rose bravely raised her voice. "Shouldn't...shouldn't we do something? Call the police or..." She trailed off. The police were already there; Christopher Adams and Michael Williams were police officers.

Kate ignored her, keeping up her nervous pacing with her head dropped and lips mumbling quiet prayers.

"Will you tell us what's going on?" Sam asked, a lot calmer this time, but anger still underlined his words.

Kate shook her head. "Just wait," she said. "Wait until Chris and Mike come with your parents. Then we'll talk."

"How will they know where we are?" Rose asked.

"They know," she said softly. "They'll come."

Aaron didn't know how long he sat there staring at his mum. She seemed determined to wear the floor thin, walking up and down the length of the room. Suddenly she came to a standstill. Her eyes opened. She turned and darted to the door. Aaron rose to his feet, his heart twisting in his chest.

Kate's hand was on the handle before the knock even happened. She pulled the door open with great haste to see both Chris and Michael. She threw herself into her exhausted husband's arms. Chris looked over at Aaron with tired, bloodshot eyes. Aaron was staring at his dad too, taking in the sight of his injuries. A faint bruise was visible at his chin. Blood leaked from a cut on his cheek, but that seemed to be the extent of it. Aaron glanced at his uncle to see that he sported a cut just under his jawline but otherwise seemed unhurt. Chris pulled away from his wife and stepped towards Aaron, embracing him with strong arms.

"Thank God!" he breathed into Aaron's hair. "You're okay. Thank God, you're okay."

Sam and Rose got to their feet. They stared expectantly at the door, waiting for their parents to walk in and rush to embrace them in a flurry of tears. But the only one to follow behind Chris was Michael, who closed the door behind him.

"Mr Adams?" Rose spoke tentatively. "Where's...where's my mum and dad?"

Chris let go of Aaron and walked over to her and Sam, his expression one of tremendous grief. He came to a stop in front of Rose and reached out, cupping her cheek. "I'm so sorry," he whispered.

Aaron's breath caught in his chest.

"There was nothing we could do," Chris said.

Rose shook her head, brown eyes wide. Beside her, Sam stepped forward, eyes narrowed and fists clenched.

"You're lying," he accused. "You're lying!"

"Samuel—" Kate started.

"NO!" Sam bellowed. "What are you saying? That they're – they're...*dead*?" The word escaped him with difficulty. "How can they be dead? They can't die! Why would anyone hurt them?"

"No." Rose was shaking her head. Her chest heaved as panic built inside her. "No, no, NO!" she screamed.

Kate crossed the room and took the girl in her arms, whispering gently to her. Rose struggled at first, but as Kate's soothing voice reached her, she crumpled in her embrace, sobbing.

Aaron wanted to go to her. He wanted to help, to offer some gesture of support, but his feet refused to move. It was as if he had lost control over his limbs and so was forced to just stand, staring at his friends as they struggled with their grief.

"What happened?" Sam asked, the words barely making it past his clenched teeth. "Who were those...those men? Did they...? Were they the ones who...?" He couldn't finish the sentence but closed his eyes, struggling to keep control.

"Come on," Michael said quietly, stepping towards Sam. "I've booked another room. We'll go in there and talk."

"No, we'll talk *here*!" Sam was shaking now, though whether it was from anger or grief Aaron didn't know. "Will someone just...just tell me what the hell is going on!" His voice rose; tears shone in his eyes but didn't fall.

"Come on. I'll tell you everything," Michael promised, "but not here. Come on."

Sam took hold of his sobbing sister, pulling her away from Kate and led her out of the room, following after Michael. The door closed after them with a click. Aaron was left facing his parents, and felt an unbearable urge to run after his uncle.

"Sit down, Aaron," Chris instructed quietly.

Aaron lowered himself down onto the edge of the bed. Long minutes stretched out but no one spoke. Aaron waited, barely breathing. He watched as his parents shared awkward glances, communicating in that strange husband-and-wife way that didn't need actual words. Finally, Chris let out a sigh and walked over to the chair, pulling it across the room so that he could sit in front of Aaron.

"I know you have a lot of questions," he started, "but I want you to keep quiet and let me explain first, okay?"

Aaron nodded.

His dad sighed again, fingers rubbing at his chin as he closed his eyes. After a moment's pause, he looked at his wife, but she stubbornly stayed next to the window, refusing to come any closer.

"What happened tonight..." Chris started. "It's very difficult to explain. Before you can make complete sense of it, you need to understand something. You're different from other people, Aaron."

"Different?" Aaron asked. "As in...?"

"As in..." Chris faltered. "You're not...human."

3

FAMILY SECRETS

Aaron blinked at him. "Sorry?"

"You're not human," Chris repeated. "Neither are we." He pointed at himself and Kate. "Neither is Mike—"

"Wait, wait." Aaron held up a hand, his eyes narrowed. "Wait...What?"

If the situation hadn't been so dire, Aaron would have laughed. It was a joke, of course it was a joke. But then he remembered that his dad didn't make jokes. After the kind of night they'd had, after what had happened to Mr and Mrs Mason, his dad wouldn't even think of making jokes.

"Aaron." Chris took in a breath. "I know what this sounds like, but you have to understand that what I'm about to tell you is the absolute truth."

Aaron nodded, but a part of him still protested wildly. It was ludicrous. He wasn't human? What did that mean? He watched as his dad drew himself closer, sitting on the edge of his seat, hands clasped together and head bowed.

"I should have told you this before, I know that," he started. "Your mum and I..." He glanced at his wife. "We hoped you'd be older when we told you, but..." He swallowed heavily. "After tonight, I guess we have no other choice." He met Aaron's eyes. "We're not human, not completely." He paused. "We're mages."

Lines formed across Aaron's brow and his eyes narrowed again. "Mages?" he asked.

"Yes, mages," his dad repeated. "We're different beings. Born into this world in the form of a man but with powers bestowed by Heaven itself."

Mages? Powers? Heaven? Aaron's head was spinning.

"You're having me on," he said. "This isn't funny, Dad."

"I agree, it isn't funny in the least," Chris replied, "but I'm not having you on. You're a mage and so are we. We've been living in the human realm since you were born, which strictly speaking isn't allowed—"

"Human realm? So....we're *aliens*? Is that what you're saying?" Aaron asked, so angry he was trembling. How gullible did his dad think he was?

"No, we're not aliens." A half smile came to Chris's face. "But we do have our own world, so to speak – our own realm."

Aaron was shaking his head, his mind screaming in denial. "This is...this is insane," he argued.

"It's difficult to believe, I know," Chris said softly, "but think about what happened today. Everything you saw. Does any of that make sense?"

Aaron fell quiet. Did it make sense? No. The ground opening to trap the out of control car, the white mist dropping from the sky and the way it chased them, the men who stepped seemingly out of thin air – It couldn't be explained, not by rational means. Aaron's insides twisted, his heart frantically beating against his chest. Mages? Powers? Was it really possible? He glanced up to see the sincerity in his dad's dark green eyes. He swallowed heavily.

"You're not joking?" he asked, half hoping he was.

Chris shook his head. "I'm not."

Aaron's mouth dried. "A...a mage?"

Chris nodded. "Different, not human, but we have humanity, Aaron. We're the same in most ways."

Aaron nodded, holding on to that small truth. They had humanity. They were still humans...sort of.

"Those...those men." Aaron asked quietly. "Who are they?"

Chris's expression twisted into one of anger. "It's a long story, Aaron, and not one that I want to get into right now." He brushed a hand through his hair, letting out a slow breath. "I promise I'll tell you everything, but we don't have much time. We have to leave. Those things are looking for us. They know where we are, and they are just waiting for the right moment to attack."

Aaron nodded, his heart beating wildly. "What are we going to do?" he asked.

"Go somewhere safe," Chris replied. "Mike's in the other room, explaining all this to Samuel and Roslyn. As soon as he's done, we're going to leave."

"What?" Aaron asked. "You're telling Sam and Rose about me? That I'm a...a mage?"

"They have a right to know, Aaron."

"A *right* to know?" Aaron's eyes widened. "I've just been told this two seconds ago and it's about *me*! Why are you telling my friends?"

"Because your friends are a part of this now." His mum spoke from the corner. "You unleashed your power in front of them. They witnessed it. Now they're involved."

"My power?" Aaron asked, turning around to look at her. "What are you talking about?"

"What happened today," Chris said, "what you did, that was an example of instinctual reflux–"

"What *I* did?" Aaron asked incredulously. "Dad, I didn't do anything!"

"The car, Aaron," Chris said. "What happened to the car, that was you. Your instinctual reflux is a flow of power, one that opened the ground to stop the car from running you over."

Aaron went rigid, as if someone had doused him with ice-cold water. His mouth opened and closed but not a sound left him. Slowly he shook his head. "No," he breathed. "I...I didn't..."

"It's okay." Chris rested a hand on Aaron's shoulder. "It was out of your immediate control. I already told you, it was instinctual. You reacted to save yourself. It's okay."

"That...that driver?" Aaron's heart twisted. "Oh God. I...I killed him!"

"No, you didn't," his dad replied. "I checked on the driver after...after leaving the Masons." He shifted in his seat. "She was drunk and had passed out at the wheel."

Aaron thought it would make him feel better to know that no lasting damage had been done by his hand, but it didn't. If anything, his stomach curled tighter.

"How did you get her out?" he asked.

"I pulled the car out," Chris replied, "then fixed the ground. I couldn't have the authorities confused–"

"You *pulled* the car out?" Aaron asked. "Fixed the ground? How? How could you–?" He paused, eyes widening. "Wait. Mages, do they have...magic?"

"No," Chris replied, with that half smile again. "It's not magic, Aaron. It's much more than that." He moved to sit next to him. "What we have are powers."

Aaron felt dizzy and a little sick. He couldn't see the difference between powers and magic. He closed his eyes but it only made him feel worse.

"That's why we wanted you to stay away from your friends," Chris said quietly. "When a mage exposes his power in front of humans, it leaves something called a Trace on the humans, so other mages can identify them. That's why we pulled you from school," he revealed. "A mage's core wakes at the age of thirteen. It continues to grow over the next six years. We let you go to school when you were younger, but we knew you could never go to secondary school. We weren't going to take the risk that you might do something in front of hundreds of children. And when that boy tried to push you down the stairs, we got a chance – an excuse to pull you out early." Genuine sadness engulfed his features. "That's why we kept you away from your friends, told you not to hang around them."

Now Aaron was definitely going to be sick. He pushed the feeling of nausea down, fighting the rise of bile clawing up his throat.

"But you continued meeting them," Kate said, accusation and anger lacing her words. "You defied our explicit demands to stay away–"

"Because he didn't understand," Chris interrupted, throwing a hard look Kate's way before he turned back to Aaron. "You didn't know why we were asking you to stay away. It's our fault. We should have been honest and told you the truth."

Aaron had always wondered why his parents didn't want him around his friends. Now he knew. It wasn't his friends who were the problem, it was *him*.

"Sam and Rose," he croaked, still fighting the urge to throw up, "they didn't see me do anything. I didn't *do* anything. How do you know they even have that…that Trace thing on them?"

"We can see it," Chris replied wearily. "You will too, once you learn how to pick up on it. All mages can see the Trace. But the problem is, those things you saw today? The ones that came out from the white mist? They can sense the Trace as well and they kill anyone who has it." He met Aaron's terrified gaze. "Sam and Rose can't stay here. It's not safe for them. They have to leave with us."

"But they have other family," Aaron said, desperate to do something – anything – right by his friends. "Their grandparents live in Scotland. And I know Sam and Rose won't say anything to anyone. They won't tell a soul–"

"It doesn't matter," Kate interjected. "Even if they did, no one would believe them. But no matter where they go, which corner of the world they hide in, they will always be found because of the Trace."

"I don't understand," Aaron began, his stomach tightening so much it hurt. "Then where are we going to go?"

His parents fell quiet. His dad looked over to meet his mum's gaze. "We have to go back," Chris said, speaking to Kate now. "We don't have a choice any more."

Kate didn't say anything. She stood with her arms crossed, lips thinned to a line. Then she looked away, staring at the window, despite the curtains still being closed.

***

Dawn broke some four hours later – the sky an array of orange, yellow and red, before it steadily turned to the cloudy blue of daylight. Chris drove through the English countryside. Acres of green land stretched before the car, and mountains lined one side, their peaks hidden behind foggy clouds.

The occupants of the car sat in silence, each one lost in their own grief-stricken thoughts. No one had spoken a single word since Chris, Kate and the three teens had piled into the car. Michael had stayed behind, mentioning something about "taking care of things". Aaron had watched his uncle as they drove away, wondering if he would ever see him again. He had no idea where they were going and he didn't have enough strength left in him to ask.

Aaron glanced at Rose, sitting next to him. She had her head resting on Sam's arm. Watery brown eyes stared ahead, not seeing, not blinking. Sam had sagged against the door, his gaze ahead. They hadn't said a word to Aaron since talking with Michael. They didn't even look his way. They had got into the car, avoided looking at him, and sat in complete silence.

Aaron turned his head, staring out of the window. He didn't blame Sam and Rose for not wanting to talk to him, but that didn't mean it didn't hurt. Aaron closed his eyes, as confusion and uncertainty stabbed at him again. The truth his parents had told him was still being protested in the back of his mind. Like thorns, it pricked at his conscience, and at his logic. Mages. Powers. A different realm. It was too ludicrous to be real – but then, what other explanation was there?

"Where are you taking us?"

Sam's voice carried clear in the car, drawing everyone's attention.

"Somewhere safe," Chris answered, keeping his eyes on the road.

"Where is that?" Sam asked.

"It's hard to explain," Chris answered. "Once we get there, you'll understand."

A moment passed in silence before Sam said, "Stop the car."

"We can't," Chris replied. "We need to keep going."

"I said, stop the car," Sam repeated, his words dripping with anger. "You can go wherever you like, but let me and Rose go."

Rose lifted her head off her brother's shoulder to stare at him.

"Samuel–" Chris started.

"No! I want out!" Sam yelled suddenly. "Who are you to take us away?" he asked, his fists curled into balls. "Let me and my sister go!"

Kate turned in her seat, looking at him through the steel mesh. "I know you're upset, Samuel, but please, just stay calm."

"*Calm?*" Sam repeated incredulously. "How can I stay calm? We were just attacked! By...by something I...I can't even *begin* to understand. And my mum and dad–" His voice broke and he stopped abruptly. His eyes glistened with unshed tears but he shook his head, as if refusing to succumb to grief. "We want out," he stated. "I need to go back, back home to my parents. I won't leave them...not like this."

"Michael is with them," Chris said. "He'll make sure everything is arranged accordingly."

Sam slammed a hand against the mesh; the loud *thwack* rang in the car.

"They're *my* parents!" he hissed between clenched teeth. "I'll do what needs to be done!"

"Samuel, you can't go back," Chris said in a tone that warned him not to argue. "None of us can go back – never again. Michael's already explained this to you."

"Those men," Sam said, his eyes glazed over in memory of the dark figures appearing out of the mist. "Who were they? What did they want? Why did they kill my mum and dad?" His voice broke again. "What did they want from them?"

Kate turned around as much as she could in her seat. "They didn't want anything. They were there to kill, simple as that." She glanced once at Aaron before her gaze snapped back to Sam. "If you or Rose go back, they will sense you because of the Trace. They will come for you." She tilted her head in remorse. "I'm sorry, really, I am. But the harsh reality is that you can't stay here. Where we're taking you, you'll be safe. We'll all be safe. So, please, just calm down and let us do what needs to be done, okay?"

Sam didn't say anything but he leant back in his seat, turning his head to stare out of the window so he wouldn't have to look at anyone else.

Aaron watched him silently. He couldn't blame Sam for getting angry. They had lost everything in the space of just a few hours: their parents, their home, their freedom, their *life*. And all for what? Because they had chosen to be *his* friend. Because they had wanted to do something nice for his birthday.

Aaron lay back, resting his head against the seat. He closed his eyes, in bitter self-condemnation. What a way to celebrate his fourteenth birthday.

***

"I don't know about this."

"Why?"

"I don't feel comfortable."

"Why not?"

Aaron turned his head to glare angrily at the older boy, squinting in the bright sunlight. "Because it's not me!"

The green-eyed boy chuckled. "It is you," he said, casually propping himself next to Aaron against the low wall. "It's a part of who you are. Deep down, you know that."

Aaron shook his head, vehemently denying it. "*This* is not me!" Aaron held out his hand, which was clutched around the foreign object.

The other boy's vivid green eyes gleamed in amusement. "Deny it all you want," he said, "but when it comes down to it, *this*," he pointed to the thing in Aaron's hand, "is in your blood. It's who you are. Why you were created." He smirked at Aaron. "Fighting it will only tire you. Fight *with* it and it'll bring you nothing but success."

Aaron looked down at his hand. "The only thing this brings is death," he said miserably, watching the sunlight gleam off the silver gun in his hand.

Aaron's eyes snapped open.

The gentle thrum of the engine and faint jostling motion told Aaron he was still in his dad's car. He sat up, lifting his head away from the side of the door where it had lolled while he slept. He rubbed a hand over his neck to soothe the crick, and shifted in his seat, easing the stiffness in his sore body. Sam was asleep; Rose looked like she wasn't far from it herself.

Aaron settled back in his seat, thinking about the dream. The same boy, the same sharp green eyes, the same overwhelming familiarity...but this time it was a different setting and a different conversation. His heart skipped a beat at the recollection of the gun in his hand. It had felt so real. So much so that he could still sense its metallic weight in his hand, feel its smoothness in his fingers. He shuddered, clenching both hands into fists. In an effort to distract himself, Aaron looked out of his window, taking in the scenery.

The road had changed into a narrow, twisting, one-lane road; mountains lay on one side, a steep fall on the other. It made Aaron nervous so he closed his eyes. He had always hated steep hills and jagged cliffs. He remembered his parents driving him to Fort William when he was younger and he had cried throughout the journey. He had been certain the car was going to slip off the narrow road. He had no idea if Fort William was their destination now, but the road seemed the same. He kept his eyes closed, hoping they would reach a main road soon.

It was the sound of Rose's terrified scream that made him open his eyes. Fear bubbled inside him so fiercely that he momentarily couldn't find his breath to cry out. His dad must have fallen asleep at the wheel because they were about to drive off the road.

"Dad!" Aaron shouted, banging a hand against the mesh to wake him up.

Too late.

The car smashed through the road barrier and went careening into the air. Screams filled the car and Aaron jolted out of his seat. The car kept going, the momentum carrying it further into the air. Just as the car began taking a nosedive to the rocky cliffs below, it began shuddering. Aaron was violently thrown forward, his seatbelt the only thing that saved him from smashing face first into the metal mesh.

"Hold on!" His mum's voice was faint against the screams.

A blinding white light, as quick as a bolt of lightening, passed over them. For a heartbeat it seemed like a shimmering, transparent bubble had encased the car. A wave of heat, more intense than anything Aaron had ever experienced, washed over them. It was gone just as quickly as it came but it left him drenched in sweat, his clothes sticking to him, his hair plastered to his head. The car hit the ground, slamming against concrete before coming to a screeching halt.

Aaron was breathing hard, his eyes wide with fear and shock. He turned to look at Sam and Rose. They looked the same: scared and covered in sweat.

"Sorry about that," Chris breathed, turning in his seat to look at them. Aaron saw the perspiration on his face too, as well as his mum's. "It's always rough going through a tear."

"Going through a *what?*" Aaron exclaimed.

"We should move. We have to get access," Kate said, unbuckling her belt.

"Access? To where?" Aaron asked.

His dad turned to hold his gaze. "To the City of Salvador."

***

Aaron stepped out of the car, staring in bewilderment at his strange surroundings. On either side of him there were what must have been hundreds of thousands of trees, standing in such perfect lines it was unnerving. They stretched along as far as Aaron could see – tall with dark brown trunks and deep green leaves, so rich in colour they looked fictional.

Aaron was standing on a narrow, concrete path, only about a metre and a half wide. Their car had landed perfectly on the pathway. Aaron looked ahead, but all he could see was the never-ending path, lined by trees on both sides. Sam and Rose had clambered out of the car behind Aaron and stood staring at their surroundings with open mouths.

"Where are we?" Aaron asked.

"The Gateway," his dad answered quietly.

With notable strain, Chris began walking down the path, trepidation clear in each hesitant step. Kate followed behind with the same look of apprehension. Aaron, Sam and Rose followed behind them, all the while staring at the trees that were too green, the sky that was too blue or the concrete path that was too smooth.

They walked along the seemingly never-ending road until Aaron was sure that the path led to nowhere, when a door suddenly appeared before them. It was only a door. No walls, no handle. Just a tall, plain door – a mass of glistening, shiny white that towered over them. The surface gleamed in the soft sunlight. Just like everything else here, the door looked like an illusion. It was impossibly tall, its top hidden behind the soft, white clouds. There was no way a structure this tall could stand unsupported in the way it was. The sight made everyone stop in their tracks.

Aaron stepped closer, staring at it with curiosity. He wanted to reach out and touch the shiny door. Before his eyes, strange markings began to appear on the surface: symbols, shapes and numbers. Some were curvy and messy, like random drawings a child might scribble. Others were straight with crisp lines, etched with meticulous precision. The markings were all over the door, at least a hundred of them, seemingly in no particular order. They were scattered across the surface, some written in sequence in a line, others engraved diagonally.

Aaron's gaze drew upon the only set of markings he could understand. Numbers. There was a fancy three etched in calligraphy, the number seven next to it, a group of nines, and the numbers seven, eight, six, thirteen and a four scattered across the surface of the door. The more Aaron stared at the numbers, the more they seemed to shine, as if encrusted with glistening diamonds caught in rays of sunlight. Aaron looked over to his dad, to see him staring at the door with just as much scrutiny, but his gaze was more intense. His parents shared another look, mirroring each other's hesitation.

Chris breathed out a strained sigh and lifted a hand. He placed it onto the door, his fingers standing out against the bright white. Kate did the same, her hand small and nimble set parallel to her husband's. She reached out, offering her other hand to Aaron. He took it at once.

"Hold on to each other," she instructed.

Perplexed, Aaron reached out and took Rose's hand, who quickly reached for her brother's hand. Chris held out his free hand to Sam to complete the chain. Sam paused, his eyes narrowed and jaw clenched. A pleading noise came from Rose, and Sam reached out, reluctantly taking Chris's hand.

Chris turned to look at the door. "I seek sanctuary," he said in a loud, clear voice.

"I seek sanctuary," Kate whispered behind him.

The door shimmered and the symbols began to glow. Each and every symbol shone like bright stars, their light beaming out across the five of them. Then, slowly, the light began to dull, and diminished completely as the symbols melted away. Only the number four remained, burning brightly on the door for a moment longer. Then, as it faded, a circle appeared. Inside the circle was an inverted V with three wavy lines behind it, and a spiral sitting between the legs of the V. The symbol flashed brightly, and then it too faded.

There was a loud click and the door slid open, disappearing as it did so, leaving behind a rectangular doorway. Chris and Kate dropped their hands, watching with blank expressions. Aaron and the twins stared in complete shock at what lay on the other side.

It was dark there – nightfall, apparently, even though Aaron was standing in dazzling sunlight. Aaron's gaze darted everywhere, trying to make sense of what was going on. It was a village, or that's what his first impression told him. Floating lanterns lit the night sky. A cobbled path led the way to a row of cottages, complete with small fences surrounding tiny front gardens.

Opposite them were three tall rectangular buildings. Far off in the distance, Aaron could make out the glistening surface of a lake.

In the middle of the road was the longest table Aaron had ever seen. It seemed to stretch on forever, and easily be able to seat hundreds of people. Aaron felt Rose's fingers tighten around his. He turned to look at her, but she was staring ahead, clearly in confusion. Sam didn't look any better.

Chris and Kate stepped through the doorway, and the others followed behind, staring all around at the calm, surreal village. They walked down the path, directly towards the cottage at the end of the row, separated from the rest by a tall fence.

Something moved in the dark. A creak, a thud and a floating light appeared in front of them, coming out from that very house. Footsteps accompanied it. As the ball of light got closer, Aaron realised it was another lantern, but this one wasn't floating. It was being carried by a man, illuminating only one side of his face in the glow.

"Jus' wait 'ere, please." He spoke gruffly, as if he had just awoken. Judging from the serene silence and pitch-black darkness, Aaron figured that might have been the case. "A'righ, who do we hav' 'ere?"

The man held his lantern up high so that the light could wash over not only them but himself as well. He was haggard-looking – a scruffy, blond beard dotted with grey covered the bottom part of his face. Beady blue eyes gazed out, the skin around them wrinkled. Aaron noticed a clipboard in his other hand.

"Come on, wha's the name?" he asked with narrowed eyes, his wrinkly brow furrowed with impatience.

"Adams," Chris said quietly.

The man went rigid. His eyes widened as he pushed the lantern closer, examining Chris's face with sudden interest. "Bless ma soul!" he breathed. "Adams? Chris'opher Adams?"

Chris nodded tightly. "That's the one," he said stiffly.

The man smiled, revealing chipped, yellowing teeth. "Well, well, isn' this somefin'?" He looked over at the others, his gaze leisurely scanning Kate, Rose, Sam and finally settling on Aaron. His smile got wider. "Tha' lad looks an awfu' lot like yeh."

"Why wouldn't he?" Chris asked, his voice furious but quiet. "He's my son."

The man laughed, a rough barking sound. "Aye? Well, yeh get yerselves comfor'able." He pointed to the row of cottages. "Any of 'em last four will do yeh fine for tonight." He held a hand to his chest. "Ma name's Jason Burns. Yeh need anyfin', yeh let me know."

Chris nodded tightly at him but didn't indulge in any formalities. He took hold of Kate's hand and turned, leading her to the nearest cottage. Aaron quickly followed behind them, acutely aware of Jason Burns's eerie gaze on him the entire time.

***

The cottage was small – tiny, in fact. The ceiling was so low, the top of Chris's head brushed against it. It was dimly lit with lanterns hanging from the wall and a few candles. They walked into the only room on the ground floor. Inside was a small three-piece sofa and a coffee table, which held a tray of dried fruit, some biscuits, a jug of water and a single glass.

Aaron sat down on the threadbare sofa; Rose and Sam collapsed next to him. He was exceptionally tired, which was strange seeing as he hadn't done anything besides sit in a car all day. He rubbed at his eyes, stifling a yawn.

"It's late," Kate said. "You three should rest. It's been a tiring day."

None of them moved.

"What is this place?" Aaron asked.

His parents shared a glance.

"It's the City of Salvador," Chris said. "It's a sanctuary. It gives protection to those who need it most."

Aaron already knew the answer to his next question, but he went ahead and asked anyway. "We're not in our world any more, right?"

"This is our realm. Well, a part of it, anyway," Kate replied. "We'll talk tomorrow. Tonight, I just want all of us to get some rest." She gestured to the door. "The bedrooms are upstairs."

Sam and Rose took the first room they came across. They shut the door without so much as a glance in Aaron's direction. Trying not to let it upset him, Aaron walked across the narrow landing and opened a second door. The room was small; a bed pushed against one wall and a worn-out bedside cabinet were the only pieces of furniture in the room. Aaron glanced at the peeling wallpaper and dust-flaked window.

Aaron kicked off his shoes and pulled off his jacket. He climbed onto the bed, ignoring the musty smell that filled his nostrils. He used his jacket to cover the pillow, so that he wouldn't be breathing in dust all night. He lay there, awake and painfully aware of every sob that came from the room next door.

How he fell asleep, Aaron had no idea, but that night his dreams were plagued with replays of those men coming out of the mist, and imagining them attack the Masons. Screams he thought belonged to Mr and Mrs Mason rang in his head, turning his stomach even as he slept.

4

THE CITY OF SALVADOR

When Aaron awoke, daylight had filtered in through the grimy window. He blinked sleepily, confused by the strange surroundings and mouldy stench. Then yesterday's events flashed through his mind and his heart dropped. He got up and pulled on his shoes. He walked downstairs and into the living room to find both his parents sitting on the sofa. His mum had found clothes from somewhere and had changed into a plain top and trousers, with simple sandals on her feet. It seemed the conversation they were having was a tense and painful one, for when they looked up at him, Aaron could see the stress in their expressions. Both smiled, though, their tired eyes brightening a little.

"Morning," Chris greeted him.

Aaron closed the door behind him. "Morning," he replied.

"How'd you sleep?" Kate asked.

Aaron gave a one-shouldered shrug in response.

"Samuel and Roslyn still asleep?" Chris asked.

Aaron nodded.

"Give them time, Aaron," Kate said, her tone soft and kind. "They're going through a terrible loss. They'll want to be alone for a while. Give them that space."

"I didn't think you cared," Aaron couldn't stop himself from replying.

His mum looked taken aback. "I do care," she said. "A lot, actually. That's why I tried so hard to keep you away from them."

There it was again, that sharp jab that twisted his heart, like a knife in his chest. Aaron didn't say anything, but his expression must have showed his guilt because his dad got to his feet and walked over to him.

"You didn't know," he consoled, "but from now on, Aaron, you must always do as we ask. Believe us when we say we know best. I can't stress the importance of this: you *must* trust us enough to do as we ask."

Aaron nodded.

Chris clapped a hand on his shoulder, offering a weak smile. "Come," he said, gesturing to the door. "It's time you saw Salvador."

***

The day was bright and warm – strange for the month of November. It was the first thing Aaron noticed when he stepped outside. Last night had been too dark and he had been too exhausted to take in much of the place. In the daylight, though, Aaron could see the City of Salvador and what he saw surprised him.

As Aaron stepped onto the cobbled path, he glanced at the long line of cottages to his right. They all looked the same: small, red-brick squares with slated roofs and green wooden doors. About ten houses down, though, the doors changed to the colour blue. There were small gardens at the front of each cottage – just a patch of grass and some flowers, nothing too impressive. A peeling white fence ran down the front of the gardens, like a worn-out barrier.

Aaron passed the gate and stared in amazement at the scrubbed wooden table, right smack in the middle of the road. Accompanying chairs were tucked in along both sides. His judgement last night had been almost accurate. It was long enough to run down the length of the road and could easily seat at least five hundred people.

On the other side of the table were three buildings – tall sandstone structures with big, thick doors. In the distance was the lake he had glimpsed last night. In the morning light, Aaron could really appreciate the sight. A clear, extraordinarily blue sheet of water, glistening in the sunlight, surrounded by trees.

"Ah, the Adams rest'd?"

Aaron turned to see the man from last night, Jason Burns, approaching. Daylight was not kind to him. His skin was wrinkled, hair straggly and dry. Long strands of grey hair hung from his eyebrows, almost down into his eyes. When he held out a hand for Chris to shake, Aaron saw that his nails were blackened with dirt.

"As much as needed, yes," Chris replied.

Jason's beady-eyed gaze jumped to Aaron and he grinned, revealing his yellow teeth again. "His fi'st time in Salvador?" he asked with a nod.

"Yes," Chris replied, and Aaron could sense the tension coming off his dad in waves.

Jason chuckled, shaking his head. "Bless ma beard! Isn' this somefin'?" His eyes locked with Chris's. "All the Adams back in our realm. A sure sign o' good times to come."

"I bet it is," Chris muttered darkly. He turned and took Aaron's arm a little too tightly. "Come on, let's go."

They passed the table and headed towards the lake, leaving the creepy-looking Jason Burns staring after them.

"Dad, what is this place?" Aaron asked.

"I told you, it's the City of Salvador – a sanctuary," Chris replied.

"It looks more like a village than a city," Aaron said.

Chris kept on walking but his grip loosened a little. "It used to be a city. Now this is all that's left of it."

Aaron glanced up at him. "All that's left?"

His dad didn't answer straight away; he looked like he was struggling to find what to say. He took in a deep breath. "There's a war going on, Aaron. A war in this realm that's tearing our world apart quite literally."

"A war?" Aaron asked. "Why? What's going on?"

"I want to tell you, really, I do." Chris rubbed at his head. "It's just...everything is kind of messed up right now. I don't know what's going to happen, so I don't know what to tell you. We might not even be allowed to stay in this realm." He let out a sigh. "Just let me get a few things sorted. Then I promise I'll sit you down and tell you everything."

"You said that before," Aaron reminded him quietly. "You said once we got here we'd talk."

"I know, but..." Chris came to a stop, halting Aaron mid-step. "The future as it stands is very unclear. I have to sort things out, make sure it even makes sense to involve you in all this." His eyes softened. "Just give me a little time. For now, take solace in the fact that you're in one of the safest places in both realms."

They walked onwards in silence, passing the lake. Even when Aaron was distracted with confusing thoughts, the sight of the beautiful lake somehow managed to calm him. The water was still, the blue too rich to be real. Aaron had the urge to climb down the bank and touch it, to see if his fingers would interrupt the glassy perfection and cause ripples in that calmness. But his dad had walked past the lake, so Aaron followed after him. They continued down the path until they arrived at a woodland area. Aaron stared at the vines that stretched up and intertwined with a brass sign hanging between two thick tree trunks that said *Orchard*.

Aaron followed his dad into the orchard bathed in dazzling golden sunlight. He couldn't help but stare in wonder at the perfectly lined trees, with branches that dipped down with the weight of their fruit, ripe and mouth-watering, ready for the picking. Aaron's stomach growled noisily, reminding him he had not eaten since yesterday's lunch – a miserable cheese sandwich his mum had got from a petrol station. At least he had eaten his; Sam and Rose's sandwiches were still in the car, untouched.

Chris led Aaron deeper into the orchard, past wicker baskets filled to the brim with oranges, apples, mangos and fruits Aaron didn't have a name for. He was tempted to reach out and grab something, but didn't.

They reached a grapevine, pitched horizontally to the trees. A dark-haired man with his back towards them was picking grapes off the vine. Despite the soft ground under their shoes, somehow the man sensed their arrival. He stopped and turned around. He had a sharp, angular face with deep-set brown eyes, which were slowly widening with shock.

"Chris?" he whispered, his brow creased.

A warm, genuine smile spread over Chris's face. "Hi, Drake."

The next moment, both men had stepped forward to embrace, like brothers would. Aaron watched in quiet surprise. The man – Drake – stepped back but clasped both hands around Chris's arms.

"By God, Chris, it's really you." He shook his head, making wavy strands of hair fall into his eyes. "What...what are you doing here?" An uneasy expression flitted over him. "I told you it wasn't safe."

"I didn't have a choice," Chris answered.

That's when Drake's gaze moved to Aaron. The brown eyes gleamed and a small smile spread across his face.

"Aaron?" he asked, looking back at Chris.

Chris nodded with a smile. "Aaron, this is my good friend, Drake Logan."

Drake held out a hand. "Pleased to meet you, son."

Aaron shook his hand, noticing the tattoo of a silver dagger on his inner wrist.

"I need to speak with you," Chris said. He paused to look at Aaron. "Why don't you have a little wander around, Aaron, see Salvador. I'll meet you at the table in half an hour."

It was a dismissal and Aaron knew it. As he turned to walk away, a spark ignited in his chest, anger burning him. His dad was purposefully keeping him from learning too much about this place, this realm. But last night's events were still fresh in his mind, so disobeying his father wasn't an option right now. His dad's words echoed in his mind. *You must always do as we ask. Believe us when we say we know best. I can't stress the importance of this: you must trust us enough to do as we ask.*

In an act of defiance, though, Aaron swiped a hand at the basket he passed and scooped out two apples.

Aaron walked out of the orchard, munching on the apples. He didn't know if it was because he was hungry or if the apples of this realm were just this good, but they were the best things he had ever tasted: sweet, juicy, refreshing and strangely filling. He wandered down another path, this one leading parallel to the lake. One look in the distance and Aaron knew where it led. The square patches of green and yellow land, the white dots grazing on the grass, a few larger black and white figures accompanying them: it was all tell-tale signs of farmland.

It took Aaron almost ten minutes to reach the end of the path. Again he found himself admiring something he had never given any thought to before. Living the city life in Chelsea, Aaron hadn't ever had the chance to admire the countryside, or even nature for that matter. He had never been camping, never visited any farms or country parks. If he was honest, he didn't have the desire to, either. But this – the sight of sheep and cows lazily grazing on fresh green grass, sunlight showering yellow fields that Aaron could only assume was wheat or something – it was all rather...serene.

Further down the path, Aaron passed by a fence, beyond which small, wooden coops were lined along one side. A dozen brown hens were gathered, clucking and ruffling their feathers, apparently feeding. Aaron didn't notice the woman until she poked her head up from behind the coops. She had blond hair gathered up in a messy bun, blue eyes that were narrowed at him and a streak of dirt on her cheek.

"Well, don't just stand there," she said. "Grab her, quickly!"

Aaron glanced down in time to see a hen dart through his legs. Aaron dashed behind it. The hen clucked at him and fluttered away, faster than he thought possible.

"Oh, for Heaven's sake!" The woman got off her knees, hurrying around the wooden huts. "I'll just have to do it myself."

"I got it." Aaron ran after the hen, hands outstretched to grab the little thing, but it was too fast.

The bird flitted this way and that, avoiding capture. Aaron scrambled behind it, almost slipping on the soft, muddy ground. In a clumsy swipe, he managed to close both hands around the feathery bird. The hen flapped her wings, clucking loudly, trying to get free. Aaron held the thing at arm's length as he turned around and walked back to the woman, who was smiling at him.

"Here we go." She took the bird from him. "This one is always trying to break free," she chuckled. She carried the hen over to the coop and placed her gently inside. She turned to eye Aaron, squinting against the sun's glare. "I haven't seen you before. You new?"

"Yeah," Aaron replied.

He couldn't help but stare at her. She was rather lovely looking. She couldn't be older than mid-twenties. Her blue eyes were dazzling in the sunlight.

"You're not a Shattered, are you?" she asked, walking around the coop.

"A what?" Aaron frowned.

"You don't look like one." She mused as she went behind the back of the coops, only to reappear with a basket full of brown-shelled eggs. "You're out and about; that doesn't happen so quickly." She smiled. "What's your name?"

"Aaron Adams."

She paused, turning with a frown. She regarded him crossly. "Adams?" she asked. "Think you're funny, do you?"

"Um...no," Aaron replied, confused.

She shook her head. "Who put you up to this? Was it Omar?" She scooped a few more eggs from behind the coops and added them to her basket. "I bet it was Ella, that little minx – or was it Julian this time?"

"It wasn't anyone," Aaron said. "I'm Aaron Adams. I'm not joking."

"Ha! Not joking," she scoffed. "That's a good one." She walked over to a wooden block and placed the basket down next to a similar one filled with more eggs. "The Adams aren't coming back. It's time everyone let that go." She picked up the towel beside the baskets and wiped her hands clean before throwing it over her shoulder. She stood with her hands on her hips, eyeing Aaron again. "Wanna give me a hand?"

Aaron opened the gate and walked across to her, taking a basket of eggs. She picked up the other one.

"Where are we taking these?" Aaron asked.

"To the artillery." She gave him a look. "The Stove, of course. I've got breakfast to prepare." She led the way past the gate.

"Breakfast?" Aaron glanced down at his basket with at least fifty eggs.

"Yeah, you know that thing you have when you wake up in the morning and fill your stomach with food?" she replied.

"I know what breakfast is," Aaron defended.

"Good for you." She winked at him, flashing a toothy smile. "I'm just playing, don't mind me."

They'd started walking when Aaron spotted his dad. Drake Logan was by his side and both seemed deep in conversation, brows lined with tension. When they looked up and saw him, though, they smiled, still whispering to each other from the corner of their mouths – no doubt saying they would talk later. Aaron pretended he didn't notice.

"Hey." Chris came to stand before him. "Having fun, I see." He nodded at the basket.

"Hello." The women greeted him with a smile. "Haven't had the pleasure yet." She balanced the basket on her hip and held out a hand. "Mary Collins."

With a smile, Chris took her hand. "Christopher Adams."

The smile fell from her face and she stood, shell-shocked, her hand still in Chris's. Aaron couldn't help but smile a little at her gob-smacked expression.

"A-Adams?" She looked from Chris to Aaron, before finally staring at Drake.

"It's really him," Drake confirmed, slapping a hand on Chris's shoulder. "The Adams are back."

Mary came out of her shock and quickly dropped his hand. "Oh, I-I thought..." Her gaze darted to Aaron and she tilted her head to one side. "I'm sorry, I thought the others had put you up to... Oh, never mind. I'm really sorry."

"It's okay." Aaron didn't expect her to be so apologetic. It wasn't a big deal. "No harm done."

She smiled at him, before her eyes widened at the basket in his hands. "Oh! Drake!" she snapped at the man. "Quick, take the basket from him!"

Drake moved forward a step before Chris held out a hand to stop him.

"It's fine," he said. "Aaron doesn't mind helping, do you, Aaron?"

"No," Aaron replied.

"But…but it isn't right," Mary said, looking rather flustered. A pink tinge started up her neck and seeped into her cheeks.

"No, it is right," Chris replied. "Treating people differently, that's what's not right." He looked to Aaron. "My son is no different to the other residents of Salvador. Please treat him as such."

Mary looked between Chris and Aaron, but she gave a little nod. "As you wish." She turned to Aaron. "Come on, we better get a move on."

Perplexed, Aaron followed behind her, shooting his father a confused glance, but he only nodded and winked in return.

***

The Stove, as Mary referred to it, turned out to be one of the tall sandstone buildings opposite the cottages. Upon entering, Aaron found himself in a vast room with a high ceiling. The roof caught Aaron's attention; it was a circular sunroof, which was currently in the process of sliding open. The sunlight lit every corner of the room. Lined along all three walls were worktops of gleaming, rich brown granite. But where ordinary kitchens had cupboards above the worktops, this one had only shelves lined over and underneath the heavy counter tops. Stacked on the shelves were normal cups, plates and glassware, along with giant-sized pots and pans, and possibly every cooking utensil invented.

But the thing that caught Aaron's attention was the monster appliance in the middle of the room. A stove, but one Aaron had never seen the likes of before. It was a square, metallic beast, wider than most cooking appliances. Fifty burners, all different sizes, were grouped in ten sets of five on the surface. Thick, black metal doors with an ornately carved design were closed over the oven. The stove dominated the room, gleaming in the spotlight cast by the sunroof. Aaron couldn't help but stare at it.

"Just put the basket there." Mary pointed at the nearest worktop. "Thank you, Aaron."

Aaron carefully put the basket down and turned, wiping his hands down his jeans as he glanced around. "This is…some kitchen."

Mary turned to smile at him. "You impressed?" she asked. "You can tell you're from the human realm, if *this* impresses you." She shook her head, chuckling.

Aaron decided not to comment. "What's next door?" he asked.

"The bakery." She pointed to her right. "And the cold room." She pointed to the left.

"Cold room?"

"Yeah, you know, to store items?" She knelt to take a humongous pot from the shelf. It was big enough to bathe a baby in. "There's a chiller in there, to store ice cream and such." She turned to Aaron with a grin. "I make the best raspberry ripple ice cream."

"You must do a lot of cooking," Aaron remarked, throwing the monster stove another look.

"It's all I do." She brought the pan to the stove. "It's my first love." She carried the basket over. "I've been living in Salvador for," she paused, eyes turned upwards as she worked through a mental calendar, "twelve years now, and that's all I've ever done. It's like my life's mission is to feed everyone."

"You've been here twelve years?" Aaron asked.

Mary's smile faded. "Yeah, twelve years." She picked up one of the eggs, holding it in her hands. "I was fifteen when...when *they* came." Her voice dropped. "My sister was sleeping in the next room. They killed my parents, slaughtered my brother while I slept." Her face fell, her eyes shadowed. "I woke up when they went into my sister's room. I heard her screams and ran to her but...but it was too late. They...they had already..." She shook her head, blinking up at Aaron with moist eyes. "When I came here, I was alone. I mean, I felt alone." She put the egg into the pot. "Neriah always lectured that we are one – a family, bound by our powers and bloodlines." She picked up the other eggs from the basket and, one by one, placed them gently into the pot. "But at the start, it's always difficult to think of strangers as your family." She turned to smile at Aaron. "Now, though, I know what he means. I consider all mages a part of an extended family that I have to take care of by feeding."

"You cook for everyone?" Aaron asked.

"Yep." She carried the empty basket over to the worktop, replacing it with the one Aaron had brought.

"Do you...uh...want any help?" Aaron asked warily. He was terrible at cooking, couldn't make toast without burning it, but he felt bad for her. She was all alone, left to cook for everyone.

"That's okay." She sent him another smile. "I have my happy helpers. They'll be here soon. Although, they aren't that happy to help." She shrugged. "But they'll be here, so don't you worry." She gestured to the door. "You go and relax. I'll have breakfast ready before you know it."

***

Aaron walked outside to find more people on the street. Several had taken seats at the table, and a few were crowded around the open doors of the cottages. He spotted his mum and dad seated at the table with Drake. As he made his way down the path, Aaron felt rather than saw stares shift focus to him. Men, old and young, stared at him. Women turned to whisper to their neighbours as he walked past. It was by far the most uncomfortable walk Aaron had experienced.

"Where were you?" his mum asked, as he took a seat next to her.

"In the Stove," Aaron answered.

"Excuse me?" Kate asked, turning to him.

"The kitchen. It's called the Stove," Aaron explained.

Kate only nodded before dropping her gaze to the table.

"Mum?" Aaron started, glancing at the people crowded at doorsteps, staring at him.

"Just ignore them," Kate said, without looking up.

"But why are they staring?"

His mum didn't answer right away. A small, sardonic smile lifted up the corners of her mouth. "Because we're the Adams."

Aaron fell quiet. He looked down the table before turning back to his mum. "Where's Sam and Rose?"

"Inside," Kate replied. "They didn't want to come out."

The bubble of guilt rose inside Aaron again. He turned, seeking out the cottage that they had stayed in last night. He stared at it for long minutes before eventually looking away.

More people started taking their seats around the table. No one introduced themselves or even bothered to speak to the Adams, but continued their sideways glances and muttering. Aaron sat in silence next to his mum. His dad and Drake continued their quiet conversation, seemingly oblivious to the staring.

A particular group nearby caught Aaron's eye. Six women, tall and fair, with long blue robes which trailed to the ground. But that wasn't what grabbed Aaron's attention. It was the way they were walking: in single file, with a hand resting on the shoulder of the person in front of them. The one at the front was staring, unblinkingly ahead of her, her pale blue eyes gazing into the far distance. When they reached the table, the six stepped out of their single file and felt their chairs with their hands before sitting down.

"Hey y'all!"

Aaron turned to see a boy, not much older than him, standing at the end of the table. On either side were two stacks of plates, almost as tall as the boy. The boy grinned and reached back to tie his shoulder-length hair into a ponytail.

"Watch yer fingers," he warned.

He pulled back his hand before extending it out fully, as if throwing an imaginary Frisbee. The stacks of plates flew across the table. Aaron pushed himself back as the train of plates whipped by him, going down the length of the table, leaving a single plate in front of every occupied seat. The boy pulled back his other hand and repeated the action, to lay plates on the other side.

"Now it's time for the cutlery." The boy grinned.

Aaron pushed himself away from the table.

"Alan!" came a shout. A girl, blond with a round face and pretty blue eyes, ran up. She was holding a large tub in her hands. "What did Mother Mary say?" she berated.

"Mother Mary worries too much," the boy replied.

"She has a point," the girl said. "She doesn't want you stabbing someone with a fork!"

The boy – Alan – only shrugged, but scooped out the cutlery from a large bucket and began handing them out. The girl reached into her tub and brought out a glass tumbler. She set one in front of everyone. When she reached Aaron, she looked up to meet his gaze, pausing slightly. Aaron couldn't help but stare at her. She looked to be around his age. Her eyes were a bright blue and her hair shone golden in the light. The girl smiled and quickly deposited the glass.

"Ava!" another girl called to her from halfway across the street. "Mother Mary wants you!"

Ava gave Aaron one last smile before turning and hurrying back towards the Stove. Aaron watched her go until she disappeared behind the doors of the kitchen.

"Aaron."

He jumped a little at the close whisper. He turned to his mum. "Yeah?"

Kate glanced once in the direction of the Stove before looking back at him. "It's impolite to stare."

Aaron shrugged. "Not staring," he argued weakly.

He looked around the street to avoid his mother's eyes. He craned his head to the side, looking at the long line of cottages, when several blue doors opened at once and out stepped groups of teenagers.

Aaron's attention went to a particular girl in the crowd. Her thick, dark hair had streaks of electric blue through it, and reached down to the curve of her back. Her long legs looked even more so in her tight jeans. A cropped top bared her midriff, flashing smooth, creamy skin. There was something on one side of her stomach: a large, dark mark that Aaron couldn't make out from this distance. Next to her was a boy, perhaps a year or two older than Sam, with hair so shockingly blond it looked white. His sleeveless top showcased his muscular arms. A strange spiral symbol was etched onto the tanned skin, just at his right shoulder cap. He was sharp-featured, with eyes so blue Aaron could see them from this distance. The other boys and girls were similar in appearance: the boys tall and muscular, the girls long-legged and stunningly beautiful. They all possessed a strange grace, and appeared strong, powerful and oddly enamouring.

The blond boy with the spiral tattoo caught Aaron's stare. Their gazes locked and for a moment, both boys just stared at each other. Aaron saw the boy lean back and say something from the corner of his mouth. The girl with the blue streaks turned to stare at Aaron.

It was his cue to look away, but Aaron found himself meeting her stare head on. The group started heading his way.

"Well, well, fresh meat on the stalls today, eh?" the blond boy said, coming to stand behind Aaron.

Kate turned, as did Chris and Drake to face him. In fact, everyone seated around the table was watching the boy, somewhat warily.

"Skyler." Drake greeted him with a curt nod. "Be nice."

"I'm always nice," the boy – Skyler – replied. He looked down at Aaron, flashing a charming smile. "So, Shattered or mage?"

"Mage," Aaron replied, finding the unfamiliar word stick to the back of his throat.

Skyler nodded. "Figured. You don't look like a Shattered." He cocked his head to one side, examining him. "What's the name?"

"Aaron," he replied. "Aaron Adams."

The boy's expression changed at once. The assembled crowd of teenagers behind him looked equally shocked. Skyler's mouth curved into a smirk, his striking blue eyes narrowed.

"Adams?" he asked. "For real?"

"Yeah," Aaron replied, "for real."

Skyler didn't say anything but simply stared at him. Then he grinned and Aaron's heart missed a beat. He knew that smile. He used to see it on Matthews, the school bully, just before there was trouble. This was the same smile: predatory, cold – and promised pain.

"What happened?" Skyler asked, addressing Chris. "Got tired of the human realm?"

"I don't believe that's any of your business," Chris replied, before turning back to continue his conversation with Drake.

"You'll find that it is, in fact, my business," Skyler said.

Chris looked up at him with a tired sigh. "And you are?"

The boy straightened up, holding his head high, as if his name was a title worthy of praise. "Skyler Avira."

Chris's expression changed. He was clearly taken aback; his eyes softened and his mouth dropped open. "You're Joseph's kid?" he asked.

"Yeah, Joseph Avira," Skyler repeated. "Remember him?"

Chris looked uncomfortable. He shifted in his seat, dropping his gaze. "I'm sorry about what happened to Joseph," he said. "You have my deepest condolences."

Skyler smirked, his eyes burning. "You know *exactly* what to do with your condolences," he hissed. "You have no right to come back here, sit at the table of Salvador like nothing happened and start spewing useless apologies!"

"Skyler," Drake warned. "That's enough."

"You have every right to be angry," Chris said to Skyler, "but you don't know what happened. Circumstances were such–"

"Circumstances are a weak man's shield to hide behind," Skyler returned. "But we already know that's what you are."

That's when the first spark of anger lit Chris's eyes. "You don't know what you're talking about, son."

Skyler's hands curled into fists and his eyes blazed with anger. "*Don't* call me 'son'!" he warned.

A mighty gust of wind blew across the table, so strong it unsettled the plates and glasses. They fell to the ground, smashing to pieces. The numerous people seated around the table had to grip onto the edge to save themselves from toppling out of their chairs.

"Skyler." The girl with the blue streaks caught hold of his arm and pulled him back. She muttered something in his ear. It didn't calm him, but the strange wind died down, leaving everyone with ruffled hair and concerned expressions.

Aaron glanced across to see his dad was holding Skyler's furious gaze, but there was no sign of annoyance or anger on his face, just quiet remorse.

That's when Mary arrived at the table, holding a large tray of food. Behind her, several boys and girls carried various trays and drinks. Mary looked surprised. Her gaze darted from the broken plates on the ground up to an angry-looking Skyler and the penitent Chris.

"Skyler?" she questioned.

But the boy only sent a scathing look at Chris and walked away. The girl and their assembled group hurried after him. Chris watched him before getting up from the table.

"Chris, don't," Drake said. "He's a hot-headed idiot; don't mind him." He gestured to the retreating form of Skyler. "He doesn't know what he's talking about."

But Chris walked away, heading back to the cottage in which they had spent the night. Kate got up after him.

"Kate, please don't," Drake tried, but she shook her head sadly.

"Come on," she said quietly to Aaron.

Aaron got up. Sending Mary a look of apology, he hurried after his parents, his stomach rumbling with hunger.

5
Difficult Decisions

It was perhaps twenty minutes later when a knock sounded on the door. Kate opened it to find Mary standing there with a tray loaded with toast, eggs and a large serving of fruit. Ava stood behind her, holding a tray with a jug of juice, several plates and glasses on it.

"It's against usual practise for mages to eat inside," Mary said, "but on this occasion, I think it can be overlooked."

"Thank you," Kate said, taking the tray from Mary. A click of Kate's fingers and the tray Ava was holding rose in the air. Kate carried her tray into the living room, with the second tray floating in after her. Aaron gaped at the sight, too shocked to make a sound. Kate knelt in front of the single rickety table and placed her tray on it. The second tray gently settled onto the floor next to her. Kate loaded a plate for Aaron and handed it to him, followed by a glass of freshly squeezed orange juice. Aaron took it warily, still gaping at his mum.

"Eat, Aaron," Kate said without looking at him.

Balancing the plate on his knee, Aaron gulped down his juice.

"Chris?" Kate held out a plate.

Chris looked over at her and shook his head. Kate pulled back her hand, hesitating for a moment.

"His anger is understandable," she said. "Even if he doesn't know what he's talking about."

Chris nodded but didn't speak. He sat with his head bowed, hands clasped together.

Kate didn't say any more. She set another two plates, filled two glasses with juice and balanced them precariously on the edge of the plates, and stood up. She left the room, heading upstairs to give Sam and Rose their breakfast.

Aaron was left alone with his dad. He glanced at him as he chewed a mouthful of toast and egg. "Dad, you okay?" he asked.

Chris lifted his head. Troubled eyes found Aaron but, regardless, a smile graced his face. "Yeah. I'm fine, Aaron." He nodded. "I'm fine."

Aaron swallowed. "Why was that boy mouthing off to you?"

An expression of pain flitted across Chris's face. "His father," he started quietly. "His father was my friend – more than that, he was like a...a brother to me." He shook his head, squeezing his eyes shut as he let out a sigh. He wiped a hand down his face. "He died after I left this realm."

"I'm sorry," Aaron said. "But why was that boy getting annoyed with you? You didn't do anything."

Chris nodded, silent for long minutes. "Yeah," he said slowly. "I didn't do anything."

Aaron watched as grief flooded his dad's features. "Dad?"

The door opened and Kate walked back in. "They're still refusing to come out of the room," she said, "but at least they've taken the breakfast."

"Good," Chris said, straightening up. "They need to eat something."

"So do you," Kate said, holding out the last plate.

Chris gave in this time and took the plate, picking up the toast and taking a generous bite. Kate didn't have a plate but she seemed content to use the serving dish. They ate in silence, Kate and Chris lost in their thoughts and Aaron in his rising confusion.

***

Aaron didn't know what to do. He had taken a shower and changed into the spare set of clothes he found in one of the cupboards. It was a simple white shirt and blue jeans. Both were a bit baggy but Aaron made do with them. Sam and Rose were still in their room. Aaron had stood outside for ten minutes, plucking up the courage to go in and see his friends, but he couldn't bring himself to do it. Dejectedly, he went downstairs and sat next to the grimy window, staring out at nothing in particular.

Drake had come by shortly after breakfast and left with Chris, going somewhere private to talk. It irked Aaron – the secrecy, the whispering, the intense looks his parents kept sharing. It was slowly driving Aaron mad. Why couldn't they just talk in the open? Why couldn't they tell him what was going on?

Aaron scoffed silently. He told himself it shouldn't be surprising that his parents were hiding things. After all, they had hidden such an enormous truth from him. He was a mage. A different being. What that meant, Aaron still didn't know. He turned his head to look at his mum, who was busy cleaning the living room, making the space a little more habitable. His mouth opened to ask her, to beg her to tell him what was going on. But before he could speak, a shadow crossed the window. Aaron pressed himself closer to the glass, craning his neck to look to the side, but he couldn't spot anyone. Not a moment later, there was a knock on the door. Kate looked up, her blue-eyed gaze snapping from Aaron to the door. She went to answer it while Aaron quickly followed after her. The door opened to a tired-looking Michael.

"Mike," Kate breathed with relief, before embracing her brother. "Thank Heavens. I was so worried."

"I'm not the one you should be worrying about," Michael said. "Everything okay, Kate? So far, I mean?"

Kate nodded. As Michael walked in, Aaron noted the two duffel bags in his hands. His uncle dropped them and walked over to envelop him in a crushing hug.

"How you doing, kiddo?" he asked.

"Fine," Aaron replied.

Michael moved into the living room. He glanced around before turning to Kate. "Chris?"

"He's talking to Drake," Kate replied.

A small smile came to Michael's face. "Drake. Damn, I'd almost forgotten about him." He ran a hand through his short hair and sat down with a sigh. "Anyone else here?"

"Not from our crowd," Kate replied.

"Your crowd?" Aaron asked before he could help it.

Kate looked around at him, pausing slightly before replying, "Old acquaintances."

Aaron clicked his mouth shut. If he was going to get vague answers, he wasn't going to bother asking her anything. He would speak to his dad instead.

Kate turned back to her brother. "I trust you took care of everything?"

Michael grimaced. "Yeah," he said quietly. "It's done."

Kate straightened up, but Aaron could see the grief in her features. "Thank you," she replied tightly.

Michael only nodded before he got to his feet. He walked to the bags in the hall and picked them up. He handed both to Aaron. "Here."

Aaron took them. "What's in them?" he asked, feeling their weight.

"Your stuff," Michael replied. "Clothes and shoes. Your friends' things are in the other one."

Aaron snapped his head up to look at him. "You went into their house?"

"I thought they'd like some of their things," Michael replied. "It's nothing special, just a few items of clothing and...and a few pictures from their mantel." He dropped his gaze. "They didn't get to attend their parents' funeral. The least I could do is get them their family photos."

Aaron didn't say anything. He glanced down at the bags before looking up at him with a frown. "Won't everyone notice that the Masons are missing?" he asked. "Us too, for that matter?"

Michael looked uncomfortable. He shared a look with Kate, before replying. "As far as that world is concerned, we're all missing."

"Missing?" Aaron repeated. "That's it? We're missing?" He looked across at his mum. "Sam and Rose have family. Grandparents, aunts, cousins." His voice rose slightly. "They're going to be looking for them."

"They can look," Kate replied quietly, "but they'll never find them."

Aaron's mouth fell open in shocked disgust. "Mum?"

"I feel for them," Kate said. "Really, I do. But there are countless people that vanish without a trace, never to be found again." Her expression stayed the same, coldly indifferent, but her eyes betrayed her turmoil. "Sooner or later, their family will learn to live with it. I don't like it, but there's no other choice. Samuel and Rosalyn cannot go back to that world. It's not safe for them."

Aaron's stomach tightened with anger. He didn't say another word but turned, making his way upstairs, shuffling the heavy bags through the narrow doorway. He was halfway up the stairs, well out of earshot, when Michael turned to his sister.

"Don't worry," he placated. "He'll understand eventually."

Kate nodded. "Yeah," she replied, sighing unhappily. "Eventually."

Michael moved towards her, his eyes dark and mournful. He reached into his inner jacket pocket and pulled out a small wooden box. Kate's eyes widened at the sight.

"Mike," she gasped. She moved forward and took the box from him. "How'd you...you knew about this?"

Michael nodded. "Chris told me," he explained. "I couldn't leave it behind."

Kate pressed her lips together tightly, to bite back her tears. Her hand caressed the box and, despite her struggle, a stifled sob escaped her. She looked up at her brother and nodded. "Thank you," she whispered.

Michael wrapped an arm around her, holding his sister close as she cried silently against his shoulder.

***

Aaron knocked on the door, shifting from one foot to the other, his fingers clutched tightly around the straps of the duffel bag. There was no answer but Aaron knew Sam and Rose were inside. With a deep breath, Aaron opened the door. Sam was next to the window while Rose was sitting on the bed, knees drawn to her chest and head resting on them. Aaron paused at the threshold, staring at her tear-soaked face and red-rimmed eyes. His heart twisted.

"Uncle Mike," he started. "He...um...he brought some of your...stuff." He held up the bag.

Neither Sam nor Rose moved, or said a single word. They simply stared at either him or the bag. Aaron lowered it gently to the floor and straightened up. His mouth was dry, voice choked. What could he say? How could he even phrase his apology? *Sorry I ruined your lives?* Even the thought of saying something so utterly useless made Aaron feel sick. No matter what he said, no matter how he said it, it was never going to be enough. Nevertheless, he couldn't stop himself.

"I'm sorry," he said, before backing out of the room and closing the door.

He was right. It was not enough. Not by a long shot.

***

"Any idea where I'll find him?"

Drake glanced at Chris before bringing the bottle to his lips and taking a large gulp. "I already told you, I don't know," he replied. "No one knows where Neriah is." He glared at Chris. "And you're risking everything to seek him out, you do know that?"

"I do," Chris replied quietly, "but I have to see him."

"Chris." Drake put the bottle down and turned in his seat to face him. "You don't know what it's like. It's ten times worse than before." His brow creased, heavy with concern. "Raoul is still looking for you. The minute he hears you're back, he'll come for you with all he's got. And with Aaron here..." He paused and took a deep breath. "You need to leave. Take your family, go back to the human realm and stay there – for good."

Chris sat for long, silent minutes before turning to look at Drake. "I spent fourteen years in the human realm," he said. "I did what I had to, to keep my family safe, but I wasn't happy, not for one single day. Neither was Kate and the both of us made Aaron miserable. All for what? In the name of safety?" He shook his head, face twisted with grief. "A lot of good that did. Because of us, because of our war, two innocent kids have lost their family, their parents, their home. All because we happened to live on the same street as them."

"It's not your fault–"

"Who you kidding?" Chris asked sharply. "Of course it's my fault!" He stopped and forced out a breath, fighting to remain calm. He leant back to rest against the sofa. "I should have told Aaron the truth. He would have stayed away from the humans if he knew–"

"It's done now," Drake cut in. "Stop worrying about others and focus on what's going to happen to *you*." His tone sharpened. "There's no knowing what Neriah will do."

"Neriah can do what he likes," Chris said quietly. "He's well within his right."

"What about your rights?" Drake asked. "You're not just an average mage, Chris. You're an Elemental too. You're just as important as Neriah."

"That doesn't matter now," Chris said.

"Of course it matters!" Drake snapped. "If you want to face Neriah and survive, you'd better change your attitude!" He lapsed into a strained silence, before slowly shaking his head. "For God's sake, Chris," he whispered, "what are you doing? Coming back here is like signing your life away. If not Raoul, then Neriah will destroy you." His dark eyes narrowed, filled with worry. "Please, go from here. Take your wife and your son and leave. Hide out and live your life. Forget about Neriah and this realm, please. I'm begging you."

"I tried living like that," Chris said, before taking a deep, steadying breath. "Neriah will hear me out, I know he will. After I've spoken to him, he can do what he likes. I don't really care." He looked across at Drake. "But I know Neriah will protect Aaron and at the end of the day, that's all that matters." His green eyes sharpened. "As for Raoul." A slight growl underlined the name. "I hope he comes for me. In fact, I'm counting on it."

Drake looked away, choosing to stare at the door rather than the quietly seething Chris. After a few tense minutes, he spoke. "I heard something about Ragdad," he said unhappily. "It's rumoured Neriah was staying there for a while." He shrugged. "It's worth a visit."

Chris nodded. "Thanks." He paused for a moment, his fingers nervously tapping against a glass bottle. "I was thinking...I want to go home first."

Drake turned to him with a frown. "Why?" he asked.

With great effort, Chris looked up to meet his eyes. Understanding flooded Drake's expression and he shook his head. "Chris–"

"I know," Chris said, nodding as he focused his sight on the half empty bottle and not Drake. "I know but...I just...It's been fourteen years. I *need* to see them, both of them."

"Did you..." Drake faltered. "Did you ever see Alex in the human realm?"

"No," Chris replied, his eyes sliding shut and his brow furrowing, as if in pain. "I expected to. I went to the usual places, stayed there for hours at a time, hoping to see him passing but..." He trailed off, swallowing heavily.

Drake nodded before taking a longer gulp of his drink. "If you're staying in this realm, then you need to first go and meet Neriah." He looked up at him. "Everything else has to wait." He swallowed heavily, his eyes dark with grief. "Alex and...and Ben, both have to wait."

Chris closed his eyes, but gave a small, resigned nod. They lapsed into silence, both men lost in their own troubled thoughts.

***

When Chris came back to the cottage, it was well into the night. Aaron was fast asleep, tucked up in the bed Kate had spent a good two hours cleaning. Chris found his wife standing at the bedroom door, her eyes fixed on their sleeping son.

"We're leaving, aren't we?" she asked without turning to him.

"Yes," Chris replied.

She nodded, her blue-eyed gaze still on Aaron. "We're not taking him with us?"

Chris paused before forcing the word out. "No."

Kate turned around at last, meeting his eyes. Slowly, she shook her head. "I don't know if I can leave him," she whispered. "I haven't lived a day without him."

Chris walked over to his wife, holding her gently by the shoulders.

"Have I?" he asked.

Kate moved into his arms and closed her eyes, breathing out a difficult sigh. Chris stared at his sleeping son. He tightened his hold around Kate. "You stay with him," he said.

Kate pulled back, looking up at him. "You really think I would do that?" she asked. "Let you and Michael face Neriah and take all the blame?"

"Maybe that would be better—"

"Chris." Kate stopped him. "All of us made that decision," she said quietly. "All of us will face the consequences."

Chris leant down, capturing her lips in a soft, gentle kiss. He pulled away and held her close to his chest. "What about Aaron?" he asked.

"He'll have to understand," Kate said. "There's no other choice."

"He's going to be so mad at us for leaving," Chris said with a heavy heart.

Kate closed her eyes, forcing the burning tears to stay back. "I know," she breathed, "but I would rather have him angry and alive, than fighting for his life."

***

The morning rays shone brightly into the room, warming Aaron's face and stirring him gently from his slumber. Aaron groaned and moved his face away, burying it under the duvet. But it was too late; he was already awake. Lifting his head, Aaron squinted in the daylight, looking around the room. Yawning, he got up and out of bed.

He dug through the bag Michael had brought him and found his toothbrush and a set of his own clothes. A quick shower later, Aaron made his way downstairs. He went into the living room, expecting to see his parents whispering suspiciously with each other again. He was surprised to find the room empty. He frowned.

"Mum?" he called. "Dad? Uncle Mike?"

He went back upstairs, to the third and last bedroom. He knocked on the door, but there was no answer. Opening the door, Aaron found the room empty. Frowning, Aaron headed to the front door. Maybe they were having breakfast. Aaron stepped outside into the dazzling sunlight. His sweeping gaze didn't find his parents at the table. Feeling a sense of dread building, Aaron hurried beyond the fence, looking up and down the street, but he couldn't spot them anywhere. He noticed Jason Burns walking back to his cottage.

"Mr Burns!" he called. "Hey, wait!" Aaron ran towards him.

"Li'l Adams." Jason grinned, coming to a stop. "How yeh this mornin'?"

"Yeah, fine. Do you know where my mum and dad are?" Aaron asked. "Or Uncle Mike?"

Jason stuck out his bottom lip and shook his head. "No' a clue." He grinned again. "They no' run off again, 'ave they?"

"Run off?" Aaron asked and his heart skipped a beat. "Again?"

Jason chuckled, his small eyes alight with amusement. "I'm jus' teasin'." He laughed. "They'll be around 'ere somewhere."

Aaron watched as the man turned and disappeared into his cottage. "Around, somewhere," he repeated under his breath. "Thanks, that helps," he grumbled, turning around and almost running into someone. He stumbled back. "Oh, sorry!"

"It's alright." Drake smiled back. "You okay?"

"Yeah," Aaron replied. "I'm just...I was looking for my mum and dad. Have you seen them?" He figured Drake would know where his dad was at the very least. He had spent the entire day with him yesterday.

"Actually, yeah," Drake replied, looking uncomfortable all of a sudden. "They left, about three hours ago."

Aaron stared at him. "Excuse me?"

"They left," Drake replied, his expression morose. "They...they left this for you." He held out a folded piece of paper.

Feeling like the bottom of his stomach had dropped out, Aaron took it, unfolding the paper quickly. He recognised his mum's neat writing.

Dear Aaron,

I know this will come as a shock and I apologise for that. I also know you will be very upset with us after reading this letter but unfortunately there is nothing I can do about that. There's so much we have to tell you – about this realm, about us, about you – but it deserves a proper conversation, not a letter. So you will have to forgive us for leaving you with so little information. Be assured that once we return, we will offer you a full explanation – that is a promise. For now, please accept this brief note.

Aaron, before you were born, your father, uncle and myself had to leave this realm. The reason can't and shouldn't be disclosed in a letter. Just understand that the situation was such that we had no choice. But with every decision comes a consequence. We all have to answer for our actions and we can't do that if you're with us.

We have left you in the safety of Salvador so no harm can come to you. You are protected as long as you stay in Salvador. If you came with us, your life would be endangered.

We've entrusted your care to Drake Logan. He is a good family friend, Aaron. He will look after you until we return. Take care of yourself, and Samuel and Rosalyn. We will see you soon, darling.

We love you.

Mum and Dad

Aaron looked up from the letter, his heart thudding so fast it felt like it was going to beat its way out of his chest. He looked up at Drake, a stranger he knew nothing about bar his name. He stared at the letter again, trying to come to grips with what had happened.

His parents were gone.

His uncle was gone.

They had left him.

They had left him completely alone in a world he knew nothing about.

6

BONDS OF FRIENDSHIP

Time passed in a slow, dreary manner, with Aaron doing nothing more than sitting at the front door for most of the day. He watched the happenings of the village with quiet, curious eyes. Every morning, he saw the petite blonde, Mary Collins, carry baskets of either eggs or fruit to the Stove. He saw groups of people, some as young as him, bustle in and out of the kitchen. The table was set and breakfast was served. It was at this point that Drake would stand at the table and look around for Aaron, gesturing to him to join them.

Aaron always got up and sat next to Drake to eat in silence. The rest of the people would chatter, glancing surreptitiously at him every so often, but no one spoke to him. Afterwards, Aaron would fill two plates with food and take them into the cottage for Sam and Rose. Wordlessly, Aaron would open the door and put the plates onto the small dresser and leave. He did the same for lunch and dinner, and so far Sam and Rose hadn't said anything to him, but quietly ate what was brought for them. Aaron would then go back and sit by the front door, watching the people carry baskets of fruit and vegetables from the fields to the cold room, or come back from the lake with nets full of fish. He watched them for three days.

Three days. That's how long it had been since his parents and uncle left him in Salvador. Aaron still couldn't believe they had gone. *His* parents – the same people who couldn't give him two minutes of privacy. The parents who demanded to know where he was every second of the day. His uncle who doted on him and would always fight on his behalf. The very same people who had been so overly protective of him had left him completely alone.

His mum's letter was still in his pocket. At various times in the day, Aaron would re-read it, in the hope of gleaning some clue or hint from it. He told himself he would find something; all he had to do was read between the lines. He pulled the letter out, unfolded it and started to read again, pondering over the words.

...before you were born, your father, uncle and myself had to leave this realm...

Leave this realm? Aaron narrowed his eyes at the words. What could possibly have happened that drove all three from their world? It had to be something undoubtedly big, something life-changing. People don't give up their world, their home, easily. What could have happened to his family to have all of them get up and leave?

The reason can't and shouldn't be disclosed in a letter. Just understand that the situation was such that we had no choice.

Had no choice. To Aaron, that meant his parents and uncle were driven out. They didn't want to leave but something or someone had made them. But who would want to get rid of them, and why?

A shadow crossed over him, snapping Aaron out of his thoughts. He looked up from the letter to see the boy with the striking blue eyes and platinum blond hair, the one who picked a fight with his dad on their first morning here. Skyler, that's what he said his name was. Skyler Avira.

"You on dog duty?" Skyler asked with a smirk. "Guarding the front door?"

Aaron folded the letter and pocketed it. He didn't fight the accusation. He didn't trust these people, these *mages*. There was no way he was going to let any of them in, not with his friends in the house.

"Can I help you?" Aaron asked.

Skyler grinned, flashing his teeth in a feral way. "Yeah, you can help me," he replied. "You can get out."

Aaron frowned. "Excuse me?"

"Get out," Skyler repeated. "I need this place vacated."

"What for?"

"For the Shattered ones," Skyler replied. "They'll be coming soon."

Aaron stood up, staring at Skyler with surprise. "Where am I supposed to go?"

"Do I look like I care?" Skyler asked. "Go wherever you want. Just have this place emptied in under an hour." He turned to leave.

"Wait," Aaron called, and Skyler turned with an amused grin. "You can't just throw me out," he protested.

"Believe me I can. Quite literally," Skyler said, his eyes glinting with malice.

"It's not just me in here," Aaron said. "My friends—"

"Hey, Adams," Skyler barked suddenly, "I don't give a crap who's with you. Just have this place cleaned out or I will personally drag you and your *friends* out of here."

Aaron's hands clenched into fists and he straightened up to stand tall. "Go for it," he said quietly.

Skyler looked surprised. "Really?" he asked, stepping towards him.

"Really," Aaron replied, sounding braver than he felt. "Drag me out, 'cause I'm not leaving."

Skyler grinned. "With pleasure," he muttered and walked towards him.

"Skyler." Mary arrived, halting him. "Behave," she muttered crossly, as she walked closer.

"What?" Skyler asked. "He's asking for it."

Mary ignored him and turned to Aaron. "Don't mind him," she said, gesturing to Skyler, "but you do have to move. There's a large number of Shattered ones coming and we need the space. These are Sanctuary cottages. They aren't meant for long-term use." She turned and pointed to the cottages at the end of the row. "The ones with the blue doors are for permanent residence."

Aaron looked at Skyler. If the boy had just explained it like she had, he would have happily moved.

"Okay." Aaron nodded. "I'll just let my friends know and gather our things."

***

Aaron knocked gently before opening the door to find Sam sitting on the floor, back against a wall, and Rose next to the window. Both looked around at him as Aaron walked in, but, just like the last three days, they didn't speak. Aaron lingered in the doorway.

"They...the people," he started. "I mean, mages," he quickly corrected. "They want this place vacated." He pushed on as alarm crossed the twins' faces. "They're moving us into a different cottage." He looked around the room, an excuse not to meet the red-rimmed, puffy eyes of his friends. "We need to leave within the hour," Aaron continued, "so if you want to get your stuff together..." He trailed off. Without meeting their eyes, he turned around to leave.

"Aaron?"

He stopped at Rose's quiet call and turned back. She was staring at him, her usually warm brown eyes looked dull, tired and bloodshot. Rose looked to Sam, just a small, fleeting glance, before turning to Aaron again.

"Is that all you're going to say?" she asked.

Aaron paused, brow furrowed. "What?"

"Five days," Sam started in a rough, husky voice. "Five days we've been here and this is all you have to say to us?"

Aaron shook his head. "I don't...I don't understand. I thought you weren't speaking to me."

"Exactly when were we supposed to talk to you?" Sam asked. Annoyance tinged his voice. "When you run in here with plates of food and hurry out like your life depends on it?"

"We thought you didn't have the time to talk to us," Rose said quietly.

"Figured you'd be too busy out exploring this new world of yours," Sam added.

Aaron's face heated up with anger. "It's not my world," he objected.

"Isn't it?" Sam asked.

"My world is where I've lived my whole life," Aaron replied.

The lines on Sam's brow disappeared and he smiled a little. "So you're not jumping onto this mage bandwagon then?"

"I'm still me," Aaron said. "No matter what anyone says. I'm the same person I always was."

Sam smiled with relief. "Good to hear it."

They fell into silence, each just looking at the other.

"Sam," Aaron said, walking two steps closer. "I...I don't know what to say." He shook his head, baring his guilt. "How do I even begin to apologise? What do I say for ruining your lives?" He looked across at Rose, seeing her tears. It made Aaron want to run out, but he forced himself to stay. "It's my fault," he said. "I did this to you, to both of you. That...that car...The ground. I did that. It was a reflux or...something." He shook his head, trying to remember what his dad had said.

Sam's expression darkened and Aaron could see the grief, thick as a coat, cover his whole being.

"It's my fault," Aaron said, so softly he was whispering. "It's all my fault. It's my fault you're stuck in this mess...in this realm..." He pushed the words out, past the bubble of guilt that was growing at the back of his throat, threatening to suffocate him. "Sam, I'm sorry." He came to kneel next to his friend. "I'm sorry. God, Sam, I'm *so* sorry." He looked over at Rose, who was furiously wiping her wet cheeks. "Rose, I'm...I'm so sorry."

Rose sniffed back her tears and looked over at him. "Did you know you were a mage?" she asked.

Aaron slowly shook his head. "No."

"Did you do that reflux thing on purpose?" Sam asked.

"No."

"Then how can any of this be your fault?" Rose asked.

Aaron gaped at her. "Wait." He looked between the twins. "You...How?" he asked in disbelief. "How can you not blame me?"

"We did, at the beginning," Sam said. "When your uncle told us about you being different and that we were marked because we witnessed you using your..." He paused. "...*power* or magic or whatever it was." He took in a breath. "God's honest truth, we blamed you. But then, over the days we've been here just sitting and thinking, we realised it's not your fault." His eyes glinted with anger. "It's your parents' fault." When Aaron didn't protest, Sam continued. "They're the ones to blame. They should have told you about being different. They should have explained what you were capable of. If you knew, you would've been able to control yourself. If you knew—"

"I wouldn't have been friends with you," Aaron said, interrupting him.

Sam stared at him with surprise. "You'd ditch us?"

"You'd still be in your world, with your family, if I had," Aaron replied.

Sam didn't say anything.

Rose took in a deep breath. "Let's not talk about that," she said. "We need to figure out what happens now. How long do we stay here? What's the plan?"

Aaron shrugged. "Dunno."

"You haven't asked your parents?" She looked surprised.

"It's not like they would tell me," Aaron said. Taking in a breath, he added, "And...they're gone."

"Gone?" Sam frowned. "Where?"

Aaron shook his head, trying hard to mask his heartbreak. "They just...left." He dug out the letter from his pocket and handed it to Sam. "Left that for me."

Rose got up and crossed the room so she too could read the letter. Quiet minutes passed as the twins read it with furrowed brows, before sharing looks of surprise.

"Your life would be endangered if you went with them?" Rose asked. "Why would they think that? Who would want to hurt you?"

"Those men from that cloud-mist thing," Sam offered. "Maybe they're after you?"

"Me?" Aaron asked, his heart leaping painfully. "Why would they be after me?"

"Think about it," Sam said. "They came right after you cracked open the ground to stop that car." He paused before meeting Aaron's gaze. "Almost as if they were waiting for you to use your powers so they could come for you. They were chasing after you," Sam pointed out. "Your mum and dad were desperate to get you out of the way. They come here," he gestured to the room, "some mad place in another *realm*, whatever that means." He rubbed at his chin. "They claim this place is safe for you." He looked at Aaron. "It makes sense. Those things came for you."

Aaron's heart missed several beats. "Why?" he asked. "What do they want from me?"

"Your parents hid the fact that you're a...That you're...different." Rose shifted uncomfortably. "If they can keep a secret that big, what else could they hide from you."

Aaron swallowed heavily. "I have to find out what going on," he said. "What it is they're keeping from me."

"Sounds like a plan," came a sarcastic voice, startling the three. Skyler stood at the door, leaning against the frame, arms crossed and cool blue eyes set on Aaron. "My advice? Take your scheming somewhere else. I need this space."

***

Aaron stepped out into the sun with a smile. He had his best friends by his side. Skyler led the way through the gate and down the long row of houses.

"What did your mum and dad say?" Rose asked. "Did they explain anything about this place?" she asked, staring wide-eyed at the long table that stretched down the road.

"What do you think?" Aaron asked.

"Considering they took fourteen years to tell you what species you are, I'm thinking...no," Sam said.

Skyler stopped at the first blue-doored cottage. "Here you go." He waved a hand at the gate. "Your humble abode."

Aaron noticed a girl, the one with blue streaks in her hair, watching them from across the street. She walked towards them, a quizzical look on her face.

"Skyler," she called, looking half amused and half annoyed. "What do you think you're doing?"

"I'm moving them to a permanent location," Skyler replied.

The girl's grey eyes flickered from the cottage back to Skyler. "You've got to be kidding."

"It's been over a week, Ella," Skyler said, his blue eyes bright with mischief. "He's not coming back." He turned to Aaron. "The place is all yours."

"Wait, wait," the girl – Ella – came forward, one hand on Skyler's arm. "This isn't funny."

"I agree," Skyler replied. "There's nothing funny about it." He pointed to the cottage. "The house is unoccupied; we have permanent residents looking for a place to stay." He held up both hands. "What's the problem?"

"The problem?" Ella asked, with a raised eyebrow. "I think the problem is six-foot tall, has black hair, green eyes and the ability to kick your ass across Salvador."

"Kyran's not coming back," Skyler said. "And even if he does, he's been gone too long. Don't use it, you lose it." He turned to Aaron. "Get a move on." He nodded to the door.

Aaron paused. "We don't want to get into the middle of anything—"

"There's nothing to get into the middle of," Skyler interrupted. "The place is all yours." He smirked at Ella and added, "Feel free to throw out anything you don't want."

Ella shook her head in disgust and walked away. With a chuckle, Skyler left as well. Aaron turned to Sam, to see him staring at Ella, watching her. Only when Ella went around the corner and disappeared from sight, did Sam blink and turn around. Seeing the raised eyebrows of both Aaron and Rose, Sam only shrugged before heading towards their new cottage.

***

The blue-doored cottage was much, much nicer than the cottage they had been staying in. For a start, it was cleaner. It was sparsely furnished, but what was there was in good condition. The layout of the cottage was the same as the previous one: downstairs was one main living room, a bathroom, but no kitchen, and upstairs was made up of three bedrooms and another bathroom. The biggest room had a bed and a small wardrobe. The second room was the same but the third room had no bed, just a wide built-in wooden cupboard that none of them could open.

From Skyler and Ella's conversation, Aaron realised the cottage had previously belonged to someone named Kyran. So when he opened the wardrobe and found clothes stacked inside, he wasn't at all surprised.

"What should we do?" Sam asked, standing in the room with both hands on his hips.

"What can we do?" Aaron replied. "We'll just push this stuff to the side, in case that Kyran bloke comes back for—"

"What are you on about?" Sam asked. "I'm talking about the beds."

"What about them?" Aaron asked.

"There's only two beds and three of us," Sam pointed out.

"Oh." Aaron glanced around at Rose. "Yeah, that's a problem."

Rose smiled. "Just a little one," she teased.

Aaron brushed a hand through his hair, thinking. "There's a sofa downstairs," he offered. "It looks pretty decent."

"Who's going to draw *that* short straw?" Sam asked, pulling a face.

"I don't mind sleeping on it," Rose said, "but I'm not sleeping downstairs on my own."

"Good point," Sam said. "We'll bring it upstairs."

Half an hour later, the sofa had been hauled and dragged up the stairs, and into the biggest room. The three of them stood staring at the sight of the sofa, pressed up against the wall.

"So," Sam started. "Who—"

"Not it!" Rose and Aaron called simultaneously.

"Damn it!" Sam turned to his sister. "You said you didn't mind sleeping on the sofa!"

"I said I didn't mind," Rose said. "I didn't say I *would* sleep on it."

"That's just trickery at its worst," Sam complained.

"Oh, don't be a baby," Rose said, turning to go to her room next door.

"I'm not the baby," Sam called after her. "You're the one that still does 'not it' to settle things."

Aaron smiled. This was the first time in days that Sam and Rose sounded, just a fraction, like their old selves again.

**

After unpacking their pitiful amount of clothing and possessions, Aaron, Sam and Rose stepped out of the cottage to explore Salvador.

"You've really not been out here?" Rose asked as they walked towards the lake.

"No," Aaron replied, "apart from the first day. My dad took me with him when he went looking for his friend."

"Is that Drake? The one mentioned in the letter?" Rose asked.

Aaron nodded.

"What's he like?" Sam asked.

Aaron shrugged. "Quiet. Doesn't get involved much. The only time I see him is at mealtimes."

"Does everyone really sit at that table?" Rose asked.

"Yeah," Aaron replied.

"Isn't that a little...weird?" she asked. "I mean, the whole village sits together to eat? What's wrong with eating in your own houses?"

"No clue." Aaron shrugged.

"Maybe it's because none of the houses have kitchens," Sam pointed out.

"I'm sure they could build one, if they wanted," Rose argued. "It's not like–" She stopped short, staring ahead.

Sam followed her gaze and his eyes widened in amazement. "Whoa," he breathed.

Aaron smiled as his friends stood, taking in the sheer beauty of the lake. The vast, glassy pool of a blue so rich it beggared belief. The green of the surrounding trees reflected in the lake, giving some areas of the water a beautiful shade of not quite blue and not quite green. There was something about the stillness of that water that calmed Aaron. A serenity that he had never experienced before. A simple glance told him Rose and Sam were affected too. Gentle lines curved around their mouths, lifting their lips up. Rose let out a soft sigh.

"It's a sight, isn't it?" Aaron said.

Sam nodded. "Does anyone else have the urge to jump in?" He looked around at a frowning Rose and Aaron. "Just me then?"

Aaron chuckled and all three turned to walk away. They headed towards the orchard, while Aaron told them what happened when he went there with his dad.

"Wait, that Drake guy said it wasn't safe here?" Sam asked. "But your mum said the opposite in her letter."

"That's what I don't get," Aaron said as they walked down the path.

"How can it not be safe?" Rose asked. "The people – I mean, mages – they don't seem dangerous."

"I don't know about that," Aaron said. "They're not exactly the friendliest bunch." He thought specifically about Skyler and the crowds of mages that sat at the table and stole glances his way, but never spoke to him. "Other than Mary, no one's even bothered to speak to me." He paused before adding, "Correction, Skyler spoke to me but I would much rather he just ignore me like the rest."

Rose shivered. "That's the boy who moved us?" she asked. "He gives me the creeps."

"That's 'cause he *is* a creep," Aaron said. "Reminds me of Matthews. The same attitude, the same smirk, the same I'm-gonna-beat-you-to-within-an-inch-of-your-life type of look in his eyes."

"Let him try," Sam glowered. "There are three of us against him."

"He has a whole gang, Sammy," Aaron pointed out. "All the same as him – big, with more muscles than brains, I bet."

"I don't know about that," a voice said from behind them, making all three turn around. A young boy with copper-brown hair pulled back in a tight ponytail stood smiling at them. "Skyler's pretty smart and, unfortunately for the rest of us, he knows it."

Aaron recognised him. He was the boy who set the table with flying plates. Aaron had seen him do the same every day for all three mealtimes.

"It's rude to eavesdrop, I know," the boy continued, his sparkling hazel eyes crinkling in amusement, "but I couldn't help myself." He stared at Aaron. "You're Aaron Adams, aren't you?"

Aaron nodded slowly.

The boy rubbed a hand down his shirt before holding it out.

"It's a pleasure." He smiled. "Alan Kings."

Aaron shook his hand.

"I've been wanting to introduce myself for a while now," Alan said, "but Logan's been sitting with you, so I've not dared."

"Drake?" Aaron asked. "Why would Drake's being there stop you?"

"Logan's warned everyone not to speak to you," Alan replied.

"What?" Aaron asked with surprise. "Why?"

"So no one badgers you with questions, I suppose," Alan said with a shrug. "It's all everyone wants to know. Where have the Adams been? Why you didn't come back?" He smiled at Aaron. "Which, judging by your dumbstruck expression, you wouldn't know how to answer. Seems like it's a good thing Logan's scared everyone into keeping quiet around you."

Aaron silently agreed. It would drive him insane if everyone kept asking him questions he wanted answers to himself.

"Why's everyone scared of Drake?" Aaron asked.

"You're joking, right?" Alan asked with a grin. "Logan was a Hunter. You don't mess with Hunters. You do what they say and you do it with a smile. Which brings me back to Skyler." He stared at Aaron for a long moment. "Don't get in his way, and if you wanna talk about him, do it behind closed doors." He gave a sweeping glance to his surroundings. "Right now, this place is Skyler's playground. Him and Ella are the ones in charge. To them does most of Salvador's allegiance lie." He looked back at Aaron. "Of course, now that you're here, they have to give you back your share, but until you gather a few friends, don't invite Skyler's wrath by talking about him." He nodded at Aaron before stepping back. "I better get back. Mother Mary will have my head if I don't get these to her in time for dinner." He gestured to the basket full of potatoes sitting by his feet. A twitch of his fingers and the basket rose into mid-air.

Aaron watched, wide-eyed as the basket floated next to Alan. Sam and Rose let out choked sounds of surprise.

"Shattereds," Alan chuckled. "So easy to spot." He grinned and set off down the path, the basket of potatoes floating behind him.

7

THE HUNTERS

When the residents of Salvador gathered around the table for dinner that evening, Aaron took his seat opposite Rose and Sam. He waited, head turned, watching the path that led from the orchard. He ignored the stares and whispers from the others. His peripheral vision told him he wasn't the only one being stared at. Sam and Rose were shamelessly gaped at as well, leading to Rose self-consciously pulling at her top. Aaron looked over at her. Meeting her eyes, he shook his head.

"You look fine," he assured her. "It's not your fault they can't stop staring."

The eavesdropping mages looked away and Rose smiled gratefully at Aaron. Skyler and Ella walked over together and sat down, roughly twenty or so chairs away from Aaron. The rest of Skyler's group spread around him. Next to approach the table, was a single line of ladies in flowing robes, all fair-haired with pale blue eyes staring ahead and hands resting on the shoulder of the woman in front.

Rose and Sam noticed them too.

"Are they...?" Sam started.

"Blind," Aaron confirmed.

He had known the moment he first saw them. Their unblinking gaze, staring unseeingly ahead, and the way they came to sit at the table made it obvious they were without sight.

Alan appeared at the head of the table, stacks of plates hovering at either side of him. He met Aaron's eyes and grinned. "Heads up," he warned before throwing out a hand, sending a line of plates flying along the length of the table.

Aaron watched Sam and Rose as the surprise, shock and overwhelming disbelief crossed their faces. Both gave a little jump as two plates came to a clattering stop before them. They looked up at Aaron, meeting his smiling gaze. Aaron shrugged and couldn't help but chuckle as an awestruck Sam watched Alan set the plates on the other side of the table.

"Ava's not here yet." Alan grinned, meeting Aaron's eyes again. "So I'm taking a shortcut."

He lifted a hand and rolls of forks, knives and spoons wrapped in white paper napkins rose into the air. A flick of Alan's hand and the sets of cutlery raced along the length of the table. For a moment, the sets hovered above everyone's heads, before they fell onto the plates with a *clink*. Alan nodded, seemingly happy with his work. He turned, picked up the empty cutlery bucket and walked away.

Sam and Rose turned to Aaron with wide eyes and gobsmacked expressions.

"That was...Wow," Rose breathed. She leant towards Aaron. "Can you do that?"

Aaron was quick to shake his head. "No."

"What can you do?" Sam asked. "Other than crack open the ground, that is?"

Aaron's heart quickened. "I don't know," he replied.

He caught sight of Mary and her kitchen helpers, trays in hand, heading to the green-doored cottages. Aaron watched as they knocked on the doors and handed the trays of food to the solemn and tired looking individuals that answered. He realised with a painful lurch of his heart that Mary was delivering dinner to the humans – the Shattereds, as they put it – that had arrived at Salvador today. He remembered Mary telling his mum that it was against protocol for mages to eat inside the cottages. There were different rules for humans it seemed.

Aaron turned to look away from the depressing sanctuary cottages, not wanting to dwell on what must have happened to the humans for them to come to Salvador.

The sight of Drake Logan, making his way towards the table, distracted Aaron. He saw the surprise flit across Drake's face when he spotted him. Drake obviously wasn't expecting to see Aaron already seated at the table. Drake's gaze moved to Sam and Rose and a look of understanding flashed on his face. When Drake sat down next to Aaron, he spoke to him for the first time in three days.

"I see your friends are out and about."

Aaron nodded. Even though Sam and Rose were seated across from him, Drake's voice was so low only Aaron could hear him.

"It was going to happen eventually," Aaron replied.

Drake nodded, unfurling his cutlery from the napkin and setting them on either side of his plate. "I wasn't expecting them out this soon," he said.

"Shattereds take their time."

"Why do you call them Shattereds?" Aaron asked.

Drake met his eyes but quickly looked away. "It's the name mages give to the humans who have to leave their realm."

"But why the term *Shattered?*" Aaron asked.

"Because," Drake replied quietly, "only those who have nothing left, whose lives have become *shattered*, leave their world behind to come to this realm."

Aaron's stomach clenched with disgust. "Don't you think that's insensitive?" he asked.

Drake smiled a little. "You'll find mages aren't the most sensitive of beings."

Mary arrived at the table with her helpers lined behind her, all carrying large platters of food. A delicious aroma filled the air, making mouths water and stomachs rumble. Silver trays heaped with grilled chicken, dishes of fried rice, and bowls of crunchy, colourful salad were lined along the table. A platter of potato skins stuffed with cheese, and another dish overflowing with roasted vegetables were placed directly in front of Sam and Rose.

Aaron and Drake ate in silence as the others chatted amongst themselves. Even Rose and Sam were whispering to each other, discussing the richer taste of the food. Aaron glanced at Drake, taking in the sight of the quiet, serious, dark-haired man.

Logan was a Hunter. You don't mess with Hunters. You do what they say and you do it with a smile.

Alan's words spoken that afternoon echoed in Aaron's head. Swallowing his mouthful of chicken, Aaron cleared his throat. "Drake?" he said softly. "What is it you do?"

Drake looked over at him. "What do you mean?"

"Like a job," Aaron said. "What do you do for a living?"

Drake smiled, just a slight lifting of the corners of his lips. "Things don't work like that here," he said. "Nobody works for a living." He gestured to the table. "Everyone uses their powers to live. Some grow food from the ground, others manipulate the water for our gain." He shrugged. "We all live together, taking care of life's necessities."

"You work in the orchard," Aaron said. "So is your power to make things grow?"

Drake chuckled, surprising Aaron and the surrounding mages. They all turned to stare at Drake, as if seeing the man laugh was a rare sight.

"Yes," Drake said, after calming down a little. "I make things *grow*." He shook his head in amusement.

Aaron shifted in his seat, knowing that Drake's little laugh was at his expense. "Have you always worked in the orchard?" Aaron asked. "Or did you do something else before that?"

Drake's amusement quickly left him and he turned to look at Aaron, his eyes once again serious. "What do you mean?"

"I heard you were once a Hunter," Aaron said.

Drake's eyebrows shot up, disappearing under the strands of the wavy hair that fell across his forehead. His mouth opened but he took a moment to speak. "Where did you hear that?"

"You hear a lot of things around here," Aaron replied. "Is it true?"

Drake seemed to be fighting the urge to answer. "Yes," he said at last.

"What did you hunt?" Aaron asked. Somehow, he didn't think mages shot down wild animals.

"Everything that needs to be hunted," Drake replied.

"Tell him straight out," a voice called from down the table. Aaron turned to see Skyler smirking at him. "Tell dear Adams what it is Hunters do."

"Stay out of this, Skyler," Drake said at once.

The table had hushed to silence, watching either Skyler, Drake or Aaron.

"Oh, come on." Skyler cocked his head to the side, icy blue eyes fixed on Aaron. "He wants to know. It's obvious daddy dear hasn't told him."

"Skyler," Drake warned.

"You wanna know what Hunters do?" Skyler asked Aaron, ignoring Drake. "Hunters do what mages were created to do."

"That's enough," Drake said.

Skyler gave him a single glance, before looking back at Aaron. "We hunt and destroy demons."

"Demons?" Aaron asked, with a furrowed brow.

"Demons," Skyler confirmed. "Entities that exist solely to cause death and destruction."

"Skyler! Enough!" Drake rose to his feet, face twisted in anger and eyes blazing. "Don't say another word!"

"Why?" Aaron asked, turning to Drake and rising to his feet too. "Why won't you let him tell me anything?"

"Because Chris doesn't want you to know!" Drake snapped.

Aaron stilled. Silence fell across the table.

"Why?" Aaron asked.

"Because," Drake breathed deeply, in an effort to calm down, "no one knows if you're staying. What's the point of learning about a world you're never going to be a part of?"

***

The lanterns floated above their heads, casting a warm glow over the two boys, but Aaron still shivered as the night's cool breeze washed over him.

"Why?" he asked, his voice soft and filled with honest confusion.

The boy turned around to look at him, blazing green eyes narrowed in agitation. "What do you mean, *why*?" he snarled. "Because it's up to me, that's why! It's my choice and I'm saying no."

Aaron swallowed. A painful stab of disappointment swelled in his chest. "I thought you would help me," he said quietly.

The boy glared at him. "Why would you think that?"

Aaron shrugged. "I don't know. I just...I felt like you would."

The boy shook his head. "It's not my job to help anyone."

Aaron nodded, his heart twisting with misery. "I get it," he said. "I have to do it myself. I'm on my own."

The boy stared at him, the vivid green of his eyes darkened a shade. "We're all on our own, Aaron," he said quietly. "It's time you got used to it."

Aaron jolted awake, his gasp echoing in the dark room. His frantically beating heart reverberated in his mouth. He forced out a long, deep breath. It was just a dream. Another strange dream of the same boy, but this one left him with an ache in his chest. He couldn't understand why. The dream hadn't been horrific. Nothing happened in it. He was just talking, or perhaps they were arguing, but even that shouldn't leave him feeling so...heartbroken.

"Aaron?" Sam's sleepy voice carried in the dark.

"Yeah?" Aaron answered.

"You okay?" he mumbled.

Aaron swallowed, closing his eyes and taking a deep breath in. "Yeah, just a bad dream," he replied.

The sheets ruffled as Sam shifted his position on the sofa. "Don't worry," he whispered. "Go back to sleep."

Aaron nodded, even though Sam couldn't see him in the dark. He turned to the side. Drake's words kept spinning in his mind. So that's why Drake hadn't bothered to speak to him. Why make the effort to get to know him when Aaron might not be around much longer? As quietly as he could, Aaron dug his mum's letter out of his pocket. It was too dark to read it, but Aaron just held it in his hands, wondering where his parents were at this very moment? How long would they be away?

The door creaked open.

"Aaron?"

Aaron sat up in bed. "Rose? What's wrong?" he asked.

The door opened wider and Aaron heard her come further into the room.

"I heard you and Sam talking," she said. "I can't sleep in there."

"Why?" Aaron asked.

"Don't know." Rose sounded afraid. "Think I can sleep here?"

"No," Sam interrupted. "You wanted the separate room. Deal with it."

"Please, Sammy?" Rose used that voice, the one Aaron knew would win most of the arguments with Sam.

Sure enough, Sam's sigh of resignation echoed in the room. "Fine." The sheets rustled as Sam sat up. "I'll sleep in there."

"I'll sleep on the sofa," Aaron offered.

"I have another idea," Rose said, stopping both boys.

Ten minutes later, all three were pushing the bed from next door into the first room. It might have been easier if they could have seen what they were doing, but the lanterns hanging from the ceilings didn't have any switches so they were left in the dark.

"Go to your left – the left!" Sam snapped.

"There's no more left...left," Aaron protested.

"Alright, to the right then." Sam groaned and pulled the bulky bed to the other side.

Somehow, pushing and shoving, and amidst a lot of yelling, they managed to get the bed situated somewhere between the first bed and the sofa. The room was cramped but none of them cared. They settled into their respective beds and sofa.

"Better, Rose?" Aaron asked.

"Much better," she replied. A few minutes passed in silence, but all three were still awake. "Aaron?" Rose whispered.

"Yeah?"

"You reckon what Drake said was true?"

Aaron paused. "Why would he lie?"

"Do you think your parents are going to leave this realm?" Rose asked.

Aaron let out a sigh. "I don't know," he replied. "According to Drake, it's unlikely we'll be sticking around."

A pause, then Rose asked, "What are the chances they'll take us along with them?"

Aaron faltered. He honestly didn't know what his parents were planning.

"We don't need them, Rose," Sam said. "We'll be fine."

"I don't know if mum and dad are planning on taking you both with them," Aaron said, "but I'm not going anywhere without you two."

"Thanks, Aaron," she whispered and Aaron could hear the relief in her voice.

***

The days passed with Aaron and the twins busily exploring the City of Salvador. They found the place wasn't small, not by any standard. First there was the farmland that stretched for miles. Past that was a whole clutter of small buildings. They looked like shops, stocking everything from clothes to books, but there was no one running them. They were just left there, doors open with stacks and stacks of merchandise on the shelves. Aaron and the twins had a look around, but didn't touch anything.

"I bet you it's alarmed," Sam said, eyeing a leather jacket suspiciously.

"I can't see any surveillance," Rose said, craning her neck back to peer at the ceiling.

"It wouldn't be very good surveillance if it wasn't hidden," Sam replied.

"You're so paranoid," Rose said. "Everything's a conspiracy with you."

They wandered around the shops for a little while before heading back. As they passed the orchard, they saw Drake Logan supervising a group of mages carrying baskets of fruit to the Stove. As Aaron passed, Drake looked around at him. A simple nod in form of a greeting was all Aaron got before Drake turned his attention back to the mages.

Ever since Drake's outburst at the table, almost a week ago, he had avoided Aaron, going back to the practice of not speaking to him. Along with Drake, it seemed that the majority of Salvador had taken an oath not to speak to Aaron. They stared at him when he passed on the street or when he sat at the table at mealtimes, but no one ever approached him – save for Alan and Mary, but even that was only when Aaron was at the table.

As Aaron and the twins made their way past the lake, they spotted Skyler with his usual group of mages making their way towards them.

"Here comes trouble," Rose muttered. "Just ignore him, Aaron. Don't react to anything he says."

Aaron nodded. He was planning on ignoring Skyler anyway. When they passed by, Skyler didn't say anything. He didn't even look in Aaron's direction. But the quiet snickers and the looks thrown Aaron's way by the surrounding mages indicated Skyler had made a snarky remark out of Aaron's earshot.

"You notice something about those mages?" Rose asked, once the group had passed.

"They're all prats," Sam said, looking back at the crowd with annoyance.

"Aside from that," Rose said. "They all seem rather fond of ink."

Aaron had noticed. From the spiral tattoo on Skyler's shoulder to the various marks adorning almost every mage in his group.

"I noticed Drake's got a dagger inked on his wrist," Aaron said.

"Drake doesn't look the type to get a tattoo," Rose said.

"Yeah," Aaron agreed. "He seems too serious."

"Maybe he got it when he was drunk," Sam suggested.

They continued walking down the path. In the distance, Aaron could see Alan carrying baskets into the Stove.

"What do you think Alan meant by this place being Skyler's playground?" Aaron asked.

Sam shrugged. "Dunno, mate."

"He does act like he owns the place," Rose mused.

"Alan said that Skyler and Ella have Salvador's allegiance," Aaron repeated, "but that I would get my share. What does that even mean?"

"You should speak to Alan," Rose said. "Ask him to explain. He'll probably tell you."

"Not if Drake's warned him," Aaron said. "You heard what he said about Hunters and doing as you're told. Drake's warned everyone not to speak to me and not to tell me anything because..." His heart jolted. "Because dad told him to."

"You reckon what Skyler said was true?" Sam asked. "About...about hunting demons?"

"I always thought demons were just metaphorical," Aaron said. He glanced up at Sam. "Then again, I didn't think half the things I've seen here were ever possible."

"I wonder why Drake stopped being a Hunter," Rose said. "He seemed really uncomfortable talking about his past."

"Drake seems uncomfortable talking, full stop," Aaron said.

"Maybe he's retired," Sam offered.

"Could be," Aaron agreed. "He's not that old, but if Skyler's a Hunter, then–"

"Wait, Skyler's a Hunter?" Sam asked, stopping in his tracks. "How d'you get there?"

"He told us," Aaron replied. "That day, at the table. He said, '*we* hunt demons'. He was talking about himself."

"How old do you reckon Skyler is?" Rose asked.

"Can't be more than twenty, if even that," Sam guessed.

Rose slowly shook her head. "Demon Hunter. Seems like a heavy title to bear."

A sudden, bright light flashed – so intense, the entire street lit up. It was gone as quickly as it had come, but it left Aaron blinking spots away from his vision. An audible click rang around them, and far in the distance Aaron saw a rectangular doorway forming. The purr of numerous engines cut through the air before Aaron saw the first of several motorbikes racing in. A group of twelve rode down the road, heading straight for the cottages.

"What the—?" Sam gasped.

A few doors to the cottages opened and people came out to see what the commotion was, but the bikers didn't slow down. They swerved to the back of Jason Burns's house and disappeared into the thick, dense wood that was the backdrop to the cottages.

Aaron shared a look with the twins. "Should we?" he asked.

Sam looked to his sister, before meeting Aaron's eyes. "Why not?"

The three ran after the bikers. Had they not seen the bikes turn into the woodland area behind Jason's cottage, they would have never noticed the dusty, narrow path there. Using the sound of the roaring engines as a guide, Aaron, Sam and Rose followed the path down a steep hill. At the bottom they found another clutter of buildings side by side, arranged in a semi-circle. The buildings were big and bulky, a mass of grey stone with no windows and chunky steel shutters blocking the entrances. There was no sign on any of the buildings to indicate what they were. The three raced past, having no time to stop and wonder what they were. The sound of the bikes drew them deeper into the woods, still on the dusty, rocky path. The sound suddenly cut off, making the trio come to a halt. Aaron leant against a tree, trying to catch his breath.

"Now what?" Rose asked, wiping a hand across her sweaty brow.

"We keep going," Aaron replied. "Come on."

He led the twins, hoping the end of the path would get them to the bikers. He was grateful when they reached the top of a hill and spotted the mages parked in another clearing at the bottom.

"Look at them," Sam gushed, his eyes twinkling. "Such beauties."

Aaron rolled his eyes. "Stop staring at the bikes and focus on the mages riding them."

But Sam was squinting, trying to make as much as he could about the dozen gleaming bikes at the bottom of the hill. "They look like Ducati Panigales," he whispered. "Those ones, over there, to the left, they're definitely Kawasaki Ninjas." He was practically drooling. "God, I just wanna touch one."

Rose whacked him on the arm. "Focus!"

"Right, right," Sam muttered.

Standing a safe distance away, under the shade of the trees, Aaron, Sam and Rose studied the bikers. They were all young, barely in their twenties. They wore boots, tight-fitting jeans, what looked like vests under zipped tops, and long denim coats with flared ends. There was something about them, something in their body language that reminded Aaron strongly of Skyler. Aaron could easily imagine them as the crowd of mages that were always by Skyler's side.

One by one, the mages got off their bikes, huddling around one particular red-haired girl. She turned to speak to the assembled group, nodding her head at several members. It was as she craned her neck to speak to a tall, brown-haired boy that Aaron caught sight of the tattoo, sprawling up her neck and disappearing behind her ear and under her hair. From this distance, it looked like an image of barbed wire, only it was a strange shade of silver as opposed to the standard black ink. That's when Aaron knew who they were.

"Hunters," he breathed. "They're Hunters."

"How do you know?" Sam asked.

"They look like Hunters," Aaron replied.

"Well, well." Skyler's drawl made Aaron turn around to see him standing with his usual group. "Look at that? Barely here a fortnight and little Adams can already tell his mages apart."

The crowd around Skyler snickered. Aaron didn't say anything.

"You should wear a bell or something," Sam said. "You're always creeping up on us."

Skyler flashed him a grin. "A bell?" he asked, walking over to Sam. "I could send a tornado and you lot'll still be unaware." He looked Sam up and down with cold blue eyes. "It's rather pathetic how clueless you are."

Skyler and his cronies swept past Aaron and the twins, heading down the hill. Aaron didn't waste a minute. He followed after them, as did Rose and Sam. They reached the bottom of the hill and walked over to the bikers, who had noticed the approaching crowd. The red-haired girl stood at the front, her beautiful sea-green eyes narrowed at Skyler.

"Bella, so nice to see you again," Skyler greeted her, with a smile and open arms.

The girl – Bella – smirked back, eyes flashing. "Skyler." She nodded. "If only it was ever nice to see you."

Skyler grinned. "Aww, Bella, baby, don't be like that."

Bella rolled her eyes before holding out a gloved hand. "Just stop it, Skyler," she said irately. "I'm here to see Scott."

"Scott's not here," Skyler replied. "So if you have anything to say, you're gonna have to say it to me."

"Contrary to what you believe, you're not in charge," Bella said. "Scott's the one I need to speak to and I know he's here."

"He's not," Skyler insisted.

"Afraid he is."

Everyone turned to see a brown-haired man with a big grin walk towards them. He was tall and broad, just like Drake, but Aaron guessed he was at least a decade younger.

"Scott?" Skyler looked surprised. "When did you get back?"

"A few hours ago," Scott replied. He looked over at Bella and nodded. "It's a pleasure, Miss Giovanni," he said. "What can I do for you?"

"Isn't it obvious?" Bella asked. She straightened up, her head held high, shoulders pushed back. "We want the next Q-Zone."

Scott's expression changed from pleasant to concerned. Behind Bella, Skyler let out a derisive snort.

"Please," he scoffed. "You and this circus don't have a chance in the Q-Zone." He gestured to the crowd around her.

"Was I talking to you, git?" Bella shot back.

Sam leant over to whisper to Aaron. "I think I'm in love with her."

"How long you been hunting?" Skyler snapped at her.

"Longer than you," Bella replied.

"Alright, alright." Scott held out a hand, gesturing for Skyler to back down. "Miss Giovanni, I've got to be honest. As successful as your hunts have been, I don't know if you have what it takes to step into a Q-Zone."

Bella reared up her head. "Well then," she said. "Let us show you what we can do."

Scott seemed to consider it. His eyes narrowed and brow lined. He took in a breath before nodding.

"Alright." He stepped to the side and held out a hand. "To the ring, please."

Wearing a triumphant smile, Bella led her group of mages forward.

"Scott?" Skyler started, shoulders hunched in agitation and eyes swimming with annoyance. "What the hell?"

"They have every right to go into the Q-Zone, if they can handle it," Scott replied.

"They *can't* handle it!" Skyler snarled.

"Well," Scott crossed both hands under his chest, not fazed by Skyler's anger, "get in the ring and prove it."

"Don't worry, I will." Skyler glowered.

He followed behind Bella and her group. One by one, the other mages followed after him. With a sigh, Scott turned but stopped short at the sight of Aaron and the twins.

"I don't believe we've met," Scott said. He held out a hand. "Scott Patterson."

Aaron shook his hand and mentally prepared for the reaction. "Aaron Adams."

Sure enough, Scott's expression morphed first into shock, then disbelief, before settling on surprise.

"Good God!" he gasped. "Are you really?"

"Yeah, really," Aaron replied.

Scott looked over to the top of the hill. "Your parents?" he asked.

"They're not here," Aaron replied, hating the way his heart twisted at the reminder. "They had to go...somewhere. I'm not really sure where," he said, feeling like a right idiot. "But they should be back soon. Hopefully," he added under his breath.

Scott nodded, but his eyes had lit up with joy. "I can't believe...You go away for a fortnight and so much happens," he chuckled. "It's an honour to meet you, Mr Adams." He shook his hand again, fervently this time.

"It's Aaron, just Aaron, please."

"Of course, Aaron." Scott beamed. He looked over at Sam and Rose. "And they are?"

"My friends," Aaron replied, "Sam and Rose Mason."

Scott shook their hands, smiling at them with a hint of sadness in the corners of his mouth. "It's nice to meet you," he said, "and I'm sorry for your loss."

Sam and Rose were shocked.

"How did you know?" Rose asked.

"Your name proves you're human," he said, "and you're here, in Salvador. No human comes here, not unless they have nowhere else to go."

Rose only nodded, whereas Sam chose to stare at the ground. Scott turned back to Aaron.

"I'm afraid I have to go. There's a competition starting soon." He paused for a moment, before smiling. "Come and watch if you like."

"Yeah," Aaron said. "Sure."

Scott chuckled, shaking his head. "I can't believe the Adams are back," he said. "To think, after so long, the Elementals are finally back in the one realm again."

"Elementals?" Aaron frowned.

Scott laughed. "You trying to be funny?" he asked. "You don't know you're an Elemental?"

"I thought I was a mage," Aaron said, confused.

"You're kidding, right?" Scott grinned, but at Aaron's lost expression, his smile slid away and his eyes widened. "You...you're not kidding?"

"My dad told me two weeks ago that I'm a mage," Aaron revealed. "He didn't say anything about being an Elemental."

Scott staggered a step back, gaping at Aaron with an open mouth. "Good God," he breathed. "You..." He trailed off, struggling to compose himself. Running a hand through his dark hair, he turned to glance behind him. "I'm...I'm sorry, but...I should go."

Aaron watched as Scott hurried away. He was just wrapping his mind around the whole being mage thing and now he was referred to as an Elemental? What was going on?

Rose's warm hand slipped into his. "Come on." She pulled gently, leading Aaron and Sam to follow behind Scott.

8

WHEN MAGES FIGHT

The ring, it turned out, was just that. A large, circular area, marked in the ground by a series of rocks. Etched in the middle of the ring was a symbol – one Aaron had seen on the tall white door upon entering Salvador. It was a peculiar mark: a circle with an inverted V in the middle. Between the legs of the V was a spiral. Three wavy lines marked on either side of the V finished the design. Aaron stared at it with a fascination he couldn't understand. Only when Rose pulled at his arm did Aaron snap out of his daze.

"What?" he asked.

"Move!" she urged, throwing a pointed look behind him.

Aaron turned to see Skyler glaring at him.

"You wanna stand and stare all day, Adams?" he asked. "'Cause the rest of us have things to do."

Aaron moved out of his way and Skyler waved a hand at the ring. The rocks trembled before lifting into the air. One by one, the rocks aligned themselves into an arch. Aaron tried not to look impressed but failed miserably.

Skyler turned to the red-haired Bella. "It's all yours," he said, waving a hand in mock-courtesy.

Bella sent four of her mages into the ring. Skyler gestured to four of his own cronies, and three boys and a girl entered the ring. Skyler snapped his fingers and the rocks floated back to their former location.

Aaron noticed that every one of the eight mages inside the ring sported some sort of a tattoo. Some had thin silver swords etched on the side of their necks. Others had strange symbols and words under their ears or sprawling across their collarbones. One had a pair of black and gold pistols on the back of his neck.

The rest of Bella and Skyler's group were crowded around the outskirts of the ring. A gradual stream of Salvador residents filled the area. They all looked excited as they joined the Hunters around the ring or stood further back. Aaron spotted Alan sitting on the wide stone steps that led up to a circular glass building. Out of all the structures Aaron had seen in Salvador, this one was the most modern-looking. Aaron and the twins walked over to take a seat next to Alan.

"Hey," Aaron greeted.

"Hey y'all." Alan grinned. "Just in time to see the fight."

"Why are they fighting?" Aaron asked.

"What all Hunters fight each other for," Alan said. "A chance to go into the Q-Zone."

"The Q-Zone?" Aaron asked. "What's that?"

Alan met Aaron's gaze with first surprise, then understanding and, finally, a little pity.

"Sorry, I forgot you've only just arrived in this realm," he said. "The Q-Zone is every Hunter's dream," he explained. "In the world of Hunters, you're not worth half your salt if you haven't gone into the Q-Zone at least once in your life."

"But what is it? This...this Q-Zone?" Sam asked.

"Don't you worry your little Shattered mind about it," Alan laughed. "It's only for Hunters."

Behind them, Scott appeared at the top of the stairs, framed against the doorway of the circular building.

"If everyone could settle down," he called. His bright, hazel-eyed stare went out to the eight mages in the ring. "The Hunters of Balt," Scott called. "Show your skills against the Hunters of Salvador." He looked directly at Bella. "Give me victory and I will give you access to the next Quarantine Zone."

A tremendous cheer erupted, with the biker mages whooping and raising their fists in the air. Bella was grinning from ear to ear.

"There will be three rounds," Scott continued. "The Hunters of Balt have to win the first two and survive the third to win. Each round lasts forty seconds." He nodded at them. "Your time starts when the ring is ready."

A rumbustious cheer went through the crowd, with literally every single mage shouting encouragement and clapping. Aaron watched as the eight mages in the ring turned to one another, determination visible on all of them. No one moved, they just each stood facing an opponent, waiting. The symbol inside the ring began to brighten, as if a light under it had been switched on. The cheering got louder and more frantic the brighter the symbol glowed. Then the light went out and the Hunters attacked.

Aaron was expecting a fight. A boxing match, maybe mixed martial arts, or even good old fist-fighting. What he wasn't expecting was the ground to literally shake as the mages unleashed their powers. Four pairs of Hunters scattered to different areas of the ring.

Aaron watched gobsmacked as the girl from Skyler's gang stood with a fireball hovering over her hand. She threw it at the biker mage who ducked, avoiding the hit. Aaron panicked when he saw it about to hit the mages standing around the ring, still cheering and clapping, but the fireball vanished when it passed above the rocks outlining the ring. It was as if there was an invisible barrier surrounding the ring – one that prevented anything from leaving it.

A biker mage threw out his hands and his opponent was thrown back by an unseen force. The Salvador mage leapt back onto his feet and twisted out of the way of another attack, retaliating by pointing to the ground and pulling his hand back, as if pulling an imaginary rug out from under the other mage's feet. The biker mage fell down with thump.

"Whoa!" Sam gasped. "I...I can't believe I'm actually seeing this." He shook his head, eyes wide and unblinking. "It's...it's magic. They're using magic!"

"Not magic," Aaron murmured, stunned at the display himself. "Powers. Mages have powers," he said, having remembered his dad's words.

Rose didn't say anything, but watched the fight with an open mouth, hands against her cheeks, with odd choking noises of disbelief every few seconds.

A shimmer ran through the ring, signalling the end of forty seconds, and the eight mages relaxed, bringing their hands to rest at their sides.

"Well done." Scott beamed. "You held your ground against the Hunters of Salvador." He gestured to Skyler. "Round two, please."

Skyler waved a hand and the rocks jumped up to make the stone archway again. The eight mages left the ring and another eight entered, four from Skyler's team and four from Bella's. This time, Aaron noticed, even Salvador's mages were wearing long coats and leather vests. Aaron leant closer, eyes narrowed at their unusual attire.

"The ring will tell you when to start," Scott's voice boomed across the grounds.

Again, the eight levelled up against one another and Skyler moved the rocks to seal the ring. It seemed that Skyler was the only one that could lift and drop the rocks. There was the same bright flash in the symbol on the ground, and the second round began. It all happened so fast, Aaron was left a little dazed. One moment he was staring at the mages, who stood facing their opponents. The next, they had pulled swords on one another. Aaron blinked, gaping hard. He even brought up a hand and rubbed at his eyes, but the swords were still there.

The clang of metal hitting metal, as the swords blocked each other, rang through the air. The surrounding mages cheered and clapped, shouting encouragement and praise. But it was frightfully obvious the mages weren't fighting to disarm each other; they were trying to impale one another.

"What are they're doing?" Rose cried. "Oh my God! Oh my God! They're going to kill each other!"

"What is this?" Sam seethed. "This...This isn't a sport! It's plain-ass crazy!"

Aaron couldn't speak. He was rooted to the spot, numb and mute with shock. The long coats made sense now. They were hiding weapons. Each of the eight Hunters had a long, gleaming sword in hand and were attacking each other with vigour. Aaron turned, tearing his gaze away from the fight to look at Alan, still seated next to him. He was cheering loudly, hazel eyes sparkling with glee as he watched the fight. Aaron twisted back to see Scott, still smiling with delight as he watched the match. They all wouldn't be so relaxed if there was even the slightest chance of a casualty, would they? Somehow, Aaron knew the mages wouldn't be killing each other in the name of sport. They didn't look savage enough for that. The sword fight must be restricted somehow. Even though it didn't look like it, maybe it was a case of pretending to hit, but not to *actually* hit.

No sooner had Aaron comforted himself with the thought, than he saw one of the biker mages knock the sword out of his opponent's hand and plunge his own straight into the other mage's stomach. Rose screamed and Sam shot to his feet, cursing blind. Aaron was left dazed with shock. He felt Sam's hand grip at his arm and haul him to his feet.

"We're getting out of here!" Sam said, clearly panicked. He had Rose's hand in his other. "Come on!"

"Aaron? Hey, where are you lot going?" Alan asked as Sam dragged Aaron and Rose down the steps.

"Sam! Sam, wait!" Rose pulled back, halting him. "Look!" She pointed to the ring, where the impaled mage simply took hold of the sword and pulled it out of his torso.

The sword was stained red. The mage grunted with obvious pain, his face twisted in agony as he doubled over after pulling the sword out. He threw the blade back to its owner and said something, which was impossible to hear in the commotion of the cheering crowd. Judging by his expression, it wasn't anything polite.

"What the–?" Sam gaped at the still-standing mage. "He just got stabbed with a sword!"

"They can't die," Rose gasped. "Mages can't die."

"We can." The voice came from behind them. Turning around, they saw Alan, who had followed them. "Mages aren't immortal," he explained. He smiled and glanced at the ring. "We can die, just not at the hands of another mage." He clapped a hand on Sam's shoulder. "Come on, you're gonna miss the final round. That's the one to watch."

Silently, the three friends followed behind Alan and resumed their seats on the steps. They watched the mages leave the ring after the second round came to an end. The eight mages carried their bloodied swords out with wide grins on their faces, and ripped, crimson-stained clothes.

"Do they have to stab each other?" Aaron asked, feeling a little sick. "They could just disarm the other."

"Disarm?" Alan frowned, like he didn't understand the word. "Why would they do that? Hunters kill, they don't *disarm*."

"Yeah, okay," Aaron said, "but they don't have to hurt each other. Even if the cut's not fatal, it would still hurt."

"Not as bad as bullets," Alan said. "Those things are murder to dig out. That's why guns aren't allowed in the ring."

"Oh really?" Sam asked with heavy sarcasm. "Well thank God for that!" He shook his head, looking away from Alan. "To think," he muttered angrily to Aaron. "I figured your parents didn't want you hanging around me because I was a bad influence." He gave a narrow-eyed glare at the mages. "Only to find that *their* community is the one with tattoos and weapons, riding bad-ass bikes and going around stabbing each other with swords."

Maybe it was the after-effect of his panic or maybe it was the way Sam said it, but it made Aaron laugh. He stifled it at Sam's annoyed look.

"Sorry, Sammy."

Sam looked away, but a slow, exhausted smile came to his lips as well.

"Well done, Hunters of Balt." Scott's voice drowned out all others. "You sustained only two hits. It all rests on this final round. Choose another four mages to enter the ring." He gestured to Skyler. "But for the final round, you face Skyler and Ella. You will have, again, only forty seconds. If any of you four remain standing at the end of the round, you get the Q-Zone."

"Wait, so it's four of them against only Skyler and Ella?" Rose asked. "That's not fair."

"Did you notice, Scott didn't say they had to defeat Skyler and Ella?" Aaron said. "All four only have to remain standing by the end of the round." He frowned. "That's weird, no?"

The crowd's yelling and cheering increased to new levels as Skyler raised the stone arch again. The red-haired Bella chose another three mages and stepped in herself as the fourth fighter. Skyler waited until Ella joined him before stepping into the ring and lowering the rocks. Sam let out a low whistle at the sight of Ella.

"Damn, look at her," he whispered across to Aaron.

"She's not really dressed for a fight, is she?" Rose asked, sounding genuinely worried.

Aaron agreed whole-heartedly. Ella was only wearing tight-fitting jeans and a white cropped top. Her long hair was left to cascade down her back. Aaron noticed that she too had a tattoo: an extensive, incredibly detailed image of a vine with open flowers along it. The black ink tattoo started just at the top of her ribcage, going all the way down to cross her navel and disappear behind the waistband of her jeans. It seemed likely the tattoo continued down her leg.

Despite her ill-suited attire for the fight, Ella looked completely at ease. Skyler stood casually next to her, looking calm, with a smirk on his face. Bella openly glared at him. The symbol on the ground lit up for the third time that day. Bella reached up, her hand going for the back of her neck, reaching for something tucked under her coat. Aaron felt his stomach turn suddenly.

"Wait!" he cried. "She's got a sword!" He turned to Sam and Rose. "That's not fair. Skyler and Ella don't have any weapons!"

"Relax, Aaron," Alan said, reaching out to hold on to his arm. "Skyler and Ella don't need weapons to fight against mages. They're Elementals."

Aaron's heart skipped a beat. "What?" he asked. "Did you say Elementals?"

Alan's answer was drowned out by the thunderous clapping and yelling as the final round began and a furious battle broke out in the ring. Aaron's attention was pulled back to the fight in time to see Bella and the other three biker mages pull out their swords and leap towards Skyler and Ella. Two boys targeted Ella, while Bella and a boy went for Skyler.

Skyler twisted out of the way, dodging the two blades with great ease. He threw out a hand and the other boy was hit by an invisible blow, causing him to stagger a few steps back. Skyler stepped out of the way of Bella's sword and turned, coming behind her. A kick at the back of her knees and Bella was down.

"Prat!" Sam cursed. "You don't do that to a girl."

"Unless the girl is trying to stab you with a sword," Rose pointed out.

The two biker mages were ruthless in their attack against Ella, but no matter how fast they swung their swords or how furiously they slashed, they couldn't get her. Ella ducked and dived, bending backwards to flip and dodge the blades. The whole time, the teasing smile never left her face. Aaron hadn't seen any of the other Hunters move like that. Ella twisted out of the way of another attack before turning to face the two boys. She clenched both hands into fists before bringing them up, opening them with her palms raised. A sheet of what appeared to be glass appeared before her, just as both mages thrust their swords forward. Both swords got stuck in the sheet, which Aaron noticed belatedly wasn't glass but a mix of water and ice. The bikers tried, but they couldn't get their swords out of the icy clutch. In a flash, Ella was behind them. She threw out a hand and a blue rope extended from her hand and coiled around one mage's neck. She pulled and the boy fell to the ground, clawing desperately at his own throat, choking against the rope's hold. The second mage gave up on his sword and sent a fireball at her. A wave of Ella's hand turned the ball to ice and it flew back to hit him square on the head. He fell with a grunt.

With Ella's two mages down, all eyes turned to Skyler. Bella was knocked to the ground again and while the last Hunter of Balt was putting up a good fight, he was clearly outmatched against Skyler's speed and agility. Skyler moved out of the path of the attacks, looking calm and collected, his defence effortless. In comparison, the mage from Balt was gasping for breath, his face wet with perspiration, making attempt after attempt to get Skyler but failing miserably. A simple twist of Skyler's fingers and the sword was wrenched out of his opponent's hand, falling to the ground with a clatter. Skyler cocked his head to the side, smirked and then kicked, sending the boy flying across the ring. He hit the ground with a groan and lay still.

The symbol inside the ring began to glow, signalling the end of the last round, prompting a deafening cheer from the mages of Salvador. As the glow got brighter, Bella struggled to get up. She raised herself to her knees. Using her sword for support, she got to her feet. The glow began to dim and Bella straightened up, wincing with pain. Before the last of the glow diminished, Skyler reacted. He kicked her feet from under her and Bella fell once again, but Skyler didn't let her hit the ground this time. He caught her, lowering her somewhat gently to the ground, kneeling next to her. Bella wasn't giving in though. She struggled against him, trying to throw him off and get up. The crowd fell silent as the light left the symbol and the round ended, with the Hunters of Balt on the ground and Bella fighting against Skyler's hold.

"No!" Bella shrieked. She tried to free herself but Skyler's grip didn't falter. "Let go of me!"

"Bella!" Skyler snapped, shaking her. "Listen to me!" His voice carried through the air, so everyone could hear him. "You're not ready. You hear me? You are not ready. You go into the Q-Zone like this, you'll get killed!"

Bella stared back at him, angry tears welling in her eyes.

"Bell." Skyler's voice softened. "You'll get yourself killed."

Bella managed to free herself, or perhaps Skyler let her go, it was impossible to tell. Without saying a word, Bella painfully got to her feet and limped over to pick up her sword. Skyler stayed where he was, his head dropped and expression darkened. He lifted a hand and the stones picked themselves up, allowing the Hunters of Balt to leave the ring, defeated and heart-broken.

***

That evening, all anyone could talk about was the fight in the ring. The crowd gathered at the table for dinner ate less and gossiped more, comparing today's fight with previous ones. Although Skyler had won the battle, he seemed to be in a bad mood. As it turned out, this wasn't very good for Aaron. Throughout dinner, all Skyler did was pick on him.

"Did you enjoy the show, Adams?" Skyler asked, down the table. "You could've caught flies with your mouth, it was open so wide."

"Leave him alone, Skyler," Ella said.

"I bet you've never seen a display of power before," Skyler said, ignoring Ella. "What with daddy dearest keeping you in the dark and all," Skyler continued.

"That's enough," Drake interrupted. "You say another word, I'll personally shut you up."

"Bring it, Logan," Skyler challenged. "I can beat you into the ground and you know it."

"Sky?" Ella grabbed a handful of his top and pulled it so he had to face her. "What's got into you?"

"Nothing." He yanked himself free. "Just sick of all this attitude."

"You're the one with the attitude," Sam muttered.

"What'd you say?" Skyler snarled. "No one was talking to you, Shattered."

"Sam, don't," Aaron warned, when he saw the reply on his friend's lips. "Just leave it." He turned his head to meet Skyler's icy gaze. "Let him say what he wants. It doesn't matter."

"Yeah, it doesn't matter," Skyler said. "It doesn't matter. Nothing matters to the Adams. They just go along, doing what they want, not giving a damn what happens, 'cause you know what? It doesn't matter."

"What do you want from me?" Aaron asked, turning in his seat to look at Skyler. "Why are you constantly picking fights?"

Skyler let out a harsh laugh. "Fight? With you?" he asked. "Have you looked at yourself, pipsqueak? I could crush you from where I'm sitting. Weren't you paying attention today?"

"Why are you getting so worked up?" Aaron asked. "I'm not talking to you. I'm not in your way. So why are you getting angry?"

"You want to know *why* I'm angry?" Skyler asked, with his eyebrows raised. "How about the fact that you can come here and sit around the table like *nothing* happened—"

"Alright, Skyler," Drake cut him off. "That's enough. No one wants to get into that."

"I don't know what happened," Aaron said, ignoring Drake. "My mum and dad didn't tell me anything. Why they left all those years ago? What happened? Nothing." He hated admitting it out loud, but the slow burn of fury inside forced the words out. "Alright? So either tell me what happened or shut up about it."

Skyler looked surprised. His eyes grew colder and a smirk raised his lips. "I'll shut up when you're out of here."

"I'm not going anywhere," Aaron returned.

"Then as long as you're here, you're the one who has to pay for your father's sins," Skyler said.

"What sins?" Aaron asked, feeling his whole body tighten with anger. A small part of his mind told him to stop, to not engage in a fight with Skyler, but Aaron's patience was wearing thin at the constant provocation. "What's my dad done to you?" he asked. Then, remembering what his dad had told him, Aaron asked, "Or is this about your father?"

A hush fell across the table. The warm air cooled all of a sudden. Skyler's face was taut with anger, his eyes blazing and fists clenched.

"My dad told me," Aaron continued. "And, look, I'm really sorry about what happened to your dad, but it's not my–"

Skyler shot to his feet, coming straight for Aaron.

"Sky! No!" Ella darted after him.

Before Skyler could reach Aaron, Drake stood before him. Several mages leapt to their feet after Skyler.

"Don't you dare talk about my father!" Skyler roared, trying to get past Drake.

"Skyler, enough!" Drake yelled, pushing him away. The ground shook, as if in warning.

It seemed to work. Skyler backed off, several hands still holding on to him, restraining him. He shook them away and glared at Aaron.

"You watch yourself," he growled in a low voice. "Mention my father again and I will tear you from limb to limb!" His eyes darkened. "Sleep with both eyes open, Adams," he warned before turning around and storming away.

***

"God, this sofa is so uncomfortable," Sam groaned.

"You want to swap?" Aaron asked.

"No, it's alright," Sam sighed. "I'll make do with it."

"Quit whining, then," Rose said.

"Shut up," Sam said irritably.

"You shut up," Rose fought back.

"Guys, please," Aaron cut in. "Just for one night – *one night* – could you stop fighting?"

They fell quiet. It was too dark to see, but Aaron would have bet money they were both pouting. Aaron's fingers traced the outline of his mum's letter. It had been a week since his parents had left. A week, by normal standards, wasn't a long period of time. But for Aaron, who had never been away from his parents, it felt like an eternity.

A bright flash outside the window distracted him.

"What was that?" Sam asked.

"Dunno," Aaron muttered but got up, pocketing the letter. He made his way to the window, pulling the curtains back. The floating lanterns outside only cast a soft light, not enough to see all of the dark street below. Aaron thought he could hear the faint roar of a motorbike, but it faded away before he could be sure he even heard it. "Can't see anything," Aaron said, returning to his bed.

"Maybe it's that Bella chick, coming in the dead of the night to kill Skyler," Sam said.

"I did hear a bike," Aaron said.

"I'm joking," Sam said. "Mages can't kill each other, remember? Which is just as well, seeing the temper on Skyler."

"What was the deal with Skyler's father?" Rose asked Aaron.

Aaron repeated the story his dad had told him.

"I don't get it," Sam said. "Why is Skyler so angry with your dad? What does his dad dying have to do with your dad?"

"I don't know what Skyler's problem is," Aaron said.

"Whatever is wrong with him, you've gotta admit he was seriously cool in that fight today," Rose said.

"Unfortunately, that is true," Sam agreed. "Although, I would've loved to see him take a beating, especially from that Bella."

Aaron turned to his side, propping himself up on one arm. He couldn't see anything in the near total darkness of the room but he still had to face his friends when he talked to them.

"Did you guys notice what the mages were fighting with?" he asked.

"Um, yeah," Sam said. "Kinda hard not to notice big-ass swords."

"No," Aaron said. "I meant their powers. The fireballs and ice?"

"Yeah, we noticed that too," Rose said.

"That guy, Scott," Aaron said. "He called me an Elemental."

The mental image of the ground cracked in two with the car stuck in it, the fireballs and icicles he saw in the ring, the way the ground trembled when Drake stood up to protect him – it all seemed to point to one thing.

"The power mages use," Aaron started. "I think...I think it's something to do with the elements." Sam and Rose didn't say anything, unnerving Aaron. "Guys?" he called.

"Yeah," Rose said quietly, "I...I think you're right."

"Makes sense," Sam said and Aaron could hear the tightness in his voice.

"The fireballs, the ice," Rose recounted. "And I think Skyler was using air to push back the other mages."

"Yeah, I think so," Aaron agreed, remembering how a wave of Skyler's hand had knocked others across the ring.

"But that doesn't make any sense," Rose said. "All the mages were using powers, using the elements," she pointed out. "So are all of them Elementals?"

"I don't–" Aaron stopped short, falling silent.

"Aaron?" Rose called. "What's wrong?"

"Nothing," Aaron replied. "I just...I thought I heard something." Even though Aaron was lying in bed, under a duvet, he felt goosebumps erupt all over him. His stomach tightened. He listened hard to catch any sound, but there was nothing. He gave himself a mental shrug. "Sorry, I was saying that I don't think all the mages are Elementals. Alan referred to Skyler and Ella as Elementals but he made it sound like they would easily defeat the others *because* of that."

"But then, technically, the other mages wouldn't have the same powers as Skyler and Ella," Rose said.

"They don't," Sam said quietly. "Didn't you see Skyler and Ella? They wiped the floor with those other mages. It was four against two, with swords no less–"

"Shhh!" Aaron urged suddenly. "Guys, quiet," he whispered.

"What is it?" Rose whispered back.

"I heard something," Aaron said. He was sure this time. It sounded like...footsteps. "I think there's someone downstairs."

Sam and Rose quietened at once.

"You don't think Skyler was serious, do you?" Rose asked. "About the sleeping with both eyes open thing?"

Sam swore. "He's just the type to try something," he said.

Aaron swallowed heavily. He didn't trust Skyler and he did seem like the brash, beat-you-up-and-deal-with-consequences-later type.

Tense moments passed in utter silence.

"I don't hear anything," Rose whispered.

"Neither do I," Sam added.

They all lay still, listening for any small creak or squeak. Nothing happened.

"You're just imagining it," Rose said to Aaron. "God, you scared me."

"Don't let Skyler get to you like that," Sam said with a nervous chuckle.

"Sorry," Aaron said, "I must be hearing things. I was sure–"

There it was again: another series of thuds, loud and noticeable this time.

"You heard that?" Aaron asked.

"Yeah," Rose whispered, sounding scared. "That I heard."

The sheets rustled as Sam sat up. "Great," he said, fear clear in his voice. "Someone's downstairs."

***

Aaron crept down the steps in near total darkness. Sam was before him and Rose behind. Sam had the bathroom curtain rail in his hand – the only weapon they could think of. Aaron's heart thudded heavily in his chest and he struggled to keep his breathing even and quiet. Being blinded by the darkness meant they had next to no chance of fighting Skyler. If that even was an option.

They came to stand at the bottom of the stairs. Faint sounds were coming from the downstairs bathroom. Aaron frowned. Had Skyler crept in here to beat them up but decided to use the bathroom first?

"Sam," he whispered as low as he could. "I don't think it's Sk–"

The door clicked and opened, and Sam reacted. Aaron heard the distinct swish of the metal rod being swung in the air and prepared himself for the smack of it hitting flesh, and possibly even the crack of bones. But he didn't hear any of that. What he did hear was the clang of the metal rod hitting the floor and Sam's yelp as he was pulled violently forward.

"Sam!" Aaron yelled.

"No!" Rose screamed behind him. "Sam!"

There was a thud, a clicking noise and a sharp intake of breath before suddenly light flickered in all corners of the hallway, as lanterns hanging from the ceilings glowed brightly.

The first thing Aaron saw was Sam, lying sprawled out on the floor, looking terrified – and rightly so. He was facing down the barrel of a gun. A pistol, to be exact. But that wasn't what stole Aaron's breath. It was the boy holding the gun, pinning Sam down with a knee on his chest and a hand around his throat. The boy looked up and met Aaron's stare.

It was him. The boy with vivid green eyes.

The boy Aaron had been dreaming about for almost two months now.

The boy who was now narrowing his eyes at them, looking absolutely livid.

"Who are you?" the boy demanded. "And what the hell are you doing in my house?"

9

Houseguests

"Don't shoot! Please, don't shoot!" Sam cried, both hands held up in surrender.

"Who are you?" the green-eyed boy asked again, his gun still pointed at Sam's face.

"I'm...I'm Sam Mason. I'm not from here, I'm from Earth – planet Earth!" Sam yelled.

"We're all from planet Earth, idiot," the boy said, but pulled away his semi-automatic. His thumb pressed a lever on the side of the gun before he let Sam go and stood up.

Rose hurried to help her brother back onto his feet. They huddled close to Aaron, who was still staring at the green-eyed boy in stunned disbelief.

"What are you doing in my house?" the boy asked again, reaching back to slip his firearm into its holster.

Sam and Rose didn't answer but looked to Aaron, who was just standing there, trying to figure out if he was awake or in fact asleep. He had only ever seen this green-eyed boy in his dreams. It was the middle of the night. Regardless of how real it seemed, this was surely just another dream. It had to be.

"I'm dreaming," Aaron murmured.

The boy's eyes narrowed. "What?" he snapped.

Aaron blinked, realising this was most definitely not a dream, and judging by how angry the boy looked, they should start explaining – fast.

"I...I...We..." Aaron stammered, his ability to form words failing him miserably.

"We didn't come here on our own," Rose spoke up for him. "We were told to move here."

The boy looked over at her and his expression softened, just a little, but his eyes were still narrowed.

"Told to move in?" he repeated.

"We...we were told this cottage was empty," Sam said in a shaky voice. "He said the previous owner wasn't coming back."

"What?" The boy moved forward. "*He?* Who told you–?" He stopped and his eyes widened with realisation. His expression twisted into fury. "Skyler," he growled and turned around, storming out the front door.

Aaron, Sam and Rose shared a look before hurrying out after him. There were lanterns floating in the air, casting a soft light on the sleeping street. It wasn't going to be asleep for long.

"Hey! Skyler!" the boy yelled as he strode towards one of the blue-doored cottages. "Get out here!"

Three houses down, a door opened and Skyler appeared, his platinum hair dishevelled and sleep lingering in his eyes. At the sight of the other boy, though, he seemed to wake up.

"Well, well," he said with a smirk, leaning against the doorway. "Look what got dragged back into Salvador."

The door to the next cottage opened and Ella appeared, sleepy-eyed with bed-tousled hair.

"What's all the rack–?" She paused, startled at the sight of the green-eyed boy. "Kyran! You're back," she cried with great enthusiasm.

The boy – Kyran – nodded at her.

"Hey," he returned before turning back to Skyler. "What do you think you're doing?"

"What?" Skyler asked, feigning confusion.

"You moved other people into my house," Kyran said. "Told them I wasn't coming back? What the hell?"

Skyler shrugged. "Call it wishful thinking on my part."

Kyran glowered at him. "Move them out."

"Why should I?" Skyler asked.

Kyran took a step forward, fists clenched. "You put them in, you get them out."

"You reckon they know we're here?" Sam asked Aaron. "They're talking about us as if they can't see us."

"We can see you," Skyler answered, not looking away from Kyran. "We just don't care."

More blue doors opened and, one-by-one, mages stepped out, rubbing sleep from their eyes. Murmurs of "Kyran" echoed in the night, but the aforementioned was busy arguing it out with Skyler.

"How about I move them in with you? How'd you like that?" Kyran snapped.

"You could try," Skyler answered. "They wouldn't get past the front door."

"Just move them somewhere else," a sandy-haired mage called from four houses down. "What's the problem?"

"The problem, Ryan," Skyler replied, "is that all the cottages are taken." He met Kyran's furious stare and smiled. "There's a huge number of Shattereds staying and they're likely to be around for a while." He grinned at Kyran. "Afraid your place is the only roof over their heads."

"I don't think so," Kyran snarled. "I'm not giving up my house. You take them – now!"

"And do what with them?" Skyler asked, "There's no place to put them."

"I don't care," Kyran replied

"Neither do I," Skyler smirked.

"It's fine, we'll move out." Rose raised her voice, making everyone turn to look at her. "We'll move out." She looked at Kyran. "You can have your place back."

"Rose?" Sam turned in surprise. "You heard what they said. There's nowhere else to stay."

"It's fine. It's warm enough. We can sleep outside," Rose said, her face tinged pink with humiliation and brown eyes darkened with anger. "I'd rather that than stand around listening to them talk about us as if we're...unwanted junk."

Skyler snorted with laughter. "You heard her," he said to Kyran. "If you want your place vacated, throw them out. They'll have no choice but to sleep in the street." He straightened up and stepped back. "Oh, and you should know, those two," he pointed at Sam and Rose, "Shattereds."

Kyran swore at him, which only made Skyler laugh before closing the door. Ella sauntered out, smiling as she came to Kyran's side.

"I did try to warn him," she said.

"He won't get away with this," Kyran seethed.

"That I know," Ella said. "But what are you gonna do about your houseguests?"

"I told you, it's fine," Rose said stiffly. "We'll sleep outside–"

"You're not sleeping outside!" Ella interrupted, glaring at Rose with annoyance. She turned back to Kyran. "I guess I can take one." She wrinkled her nose. "I'll take the girl, you keep the boys."

White hot anger swept up in Aaron, snapping him out of his dazed surprise. His fists clenched and jaw tightened. They were talking about them as if they were homeless puppies.

"Rose is not going anywhere without me," Sam objected at once.

"You don't get a say in this, Shattered," Ella replied. "Come on." She beckoned Rose and turned to lead the way.

"I'm not leaving my sister," Sam protested.

Aaron reached out and held onto Rose's hand. "We're not splitting up," he said.

Ella stopped and turned around. "Excuse me?" she asked with a raised eyebrow. "Did you say something?"

"Yeah, I did," Aaron replied. "Rose isn't going with you, not without us."

"Damn right," Sam added.

Ella snorted. "Suit yourself." She looked once at Kyran before turning around and walking back to her cottage.

The other mages retreated back inside their respective cottages too, leaving Kyran with his trio of houseguests. He let out an exasperated sigh before pinching the bridge of his nose and closing his eyes. He looked up at them and held up a finger.

"One night," he said. "You can stay one night. As soon as it's daybreak, you find yourself somewhere else to stay."

"Yeah, cool," Sam agreed.

Rose didn't say anything. Sam wrapped an arm around his sister and led her back. Aaron gave Kyran a last look before turning and following behind the twins.

* * *

The next morning, when Aaron woke up, he wondered if the night before had been just another strange dream of the boy with the vivid green eyes, but when he sat up in bed to see Sam and Rose already awake and whispering about Kyran, he knew it was all real. He looked across at the door, wondering where Kyran had slept. When they had returned upstairs last night, Kyran had discovered the beds and sofa in the main bedroom. Without a word, Kyran turned and left the cottage, slamming the door behind him. As far as Aaron knew, he hadn't returned at any point in the night.

"What are we going to do?" Rose asked. "If we can't get another place, they'll split us up."

"That's not happening," Aaron said. "We stick together."

"What if we don't get a choice?" Sam asked. "You saw them yesterday. They didn't care what we wanted. They were acting like we were trash, fighting over who gets stuck with us."

"They're just gits," Aaron said. "They can't force us apart. I won't let them."

They fell quiet, listening to the sounds of Salvador outside as breakfast was set. They could hear the rattling of the plates flying across the table, yet none of them moved to get up and go downstairs.

"Where do you think that Kyran boy slept last night?" Rose asked.

Sam shrugged. "No idea."

"I feel kinda bad," Rose admitted. "I mean, we took both the beds and the sofa in his house. Where was he supposed to sleep?"

"Well, he's throwing us out," Sam said. "Don't feel too sorry for him."

"He has every right," Rose argued. "We're in his house without permission. Why should he let us stay?" She turned to see Aaron sitting quietly on his bed, deep in thought. "Aaron?" she called. "What's wrong?"

Aaron slowly shook his head.

"Don't worry," Sam comforted. "We'll figure this whole somewhere-to-stay thing out. Don't look so down."

Aaron cleared his throat. "It's not that," he said. "There's...something I need to tell you."

Sam got up and moved onto Rose's bed, coming closer to Aaron. "What is it?" he asked.

"I know how...bizarre and...and completely crazy this is going to sound," he started.

"My favourite way to start a story," Sam teased.

"That...that boy, Kyran?" Aaron said. "I've seen him before." He swallowed heavily. "In my dreams."

Rose and Sam looked exactly as Aaron had imagined. Their eyes widened and eyebrows rose.

"Excuse me?" Rose asked.

"I know, crazy, right?" Aaron said. "But it's true. I've...I've been dreaming about him – Kyran – for two months now."

"How's that possible?" Rose asked. "You never met him before last night, right?"

"Right," Aaron confirmed.

"You sure?" Sam asked. "It's more than a little creepy that you dreamt about a complete stranger and then, two months later, you met him in the flesh."

"Exactly," Aaron said. "It is creepy."

Sam's face darkened. "Is it a...mage thing?"

"What do you mean?" Aaron asked.

"Like, do mages have dreams about the future?" Sam asked. "What were the dreams about? What were you and that Kyran boy doing?"

Aaron hesitated, thinking about Sam's words. *Was* it a mage thing? Did his dreams hold more significance than he first thought? He brought up the mental image of what he could remember of his dreams: the conversations he had with Kyran, the cave with the lava, the time he was holding a gun, when he asked for help but was turned down. Could that be the future? He shivered, as a trickle of fear ran down his back.

"Oh," Sam's voice made Aaron look up. "Was it *those* kinds of dreams?" he asked, misinterpreting Aaron's little shiver.

"What?" Aaron frowned. "No, no! Don't be stupid!"

Sam grinned and held up both hands. "Hey, you're the one dreaming about dudes."

"Shut up, Sam," Aaron said.

Both Sam and Rose were giggling.

"I'm sorry," Rose apologised, "but your expression was priceless."

Aaron threw a pillow at her. "Glad you're amused," he said, but a smile came to him at the sight of Rose laughing again. "Come on, we'd better get some breakfast before it's all gone," he said, getting up.

"You didn't answer," Rose said as they headed to the bathroom to wash up before breakfast. "What were the dreams about?"

Aaron shook his head. "Nothing special," he answered. "Just some weird conversations and..." He remembered the dark, the running, the cave, the lava and the feeling of helpless frustration that squeezed his heart. He swallowed heavily. "And just normal dream stuff."

***

As soon as Aaron walked outside, his searching gaze spotted the tall, dark-haired Kyran seated at the table, already halfway through his breakfast. Aaron, Sam and Rose joined him. Most of the table's occupants looked up at them, except Kyran. He had his head lowered over his plate and steadily worked on emptying it.

"How'd you sleep?" Skyler asked Aaron, with his usual condescending smirk in place.

Aaron ignored him.

"What's the matter?" Skyler grinned. "Not in the mood to mouth off today?"

"Can't you eat in peace, Skyler?" Drake asked, his mood notably darker than usual, evident in his shadowed eyes and tightened jaw.

Skyler shrugged but he looked away from Aaron, his piercing blue-eyed gaze resting on a new target instead.

"You're awfully quiet too, Kyran," Skyler taunted. "What's up?"

Kyran didn't say anything.

"Oh come on," Skyler teased. "Tell us what's on your mind?"

"Can't," Kyran replied. "No one plans a murder out loud."

Skyler chuckled. "Still mad about your place?" He tilted his head to the side. "Have a sense of humour, Kyran."

"You're the one who's going to need the sense of humour," Kyran replied, looking up at Skyler at last.

"Oh?" Skyler raised an eyebrow. "How's that then?"

Kyran didn't say anything, but the green of his eyes darkened a shade. He lifted both hands, clasping them together, elbows on the table, stare fixed on Skyler. Aaron noticed that Kyran too had a tattoo: four thin, silvery lines across the back of his right hand. Behind Kyran, the roof of one of the blue-doored cottages suddenly tore away. Aaron jumped at the thunderous sound, as did most of the table's occupants. They all turned, all except Kyran, to see the roof of Skyler's cottage spin into the air, raining debris all over the place, before streaking across the sky and disappearing out of sight.

Aaron turned back around to see Skyler's jaw clenched and face pink with suppressed fury.

Kyran smirked. "Sense of humour," he repeated. "Have a laugh, Skyler, before you rupture something."

Skyler's fists were clenched and a muscle twitched in his jaw. He looked seconds away from leaping across the table and tackling Kyran, but he forced a smile instead and nodded.

"Very funny," he said. "Not very original, but–"

"It's payback," Kyran said, scooping the last of his breakfast up. "You give away my roof, I'll take yours."

Aaron shared a grin with his friends. This was the first time they'd seen anyone get to Skyler. Aaron had to admit it felt good.

"It's your fault your place was given away," Skyler shot back. "You were missing for over a fortnight–"

"I wasn't missing. I was on an assignment," Kyran corrected.

"Much the same to me." Skyler shrugged. "Point is, you were gone. Your place was empty, so it was used." He cocked his head to the side, looking intrigued. "Hang on, what sort of assignment takes over a fortnight?"

Kyran didn't answer. Suspicion narrowed Skyler's eyes to slits.

"Where were you?" he asked. "What assignment were you on?"

"Any particular reason I should tell you?" Kyran asked.

"Why so secretive, Kyran?" Skyler smirked, baring his teeth in a feral way. "Come on, share. Where were you?"

"With me," Scott replied, a few seats away.

Skyler turned to look at him, his eyes so wide that they were at risk of popping out. "What?" he asked. "You...you took *him* with you?" He pointed at Kyran.

"I needed an experienced Hunter, so I took Kyran," Scott replied.

Skyler turned to see the smug smile on Kyran's face.

Mary approached the table, carrying a tray of steaming mugs. Her expression morphed to shock when she spotted the roofless cottage surrounded by debris.

"My goodness," she said, settling her tray down. "What happened?"

"Kyran blew Skyler's roof away," Ella said in an exaggerated tell-tale tone.

"Kyran," Mary chastened. "You've been back a few hours and the hurricanes have already started?"

Ryan, the sandy-haired mage, chortled. "Skyler and Kyran in the one place? There's more than hurricanes on the horizon."

Mary tutted at both Kyran and Skyler but passed them mugs of tea. "Honestly, boys," she said. "Learn to get along. Remember: in unity lies power."

Kyran groaned while Skyler turned to look at Mary.

"Please, Mother Mary, don't repeat Neriah's sermons," he said. "I've just started to get over them."

Mary playfully smacked him on the arm. "Actually, it's Aric's teachings."

"Sure, if you're gonna get technical," Skyler mumbled.

Mary walked away, heading back to the Stove, leaving everyone sipping the sweet, hot tea. Aaron looked up at Drake over the rim of his cup.

"Drake?"

"Yes?"

"Why does everyone call Mary mother?" he asked.

Drake gave a crooked half-smile. "Because she acts like one," he replied. "She cooks for everyone and fusses over them. No one takes her scolding to heart and she's probably the only one who can get away with telling Skyler off."

"But still, mother?" Aaron frowned. He nodded at Skyler. "How old is he?"

"Eighteen," Drake replied.

Aaron looked across the table at Kyran. He seemed about the same age as Skyler, so did Ella. In fact, all the mages that hung around with Skyler looked around that age.

"And Mary?" he asked.

"I think she's twenty-four," Drake replied.

"So an eighteen year old calls a twenty-four year old, mother and you don't find that weird?" Aaron asked.

Drake paused for a moment. "In this place, Aaron, being called a mother isn't weird. If anything, it's comforting." He turned to look at Aaron. "Making someone your family, when you've lost your own…What's strange or weird about that?"

Aaron fell quiet. Slowly, the residents of Salvador finished their tea and started to get up from the table. Aaron waited, watching Kyran as he drained his mug and got up. Aaron rushed to his feet, quickly making his way over.

"Hey, um, Kyran?" he called.

Kyran turned and his bright emerald gaze rooted Aaron to the spot. Aaron swallowed. How many times had he looked into those eyes in his dreams? For almost two months he had met those fierce green eyes. To have those same eyes meet his with a glint of annoyance was a little heartbreaking. Realising that he was just standing there staring at him, Aaron cleared his throat.

"Hi," he said.

Kyran didn't say anything.

"I wanted to say thank you for letting us stay last night," Aaron said. "I know that we were an inconvenience, and I'm sorry."

Kyran gave him a look before nodding. "Okay," he said. "Make sure you're out by tonight."

"Yeah, sure." Aaron stepped forward when Kyran made to leave. "You let me and my friends stay in your house without even knowing who we are." Aaron extended a hand. "I'm Aaron—"

"Adams," Kyran finished for him. "I know who you are."

Aaron stared in surprise. "You do?"

Kyran's mouth curved into a smirk. "You look like your father."

Aaron's hand slowly lowered back to his side. "You know my dad?"

Kyran's smirk deepened. "Everyone knows Christopher Adams."

"Right," Aaron muttered, hating the cold tone almost everyone adopted when talking about his dad. "Okay, well, I just…I wanted to say hi and…you know…just introduce myself."

Kyran nodded. "Well, you've done both." He stepped closer, leaning in to whisper. "Now get your stuff and get the hell out of my house."

Aaron stared at him in surprise. "I told you, I'm going–"

"Good," Kyran cut across him. "Make it quick, and put my rooms back the way they were before you leave." He turned and walked away.

"What do you know?" Sam said, coming to stand next to Aaron. "He's just as big a git as Skyler."

"You're definitely not a mage, Aaron," Rose said. "It seems being a mage automatically makes you an inconsiderate moron."

Aaron didn't say anything. He was about to turn around and make his way to the cottage to start his packing when he caught sight of Jason Burns stopping to talk to Kyran. Jason was quick to point in Aaron's direction. Kyran turned and his sharp green-eyed gaze cut into Aaron. Whatever it was he was saying, Aaron doubted it was anything pleasant. Jason shook his head and Kyran turned back to him with a frown. They started arguing.

"What's going on there?" Sam asked, staring at Kyran and Jason too.

"Let's go find out," Aaron replied.

They walked as close as they dared to pick up the conversation.

"What do you mean?" Kyran snarled.

"Whit I'm tellin' yeh," Jason shook his head. "They's nothin'. All houses ar' taken."

"I need them out," Kyran said, his brow furrowed with annoyance. "They're not staying with me."

"I'm hearin' yeh," Jason said, "but I cannae dae anythin'. Yeh hav' to wait till the Shatte'ed ones leave. Then I can gee them they're own p'ace."

Kyran let out a growl of frustration, running a hand through his hair. "So what? I'm stuck with them? Is that it?"

"I ain't the one who mov'd 'em in," Jason said.

Kyran cursed again, standing with both hands on his waist, head dropped. "Fine," he breathed. "They stay. But the minute the Shattereds leave, so do they."

Jason nodded, his crooked smile in place. "Aye, nae problem." He started to walk away.

Kyran turned and spotted Aaron and the twins watching him, wearing cheeky smiles.

"Jason," Kyran growled.

"Aye?" Jason turned around.

"Get me some damn beds!"

***

Sam, Rose and Aaron did what they could to not threaten their reluctant welcome. They returned to the cottage and began rearranging the furniture. They put the sofa back downstairs and pushed the second bed out of the first room. They were done when Kyran returned with two beds floating behind him. He dumped the beds in the hallway.

"*Only* until another cottage becomes available," he warned and went upstairs, slamming the door shut.

The trio shared looks.

"Well, isn't he nice?" Sam joked.

"At least he got us beds," Rose said, walking closer to the pair of single beds, complete with pillows and duvets.

"He could have used his powers to take them upstairs," Sam said. "Now we're gonna have to carry them ourselves."

"It's a disgrace how lazy you are," Rose said.

"I'm not lazy, I'm just tired," Sam replied.

"Come on," Aaron said, picking up one end of the bed. "We'd better get these upstairs."

Kyran had taken the first room, leaving the trio with the slightly smaller second bedroom. They heaved the two beds inside but had to move the wardrobe out to make space. When they finished, they stood at the door, taking in the crowded looking room. There wasn't much space left around the three beds.

"It looks like a cheap hotel room," Sam said, pulling a face.

"A hotel room with three beds?" Rose asked.

"Ever heard of family rooms?" Sam retorted

"Every heard of making sense?" Rose returned.

"What are we going to do with the wardrobe?" Aaron asked, distracting them from another fight.

Having no other option, they moved the wardrobe into the last room with the built-in locked cupboard. They came back to their room and collapsed onto their respective beds.

"God, I'm exhausted," Rose breathed.

"Wonder why," Sam muttered. "You were only pretending to hold most of the stuff."

Rose turned her head to glare at him. "You're lucky I'm too tired to come over and smack you."

"Come on," Aaron said, feeling his stomach rumble. "I'm hungry. Let's go to the orchard and get something."

"Good idea," Sam said. "I've worked up an appetite."

All three got up and made their way outside. As they walked past the row of cottages, Aaron saw near enough all of the debris had been lifted away from around Skyler's cottage. It was also no longer roofless.

"How did Skyler get his roof fixed so quickly?" he asked.

"More magic or power or whatever the hell it is mages use," Sam said.

"If it takes them half a day to build a new roof, then how long would it take them to build a new cottage?" Rose mused.

"Good question," Aaron said, wondering why they couldn't build a new place for him, Sam and Rose to stay in.

"You know what else is a good question?"

Aaron groaned and came to a stop. He turned to see Skyler saunter up behind him. For a change, he was on his own.

"How you manage to sneak up on people?" Aaron offered.

Skyler's smirk deepened. "No. How you can tolerate their clear disrespect for mages." He nodded towards Sam and Rose.

"What?" Aaron frowned. "What disrespect?"

"*Magic or power or whatever the* hell *it is mages use*," Skyler repeated. "Doesn't that bother you? The way these humans talk about mages?" He cocked his head to the side, examining Aaron with cold blue eyes. "Or has living in the human realm for so long made you think you're a human too?"

"Hey, man," Sam started. "I didn't mean anything by it. I was just–"

"Showing your lack of understanding, I get it," Skyler said. "Because you're a human. A pathetic useless burden who can't grasp the first thing there is to know about mages, but Adams here? He's a mage. More than that," he moved closer, practically in Aaron's face, "he's an *Elemental*." He emphasised the word. "It makes it even more of a tragedy that he stands around letting no good humans disgrace mages."

"Sam wasn't disgracing mages," Aaron said, making an effort to keep calm. "He made an offhand comment. It wasn't intended to be disrespectful, but everything you just said about humans? *That's* all intentional."

"Too right it is," Skyler admitted. "Difference is I'm right. Humans *are* useless. They can't even *survive* without our help."

"Your help?" Rose asked, appalled. "What are you talking about?"

"I'm talking about the very survival of your species," Skyler said. "If it wasn't for us mages, who you show very little respect for, your entire species would be long dead."

"What are you talking about?" Aaron asked.

"Do I look like your freaking tutor?" Skyler asked with narrowed eyes. "Go ask that no-good father of yours! Tell him to do something worthwhile and teach you your own damn history!"

Aaron's fists clenched. "Don't talk about my dad," he warned.

"Oh, yeah?" Skyler asked. "What you gonna do, squirt?" He grabbed Aaron by the front of his shirt. "Tell me? What you gonna do?"

"Hey!" Sam yelled. "Let go of him!"

"Stop it, Skyler!" Rose shouted, but Skyler was ignoring them. His gaze was fixed on Aaron.

"Go on, show me, Adams." He shook Aaron violently. "Let out some power. Snatch the ground out from under my feet!" He shook him so hard, Aaron's teeth rattled. "Go on! Fight me if you have the nerve." His mouth curved into a smirk. "Or are you a bloody coward? Just like your father."

Aaron didn't know what came over him. His breath hitched in his chest, blood pounded in his ears. A strange burning started inside him and before he knew what he was doing, he had swung his fist right into Skyler's face. The force of the blow whipped Skyler's head to the side.

The punch surprised Aaron just as much as Skyler. Sam and Rose gasped but Aaron couldn't even do that when he met Skyler's furious gaze. Skyler's grip around him tightened before Aaron was thrown bodily into the air. He went careening across the street, smashing into the fence that surrounded the cottages. Aaron fell to the ground with a thump, his back ablaze with agony. He pulled himself onto his knees as a shadow passed over him. He looked up to see Skyler standing before him, fists balled. With a snarl,

Skyler raised a hand to strike.

"Skyler!"

Both Aaron and Skyler looked across the street to see Ella hurrying towards them, outrage in every inch of her face.

"What are you doing?" she demanded, coming to kneel next to Aaron.

Sam and Rose caught up, looking terrified.

Skyler didn't say anything but stood where he was, jaw clenched and eyes burning with anger. Ella helped Aaron to his feet. His back protested but Aaron managed to straighten up, although he had to stoop over almost immediately, biting his tongue to stifle a cry as a shooting pain raced along his spine. Sam and Rose quickly came to his side, supporting his weight by looping his arms around their shoulders.

Ella glared at Skyler. "Get your head sorted, Sky," she said, "before you end up losing it." She turned to Sam and Rose. "Come on."

She led them away, with Sam and Rose helping Aaron, while Skyler watched them with cold blue eyes.

***

Ella led them up a path bending behind the Stove. They came to a single white building that was just as wide as it was tall: a strange square block with many rectangular windows lined along the entire length.

Ella headed to the door and walked in without knocking. Sam and Rose helped Aaron into a large hallway with marble floors and creamy walls. White net curtains hung over the windows, bathing the room in soft light. Wicker chairs lined one wall, and a similar sofa pressed against the other.

"Sit him down there," Ella said, pointing to the sofa while she walked over to one of four doors on the right.

Sam and Rose complied and slowly lowered Aaron down, taking their seats next to him. Rose held on to Aaron's hand.

"You okay?" she asked, near to tears.

"Just...perfect," Aaron managed to say through gritted teeth. He stooped over to try to relieve some of the agony blazing from the small of his back up to his shoulder blades.

"I can't believe he blasted you across the street!" Rose said.

"I can't believe you decked him," Sam said, looking a little flushed but there was a spark of pride in his eyes. "Good on you, mate."

Aaron grimaced, in too much pain to feel good about punching Skyler.

Ella had disappeared into one of the rooms, leaving the three of them to just sit in tense and worried silence. She walked back out after a few minutes with a fair-haired girl in tow. The girl was tall, with the palest blue eyes Aaron had ever seen. Her skin glowed with beauty and her elegant flowing robes made her look even more delicate and serene. Her eyes stared past Aaron and the other two, but she walked with Ella, coming to rest before them. She smiled as Ella pulled one of the chairs closer for her to sit on.

"Thank you, Ella," she said in a soft voice. "Aaron?" she called.

"Yeah...Yes?" he groaned.

"Ella told me what happened." She stared past Aaron's ear. "I'm sorry about Skyler. He shouldn't have hurt you."

Rose let out an indignant huff. "Yeah, he shouldn't have!" she glowered.

The girl moved her head in Rose's direction. Her expression changed slightly to a pained look, before it settled back and she turned to Aaron.

"My name is Armana," she said. "I can help you."

"Help me?" Aaron asked, surprised. "How...how can you...I mean aren't you...erm..."

"What?" Armana asked and her lips twitched up into a smile. "Blind?"

Aaron looked over at Ella, but she seemed lost in her own thoughts – a scowl on her face and eyes lowered to the ground.

"Yeah," Aaron answered, his voice tight with pain.

"You don't need eyes to help people," Armana said. "Pain can only be felt, not seen." She extended a nimble hand towards him.

Aaron hesitated before slowly reaching out and taking her hand. As soon as he touched her, a look of pain crossed her face and she sucked in a breath. Aaron made to move his hand back but Armana grabbed it, holding on tightly.

"No," she breathed. "It's okay," she assured him. "It's o-okay."

She took in a breath and let it out slowly. Her eyes slipped shut and she sat in concentration, holding on to Aaron's hand. A blissful cool began spreading across Aaron's back, taking away the agony in a single breath. Aaron straightened up, relieved of the twinges and stabs of pain in his back.

Armana opened her eyes and smiled, letting go of Aaron's hand.

"There you go," she said. "All better."

"How did you do that?" Aaron asked.

"You're asking for trade secrets," Armana teased. "It's my gift."

"Gift?" Aaron asked. "You can heal people through touch?"

"Not exactly, no," Armana replied. "I heal mages, not people." Her head inclined towards Rose, even though she couldn't see her. "I can feel everyone's pain, but unfortunately I can only heal mages."

Rose shared a look with Sam and Aaron before turning to stare at Armana again.

"So you're a...a mage as well?" Rose asked.

Armana smiled brightly. "I am," she said. "I'm a mage, but also an Empath."

"Empath?" Aaron frowned. "So...you feel...empathy towards others?"

Armana laughed, and Aaron was strongly reminded of wind chimes. The tinkling sound even pulled Ella out of her thoughts and she looked around at them.

"No." Armana chuckled. "Well, I mean, I empathise with others as much as the next mage, or even human for that matter." She smiled. "But that's not what an Empath is. I sense the pain of others. When I hear their voice, or touch their skin, I feel their agony – be it physical or emotional." Again her head tilted towards Rose. "If their injury is physical, I can heal it through touch. Emotional pain…Well, that's not quite as easy to heal."

Aaron glanced over at Sam and Rose but didn't say anything. If only it were as simple to take away their pain. Just a touch, a brief moment and that would be it: the pain all gone.

"Are you...I mean, don't be offended…" Aaron shifted in his seat. "But are you really...blind? I mean, in the sense that you can't see anything or that you can see things...differently?"

"You mean because I'm a mage?" Armana asked. She paused briefly. "Yes, I can see," she said. "I can see how badly you need to learn about mages." She giggled and even Ella smiled, shaking her head at Aaron. Armana leant forward. "I'm blind, Aaron. I can't see anything. Mage or not, it's still only darkness in front of my eyes."

"I'm sorry," Aaron said quietly.

"Why?" Armana asked. "I was born an Empath. It's who I am."

Aaron remembered the group of ladies in flowing robes similar to Armana's, hands resting on each other's shoulders as they came to the table at mealtimes. They were all Empaths.

"Are all Empaths born blind?" he asked.

"Yes," Armana answered. "What's the point of sight if all you're going to do is feel?" she asked. "Eyes deceive you; you only see what others want you to see." She reached out for Aaron's hand again, taking it into both hands. "But when you touch, you feel what cannot be seen. There are no lies, no deceit. It's a more honest and open relationship. Something I prefer."

"Makes sense, sort of," Aaron said.

"Alright." Ella clapped her hands. "You're all healed and it's time to go." She narrowed her eyes at Aaron. "I suggest you stay out of Skyler's way."

"He's the one who follows us around," Sam said.

Ella rolled her eyes. "Yeah, 'cause Skyler's got nothing better to do than follow you lot around."

"It's true," Aaron said. "He sneaks up on us."

"Then get vigilant!" Ella snapped. "Notice when he's around and when he is, get out of his way."

She walked out before Aaron could reply. Aaron and the twins got to their feet too.

"Thank you, Armana," Aaron said.

Armana smiled and rose to her feet. "You're welcome," she said. "And please, just ignore Skyler."

"Believe me, I try," Aaron replied.

"I know how he comes across, but really Skyler's not all that bad," she said.

Aaron gaped at her. "You must be joking."

"Skyler's got a good heart," Armana said. "I've known him for a long time. He's just a little...sharp-tongued."

"That's one way to put it," Aaron muttered.

"Give it time," Armana said. "You'll start to warm up to him. Everyone does in the end."

10

WORKING TEENAGERS

Aaron didn't know if it was the boredom of wandering around doing nothing or Skyler's taunt about being useless, but the very next day Sam and Rose offered themselves up for work.

"You don't have to," Aaron tried to tell them. "No one expects you to work."

"It's better if we find something to do," Rose replied quietly. "Besides, how much more of Salvador is there to see?"

So Aaron decided to join them and find work around Salvador. They went to see Mary, who was only too happy to get more helpers.

"That would be great." She beamed. "Rose, you can work with me in the Stove, and Sam and Aaron can help in the orchard."

Sam and Aaron trotted off towards the sun-kissed garden, leaving Rose behind at the Stove.

"Rose'll be okay on her own?" Sam asked, lines of worry creased his forehead.

"Mary's really nice," Aaron assured him. "She'll take care of Rose."

Sam hunched his shoulders as he walked, his face fallen and eyes downcast. "Rose isn't exactly great at cooking."

"I doubt Mary'll have Rose preparing meals straight away," Aaron consoled. "She'll probably just ask her to....peel potatoes or something."

Sam turned to look back at the Stove, anxiety in every muscle of his body. "I don't like leaving her on her own."

"We can go back for her if you want," Aaron offered. "She can help in the orchard."

Sam thought about it before shaking his head. "The kitchen might be better than working out in the sun."

Aaron tilted his face up, feeling the heat of the day prick at his skin. "It's the middle of November," he said, "and it feels like summer."

"I know," Sam said, looking up at the clear blue sky. "The weather in this realm is messed up."

They arrived at the orchard and happily hurried under the shade of the fruit-bearing trees. There were plenty of mages working here, picking ripe fruit and filling wicker baskets to the brim. The aroma of fresh oranges and sweet plums filled the air, making Aaron's mouth water. They walked deeper into the orchard, across the soft ground, breathing in the delicious scent of different fruits. They spotted Drake helping two boys pick pears from a tree.

"Aaron?" Drake narrowed his eyes at him as Aaron and Sam approached. "What can I do for you?"

"We want to help," Aaron said.

"Help?" Drake looked from Aaron to Sam in confusion.

"Yeah." Aaron gestured to the baskets. "You know, work here."

Drake's eyebrows shot up and he quickly shook his head. "No, no, no. I don't think so. Go back to your cottage."

"Why?" Aaron asked.

"Why can't we work here?" Sam asked.

Drake looked at Sam with a sour expression, almost as if he didn't appreciate being addressed by him. "Because I said so," he replied.

"That's not a reason," Aaron replied. "Mary said we could work here."

"Mary is not in charge of the orchard," Drake snapped. "Besides, why would you want to work in this heat?"

"Because I'm bored," Aaron replied.

Drake paused, his dark eyes studying him, before he shook his head again. "No, I'm not comfortable with you working here." He reached up to pinch the bridge of his nose. "Chris will have my head," he muttered.

Aaron felt a jolt in his stomach. He stepped forward. "I'm bored," he repeated, speaking slowly and emphasising each word. "I want to work here. It's got nothing to do with my dad."

Drake opened his mouth to protest.

"You're better off just letting us do it," Sam said. "He's very stubborn," he added, gesturing to Aaron. "He's not gonna take no for an answer."

Drake looked over at Aaron and, surprisingly, smiled. "No, I bet he isn't," he said. He let out a deep sigh and ran a hand down his face, rubbing at his chin. He looked over at Aaron. "Okay, you can work here. But if

Chris gets angry, you take the heat."

Aaron nodded. "Cool."

Drake scratched the back of his head and turned to the mages standing with baskets full of pears, apparently awaiting his instructions.

"Let me just deal with this and then I'll show you what you need to do," Drake said before leading the group of mages away, leaving Sam and Aaron by the tree. As soon as Drake was out of earshot, both boys turned to each other with big grins.

"He gave in." Sam laughed. "He actually believed me when I said you were stubborn." He paused for a moment before asking, "What's with your dad, though? Why wouldn't he want you to work here?"

Aaron's smile fell away. "I don't know," he admitted. "It seems like he doesn't want me to get involved in anything." He reached down and picked up an empty basket before meeting Sam's eyes. "Too bad."

Sam looked surprised. "Damn, Aaron," he chuckled. "Since when did you become a rebel?"

"If they didn't want me doing this," Aaron said, quietly, "then they should've been here to stop me."

***

"Armana?" Rose called softly.

The Empath seated at the table looked up at once, eyes staring past Rose. "Rose, hello."

"Hi." Rose pulled out a chair and sat next to Armana. "You asked to see me?"

Armana's lips twitched, as if resisting the urge to smile, and Rose gasped at her slip.

"I'm sorry!" she gushed. "God, I'm...I'm so sorry. I didn't mean...!"

"It's okay." Armana smiled. "It's perfectly natural for you to say that. I did come to see you, in a manner of speaking."

Rose cringed, blushing pink. "What...erm...What can I do for you?"

Armana went silent for a moment. "How's Aaron?" she asked.

"Aaron? He's fine," Rose said. "He's not said anything about his back, so I think he's all healed."

Armana smiled again. "That's good. I'm glad he's okay."

Rose nodded in agreement, confused why the Empath had Ava call her out of the Stove, just to ask about Aaron.

"Um, was that all?" Rose asked. "It's just....it's my first day working and I'm...I'm already struggling to keep up."

Armana shook her head. "No," she said softly. "I wanted to speak to you. Ever since you came in with Aaron yesterday, I've not been able to forget your voice."

Rose blinked in confusion. "My voice?"

"Yes," Armana replied. "The pain, it's overwhelming."

Rose understood then. She remembered Armana had said Empaths picked up on others' pain by touching their skin or hearing their voice.

"Who did you lose?" Armana asked.

"My...my parents," Rose answered.

Armana's brow furrowed and her pale blue eyes glistened. "I'm so sorry."

Rose shook her head and dropped her gaze to her lap. Then, remembering the girl was blind, she forced her words out. "It's okay – really."

"No, it's not okay," Armana's soft voice soothed. "It's never okay to lose loved ones."

Rose fell quiet, not knowing what to say.

"Rose?" Armana lifted a hand towards her and Rose held it. She knew the Empath's healing powers wouldn't work on her. She was a human; Armana could only heal mages.

"You have so much pain," Armana said. "So much...loneliness...guilt."

Rose could feel the tears burning in her eyes, blurring her vision.

"Why do you feel guilty, Rose?" Armana asked. "What happened wasn't your fault."

"No, it was my fault," Rose said. "Me and Sam...We...we ran home." She squeezed her eyes shut, leaking out hot tears. "When we were being chased by that...that mist thing, we ran to our house. We weren't thinking. We just...We wanted to get home, to get inside to safety. Because of us, because of me, my mum and dad are..." She faltered, unable to finish. She sniffed back her tears, taking a moment to rein back her pain. "Michael, Aaron's uncle, he told us that because we saw Aaron using his powers, it put a Trace on us. He explained that because we ran home, the...the things chasing us, they came to our home with us." She looked up at Armana. "*We* brought those things to our house. It's our fault, mine and Sam's. If we had stayed with Aaron, we would have gone straight into the car and my parents would still be alive today."

"You can't think like that," Armana said. "You don't know what could have happened."

"I'm responsible," Rose said. "I grabbed Sam and pulled him towards our house. I...I stopped him from following Aaron. It's my fault–"

"Rose." Armana's grip tightened around her hand. "What happened wasn't your fault."

"I just...I wish I could see them," Rose whispered. "Just...one last time. Just to...to say..." She dissolved into tears, sobs breaking her words.

Armana pulled Rose into an embrace, running a hand down her back. "People die, Rose," she said. "Their souls leave this existence, their bodies perish, but their hearts live on forever."

Rose pulled away, staring at Armana with wide, tear-filled eyes. "What do you mean?"

"The heart," Armana said. "It never dies, not truly. It leaves something behind."

"What?" Rose asked.

"An echo." Armana smiled sadly. "The ones who die and leave us, they're not truly gone. Their echo lingers in their wake."

"You mean like...like ghosts?"

"No," Armana said. "Not ghosts. Just echoes."

Rose leant closer. "Is...is this a...a mage thing or...?"

"Humans have it too," Armana said. "Anything that once lived, that once loved with a heart and soul, will leave behind an echo." Her unseeing eyes stared past Rose but she managed to reach out and touch Rose's cheek. "You don't have to mourn. Your parents have left behind their echoes. A part of them is still here, still alive."

"How...?" Rose asked, her voice desperate and raw with pain. "How do I find them? Their echoes?"

"You can't," Armana said with great regret. "Not here at least. An echo can only be found at the place that person once lived, in the streets they walked, the house they slept in, the things they touched or wore. It's there that their memories reside."

Rose felt her hope break into a thousand little pieces. She would have to go back to her own world, her realm to see if she could find her parents' echoes, but the human realm was a place she could never go back to. Despite knowing this, she asked, "Can...can I speak to these echoes? If, somehow, I get the chance to go back to my world, back to my house, will...will my mum and dad...their echoes, will they be there? Could I speak to them?"

A tear rolled out of Armana's eye, trailing down her cheek. "They'll be there," she whispered, "and if you were close to their heart, you'll see them too. But you can't talk to them," she told her sadly. "I'm sorry, Rose. The echoes are just that: an echo. Their souls are gone to another plane of existence. Their bodies are no more. The echo is all that's left behind, retracing the steps they once walked, over and over again. They don't interact with anyone. They don't see you. They are nothing more than a memory. All you see is a glimpse of what once was." She caressed Rose's cheek. "But, sometimes, a glimpse is all you need."

***

The days slowly passed and, to his surprise, Aaron found he actually liked working in the orchard. With Sam by his side and under Drake Logan's guiding hand, Aaron quickly picked up the basics, but realised very quickly how different this realm was. For a start, things grew in a matter of hours, not days. All Drake had to do was put his hand on the trunk of a tree and the fruit slowly grew before their eyes. Small, red bobbles grew into big, shiny apples in only two hours. The first time Sam and Aaron saw this, it left them open mouthed.

Drake taught Sam and Aaron the correct way to sever fruit from its tree, how to plant new seeds, and even corrected the technique of piling fruit into baskets so as not to bruise them.

"Treat them gently," Drake had said, taking the peach from Sam's hand and placing it carefully inside the basket. "As if they are newborn babies." He'd smiled to himself. "Which they are."

Sam had turned to Aaron the moment Drake walked away and whispered, "That dude needs help."

Working in the orchard for the majority of the day meant Sam and Aaron were exhausted by nightfall. With an equally tired and unusually quiet Rose, all three would fall asleep the minute they lay down in their beds.

It was on the fourth day of this routine that Aaron realised he had barely seen Kyran. Despite living in the same house, he never saw Kyran around the cottage. In the last two days, he hadn't seen Kyran at the table at mealtimes either.

As Aaron and Sam carried smaller baskets of assorted berries to the Stove, they saw Kyran walk down the path from the entrance. Aaron slowed down, staring at the older boy as he passed Jason Burns's house and disappeared down the dusty path.

"Haven't seen him around for a while," Sam commented. "Wonder what he's been up to."

"On assignment again?" Aaron guessed. "Wonder what kind of assignments mages have."

"Something tells me I don't want to know," Sam said.

They dropped the berries at the Stove, and spent a few minutes talking to Rose – who was struggling with preparing the dough for pizza – before making their way back. They were barely ten steps away from the Stove when they saw Skyler and Ella, along with their entourage, coming up the path from the lake.

"Ignore, ignore, ignore," Sam chanted in Aaron's ear.

"Don't worry, I will." Aaron replied quietly.

Skyler smirked at him but didn't say anything. They had just passed each other when a yell sounded across the street.

"Skyler!"

Everyone stopped and turned to see a furious Kyran, his fists clenched and jaw set, coming straight for Skyler.

"What do you think you're doing?" Kyran spat, livid. "You messed around with Lexi!"

Everyone turned to Skyler with expressions of surprise and disgust, including Ella.

"Sky?" she groaned. "Tell me you didn't."

Skyler, for his part, looked completely calm. "I had to get him back for his little 'joke' with my roof."

"So you used Lexi?" Ella asked, outraged. "That's sick!"

Kyran got near enough to throw a punch, and would probably have clocked Skyler right in the jaw if four mages hadn't stopped him.

"Hey, Kyran!" Ryan called, holding him back. "Whoa! Take it easy."

But Kyran's narrowed eyes were on Skyler, ignoring everyone else. "How dare you touch her!" he growled, fighting their hold.

"Calm down," Skyler drawled. "You deserved it and you know it."

"Oh yeah?" Kyran freed himself but didn't lash out this time. He stepped closer until he was right in Skyler's face. "Come on then, Sky."

Skyler's eyes brightened with glee. "Yeah?" He grinned. "Eager for another beating?"

Kyran smirked. "We'll see who takes the beating this time."

Skyler chuckled. "When you gonna get it?" he asked. "I'm an Elemental. You can't beat me."

"No," Kyran agreed, "but I can make you bleed."

Skyler's eyes narrowed, the mirth and amusement gone. "Let's go," he said.

Aaron and Sam watched as the group hurried behind the two boys, headed for the path behind the cottages.

"Are they going to that ring place again?" Sam asked.

"Think so," Aaron replied. "Should we follow them?"

"You seriously need to ask?" Sam grinned.

Both boys threw down their baskets and ran behind the mages.

***

It turned out that Kyran and Skyler were indeed headed to the ring. This time the only ones watching the fight were members of Skyler's gang. Aaron and Sam inched closer and closer to the ring, and found that no one stopped them. It seemed the surrounding mages had eyes only for the two boys stepping through the stone archway that Skyler had lifted, to enter the ring. The crowd was thinner, yet the rumbustious cheers were just as loud and energetic as last time. Ella, Aaron noticed, wasn't looking very happy, and stood to the side with her arms crossed, glaring at Skyler and Kyran.

The symbol on the ground – the strange circle with the inverted V, spiral and three wavy lines – started to glow. The light had barely faded when the two boys started. Kyran leapt at Skyler, his fist raised but it didn't touch the other boy. Aaron thought Kyran had missed, that his punch was ridiculously badly aimed, but something hit Skyler, making him stagger a few steps back. Skyler recovered and threw out his hand, sending an unseen jolt of what Aaron now realised was power in retaliation. Kyran twisted out of the way, so fast that Aaron would've missed it if he had blinked.

"Whoa," Sam breathed. "Did you see that?"

Aaron nodded, open-mouthed, staring at Kyran.

Kyran threw out his hand and Skyler was hit again. Gathering himself, Skyler kicked out, but Kyran dodged the blow. Twisting to the side, Kyran punched, and this time his fist connected with Skyler's face, knocking him aside. Before Skyler could catch his breath, Kyran sent him flying across the ring with a sweep of his hand.

Aaron stared, awestruck to his very core. He had thought the Hunters of Balt were impressive, but none of them had managed to strike Skyler. Kyran, on the other hand, was knocking the Elemental to the ground.

Skyler swung his arm, like a punch in the air, and Aaron could hear the wind whistling as unseen power tore its way towards Kyran, who ducked to avoid it. The surrounding mages cheered, some calling out praise to Kyran while others yelled at Skyler to, "Make a hit already!"

Before long, Skyler and Kyran were both out of breath, a fine sheen of perspiration covering their faces. Most of their punches and kicks were in the air, but the jolts of power flew across the ring, sometimes hitting their mark, other times swiftly avoided. The stones around the ring were keeping the blows of power from crossing outside, but this time Aaron could hear the strain. Even through the cheering, clapping and shouting, Aaron could detect the whistle of every throw and a faint zap as the power hit the invisible barrier.

One of Skyler's kicks caught Kyran, sending him careening backwards. He hit the ground, visibly winded but quickly rolled out of the way of Skyler's next attack. Leaping onto his feet, Kyran pulled back his hand and then shot out, as if wielding a whip. Skyler doubled over, pain lighting his features. Kyran lifted up his hand and Skyler was thrown up into the air, like a weightless doll.

"Whoa!" Sam cried.

Kyran pulled downwards and Skyler smacked to the ground, face first, hitting it so hard that Aaron swore he felt the ground tremble. Being thrown around like a ball didn't keep Skyler down for long, though. He was soon up on his feet, enraged, his platinum hair messed up and falling into his slitted blue eyes. Both of his hands were balled into fists and he swung them, double punching the air. Kyran stumbled back, taking both hits and falling to the ground. When he straightened up, he froze, green eyes widening. Aaron saw why and it stole his very breath.

Skyler was holding a gun, and it was aimed at Kyran.

Sam cursed before gripping Aaron's arm and pulling, trying to get away, but Aaron refused to move. He felt as if he were glued to the spot, watching in numbed terror as Kyran regarded Skyler warily. The surrounding mages quietened too, surprised at Skyler's tactic.

"Sky! Don't!" Ella shouted, but Skyler didn't look like he was listening.

He cocked the pistol and glared at Kyran. The shot rang out, so loud it almost popped Aaron's ears. Sam ducked, taking Aaron with him, not trusting the invisible barrier to block bullets. Aaron's gaze never left Kyran, who twisted out of the way with speed no human could match. Kyran pulled out both of his handguns.

"We're getting out of here!" Sam pulled again but Aaron refused to be dragged away.

Kyran fired three shots from each gun but Skyler dodged them all. They were fighting with bullets now and the surrounding mages were yelling their disapproval.

"Stop it, Sky!" Ryan yelled. "Not cool, man!"

"Kyran, don't!" Ella was yelling. "You both are going to get hurt!"

"Boys! No! STOP!" a voice thundered, and Aaron looked around to see Scott come belting towards them. A wave of Scott's hand and the rocks lifted to give him access. "Stop it! Stop!" Scott cried, grabbing Skyler and pulling him back. Scott stood between them, his expression twisted in rage.

Kyran and Skyler were out of breath and stood glaring at each other, but had lowered their guns

"What is the matter with you two?" Scott yelled. "Shooting at each other? Really?" he asked with fury. "There are enough forces trying to *kill* mages, without the two of you hurting each other! You want to have a go at each other? Fine, so be it! But keep guns out of it!"

Both boys looked away, fidgeting where they stood. Scott ran a hand through his hair, struggling to calm down.

"There's a meeting starting in two minutes," he said a lot quieter. "Get inside, both of you." He looked around at the surrounding mages. "All of you, inside the Hub – now."

The crowd walked towards the circular building, climbing up the steps. Kyran and Skyler followed after them, quiet but with furious expressions and darkened eyes, their weapons slotted back into their holsters. Scott lowered the rocks, sealing the ring and walked up to the building.

Aaron followed after them with Sam, but had only set one foot on the wide steps when Skyler held up a hand.

"Where do you think you're going?" he asked, face still pink and beads of perspiration on his forehead.

"Scott said all of us–" Aaron started.

"I don't think so," Skyler growled. "Get lost, Adams."

"What's going on?" Scott asked, anger still in his voice. "What's the problem?"

Aaron quickly spoke up. "I want to join the meeting."

Scott didn't say anything right away. He studied Aaron with quiet eyes before nodding. "Come inside."

"What?" Skyler turned in fury. "Scott, he's not a Hunter!"

"He's a mage, isn't he?" Scott replied. "Every mage has the right to get involved."

"He may be a mage," Skyler argued, "but he doesn't know the first thing–"

"That's irrelevant," Scott cut him off. "Besides, Aaron is an Elemental." He held Skyler's gaze. "Are you really going to stop an Elemental, Skyler?"

Skyler didn't say anything. His jaw clenched and he threw a furious look at Aaron before turning and walking past the doors into the building. Scott gave Aaron a tired, weak smile.

"Come on in," he said, "but only you." He looked pointedly at Sam. "Sorry, but it's mages only."

Sam took a step back. "Yeah, sure. That's okay," he said. "I've got to get back to work, anyway."

Aaron looked back at Scott, ready to protest but Sam had grabbed his arm. "It's cool," he whispered. "Go. Tell me everything."

Aaron nodded and turned to follow Scott into the Hub, feeling horribly guilty at leaving Sam behind.

11

The Hub

Scott led Aaron down a set of metal stairs, heading for the double doors at the end of a wide corridor. Aaron looked around at the glass-panelled walls, silver rafters and white marble floors. It all looked completely out of place in the otherwise very rural city of Salvador. Aaron stepped past double doors and entered a chamber. Like the building, it was round, with six lines of benches circling the entire room. In the middle of the chamber was a gleaming white table which, in keeping with the style of the building, was also round, but with a concave top.

Aaron walked up to the table to see what lay in its hollow. He couldn't make sense of it. It looked like an image, depicting of a whole mess of lines with letters dotted around in a random order. Thick wavy lines made odd blob-type shapes with fine spidery lines sprawling every which way inside.

"Admiring the table?" Scott asked, coming to stand next to him.

"Sort of," Aaron replied. "What is it exactly?"

Scott turned to look at the table with a smile. His previous anger and agitation seemed to disappear. "This," he held the edge with both hands, his eyes sparkling with pride, "is the Hub."

"And this," Skyler called, "isn't a class. Can we get on with the meeting already?"

Scott gave him a cold look before turning back to the table. He extended his hand over it and the image started to change. The fine lines began to fade and the thick-lined, random shapes began to lighten until they were barely visible. A different image began to take form, one that Aaron recognised at once.

"See what it is?" Scott prompted.

Aaron nodded. "A map of the world."

"Wrong," Skyler called out. "A map of the human world."

"The human realm," Scott corrected. His hand hovered over the table again and the map changed to the first image. "This is our world," Scott said. "The mage realm."

Aaron stared at the thin stretches of ink, circling and outlining a whole map of different shapes and sizes. He noted the increased number of marked areas when compared to the continents of the human world. What he recognised as South America had three areas marked on it. Africa was divided in eight areas – some big, some small. A quick glance and Aaron counted twenty-six areas covering the world map.

"These are zones," Scott explained, pointing to the thick-lined areas, each with a letter of the alphabet on them.

"Where are we?" Aaron asked.

Scott pointed to a small area, with the letter *I* on it. "Salvador is located here."

Aaron smiled. On the map of the world he had lived in, Scott was pointing to the United Kingdom. It seemed he was somewhat close to home after all.

"If we're done playing 'Where in the Realm is the Idiot?' game, maybe we could start the meeting?" Skyler asked.

Aaron didn't let Scott fight this time. He silently moved away from the table and took a seat on the wooden bench next to Ryan and a pretty, dark-haired Asian girl.

"Alright." Scott rubbed both hands together and stood before them. "Today's meeting has officially started." He raised both hands to gesture to Kyran and Skyler, both seated at opposite sides to each other. "That is, if two of our best Hunters have recovered from trying to kill each other?"

Kyran shifted in his seat and Skyler looked away, avoiding Scott's gaze.

"Good, so we can start," Scott said. "First, the update. Kyran accompanied me to Harban, where we spent ten days trying to get the Pecosas to talk."

"Any luck?" Ella asked.

"No," Scott replied. "The Pecosas maintain they know nothing about the Scorcher."

"You don't believe them?" a tall, dark-skinned boy asked.

"I didn't at first," Scott replied, "but after ten days of the same answer, I had to give in."

"But the Pecosas were sighted," the Asian girl next to Ryan said. "We know they're with him. They're helping the Scorcher."

"They say they're not," Scott replied. "The chief claims some of their people have turned. Those are the few Pecosas that have been sighted with the Scorcher. The majority of them have nothing to do with him."

Skyler snorted. "You believe that tripe?"

"I have no other option," Scott replied.

"The Pecosas are up to something," the Asian girl said. "They might not be enemies, but they're not allies either."

"I agree with Zhi-Jiya," Ella said. "We can't trust them."

"I never said we had to trust them," said Scott. "But I do believe them."

Aaron was confused. Not only with what Scott had said but with the whole discussion. It didn't make any sense to him, not that he expected it to. He had walked into a mage meeting with no prior knowledge. It was bound to be confusing.

"Anyway, next call of business." Scott waved a hand and the mages got up, walking to the circular table. Aaron joined them. "I'm setting up a Q-Zone in a week's time." Every mage became tense, standing still. "The others will arrive over the course of the week. I want everyone trained up and ready. This one is going to be big."

"Where we going?" Ella asked.

Scott turned to the table and pointed to the zone labelled *M*.

"Here," Scott said. "Zone M-25." He pointed at one of the areas outlined by the fine, spidery lines criss-crossing inside Zone M. "Tobo, Japan," Scott said, the map shimmering to show the map of the human world for a moment before reverting back. "The Q-Zone will be set up here." Scott pointed to another area of the map. "I want everyone to start their training. You don't impress me, you don't get to go. Understood?"

"Understood, Scott," came the response.

"Alright, you can go now," Scott dismissed. "Kyran, Skyler, Ella – hold back, please. I want a word."

As the rest of the mages moved out, Aaron stayed where he was, confused to his core.

"Aaron?" Scott smiled softly. "You okay?"

"I'm...I'm a little lost."

"I would expect you to be," Scott replied.

"You said you were setting up a Q-Zone," he said, "but isn't that the Q-Zone?" He pointed to the zone with the letter Q on it.

Scott laughed. "I can see why you would think that," Scott said, "but this is Zone Q. What I'm talking about is a Q-Zone, short for Quarantine Zone."

"Quarantine?" Aaron felt his mouth go dry. "What are you planning on isolating?"

"Things that need to be put down," Scott replied.

"Like?" Aaron pushed.

"In this particular instance," he met Aaron's eyes, "Lycans."

Aaron blinked. "I'm sorry?"

"Lycans," Scott repeated. "They're terrorising the people of Tobo. Over the last two months, there have been countless disappearances and mutilated bodies found almost every night."

"In Tobo?" Aaron asked. "As in Japan? In my world?"

Scott paused, his eyes narrowed slightly. "The human realm," he corrected. "Yes."

Aaron gaped at him. "You're talking about...werewolves?" he asked with disbelief.

"Lycans aren't werewolves," Ella said. "Humans confuse the two, but Lycans are very different to werewolves."

"Werewolves are nothing more than dirty dogs that've had their fangs pulled out," Skyler added. "Lycans are beasts that will rip you into a thousand shreds if you let them get near enough."

"Which is why you lot need to be prepared," Scott said.

"We are prepared," Ella said. "Send me out today. I'm ready."

"Easy there, Ella," Kyran said. "Lycans are a big game."

"You need to hold your ground against me," Skyler said to her. "Then we'll see if you're ready."

"Pfft, please." Ella turned to him. "Kyran was smacking you around minutes ago. I'll train with him, thank you very much."

"I'll supervise the training," Scott said, before Skyler could reply. "That's why I held you three back. I know you will pass the training and I need you three to get the rest in shape."

The trio nodded their agreement.

"I'm sorry, but I can't get past this," Aaron said, shaking his head.

"Lycans in Japan? How is this possible?"

"What's so unbelievable about it?" Scott asked.

"Lycans!" Aaron exclaimed. "Big hairy beasts with claws and…and fangs and…they're going around killing people? How does no one notice that?"

"They do notice," Scott replied calmly. "Where do you think these human legends and myths come from?"

"But surely there would be panic and chaos," Aaron said. "The humans would know for sure that werewolves exist."

Skyler chuckled. "Is this kid for real?" he asked.

Aaron turned to see Skyler, Ella and Kyran all grinning, chortling at him.

"What?" Aaron demanded, annoyed.

"They're humans," Skyler said, as if that explained everything. "They could have Lycans break-dancing in front of them and they'll still come up with something to explain it. *I was drunk. I was high. It was just the light. It was my overactive imagination*," he mimicked in a high-pitched voice. "And the poor sod who does get it right and tries to tell the world gets locked up in a padded room for losing his mind." He grinned. "Humans are the single most frustratingly naïve creation in all the realms."

"That's not true." Aaron shook his head. "Humans aren't stupid. If they see monsters—"

"They run," Ella said. "That's what they do. They see a threat, they run. That's what they're *supposed* to do. It's the job of a mage, of a Hunter, to face the demons."

Aaron turned to stare at the map. "The Q-Zone," he said quietly. "That's what the mages of Balt came here for. They wanted permission to go to it?"

"Every Hunter wants to prove their worth," Scott said. "Hunters will fight with everything they've got, down to their last breath, to get a chance to go into the Q-Zone. But only the most skilled of Hunters can execute a perfect Q-Zone kill."

Skyler, Ella and Kyran all sat up with pride, smirking at one another.

"What exactly is it?" Aaron asked.

"It's a temporary zone that is created for only one purpose," Scott explained.

"Trap and burn." Skyler grinned.

Aaron looked questioningly at Scott.

"The threat, whatever it may be, is in the human realm," Scott said as his hand hovered over the table to show the map of the world again. "We can't go into the human world and end it, lest we reveal ourselves and put the Trace on half of the population." Aaron tensed but remained quiet. "So the Hunters have to lure the demons out of the human realm and back into our realm to destroy them." The map shimmered and went back to the mage realm. "But, of course, the demons aren't stupid and they won't let themselves be drawn out and brought back to a place they can be killed, so I make what's called a Quarantine Zone. A temporary area, as big or small as required, that traps the demons. I can make Q-Zones in either realm, but it's only visible to mages, so it allows them to lure the demons into the Q-Zone without them realising."

"What happens to the demons once they enter the Q-Zone?" Aaron asked.

"Hunters can fight the demons whichever way they like in the Q-Zone," Scott said. His expression darkened and he looked down at the map. "But like I said, the Q-Zone is only temporary. It collapses forty minutes after it's created. Anything still inside the zone is destroyed."

Aaron could read the grief on Scott's face. "I take it the Q-Zone doesn't distinguish between mages and demons?" he asked.

"We've lost many Hunters in Q-Zones," Scott revealed in a quiet, morose voice. "An ideal execution is to trap the demons and have every single Hunter out of the zone before it collapses." He shook his head and sighed, closing his eyes. "But that doesn't always happen."

"It'll happen this time," Skyler said, coming to stand next to Scott. "We're not losing any more Hunters." Then, with a look at Kyran he added, "Well, maybe just the one."

Kyran rolled his eyes, but didn't say anything.

"Don't," Scott warned Skyler. "I don't want to hear you even joke about something like that."

"Let him," Kyran said. "He can say what he wants. I'm not going anywhere."

Skyler only smirked back at him.

"So that's what Hunters do?" Aaron asked. "They go to the human world to lure out the demons and bring them to the Q-Zone to be destroyed?"

"No," Ella replied. "We do a lot more than that."

"We have our own world to protect too," Skyler said.

"Here?" Aaron frowned. "But I thought this realm was safe?"

The faces before him darkened.

"Our realm isn't safe," Ella said quietly. "Not by a long shot."

"Not yet, it isn't," Skyler corrected. "But we'll get there."

Scott, Aaron noticed, looked downright miserable. His face was lowered, shoulders hunched and eyes closed, with deep lines on his brow.

"Scott?" Aaron called, making the man open his eyes and lift his head up before offering a tight smile.

"We don't go to the human realm often," he said. "Only when we learn about demons crossing realms and terrorising the humans. It's the duty of a mage to protect human life." His hand lifted and once again the map changed, but this time the black lines grew until the areas all shaded to black. The individual letters of the alphabet disappeared and in their place came only two letters. Either an *H* outlined in red, or the letter *N* outlined in blue. Just a glance showed Aaron that there were more red zones than blue. "But we have to protect ourselves too," Scott said and gestured to the map. "The blue zones are our safe zones, ones that are Gated."

"Gated?" Aaron asked. "What does that mean?"

Scott paused before sharing a look with Skyler and Ella. "When you first arrived at Salvador, you came across a Gate," Scott said.

Aaron thought for a moment. "You mean that big white door?"

Scott's lips lifted into an amused smile. Behind him, Skyler facepalmed.

"Yes, that *big white door*," Scott repeated. "That door is a Gate – a pretty important Gate. It protects us from demons as well as protecting the human realm."

"The human realm?" Aaron asked. "How?"

Scott paused, narrowing his eyes. "Your dad really hasn't told you anything?"

Aaron tried to ignore the dirty look Skyler threw him. "No," he admitted quietly.

Scott took in a breath. "Aaron, do you know what being a mage means?"

Feeling his face burn, Aaron shook his head. "No."

Scott nodded again, growing more frustrated, as was evident by the red tinge in his cheeks. "I can't understand why Christopher Adams would treat his own son like this." He rubbed a hand over his eyes. "Alright." Scott reached out to pull Aaron closer, turning him to face the map. "A mage has powers, you know that much?"

"Yeah." Aaron nodded.

"When a mage in this realm uses their power, it generates an immense amount of energy," Scott explained. "The Gates," he pointed to the blue *N*-marked zones, "take in that energy. They utilise it to remain strong and protect the zones." He pointed to the red *H*-marked zones. "But these areas don't have Gates. The power flows directly from these areas into the human realm and it causes tremendous damage to their world."

Aaron felt goosebumps erupt over his flesh. "What kind of damage?"

"You've seen the power we have," Scott said. "You've been in Salvador long enough. Can't you tell what kind of damage it would inflict?"

Aaron felt his skin prickle with dread. "Elements," he replied. "The mages use the power of the elements."

"Wahey," Skyler mocked. "He actually got it."

"Mages have power over the elements," Scott confirmed. "They can do almost anything with that power, but if that release of energy isn't contained, then that power leaks out and affects the human realm. If the power of Earth is used, then the energy would affect the earth of the human realm. If it's the power of Water, it'll affect the water of the human realm."

Aaron's eyes widened. "No," he gasped. "You don't mean...?"

Scott's face fell and he nodded sadly. "Nine times out of ten, it's our power that upsets nature's balance."

"Turns out natural disasters aren't so natural after all," Skyler said.

Aaron, horrified to his very core, shook his head in denial. "It can't be," he said, feeling a pressure twist at his heart. "Earthquakes," he whispered. "Tsunamis, floods, hurricanes, all of it...We...we're responsible?"

"No." Scott held on to Aaron's arm, his grip brutally tight. "*We're* not responsible," he said. "We safeguard our zones. We set up Gates so we don't kill thousands of humans. We have Gates so that our powers *don't* create earthquakes and tsunamis and floods! We aren't the ones wiping out the human species." He jabbed a finger at the red zones. "*They* are responsible!" he said. "They are the ones that use their powers freely and without a care!"

"Why?" Aaron asked. "Why would mages do that?"

"They're not mages." It was Kyran who spoke. "They're nothing like mages."

"Who are they, then?" Aaron asked.

"Demons," Ella replied, with a disgusted expression.

"Got that right," Skyler said, his voice holding a slight growl and his expression twisted to show his revulsion. "The worst of all demons."

Scott let go of Aaron, looking a little calmer. "They live in these zones." He pointed to the red H-marked zones.

Aaron looked across the map, noting that there were only seven zones marked with a blue N. The other nineteen had the red H – areas that didn't have Gates to protect the human world. These zones, Aaron realised, coincided with the areas of the world that were thought to be prone to natural disasters: South America, Canada, the United States of America, Russia, Italy, Japan and Australia.

"Why can't you set up Gates in these areas as well?" Aaron asked.

"What a good idea," Skyler said in an exaggerated tone. "Thank Heavens you came, Adams, with such revolutionary ideas. We would never have thought of putting up Gates there on our own."

"Skyler," Scott said harshly, before turning back to Aaron. "That's what we're trying to do," he explained. "Each of these zones are divided into sub-zones." The map changed to show Aaron the twenty-six zones with thin, fine lines criss-crossing the inside of each – detailing the sub-zones. "We take one sub-zone at a time and eradicate the enemy. Once we have all sub-zones cleared out, we set up a Gate for that zone. That becomes a safe zone – Neriah's zones."

Neriah, Aaron repeated mentally. He had heard the name before. He was sure Mary had mentioned him once or twice. Aaron looked at the seven zones that had been marked with a blue N. These were places that had been cleared out and safeguarded. Consequently, these were the very few locations of the world that didn't suffer as much from natural disasters.

"The N stands for Neriah," Aaron said. "So what does the H stand for?"

Scott went very quiet. A hush fell across the room with even Skyler looking uneasy.

"Hadrian," Scott said, struggling with the name. "The red zones belong to Hadrian."

"Who's Hadrian?" Aaron asked.

Scott, Skyler and Ella all looked uncomfortable, glancing to one another. Aaron tuned to see that even Kyran's expression had darkened.

"He's the enemy," Scott said with notable difficulty. He clicked his fingers. The map disappeared, leaving only a dark, blank space in the hollow of the table. "I have a lot to do," he said to Aaron. "Q-Zones don't get set up on their own." He attempted a laugh but it sounded fake and empty. "I'll see you around, Aaron."

"Yeah." Aaron nodded. "See you around."

***

"What the hell?" Sam exclaimed, eyes narrowed in disbelief. He stared at Aaron, who was sitting on the front steps to their cottage with Rose. "What do they mean they cause natural disasters?"

"Exactly that," Aaron said miserably. "If they don't set up Gates, the power they use causes disasters in our world."

"But that makes no sense," Rose said. "How can this realm affect what happens in our world?"

Aaron shrugged. "Dunno," he said. "I think this is the war my dad was talking about." He met Sam's eyes. "He told me this world was in the middle of a war, one that's tearing it apart – literally." The image of the map, with its N- and H-zones swam to the forefront of his mind. "That's what he meant: a war over the zones. It seems the fight is between this Neriah and the demon Hadrian. From the looks of things, this Neriah guy is the leader of the mages and Hadrian must be the leader of the demons. Neriah's trying to drive out the demons and take Hadrian's zones, to make them safe by setting up Gates so the human realm's not affected by the flow of power."

"They're having you on," Sam said. "They think they're being funny, telling you crap. Besides, think about it: if the mages' power is responsible for natural disasters in our word and they really have set up Gates to stop that power getting out, then those demons in those...those H-zones, the ones without Gates, must be using the same power as the mages to cause the same damage."

"You're right," Ella said, making all three look up at her. She stopped at their fence. "They do use the same power as us."

Sam walked over to her, jaw set and shoulders lifted in anger. "What do you think you're doing?"

Ella blinked at him. "Excuse me?"

"Telling him rubbish!" Sam pointed at Aaron. "I don't know what you mages are playing at, but telling outright lies to make fun of him–"

"Get off your high horse, Shattered," Ella cut him off. "We're not lying to him."

"Oh really?" Sam screwed up his face, eyes narrowed to slits. "So what you're saying is that you wave your hand here and in our world an earthquake happens?"

"Not here," Ella said. "But if you were in one of Hadrian's zones, then yeah, pretty much."

"Please," Sam said. "Pull the other one! That's not how earthquakes happen."

"Really?" Ella asked, crossing her arms at her chest. "Go on, then. How do earthquakes happen?"

Sam flustered. "They...It's...a...a..."

"Seismic waves."

They all turned to look at Aaron.

"Earthquakes happen when there's a build up of force on the tectonic plates," Aaron continued. "The rocks underground break from the pressure and friction, and the sudden movement and readjustment of the tectonic plates releases energy, which causes seismic waves, making the ground shake." He remembered studying natural disasters in excruciating detail with his mum.

Sam looked back at Ella. "What he said." He nodded at Aaron.

"That's the science behind it," Ella said, "not the cause." She looked past Sam, her soft grey eyes on Aaron. "It's not the build up of force or pressure on the tectonic plates underground, it's the power leaking through the tears that shifts the tectonic plates, which in turn cause seismic waves, meaning earthquakes." She straightened up, dropping her arms to her side. "Anyway," she looked at Rose, "I only came to tell you that Mother Mary wants to see you." She gave Sam an annoyed look, turned and walked away.

Rose stood up, dusting the back of her jeans. "I better go. I'll catch you guys later."

"Hold up, I'll come with you," Sam said. "I'm finished in the orchard, so I'll give you a hand." He turned to Aaron. "Coming?"

"Yeah, why not?" Aaron stood up. He had taken two steps when he saw

Kyran crossing the street, making his way to the back of the cottages, heading for that dusty path again. "You guys head on," Aaron said, watching Kyran. "I'll catch up with you."

Sam followed his stare. "What're you doing?" he asked.

"Nothing," Aaron said. "I just wanna see where he goes."

"Why?" Sam asked. "Didn't you see the beating he gave Skyler? You should stay out of his way."

"Whoa." Rose stopped mid-stride and turned around. "Kyran beat up Skyler?" she asked with wide eyes. "Why?"

"Skyler was messing around with Kyran's girl," Sam explained.

"What?" Rose exclaimed. "When did this happen?"

"I dunno." Sam shrugged. "Point is," he turned to Aaron, "don't get Kyran angry."

"Kyran has a girlfriend?" Rose asked, looking shocked. "Is she here? In Salvador?"

Both Aaron and Sam looked over at her.

"What do you care?" Aaron asked.

"I don't care," Rose said, but her nose and cheeks began to turn pink, like they always did when she became embarrassed. "I'm just...curious."

Aaron gave her a long look.

"I'm going to the Stove," Rose said, turned quickly, and headed down the street.

Sam looked back to Aaron. "Be careful," he said, before following after his sister.

Aaron hurried to the narrow path behind the cottages. He just caught sight of Kyran as he turned the corner. Aaron rushed after him, turning the corner to come face to face with Kyran, who was leaning against a tree with his arms crossed. His vivid green-eyed stare pinned Aaron to the spot. Slowly, his gaze trailed over Aaron, from top to bottom, before meeting his eyes.

"Care to explain why you're following me?"

12

Conversations

"I'm...I'm not..." Aaron cleared his throat. "I'm not following you."

Kyran raised an eyebrow. "So what are you doing here?"

"I was just..." Aaron glanced around. "...taking a walk."

"A walk?" Kyran straightened up, uncurling his arms from under his chest. "Seemed like clumsy running to me."

Aaron mentally cursed. He should have been more discreet. "Sorry," he said. "I just...I..." He took in a breath, resolving to stay strong and not get intimidated by those fierce green eyes that were staring at him. "I wanted to talk to you."

"About?" Kyran asked dryly.

Aaron fell quiet, struggling to voice a thousand and one questions. Kyran raised an eyebrow at his silence before shaking his head and turning to walk away.

"I've been dreaming about you!" Aaron yelled after him.

Kyran stopped and Aaron grimaced. He didn't mean for it to come spilling out like that. It had sounded decidedly odd, but Aaron had no choice but to go along with it now. Kyran turned to face him with a baffled expression.

"I've...I've been having these...dreams," Aaron continued, walking closer. "Weird dreams, actually. For about two months now. I never thought I was actually dreaming about a real person. Figured you were just in my imagination." He smiled awkwardly. "But here you are." He gave a rather uncomfortable laugh.

Kyran stared at him before nodding slowly. "Okaaay." He dragged the word out, long and slow. "That's...nice and everything but, the thing is, I drive my bike on the other side of the road, so..." He wrinkled his nose and shook his head. "No thanks."

Aaron looked confused, then his eyes widened.

"What? No, no! You think...?" He shook his head. "I'm not...I don't like you— I mean, I do like you, it's not that I hate you or anything, but I don't…It's not like that…I like girls!"

"Okay." Kyran nodded and turned to walk away.

"Wait!" Aaron shouted and ran behind him. "It's not what you think."

Kyran looked at him. "You've been having *weird* dreams about me." He shook his head. "Seems pretty straight forward." He started walking down the path.

"No, no," Aaron objected, following after him. "Not like *that*!"

Kyran chuckled. "Whatever you say."

"The dreams were mostly just us standing around, talking," Aaron explained, as he walked alongside Kyran. "But it's strange that I dreamt about you before meeting you."

"It is strange," Kyran agreed.

Aaron blinked. "That's all you're gonna say?"

"What were you expecting?" Kyran asked.

"I was hoping for more of an explanation."

"And you thought I would have the answers because…?"

Aaron fell quiet. Why did he assume Kyran would know the answer? Kyran wasn't the one having the dreams, so why would he know what they meant? In silence the two boys continued through the woods and down a steep hill. They came to a clutter of buildings arranged in a semi-circle. Aaron recognised them as the ones he, Sam and Rose had raced past the day they were chasing after the bikers. That day the buildings were deserted, with thick steel shutters blocking their entrance. Today, however, three of those shutters were lifted.

Two of them were workshops. One reminded Aaron of a mechanic's garage, with tools and spare pieces assorted onto metal shelves behind a heavy-looking trolley. Paint cans and oil containers were stacked to one side. The smell of motor oil was so thick that Aaron's eyes watered.

The second workshop held something that made Aaron's mouth drop open and eyebrows disappear behind the hair that fell across his forehead. In this second building, lined along three walls were doorless floor-to-ceiling cabinets that held an assortment of weapons. Swords, knives, dagger sets, ninja stars – all gleaming a shiny silver as they sat mounted proudly on the wall or displayed on the many shelves. In an opposite cabinet, Aaron found another collection of weapons, one that ran a chill down his spine. Firearms. All types and styles of handguns lay in pristine condition: shiny black revolvers, gleaming semi-automatic and machine pistols made up the collection. In the middle of the room was a massive anvil – a big, heavy block of iron. On a table next to it were hammers of various sizes and tongs. A wooden drum stood on the other side of the anvil.

The third building wasn't a workshop. It looked like a garage, holding at least twenty bikes, lined in rows. Aaron stared at the beauties, mentally imagining the look on Sam's face when he saw these.

Aaron and Kyran weren't the only ones here; Ryan and Zhi-Jiya were in the garage, crowded around a gorgeous red and black bike with silver spokes in its big black wheels. Every inch of it was gleaming, polished to a shine. Aaron didn't know all that much about bikes, that was Sam's territory, but spending so much time with the motorcycle enthusiast had taught him enough to deduce that the bike resembled a Honda CBR.

Ryan looked up as Kyran approached and grinned. "Just in time," he said, stepping away. Zhi-Jiya did the same.

"How is she?" Kyran asked, hurrying over to kneel before the bike.

"As good as new." Ryan beamed. "You can't even see it."

"Oh baby." Kyran ran his hand down the shiny red metal. "Don't you worry. I taught him a lesson. He won't touch you again."

Zhi-Jiya looked amused. "As long as you don't piss Skyler off again," she said.

Kyran looked up at her. "Skyler should act like he has a pair and come at me, not my Lexi."

Aaron's eyes widened. "*That's* Lexi?" he asked.

Kyran turned to him with a frown. "Yeah. Why?"

"Nothing," Aaron said. "It's just...when I heard Skyler was messing around with Lexi," he shrugged, "I figured she was your...girlfriend."

Kyran raised an eyebrow. "Skyler's stupid, not suicidal."

"What's he doing here?" Ryan asked, jutting his chin out towards Aaron, a steely look in his eyes.

"Dunno," Kyran replied, standing up. "He sorta followed me here."

"I feel for him," Zhi-Jiya said. "He's so clueless. I heard he didn't even know he was an Elemental! Can you just imagine?"

"You do know that I can hear you, right?" Aaron asked.

Zhi-Jiya faced him. "Of course," she replied, before smiling at him.

Aaron shook his head and turned to the workshops. "These are pretty impressive," he commented.

"Damn right, they are," Zhi-Jiya said, walking closer as Kyran and Ryan fussed over the bike. "Salvador's workshops are the best in this realm," she said. "Well, maybe second to the workshops of Marwah."

Aaron stared at the weapons. He noticed that each blade and firearm bore the familiar mark of a circle with an inverted V holding a spiral between its legs, while three wavy lines passed behind the V.

"Most of us have our own familiars," Zhi-Jiya said, stepping into the workshop, "but there comes a time when you need new companions." Her fingers reached for a dagger and she slowly traced the insignia on its hilt. "It sucks, but when it comes to survival," she turned to look at Aaron, "you have to learn to let go of old friends and make new, stronger ones."

Aaron met her eyes. "If it's calculated, it's not friendship."

Zhi-Jiya grinned. "Oh? So what is it then?"

Aaron smiled. "A matter of convenience," he said, "and friends aren't made for convenience."

***

Aaron came to sit at the table while Alan was setting it out. Rose and Sam were already seated, waiting for him.

"You're in one piece," Sam said, his tone light and mocking but there was anxiety in his eyes. "I take it Kyran didn't realise you were following him?"

"No, he knew," Aaron said, raising his hand to catch the cutlery as it came hurtling through the air. "He was waiting for me."

"What did he do?" Rose asked nervously.

"Nothing," Aaron said. "I walked with him and we went to those buildings – the ones at the bottom of that hill?" The twins nodded in understanding, so Aaron went on. "You're not going to believe what's there."

"What?" Sam asked, intrigued.

Aaron was about to answer when Drake came to sit opposite him. Aaron didn't want to say anything in front of him, not when he knew the man was practically a spy for his dad. He expected Drake to give his dad a full report of everything he had done while they had been away. Aaron's heart gave an uncomfortable lurch when he thought about his parents. It had been two weeks since they had left Salvador. A part of him had expected them back by now. *Any day,* he kept telling himself. *They'll be back any day now.*

"Aaron?" Rose touched his arm, bringing him out of his thoughts.

Aaron threw a look at Drake and shook his head slightly. "We'll talk tonight," he whispered. "When we're alone."

Gradually, the rest of the mages joined the table. Aaron watched as Kyran sat down with Ryan, Ella and Zhi-Jiya. He leant across to whisper to Sam and Rose.

"By the way, Lexi isn't a girl," he said. "It's his bike."

"A bike?" Sam asked. "Bloody hell, he got that angry because Skyler touched his bike?"

"He didn't touch her, he *messed* with her, remember?" Aaron pointed out.

Sam nodded, but he was grinning. "He named his bike Lexi?"

"Shh!" Aaron urged when Kyran looked around at them, eyes narrowed slightly. When he seemed occupied with Ella, Aaron gave Sam a lopsided grin. "Yeah, and he seems really attached to the thing. I can't really blame him – it's a beauty. Wait till you see it."

Rose was smiling, shaking her head as she played with her ravioli. "His bike," she chuckled softly. "It was his bike."

Aaron frowned at her in confusion. She seemed rather happy at that revelation. Really, *really* happy.

***

Six days passed and it seemed the whole of Salvador was in preparation for the Q-Zone that was opening the next day. The Hunters had spent every waking minute of the last week in or around the ring, training and practising. Mary had gone into a frenzy, preparing dishes rich in protein and practically forcing warm milk down all the Hunters' throats every night, insisting it was essential for strong bones.

The sanctuary cottages were being emptied. The great number of people – the humans who mages referred to as the Shattered ones – barely came out of their cottages the whole fortnight they were there. Mary made sure three meals a day were delivered to them. Now the Shattered ones were leaving, moving to different cities in the mage realm to restart their lives.

"They got plen'y of places tae go," Jason reassured Aaron, as they watched the saddened and forlorn-looking people follow the Hunters out of Salvador.

"Why can't the mages help them settle in their own world, in the human realm?" Aaron asked.

Jason laughed, shaking his head, ticking the paper on his clipboard as he examined the cottages from outside. "Forgettin about tha' little thing called the Trace?" he asked.

"Do all Shattereds have the Trace?" Aaron asked.

"Aaron, ma boy." Jason stopped to look at him. "They wouldnae be a Shattered if they dinnae hav' a Trace." He looked down at his clipboard. "Now, normally I would gee you yur own p'ace, but we're gettin' an awful lo' of Hunters soon." He looked up at Aaron. "I'm sorry, but yeh gonna hav' tae share with Kyran for a wee bit longer."

Aaron nodded and turned away. He had just started walking over to help Sam carry their baskets of fruit to the Stove when the Gate opened and a group of twenty or so mages came in, riding on their bikes. Aaron watched as the bikers, a mix of girls and boys in their early twenties, rode down the street and disappeared down the path that led to the ring.

"Where do you reckon they're going?" Sam asked, watching them intently through the cloud of dust kicked up by the racing wheels.

"To see Scott at the Hub, I guess," Aaron replied.

"How many Hunters do you think this realm has?" Sam asked.

"Not enough," Aaron replied quietly. "Otherwise, there'd be more blue zones on the map."

**

Hunters continued to arrive throughout the day, filling the streets of Salvador with carefree, high-spirited youths, who met one another with big grins and wide-armed hugs. There were easily more than a hundred Hunters in Salvador by sunset. Aaron watched from the front steps of Kyran's cottage as Skyler and Ella met their fellow Hunters with great warmth, smiling and laughing with them, clapping hands on their backs and ushering them to the table where Mother Mary was distributing drinks.

Aaron noted that each and every Hunter bore some sort of a tattoo. Black or silver inked images of swords, daggers or guns were the norm it seemed, marked on the back of necks, upper arms and wrists. Some girls had bronze or gold-tinted images of animals, flowers and strange symbols, visible on their exposed midriffs or arms and necks.

The flash of light swept through the City of Salvador for the tenth time that day, and the Gate opened to permit entrance to yet another team of

Hunters. Another crowd of youths, clad in jeans and long, flowing coats came inside on their motorbikes. But this particular group didn't ride to the back of the cottages like the others had done. They parked in the middle of the road and dismounted their bikes. The one at the front caught Aaron's eye. Like most of the Hunters, he was tall, with that same predatory grace. The sleeveless top he was wearing not only showcased his powerful build, but a tattoo of a lion's face inked on the tanned skin of his arm. The boy's hazel-eyed gaze scanned the thick crowd. He didn't seem to find who he was looking for and held up both arms, a quizzical look on his face.

"Where is he?" he called to the table.

"You can say hello to us too, you know?" Ella replied, getting to her feet.

"Hello, Ella," the boy replied. "Now, where is he?"

"Lost," Skyler replied. "Hopefully."

The boy narrowed his eyes. "Skyler." He nodded. "A pleasure as always."

Skyler nodded back with a grin.

"Seriously, where is that idiot?" the boy asked, looking around.

"Over there." Omar, one of Salvador's Hunters, pointed to the path leading up from the orchard.

Aaron had to stand up to see past the crowd. He saw Drake, deep in conversation with Kyran. Both seemed engrossed, with lines on their foreheads and shadowed expressions as they made their way up.

"Ah, there he is," the boy with the lion tattoo said, grinning broadly. "Kyran! Hey!"

Kyran looked up and his frown melted at the sight of the other boy. His eyes brightened and he left Drake's side, hurrying up the street with a broad grin.

"Zulf!" he called.

"I thought you would be waiting for me with bated breath at the Gate," the boy – Zulf – said with an identical grin.

"You hit your head again? Having hallucinations?" Kyran asked.

They hugged each other like brothers would – a tight embrace with a hand on the back of the other's neck.

"It's been too long," Zulf said, stepping back, still smiling at Kyran. "The last Q-Zone was what? Two months ago?"

"Something like that," Kyran replied.

"I heard you went with Scott to see the Pecosas," Zulf said, his eyes gleaming with curiosity. "What's the score?"

"A complete loss," Kyran replied. "They claim they're not with the Scorcher."

"Bull." Zulf shook his head. "Bunch of liars!"

Kyran grinned. "That's what I said."

"Bet they loved that," Zulf chuckled.

"More than being accused of helping the enemy," Kyran replied.

Zulf and his team of Hunters followed Kyran to the table and sat down. Aaron caught sight of Sam and Rose as they walked out of the Stove, carrying platters of food. He hurried over to help them.

"It's okay, I got it," Rose said, rather tersely, when Aaron tried to take the heavy tray from her.

The kitchen helpers laid out the feast and Aaron noticed the difference in tonight's dinner. Normally there were two main dishes with plenty of sides, but tonight an extra effort had been made. Platters of grilled chicken, beef steaks, lamp chops, grilled fish, roasted potatoes as well as chunky chips, stir-fried vegetables, corn on the cob and slices of buttered crusty bread were arranged down the length of the table. The Hunters started filling their plates with vigour, grinning and chatting with one another.

"Did you hear about the Ichadaris in Danwan?" a slightly older-looking Hunter was asking Skyler. "News is they're causing quite a commotion."

"I thought they were taken care of," Skyler said with a frown.

"Not a chance," said a girl with an elaborate snake design tattooed along the length of her arm. "There are very few teams that touch Ichis. Rumour has it that the Ichadaris in Danwan took out the last two teams that went in for them."

"No way." Ella shook her head, making the blue streaks in her hair flash through her dark hair. "There's no way we lost two teams, not to Ichis."

"Ask Scott if you don't believe me," the girl said.

"I will," Ella replied. Then, glancing around the table, she asked, "Where is Scott?"

"At the Hub," Ryan said. "He's fretting over last-minute details."

"He's such a worrier," Zhi-Jiya said. "When's the last time we lost anyone in a Q-Zone?

"It's *because* Scott's a worrier that we haven't lost anyone," Skyler said. "He's the best Controller since–" He stopped abruptly, looking uneasy. The surrounding mages shared his discomfort, looking down at their plates. "As long as we've got Scott doing the worrying, we don't have to do it ourselves," Skyler finished.

Sam turned to Aaron. "Controller?"

Aaron shrugged. "Maybe because he controls the Hub?" he offered.

"Makes sense." Sam nodded. "I thought he just liked telling people what to do."

"If we had lost two teams, Scott would have told us," Ella continued to argue.

"I'm just saying what I heard," the snake-tattooed girl replied.

"You should know by now, Heidi, not to listen to rumours," Ella said sharply.

"Exactly. All sorts of ridiculous stories get passed around," Zulf said. "Have you heard the latest? Apparently the infamous Adams are back."

Aaron felt his hair stand on end. His mouthful of chicken struggled to make its way past his throat.

"If anyone believes that steaming pile of crap, they deserve to get their heads blown off," Zulf said. "It's been what? Fourteen years? And still all anyone can talk about is the freaking Adams!"

"Um, Zulf?" Ella started. "You might *not* want to talk about the Adams, since the youngest one is sitting five seats down." She tilted her head towards Aaron.

Zulf's smirk melted and eyes widened. He turned to look down the table and spotted the three unfamiliar faces of Aaron, Sam and Rose. Zulf examined Sam and Aaron, obviously trying to decipher which one was an Adams. He glanced at Rose and then Sam, obviously noting their resemblance, before his eyes settled for a long moment on Aaron.

"Shit," he breathed. "Hey, man, I'm sorry. I didn't know you guys were actually back."

Aaron shook his head. "It's okay," he said. "Forget about it."

Annoyed, Zulf turned to Kyran, who was grinning unashamedly. "A heads up would've been nice." Zulf glowered at him.

"What? And miss this?" Kyran asked. "You'd think your mouth's the same size as your foot by now."

Zulf glanced down the long table, searching for someone else. "Where are your parents?" he asked Aaron.

Skyler snorted but didn't say anything.

"They're not here," Aaron replied, his chest tightening at the reminder.

"Where did they go?" Zulf asked with a frown.

"Where'd you think?" Skyler interrupted.

Zulf's frown disappeared and he nodded in quiet understanding. "Right," he said. "Damn, I wouldn't want to be them right now." He gave a little shiver.

Aaron looked over at him with a furrowed brow. "What do you mean?"

"They have to face Neriah and answer to him for disappearing for fourteen years." Zulf leant over in Aaron's direction. "Where have you been all this time?"

"Living in the human realm," Aaron answered.

Many murmurs broke across the table, with several mages turning to one another, nodding with I-told-you-so expressions.

"Damn." Zulf sat back. "So it's true then? You've been living like a... a *human*?"

"You don't have to say it like it's a bad thing," Aaron said.

"Idiot," Skyler muttered. "Of course it's a bad thing. You're a mage, not a lame human."

Aaron's fists clenched into tight balls. "I don't get it," he said. "Scott said it's the duty of a mage to protect human life. What you lot are doing tomorrow, you're doing it to protect humans, yet you take every opportunity to insult them."

"We save them; doesn't mean we have to like them," Skyler replied.

"That's obvious," Rose muttered.

"You say something, Shattered?" Skyler asked coldly.

Rose turned her head to meet his blue stare. "The name's Rose," she stated. "If you're going to address me, use my name."

Skyler looked amused. He shared a look with the other mages before turning in his chair to face her. "I don't give a shit what your name is," he said. "You're not important enough for me to remember."

"Yeah, no surprise there," Rose said. "It's clear what importance you give to humans. If you mages actually cared, you wouldn't treat us like we were scum!"

"Hey, hey, wait up." Ella held up a hand, eyes narrowed. "You can't say that."

"Please," Sam scoffed, joining in. "Don't tell me you actually think you treat us well?"

"What?" Ryan asked, frowning. "What are you talking about? What have we done that's so terrible?"

"Where should we start?" Rose asked. "Your whole attitude towards us is horrible. None of you show even the slightest bit of empathy towards any of the humans that come here, yet you know they're suffering." She pointed a finger at the line of cottages. "The houses you stay in are nice and clean, but you give dirty ones to the people that come here after losing their homes. At every step, you belittle and insult us, telling us we're worthless and useless. You call us the Shattered ones. *Shattered?*" She shook her head, lips turned up in disgust. "Is that appropriate? Is that what to label people who have lost everything? Humans that have no choice but to leave their life, their *world*, come here and are treated like second-class citizens. You have no compassion for humans, even while knowing that we've lost our family—"

"Big deal." Skyler glowered, cutting her off. "You've lost family? Take a look around," he prompted. "Everyone here has lost someone. If they hadn't, they wouldn't be in Salvador." His eyes glistened a dark blue. "You think you're the only one to lose your parents? Count yourself lucky you didn't *watch* them die. You didn't hear their screams." He glanced once at Aaron before looking back at Rose. "You suffered, lost your family, had to leave your world and come here. Suck it up and live with it. If you can't, then go kill yourself, but quit this pity-me bull 'cause no one has the time for it."

"Sky?" Ella looked affronted.

"Hey, man," Ryan shook his head. "Too much."

Zulf and Kyran shared a look with one another before glaring at Skyler.

Rose didn't say anything. She got up from the table and walked away. Sam and Aaron got up after her.

"Rose! Rose, wait," Sam called as she hurried up the pathway.

"Leave me alone," Rose called back. Her voice softened. "Please, Sam, just leave me alone." She disappeared into the cottage.

"Should we go in?" Aaron asked.

Sam paused, trying to figure out what they should do. Finally, he shook his head. "No," he said. "Give her a few minutes."

They walked back to the table, where an awkward silence had fallen over the mages. Sam and Aaron walked past the table, heading to the Stove. They would rather help Mary clean and tidy the kitchen than spend another minute sitting with Skyler.

***

Rose sat next to the window, using the soft glow of the setting sun to look at the framed picture in her hands. It was a family portrait, taken two years ago – one of the five framed photos Michael had brought for her and Sam.

Rose stared at the picture. Her tall and balding dad sat next to her mum – a short, plump woman with a broad, uninhibited smile. Standing next to her dad was a grinning Sam, his hand on their dad's shoulder. She was sitting next to her mum, perched on the arm of the chair, smiling happily at the camera. Rose stared at her mum's face. Slowly, her fingers stroked the photo, caressing her mum's image.

A gentle knock on the door made Rose look around. She expected it to be Aaron. Sam wouldn't knock. He had never in his life knocked on her door. He would just come barging in, no matter how many times she screamed at him for doing it. But it wasn't Aaron. Her lips parted in surprise at the sight of Kyran framed in her doorway.

"You okay?" he asked.

They had been living in the same cottage for two weeks but Kyran hadn't said a word to her until now. Rose felt rather thrown by his sudden concern. Looking down at the frame in her hands, she nodded.

"Yeah," she said.

A creak sounded as Kyran shifted from one foot to the other.

"Don't listen to Skyler," he said.

Rose shook her head, her lips quivered but she forced them into a steady, hard line. "He's such a jerk," she said, her voice no more than a whisper under the strain of keeping her tears back.

"I'd have used more colourful words," Kyran commented, "but yeah, he's a jerk alright."

"Does he really not care about the humans they save?" she asked, looking up at Kyran. "Does he have no compassion? Is he really that cold-hearted?

"Skyler says what he believes," Kyran replied. "And he reckons everyone should just shut up and get on with things, regardless of how they're feeling."

"Well, someone should tell that idiot that's not how humans work," Rose said. She looked down at the photo again. "When we're – as you lot put it – *shattered*, it takes time to pick the pieces back up."

Silence fell between them.

"It's not like that, you know," Kyran said.

"What?" Rose asked.

"The term Shattered." He shook his head. "It's not meant to be derogatory."

"Well, it is," Rose replied. "Even if it's true." Her voice dropped low as her fingers ran over the portrait of her parents. "When you've lost everything, the last thing you want to be told is that you're broken too."

Kyran stared at her for long silent moments. "Ignore Skyler," he said at last. "I know it seems impossible but you'll learn to tune him out."

"Yeah," Rose said, quietly. "Thanks."

Kyran nodded at her. He turned to go but paused briefly. "You should know, though, that not all mages are like Skyler. Some of us do have compassion." His eyes met hers. "Some of us do care."

Rose didn't say anything. Kyran smiled before he walked away. With his back turned to her, he lifted a hand and two of his fingers twitched. A flickering light filled Rose's room. She looked up to see hanging lanterns in all four corners of the room, glowing softly as flames danced in them.

She looked to the door again, just catching a fleeting glimpse of Kyran as he walked downstairs. She smiled gratefully after him, for the comfort of a little light in the approaching darkness.

13

THE Q-ZONE

Breakfast was unusually quiet, especially for such a large number of people sitting at the table. Most of the Hunters were subdued compared to the night before. They sat with their heads bowed and worked their way through the light breakfast of crumpets and fruit. The residents of Salvador seemed nervous, glancing at the Hunters, whispering to one another with worried expressions. Aaron noticed that even Drake seemed quieter and moodier than usual, which was a feat in itself.

As soon as breakfast was over, all the Hunters went into their respective cottages to get ready. Aaron, Sam and Rose climbed upstairs, heading to their room, when they noticed the door to the third room was left ajar. Kyran was inside, standing before the built-in cupboard that none of them could previously open.

Aaron stilled, his body tensed in a mixture of fear and fascination. The top of the cupboard was flipped down, to act as a shelf. Inside, hanging on various hooks and mantels, rested a whole inventory of weapons. An assortment of shiny silver daggers, and four pairs of semi-automatic pistols with numerous magazines were lined underneath them – but what caught Aaron's breath was the silver sword which sat proudly in the middle of the cupboard. It was narrow and long, with a white hilt that made the black insignia carved into the grip stand out. Like all the other weapons Aaron saw in the artillery hut, this sword too had the same mark: a circle with an inverted V, three wavy lines behind it and a spiral between its legs.

"Whoa," Sam breathed. "Now we know why that thing was locked."

Kyran, who was in the process of lining the inner pockets of his coat with daggers, turned to see the three watching him. He ignored them and reached into the cupboard, taking out a pair of black and silver pistols and slid them into the twin holsters fitted to the back of his belt. Next he lifted out a chain with a small spiral dangling from it. Kyran slipped the chain over his head. Lastly, he pulled out the sword, flipped the lid up, and closed the cupboard. A wave of his hand and Aaron could hear the bolts sliding into place, locking the weapons cupboard once more. Kyran raised the sword and slotted it into its sheath, hidden under his coat. When he was done, Aaron could only see the pommel of the sword, peeking out from behind the collar of his coat. Kyran walked past the trio and went downstairs. Aaron shared a look with Sam and Rose before all three hurried out after him.

The street was busy with mages. The sun beating down on them was so bright it hurt Aaron's eyes. Everyone was gathered at the end of the table, talking with each other, but the babble was impossible to understand. Aaron spotted the kitchen staff, Alan and Ava included, standing together in a separate group. Jason was to one side, nodding along to whatever it was Drake was saying to him. Even Mary was there, outside of her precious Stove. The only group missing were the fair-skinned Empaths.

A thunderous roar of a hundred engines cut through the air. Aaron turned to see bike after bike come zooming out from the behind the cottages. The gathered crowd cheered loudly, whistling and shouting encouragement as the Hunters rode out. The bikes came to a stop, grouped together in a messy huddle. The residents of Salvador hurried forward, squeezing their way past the bikes to get to individual Hunters. Aaron watched as the mages pulled out black threads from their pockets and tied them around the Hunters' right wrists.

"What are they doing?" Rose asked.

"No idea," Aaron replied. He moved through the crowd until he came next to Alan and Ava. "Hey," he greeted them.

"Hey y'all." Alan smiled back.

"What's going on?" Aaron asked. "What's with the threads?"

"It's a reminder," Alan replied. "The mages tie a black thread on the wrists of the Hunters they care for, so every time that Hunter lifts a hand to fight, they see the thread and are reminded that there's someone waiting for them." He gave a light shrug. "Makes the Hunters a little less reckless when in the Q-Zone."

Aaron looked through the swarm of bikers again to see almost every Salvador Hunter sporting a black thread around their wrist. The Hunters that came from other cities also had black threads looped around their wrists. Aaron realised they must have got them before arriving at Salvador.

A lone bike revved its way up the path, appearing from behind Jason Burns's cottage and joined the front of the crowd. Skyler parked and sat back, straightening up. He was dressed in similar attire to the rest of the Hunters: dark jeans, boots, a top under a long coat, but his coat was very different to the rest. Skyler's coat was an ivory white with a large spiral shape glittering at the back in studded silver. The tips of his coat were silver, as were the folded down collars. Aaron spotted the black thread on his wrist when Skyler lifted his hands, adjusting his fingerless gloves.

"Who would want Skyler back?" Sam asked next to Aaron's ear.

"Must be someone," Aaron replied. "Skyler's got plenty of friends."

"Hunters don't tie threads on one another," Alan explained. "It's only by the mages left behind, waiting for the Hunters to return."

"So there's someone, other than his Hunter buddies, that cares enough for Skyler to return?" Sam asked. "They must be mad."

"Shh," Alan warned but chuckled nonetheless.

Aaron searched the crowd until he found Kyran, parked near the front. He had to strain his neck, going on tiptoes to see Kyran's hands, holding on to the bars of his bike. He couldn't see anything around either wrist.

"Kyran doesn't have any," Ava said, making Aaron look around at her. "He never does."

"Why?" Aaron asked. "Doesn't anyone care for him?"

"Of course they do." Ava smiled. "But they can't tie a thread on every single Hunter. It would defeat the purpose." She rubbed the black string held in her hand. "The thread symbolises a special connection between the mage and the Hunter. You can't have a special connection with everyone, can you?"

A bike came belting its way up and stopped right beside Aaron. Ella grinned, a twinkle in her grey eyes as she straightened up on her dazzling blue bike.

"Whoa," Sam gasped, but for once, he wasn't referring to Ella. "Is that a Ducati Panigale 1199?" he asked, staring at her bike.

"You know your bikes," Ella commented. She turned to Aaron. "Ready for the show, Adams?"

"Show?" Aaron frowned.

"At the Hub." She tilted her head towards the path behind the cottages. "You can keep up with the hunt."

"Really?" Aaron was intrigued.

"Yeah, really." She slipped off her glove from her right hand and held it out.

Ava stepped forward with a smile and wrapped the black thread around Ella's wrist before knotting it. She smiled at Ella, who smiled back just as warmly and slipped her leather fingerless gloves back on.

"Be careful," Ava said.

"As always," Ella replied.

Aaron noticed the hilt of a knife slotted into a holster strapped to Ella's thigh. The silvery-white insignia was clearly visible on the black handle. Aaron couldn't hold back his curiosity any longer.

"Ella?"

"Yeah?"

"That mark." Aaron nodded at the knife. "The circle with the markings inside. I've seen it everywhere. What is it?"

Ella didn't even look down to see what Aaron was referring to. "It's the mark of the Elementals," she said. "Or, to call it by its official name, Aric's mark."

Aaron frowned. "Aric?"

Ella's smile vanished and she stared at him. "Are you freaking kidding me?" she asked, her tone cold all of a sudden. "You don't know who *Aric* is?"

"I don't know who anyone is," Aaron said.

"Oh for–!" Ella bit her tongue, eyes clenched shut as she swallowed back obscenities. "You...!" She took in a breath, clutching onto the bars of her bike. She looked around at Aaron with blazing eyes. "You're telling me that you *seriously* don't know who Aric is?"

"No," Aaron said. "I *seriously* don't know."

"Do yourself a favour," she said. "When your no good parents return, shoot them!"

"Hey!" Aaron objected.

"No, they deserve it," Ella said. "I just, I can't..." She twisted the gear and rode off, leaving a cloud of dust in her wake.

Aaron turned to Sam and Rose. "What just happened?" he asked. "She was being somewhat decent and then–"

"She threw a hissy fit?" Sam finished for him.

"Exactly." Aaron nodded. "She knows I don't know anything about mages. Why would she assume I know who this Aric person is?"

He looked around to see Alan shaking his head at him, eyes narrowed.

"For shame, Aaron," he said. "You're a mage and you don't know who Aric is?"

Aaron opened his mouth to protest when a rumbustious cheer broke out amongst the mages. Aaron looked over to see Scott, standing before the Hunters, his face grim and dark bags under his eyes. He had obviously not slept last night, or for a few nights even.

"This is it," Scott called, as soon as the cheers died away. "You're heading out to execute a Q-Zone kill. You all know the rules." His gaze swept through the crowd. "You will stay within your designated roles. No one will act the hero." He stared at Skyler for a moment longer than the rest. "You do what you need to, to get the Lycans into the Q-Zone. You do what you have to, to *keep* them in the Q-Zone. When I tell you, you leave the zone – no questions, no exceptions." His mouth thinned as he pressed his lips together and took in a breath through his nose, letting it out slowly. "And remember: if anyone is left behind in the Q-Zone after you've been ordered out, no one goes back for them. You never go back. Is that understood?"

The Hunters let out a tremendous 'Yes!' and roared their bikes in agreement.

Scott nodded and turned, waving a hand so the rectangular cut in the distance slid open after a blinding flash.

"Go," he said. "May the fates bring you back to us."

The bikes revved and the Hunters rode towards the open Gate, with Skyler and Ella leading them. The Hunters disappeared through the Gate, their long coats whipping behind them. The rest of the mages cheered, wishing them luck and success. When the last bike crossed the threshold, the Gate slid closed, melting into the background again.

Scott turned to face the rest of the mages. "You can make your way to the Hub now."

The crowd moved with Scott, with the exception of the kitchen staff. Mary and her helpers started clearing up the table.

"Let's go and see what happens in this Q-Zone," Aaron said, hurrying forward.

He turned to see Sam and Rose hadn't moved.

"Forgetting something?" Sam asked. "Humans aren't allowed inside the Hub."

Aaron's face fell. "Oh yeah," he muttered, his shoulders dropping in disappointment.

"It's okay," Rose said. "You go and check it out."

Aaron really wanted to go. He had a strange desire to see the Q-Zone in action. At the same time, though, he couldn't leave his friends to be bored senseless.

"Nah." He shook his head. "It's alright. We'll hang."

"That's all we do every day," Rose said, smiling. "It's okay. You obviously want to go. You can tell us what it was like."

Aaron couldn't make himself leave. "It's such a stupid rule," he moaned. "Everyone should be allowed in the Hub."

"But they're not," Rose said. "It's fine, just go."

Aaron shook his head. "Not without my friends," he said. "Besides, it's not like I'll understand what's happening anyway. I'll probably just make all of them mad at me because of my complete lack of understanding about all things mage."

Ava was clearing the table but she was taking her time to stack the plates. When the rest of the kitchen staff moved towards the Stove, she turned to Aaron and the twins. "You know what's remarkable about Salvador?" she asked, addressing all three of them. "The stores. You must have seen them? Past the farm?"

Aaron remembered the unmanned shops he had discovered with Sam and Rose.

"They're very useful," Ava went on. "You can get almost anything there: clothes, shoes...books. There are so many books, including ones about mages and their history." She smiled at Aaron's surprised expression. "You could read all there is to know about mages, especially the famous ones that all mages ought to know about." She held Aaron's gaze for a moment longer before walking away, the plates floating after her.

Aaron turned to Sam.

"I'm on it," Sam said before Aaron could speak, turning to run to the stores.

"I'll go with him," Rose said. "You go to the Hub, and tell us all about it tonight," she said, running after Sam.

"Look for books that mention Aric," Aaron called after them.

Both turned to give him a thumbs-up before racing down the street. Aaron turned in the other direction and set off towards the Hub.

***

The Hub was crowded with mages. When Aaron walked in, he saw almost every row in the circular room occupied by seated mages. Around the white table were the fair-skinned Empaths, sitting in high-backed chairs. The group of twelve looked as calm and serene as always in their floor-length, pale blue gowns.

Aaron found Drake waving at him, and gesturing to the seat next to him. Aaron climbed up to the third row and sat down by his side. From the raised platform, Aaron could see the map in the hollow of the table. It was the image of the mage realm, with its spidery black lines and thick-outlined blobs that represented different zones.

Scott was already there, leaning over the table, hands gripped at the rounded edge. His head was lowered but Aaron could just about make out the quivering of his lips as he muttered prayers under his breath. When he lifted his head, Scott's eyes were still closed, but his lips were now pressed together, so tightly they were turning white. He lifted up both hands, and that's when Aaron saw the chains looped around his fingers. Four silver symbols dangled from the ends of the chains: a circle, an inverted V, a spiral and three wavy lines. Scott opened his eyes and held up the circle, his lips still moving in silent words. He fitted the three wavy lines into the circle with an audible click. Then came the inverted V, which went into the middle of the circle and on top of the wavy lines. The last symbol, the spiral, slotted perfectly between the legs of the V. Scott finished his prayers and brought the silver mark to his lips and kissed it. He slipped all four chains around his neck, so the makeshift pendant sat proudly on his chest.

Scott sat down, hands pressed together, fingers resting against his lips and eyes trained on the map. Long minutes passed but nothing happened. The crowd gathered in the Hub were talking in hushed voices, worry and concern lacing their tones. Aaron looked around, waiting and watching, but nothing seemed to be happening.

"What's going on?" Aaron asked.

"We're waiting," Drake replied.

Aaron rolled his eyes. "Yeah, I kinda got that," he said, "but for what?"

"For the Lycans to be tricked out of the human world and into the Q-Zone," Drake replied.

Aaron frowned. "That could take hours."

Drake smiled. "It could take days."

"But Scott said the Q-Zone can only be sustained for forty minutes."

"Yes," Drake replied. "Which is why the Q-Zone is set up, but not opened yet." Drake glanced at the table, at Scott's visibly strained concentration. "Scott will open it at the last possible moment, just before the Hunters lead the Lycans out of the human realm. It gives the Hunters as much of the forty minutes as possible to gather all the Lycans into the Q-Zone."

"How is Scott going to know when that's about to happen?" Aaron asked, feeling a flutter of nerves in his stomach.

"They'll tell him." Drake replied. "You see that pendant he's wearing?"

"Aric's mark, yeah." Aaron nodded.

Drake looked surprised. He turned to stare at Aaron. "Starting to pick things up?"

"Shouldn't I?" Aaron asked.

Drake paused for a moment before going on, ignoring Aaron's last question.

"The Hunters have similar necklaces, depending on their individual talents. Scott can communicate with all of them through that pendant," he said.

Aaron turned to stare at Scott. Now he understood the careful consideration Scott was showing the four symbols when he slotted them in place; it was his link to his Hunters.

The minutes rolled into hours. Mary arrived at the Hub with trays of sandwiches and pitchers of apple juice. Everyone had a little to eat except for Scott, whose sole concentration was on the map. When it reached three solid hours with no action, Aaron wanted to get up and leave. He thought about all the information Rose and Sam may have acquired by now. He wondered how many useful books they would have found in those stores. He was sure they were back at their cottage by now, reading through mage history. He felt a pang of annoyance at himself. He should have gone with them. He would have been doing something, instead of sitting here.

Just as he tensed his muscles to get up and leave, he heard Scott's gasp. Every eye turned to Scott, to see him drop his hands and grip onto the edge of the table. His eyes were wide, mouth open as he listened to something only he could hear. One hand closed over the silver necklace.

"How many?" he asked. "Okay." He stood up and ran his hand over the map, making the image shift and change. A white blob began materialising, just above the location Aaron recognised as Japan. "Go!" Scott said.

No sooner had he said the word than a strange shadow began clouding the sky. Aaron turned in his seat to look outside, past the glass walls. Thick grey clouds rolled in, stealing over the brightness of the day. Thunder boomed ominously and a streak of forked lightening lit the darkening clouds.

"Start praying," Scott said, speaking to the Hub this time. "The Q-Zone's open."

***

The atmosphere in the Hub was by no means relaxed before, but after Scott spoke, the tension was so thick it was stifling. Aaron drew closer to the edge of his chair, eyes narrowing at the map on the table, and in particular at the white cloud. Small green dots – tiny pinpricks – began appearing in it, spreading across the cloud.

Scott's hands roamed over the map, etching thin white wisps leading to the cloud. One hand closed over his pendant and he spoke to the Hunters.

"Portals are open," he said while one hand traced more spidery lines into the cloud.

"Portals?" Aaron frowned.

"Shortcuts," Drake said, his gaze on the map also. "They're like tunnels that lead from the human realm into the Q-Zone," he explained. "All the Hunters have to do is lead the Lycans to one of the portals and they'll be zapped straight into the Q-Zone."

"*All* they have to do?" Aaron asked. "You make it sound like it's the easiest job in the world."

Drake smiled. "Trust me," he said. "Tricking demons into portals *is* the easiest part of the job."

"Is that how we move from the human realm to this one?" Aaron asked. "By portals?"

"Not always," Drake replied. "Portals are set up and controlled by Scott. He doesn't leave any open unless there's a hunt. The other way to travel between the realms is through a tear."

"A tear?" Aaron asked, remembering the way they had arrived in his dad's car. The fall off the road, the intense heat, the bright flash before hitting the bricked road leading to the Gate.

"There are rips, little tears that allow access from one realm to the other," Drake explained.

"Can't humans see them?" Aaron asked.

Drake chuckled. "Humans don't know what to look for," he said. "Even mages have to work hard to see them." He turned to look at Aaron, a small smile on his lips. "When you were in the human realm, did you ever see a flash of lightning but hear no thunder following it?"

"Plenty of times," Aaron replied.

"That's someone passing through a tear," Drake said.

Aaron frowned at him. "Thunder is always there, it's just sometimes too far away to hear," he objected.

Drake chuckled. "Don't get caught up in human explanations. They'll come up with anything to explain that which they don't understand."

"So you're saying every time there's a thunderless flash of lightning, that's a mage passing through a tear?" Aaron asked.

Drake shrugged. "Sometimes mage, sometimes demon."

Within minutes, the cloud steadily changed from white to green, as Hunters and presumably Lycans entered the Q-Zone under Scott's instructions. Scott leant over the table, both hands closed around the pendant, eyes fixed on the cloud.

"Get them in," Scott instructed. "How many?" he asked incredulously. "No, no! There's more!" His expression relaxed and he closed his eyes. "Good, good." He looked to the small clock hung on the adjacent wall, where red luminous numbers had started a countdown. "You've got just under thirty-eight minutes," Scott told the Hunters. "Get them in, *all* of them."

Aaron watched with bated breath, even though there was nothing to see, only Scott standing over the table. A few minutes passed with Scott doing more of the same, instructing the Hunters. He glanced across to the clock.

"Thirty minutes," he said. "How many?" He closed his eyes and one of his hands made a fist. "Fantastic! I'm locking it down. End those sons of demons!"

One by one, Scott shut down the portals, so the white wisps disappeared, leaving behind the now pulsing green cloud. The murmur in the Hub picked up volume, with many smiling faces and nods of approval. Aaron saw others with their hands clasped, rocking back and forth, eyes closed in silent prayers.

"Alright, twenty-five minutes to go," Scott said. "Fred, Rachel, get your teams and move out."

Aaron saw a few of the green dots that were swimming around in the cloud disappear. Four minutes later, Scott issued his next order.

"Sarah and Joshua, move out."

Another few dots vanished.

Over the course of the next ten minutes, Scott instructed more and more teams to leave, turning the cloud back to its white form, with only a few green dots left squirming inside.

"Fifteen minutes," Scott called. "Where are we?" He nodded, lines on his brow relaxing. "Okay, good enough," he said. "Zhi-Jiya, Omar and Lilah – get your teams and move."

The surrounding mages began giggling in relief, shaking their heads at one another with whispers of, "I told you there was nothing to worry about," and "Good thoughts lead to good results." Aaron looked around to see that even Drake was smiling.

Scott instructed another team to leave. Now there were only twelve dots inside the cloud, Aaron could easily spot them.

"Good, good." Scott was smiling. "Just ease them out, just–" He gasped, eyes widened and his mouth twisted with horror. "Skyler!" he called. "Skyler?" His hands pressed into the necklace, palms crushed together in force. "No!" he gasped. "Skyler!"

Aaron's heart skipped a beat.

"Skyler's down," Scott said, making practically everyone in the Hub suck in a breath.

It felt like the temperature in the room had plummeted, making everyone shiver.

"Get over to him. Get him out!" Drake instructed the other Hunters.

Aaron's gaze was pulled to the Empaths who had closed their eyes, their breathing calm and even. The twelve women held on to each other, forming a circle. Armana breathed in, held her breath, and then her features twisted with pain and she cried out. Her eyes squeezed tighter, her delicate fingers clutched around the hands of another Empaths. Beads of sweat gathered on Armana's brow, making her pale skin glisten. Slowly, panting softly, Armana relaxed, her shoulders dropping back down. The lines on her face disappeared and she let out a shaky breath. Her pale blue eyes fluttered open and she smiled.

Scott paused for a moment, tensed and worried. Then relief flooded him and he threw back his head, both hands covering his face. He straightened up and clutched the pendant again.

"Skyler," he breathed. "Get yourself out of there. Go, take your team and leave." He glanced at the clock. "Ten minutes. I want all of you out in five, got it?"

The minutes trickled down and when the clock glowed with a singular number five, Scott instructed the remaining four dots to get out.

"Go in pairs and get out," Scott said, smiling in relief as two dots disappeared.

It came to the last two minutes and there were still two dots remaining.

"Alright, you two," Scott said. "Leave now and stand guard."

One dot disappeared, just as the clock flashed the end of a minute, and the seconds started their steady decline.

Scott frowned. "I told *both* of you to leave," he said, holding onto the necklace. His eyes narrowed. "Kyran, get out."

Aaron felt like the bottom of his stomach had dropped. He looked at the clock. Forty seconds left. The map still showed a singular green dot.

"Kyran!" Scott yelled. "What's going on?" His eyes widened and he cursed. "Find a way past them. Get out now!"

Thiry-five seconds...Thirty-four...Thirty-three...

"Damn it, Kyran!" Scott's face was now pink, one hand gripped around the pendant while the other balled into a fist. "Dodge them and get out!" He glanced to the clock. "Thirty seconds!"

Aaron could feel panic ballooning inside him, clawing its way up his throat, making him feel short of breath.

"He's cornered," he whispered in realisation.

"Don't worry," Drake said in a bored voice. "He'll get out."

"How do you know?" Aaron asked, angry at Drake for being so calm.

"It's Kyran," Drake said. "He always finds a way out."

"Twenty-five seconds!" Scott yelled.

It seemed that only Drake was indifferent to Kyran's fate – or perhaps Drake was the only one with faith in Kyran's death-defying tricks, because everyone else in the Hub was panicking, just like Scott. Murmurs were breaking out, mages shifted in their seats, clasping hands together to mutter prayers.

"Weave your way to the door!" Scott was saying. "Don't stop, just keep going!"

Aaron was close to hyperventilating. He looked at the clock to see fifteen seconds left.

He's not going to make it. The thought echoed in his head, making Aaron's insides go cold.

"Ten seconds!" Scott was shaking now. "Kyran, get out or I swear, I'll...!" He stopped as the sole green dot disappeared from the cloud.

A tremendous cheer erupted all around the Hub and Scott collapsed in his chair, head in hands, shoulders shaking. At first, Aaron thought Scott was crying, but when the man pulled his hands away, Aaron saw he was laughing a deep, rumbling, relieved laugh.

The clock reached zero and flashed for just over a minute. The white cloud that had been the focus of the day went out in a puff, evaporating until nothing was left.

***

Aaron waited, along with the rest of the mages, at the same place he had been in the morning when the Hunters had left. The sun was shining again. Gone were the ominous black clouds, and the thunder and lightning. As soon as the Q-Zone ceased to exist, so did the bad weather.

The Gate slid open with a flash and a stream of bikes entered. The mages had made two lines, creating a pathway for the Hunters to ride down. Everyone cheered and welcomed their Hunters back with glee and relief.

The Hunters smiled at their warm welcome, but Aaron could see the tiredness in them even from a distance. Their faces were pale, shoulders drooped, backs curved – even more so than normal when riding a bike. They didn't drive down the garage path to park their bikes; they drove to the row of cottages and parked next to the fence. Aaron watched the Gate, waiting for Kyran, but he saw Skyler first. The sight of him made Aaron recoil, drawing in a sharp breath. Three long scratches disfigured his face, starting from his left ear going across his nose and lips, down to the bottom of his right cheek. A gash across his shoulder had stained his coat red.

Behind Skyler was Ella, looking tired and weary. Aaron spotted Kyran with the last group of bikers. A first look confirmed he was unhurt, but his expression held the same tiredness and fatigue as his fellow Hunters.

All the Hunters parked their bikes carelessly in the street. The majority of them dragged themselves off their bikes and into their cottages, struggling to keep upright. The mages of Salvador offered a helping hand, but most shrugged them away, choosing to go by themselves. There were some Hunters, like Zulf, that seemed less worn out. These few dismounted their bikes and walked over to speak with Scott.

Aaron followed behind Kyran, keeping a few steps back. He watched as Kyran staggered his way upstairs, his footsteps dragging loudly on the stairs. Kyran opened his door, so tired he could barely keep his head up. He swayed on his feet before he made his way over to the bed and fell face first onto it, without even taking off his coat. Aaron closed the door for him before going into the next room, finding Sam and Rose seated on their respective beds, surrounded by books.

"Hey," Sam greeted him. "Good show?"

Aaron shook his head. "Scary show, more like it," he said. He glanced at the dozen books scattered across both beds. "Wow, you were busy," he remarked. "Find anything good?"

The twins shared a look.

"You can say that." Sam teased.

"Oh my God, Aaron." Rose grinned. "Wait till you hear this."

14

A Lesson in History

"Here, sit." Rose patted the spot next to her.

Aaron sank into it, feeling nervous all of a sudden, eyeing the thick book in her lap. It was leather bound, brown with silver writing across the front and spine: *Mages Who Made History – Cornelius Backbroth*.

"So me and Sam looked through a few of these," Rose said. "Skimmed them, actually. You know what I'm like with history books."

"Give her thrillers and she's all eyes, but history?" Sam wrinkled his nose and stuck out a tongue. "Uck, no, she'll be sick!"

Rose whacked him with the book, making Sam and Aaron both yelp.

"Ow! That hurt," Sam whined.

"Careful!" Aaron cried. "That book looks ancient. It'll fall apart."

"It's supposed to hurt and no it won't," Rose answered both boys. "Now, as I was saying..." She rested the book in her lap and turned to Aaron. "We were looking for books about Aric. It was so annoying – there's absolutely *no* order or catalogue in those shops. Books are just dumped at random. It took us hours to find anything useful." She paused to glance at the book in her hands. "But after reading this, I can see why Ella got mad at you for not knowing who Aric was."

"Why?" Aaron asked. "Who is he?"

Rose leant in closer, wearing a smile. "The first mage to walk the Earth."

Aaron gaped at her. "You're kidding."

"Nope." Rose held up the book. "This has references to all mages who have done extraordinary things to help not only this realm, but the human one too." She opened the book, drawing the pages apart to almost midway, and began to read.

"*But these brave and courageous mages pale against the one who came first,*" she read. "*The Legend of Aric goes back centuries, though some argue it may have been the beginning of time itself. Of course, there is no way to know for certain.*" Rose cleared her throat. "*Tales of Aric have always been popular. Parents tell their young the heroics of Aric as a bedtime story to give inspiration and comfort, to tell the coming generations who we are and why we came into existence."*

Rose glanced up at Aaron, who tried to keep his expression clear. Perhaps he was the only mage who hadn't grown up with stories of Aric. He nodded stiffly at Rose to go on.

"It is said that when the realms were first created, it was deemed impossible to pass between them," Rose read. *"No one knows how the demons came to this realm. Some say the mouth of Hell itself opened and spewed these creatures out. Some insist the demons were always a part of this world. However they came to be, the demons ravaged this realm. They killed the life forms that resided here until none were left – no one to torture but each other. These vicious beasts turned into monsters, left tormented and twisted by their attacks on one another. They became hungrier with time, thirsting after the flesh of the innocent. They clawed and thrashed at the barrier that separated the realms. Their brutal attack didn't stop, continuing for decades, until finally the barrier gave way and tore."* Rose looked up at Aaron to see his horror. *"The demons, driven mad by hunger, ripped their way into the realm of the human race."*

Aaron had already worked out which realms were in question, but the revelation still made goosebumps erupt along his flesh.

"The demons feasted on the defenceless humans. They caused such havoc in the world of mankind that the Heavens could take no more. They sent a being, one with untold powers, to Earth. His name was Aric."

Sam let out a whistle. "Neat, huh?" he said. "Imagine having that title: Aric, saviour of all the realms."

"Aric was created for the sole purpose of protecting mankind." Rose continued. *"Heaven bestowed powers upon him, so Aric could control the four elements of all the realms: Fire, Earth, Water and Air."*

"We already figured that out," Sam said, sounding rather pleased with himself.

"We?" Aaron inquired with a raised eyebrow.

Sam rolled his eyes. "Fine, fine. You figured it out. Well done."

Aaron nodded at him.

Rose cleared her throat to get the boys' attention. *"Aric vowed to purge the demons from the human realm. He fought like no other could and killed like no other would. 'Ruthless' and 'fearless' are two words often associated with the great Aric. His battles have become legendary, often held as an exemplary model to Hunters."*

"Everyone wants to be like Aric the hero," Sam said. "Understandable."

"But Aric, as fierce as he was, soon came to realise that he was but one mage against an army of hundreds of thousands," Rose continued. *"No matter how much he*

fought, or how many demons he killed, it was not enough to save the humans. So Aric raised his hands to the Heavens and asked for his own army – a band of brothers that would fight alongside him, shoulder to shoulder. Aric's prayers were answered and he was blessed with a brotherhood, so loyal and strong it terrified the demons. Years passed, and Aric led his hidden army across the human realm, eradicating the demons whilst keeping the human race oblivious. Over time, the demons grew weaker, their numbers diminishing at the hands of Aric and his army. The demons were forced into hiding, fleeing from the human realm. Aric claimed victory."

"Whoa," Aaron breathed. "Wonder how long that took?"

"It doesn't say," Rose replied, lowering the book and closing it. "Maybe in one of the other books it might give exact timelines." She shook her head. "But wait till you hear the interesting part." She lifted up another book, a thin, grey one with a faded title. "According to this, when it was deemed safe again for the human race, the Heavens called the mages back," Rose said. "Their purpose was complete. Aric and his brotherhood had brought the demon race to their knees. All the mages were willing to return – all but Aric. He didn't want to go back because he had fallen in love." She smiled. "With a human."

"What?" Aaron gasped. "He fell for a human?"

"Yep," Sam said. "Couldn't believe it myself." He nodded at Rose. "Keep listening, it gets better."

"I've read three accounts of the same story," Rose said. "All of them state that the Heavens granted Aric his request as a reward for all he had done. But they warned him that although he could live on Earth, he wasn't permitted to stay in the human realm. Aric could visit the girl he was in love with but he couldn't be with her."

"What's the point in that?" Aaron asked.

"See from afar, but never get close," Sam mused. "Sounds like my relationship with Ella."

Rose rolled her eyes at Sam, while Aaron ignored him, too engrossed in the tale of Aric.

"What did Aric do?" Aaron asked.

"He agreed." Rose replied. "He stood back and watched as his family of mages ascended to Heaven, while he was left behind." The corners of her mouth dropped. "Alone in the mage realm."

"That's...kinda sad," Aaron said. "Imagine being the only one left of your kind."

"Extinction doesn't sound fun at all," Sam commented.

"According to legend, Aric obeyed the rules," Rose said, holding up the thin, grey book. "He often visited the girl, known only as Angela, but he didn't stay in her realm. It turns out the human realm can't tolerate mages and their power." She flipped open the book to the relevant page and held it out for Aaron to see. "Aric had protected and saved the human realm from demons. He couldn't allow its destruction by his own power."

"But that's not really true." Aaron frowned. "I've lived all my life there and nothing happened. I mean, not until..." He trailed off.

Sam and Rose shifted, clearly uncomfortable at the mention of the power Aaron had displayed and that resulted in them losing everything they had.

Rose cleared her throat. "Maybe it was different for Aric," she said. "You never did anything for fourteen years, but Aric had already been using his powers for years, fighting the demons. Maybe his presence was too strong," she suggested. "Anyway, Angela started a relationship with Aric, ignorant of his origins," Rose continued, "but when Aric's visits became less frequent, Angela grew worried and distressed. When they met again, after months, Angela demanded to know where Aric had gone. Why did he stay away from her for months at a time?"

"In other words, 'Who you messing with behind my back?'" Sam grinned.

"Basically." Rose nodded. "Aric proclaimed his fidelity, assuring her that she was his one true love. But when Angela refused to back down and demanded the truth from him, Aric took a leap of faith and revealed his identity."

Aaron grimaced. "That couldn't have gone well."

Sam chuckled. "Hey, honey, I'm not cheating on you, but I do have superpowers that will destroy your world. She must have loved that."

"Loved it enough to run screaming to the hills," Aaron commented, shaking his head. "She probably figured he was a mental case." He looked back at Rose. "So that's the nail in the coffin of Aric and Angela's relationship then?"

"Actually, she believed him," Rose said with a smile. "There are accounts that state she said that she'd always known deep down that Aric was different to other men. She told Aric that if he couldn't live with her in her world, then she would go with him and live in his." She grinned. "They moved to this realm and got married."

"They got what?" Aaron exclaimed.

"Married," Sam repeated. "The whole 'I take you to be my lawfully wedded husband that is a superhero and a kick-ass demon Hunter, blah-blah-blah.'" He waved a hand. "You know, married?"

"I don't understand," Aaron said. "Married? Aric married a human?"

"Yes," Rose replied, "and they lived the rest of their life in this realm with one another. They had six children, giving birth to the lineage of mages."

Aaron snapped his head up to look at Rose.

She nodded, her smile widening. "The mages," she started, "have Aric as their forefather and Angela – a *human* – as their foremother."

"We're part human," Aaron breathed. The revelation felt like a huge weight had been lifted from him.

"Exactly!" Sam sat up. "All of the mages are part human."

Aaron remembered what his dad had said, the night he told him he was a mage. *Different, not human, but we have humanity, Aaron. We're the same in most ways.*

"Humanity," Aaron murmured. "That's what my dad meant," he said, a little louder. "We have humanity because we're part human."

"It makes you think, doesn't it?" Sam said. "All their bellyaching about humans being weak and useless, and they're part human themselves."

"From their attitude, it doesn't look like the mages embrace their human side," Rose said.

Aaron couldn't imagine Skyler or Ella or even Drake admitting they were part human.

"There's something you should see," Rose said. She picked up another book, one that was already open and lying face down next to her. She turned it over and pushed it closer to Aaron. It was a flow chart, taking over both pages. "Aric and Angela had six children." Rose pointed to the top of the page.

Aaron leant closer, staring at the names inked on the paper. It was a family tree, starting with Aric. A cross linked him to Angela. A horizontal line connected to both names split into six descending lines. Aaron read the names under each one.

'*Aedus, Afton, Avira, Adams–*'

Aaron stopped on his own surname, eyes widening in shock. He looked up at Rose, who was staring at him.

"Since Aric married a human, his children were unable to take on all of his powers," Rose continued. "The eldest four got one power of the elements each. The youngest two," she pointed to the last two names on the chart, Aargon and Athona, "while still being mages and having some power over the elements, didn't get complete power over any."

"Complete power?" Aaron asked, his head spinning at the information. "What does that mean?"

"I'm not sure," Rose replied. "I've not read that far yet." She moved closer, sitting shoulder to shoulder with Aaron while studying the pages. "But I think it means that the eldest four got ultimate control over one elemental power each, but the last two got a weaker version of their siblings' powers."

"You know what I think?" Sam said. "I think the youngest two got cheated. They're still mages, but they don't have power of the likes of their father or older siblings. All because their father hooked up with a human."

Aaron stared at his surname, sitting with the others. *Aedus, Afton, Avira.* A memory flashed in his mind. Skyler, standing tall and proud. *Skyler Avira.* His voice echoed in Aaron's head.

"The Elementals," he said in realisation. "That's why we're called that." He held up the book, staring at the names. "The eldest four – Aedus, Afton, Avira and Adams – they got complete power over one element each," Aaron said. "Skyler's last name is Avira and he's referred to as an Elemental. My name's Adams and I'm referred to as an Elemental. I bet you Ella's surname is either Aedus or Afton." Aaron was talking fast, voicing his thoughts out loud as they came tumbling out in a mess. "That's why Skyler and Ella couldn't be defeated in the ring. That's why they seemed more skilled than the rest – 'cause they *are* more skilled than the rest."

"So you reckon the rest of the mages—" Sam started.

"Must have come from Aargon and Athona," Aaron finished. "They were just mages, whereas the other four got *complete power* over one of each element, so their future generations are referred to as the Elementals."

"Whoa," Sam said, "Aargon and Athona must have been busy. Have you seen how many mages there are compared to Elementals?"

"One power of the elements each," Rose repeated, staring at the names in the book. "Adams?" She looked up at Aaron. "So your family has the power of..." She paused, but Aaron could tell from her expression alone that she was remembering their last day in their world. The way the ground had split open to stop that car.

Skyler's angry taunt came back to Aaron. *Go on, show me, Adams. Let out some power. Snatch the ground out from under my feet!*

"Earth," Aaron said quietly. "My elemental power is Earth."

***

It was time for dinner. True to her intentions, Mother Mary went all out preparing countless dishes, similar to the feast they had the night before. Rose had left to go to help, leaving only Sam and Aaron with the books. Aaron tried to read, but his mind was on one thing: Aric. The first mage. Sent to the world to protect humankind from demons. The mage who chose to forsake Heaven in the name of love. Love with a human girl. It was like a strange fairy tale, but with mages, humans and demons instead of princes, princesses and evil witches.

Sitting on his bed, book open in his lap, Aaron read one sentence over and over again.

Aric was created for the sole purpose of protecting mankind.

There it was, written down, forever immortalising it. Mages were created to protect humans. Yet the attitude of some, like Skyler, was as if humans were not worth their time. Aaron wondered how mages got like that From Aric to Skyler. Did the passage of time really change the mindset of mages so much?

"Hey, listen to this." Sam sat up, holding a leather-bound book in his hands. "*The effect elemental power has on the human realm was not discovered until almost five years after Aric's army had come to Earth,*" he read. "*It's a well-known story that, one day, Aric happened to come across the effects of elemental power on the mortal realm when he was passing from the human realm to his own. He experienced the start of an earthquake as he was passing through one of the tears. When he came to this realm, he found two of his brothers growing apple trees from the ground.*" He paused to look over at Aaron. "*Aric realised the tears in the barrier, left by the ferocious prolonged attacks by the demons, were allowing the flow of elemental energy to seep through and disrupt the human realm.*" Sam paused, licking his lips nervously before reading on. "*Aric tried to mend it for days on end, but the damage done to the fabric of the barrier was irreparable. Nothing could fix the tears, so Aric blocked them. He set up what are now known as the famous Gates of Resistance.*"

Aaron's eyes went wide. "The Gates," he said. "The ones Scott was talking about, like the one we saw when we first arrived." The image of the towering white door with strange glowing symbols and numbers came to his mind. "That Gate was set up by Aric?"

Sam nodded. "All the Gates were set up by him."

Aaron let out a long breath, brow furrowed as he worked the information out. "Scott said they set up the Gates once they take over a zone." He recalled the map, with its red- and blue-coloured zones. "So Aric initially set up all the Gates, protecting the human world from the destructive power of mages."

"Plugging the holes, so to speak," Sam said.

"Right, but somewhere down the line of history the Gates were destroyed," Aaron deduced. "The mages are now trying to do what their ancestor once did: hunt down demons and set up Gates to protect the human world."

"Talk about history repeating itself," Sam said.

"Strange history, huh?" said Aaron.

They fell into silence, until chatter from outside filtered in through the window.

"Sounds like the table's being set," Sam said.

Aaron could make out the sound of plates clattering and the tinkle of cutlery hitting the wooden table. His stomach grumbled in response. They got up and made their way out, but Aaron paused next to Kyran's door. Sam waited at the top of the stairs, frowning at him as Aaron gently knocked on the door. There was no reply.

"What are you doing?" Sam asked, as Aaron reached for the doorknob.

Aaron didn't answer but opened the door. The room was lit with the orangey glow of the setting sun shining in from the window. The corners of the room were already shadowed. Kyran was still sleeping, lying on his stomach, clad in his long coat and boots. His soft breaths sounded slightly muffled against the duvet. Aaron stepped inside.

"Kyran?" he called, quietly at first.

There was no response.

"Kyran?" Aaron tried a little louder. "Erm, it's...it's time for dinner."

Kyran grunted and shifted a little, but didn't get up.

Aaron waited for a moment before stepping closer and calling to him again.

"Aren't you hungry?" he asked. Breakfast was the last time he had seen Kyran eat anything. "Kyran? You don't want dinner?"

Kyran lifted his head, rubbed at his eyes and turned over. His eyes were still shut but he grunted out, "Aaron?"

"Yeah?" Aaron replied.

"Disturb my sleep, I'll disturb your breathing. Got it?"

Aaron smiled, finding the murmured threat funny rather than alarming. He chuckled and turned to go. "Okay. Night, Kyran."

There was no reply.

***

It seemed Kyran wasn't the only one skipping dinner. All of Salvador's Hunters were missing from the table, which was a shame really as Mary had prepared a feast fit for a king. There were so many dishes lined along the table, Aaron didn't know where to start.

"Which ones did you make?" Sam asked his sister as she sat down.

"None of them," Rose replied a little tightly. "I've not really got the cooking bit down yet. I helped peel the potatoes and carrots."

"Oh." Sam paused. "You know you don't have to work in the kitchen if you don't want to."

Rose didn't say anything and quietly started on her dinner.

Aaron couldn't help but watch Zulf as he tore his way through almost an entire lamb's leg. Zulf, although busy eating, eventually noticed Aaron's unwavering gaze.

"Somefin' w'ong?" he asked through a mouthful.

Aaron shook his head. "Sorry, didn't mean to stare."

Zulf waved a hand at him before swallowing. His eyes twinkled with amusement. "Don't worry about it." He smiled. "You impressed with my eating habits?"

Aaron grinned. "I've never seen anyone eat so fast or...so much."

Zulf laughed. "I have only two rules that I live by," he said, holding up two meat-stained fingers. "Eat till you're fed and fight till they're dead."

Aaron laughed. "Nice rules."

"Thank you." Zulf inclined his head. He took another mouthful of rice and lamb, glancing at Aaron. He leant over the table towards him. "Hey, about last night," he started. "I'm real sorry, man. I didn't mean to give Skyler an excuse."

"It's okay," Aaron said. "You were only curious." Aaron looked over to the cottages. "It's so quiet when Skyler's not at the table."

Zulf and a few of the others chuckled.

"Ah, that's the Skyler effect," a Hunter commented. "You notice when he's not here."

"Seems like a lot of people aren't here today," Aaron said.

"They're asleep," Scott informed him.

"That must have been some battle in the Q-Zone," Aaron remarked, playing with the potatoes in his plate, "to make the Hunters skip out on dinner to sleep instead."

"It's not that," Zulf said. "The Hunters are wiped 'cause they're not of age yet." At Aaron's confused look, he elaborated. "You have to use a substantial amount of power in a Q-Zone, so it tires you out – drains you. It gets easier once you come into your full powers."

"Full powers?" Aaron asked. "When does that happen?"

"When you're nineteen." Zulf grinned. "Like I am."

"So the Hunters of Salvador, they're all under nineteen?" Aaron asked.

"Pretty much," Zulf said. "Kyran, Skyler, Julian, Omar and Ryan just turned eighteen a few months ago. Ella, Zhi-Jiya, Sarah, Jean and Danielle are all seventeen. The rest are sixteen."

"Sixteen?" Sam exclaimed. "They're only sixteen?" he asked, flabbergasted that mages the same age as him were out fighting demons.

"A mage comes into their power at the age of thirteen," Zulf explained. "Their core continues to grow and develop until they turn nineteen. That's when they come of age, meaning that their core matures. Then they can use their powers with much more ease. They don't get fatigued by excessive use and a fully developed core means precise and accurate control." He scooped up another spoonful before adding, "Oh, and they heal faster too."

"If that's the case, then why don't they wait until they're nineteen to start hunting?" Aaron asked.

Zulf's smile faded. A strange silence fell across the table, with most of the occupants staring at their plates.

"Because," Zulf said, "we don't have the time." He smiled wryly. "Waiting to grow up is a luxury we can't afford."

15

Flesh Memories

The days were getting warmer. The sun was blazing overhead; the heat so intense it reduced many to stripping out of their tops and swapping their jeans for shorts. Aaron and Sam struggled in the warmth, carrying their baskets of fruit to the Stove. As they got closer, they saw the table being set with a wide assortment of food, despite breakfast being served only two hours before. Ever since the Hunters returned from their Q-Zone hunt three days ago, Mary had ensured the table was always laid for them. It was just as well, seeing how the majority of Hunters seemed to have divided their time between their beds and the table.

Having delivered the fruit to the Stove, Sam and Aaron made their way back to the orchard, empty baskets in hand. By the time they got to the lake, they were covered in sticky sweat, their faces reddened by the scorching heat. Both boys stopped for a rest and sat down at the bank of the lake. They peeled off their thin, sleeveless tops and lay back on the grass. Aaron propped himself up on his elbows, legs stretched out before him. The grass felt pleasantly cool against his bare back. His gaze followed a group of mages in the distance, walking down to the lake and carrying fishing nets.

"You know what I was thinking?" Sam asked.

"How do they fish with no rods?" Aaron said.

"What?" Sam's brow knitted in confusion. His eyes followed Aaron's. "No, not them," he said, shaking his head at the mages. "I was thinking about the day we met Alan for the first time."

Aaron turned to him, eyes squinting in the harsh sunlight. "Yeah?"

"Alan said something about Skyler and Ella having Salvador's allegiance, but he mentioned them giving you back your share. What do you reckon he was on about?" Sam asked.

"No idea," Aaron replied. "I had forgotten about that, actually."

"Here's the thing," Sam said, turning so he was facing Aaron. "What if Alan meant it in a literal sense. As in, you own a part of Salvador or the mages' loyalty? Maybe with the Elementals being more powerful that an average mage—" He paused and then grinned. "Can you believe I just said that? An average mage?" He chuckled. "They can make fireballs from thin air, fight demons and ride motorbikes through portals or whatever, but yeah, they're just *average*."

"Makes me more than worried what Elementals can do," Aaron confessed.

Sam nodded in agreement before squeezing his eyes shut and shaking his head. "Going off topic. What was I saying? Oh yeah." He looked back at Aaron. "What if the Elementals being more powerful than the rest of the mages means that the Elementals rule the mage realm?"

Aaron was taken aback by the suggestion. "You reckon?"

"Yeah, think about it," said Sam. "Skyler practically walks around like he owns the place. Ella does the same, although," he grinned, his eyes softening, "she looks damn hot strutting around." His eyes glazed and he smiled dreamily.

Aaron rolled his eyes. "Focus, Sammy."

"Sorry," Sam said. "So that's two Elementals. You're the third and the fourth must be that Neriah bloke everyone's always talking about."

Aaron felt an uncomfortable churn in his stomach at the mention of Neriah. "He's the one my mum and dad have gone to meet. Zulf said they had to answer to Neriah, explain to him why they went missing." His fingers brushed against his trouser pocket, feeling the edges of the folded letter resting inside. "It's been three weeks since they left," Aaron said. "Shouldn't they be back by now?"

Sam didn't say anything, but his darkened expression and clenched jaw told Aaron his parents were the last thing Sam wanted to talk about. Aaron couldn't really blame him. He knew Sam and Rose held his parents accountable for everything that had happened to them. It was his parents' decision to keep the truth from him, about his identity and his capabilities, that had led to all of them ending up here.

Something caught Sam's attention just as it entered Aaron's peripheral vision. Eyes widening, Sam opened his mouth to cry out. He made a sudden move to jump to his feet, but didn't make it in time. Aaron had just turned his head when he saw it: the huge wall of water collapsing on them.

For a blinding moment, Aaron was suffocating. His involuntary gasp when the cold water hit him made him swallow. The force of the water slammed him and Sam into the ground and pulled them forward, sliding them to the very edge of the bank. Somehow, both of them managed to not go over. The water spilt back, taking the boys' baskets and shirts with it, running down the bank, filling the lake once again.

Drenched in cold water, coughing and spluttering, both Aaron and Sam pulled themselves up. The soft, muddy ground squished under their shoes. They stared in incredulous shock as the mages pulled the nets back filled with squirming fish. Aaron saw the ginger-haired kitchen helper, Henry, roll one of his sleeves back up in place before holding out both hands, waiting. Another net was set up and Henry pulled up his shoulders, and leant back on one foot before slamming it down, pushing his hands out. His power hit the lake and the water lifted back and up into a towering wave. The net swept through the pool, collecting the small, ivory fish that had been exposed. The net floated back to its two owners and the wave of water crashed backwards, spilling out.

Sam cursed as they were hit once again.

***

Their shoes made odd squelching sounds as both boys walked back to their cottage. Every step pressed more moisture out of their soaked shoes, leaving water marks of their soles on the cobbled ground. Droplets fell from their hair, some trailing down their bare backs. It was a testament to how hot the day was that both boys were almost dry by the time they reached the cottage fence.

"My, my," Ella chuckled, stepping out of her house, running a hand through her messy hair. "Trying to drown yourselves already?"

Sam pulled a face. "You lot can't even fish properly," he grouched. "Fishing is supposed to be a calm and relaxing activity, not a game of 'Dodge the Tsunami'!"

Ella laughed, her eyes sparkling with amusement. Her small top bared her midriff, exposing her tattoo. Her shorts showed Aaron that he was right: the tattoo did indeed continue down her leg, stopping just above her knee. Seeing it this close, Aaron realised the tattoo was an intricate design of a vine with fully blossomed water lilies growing down it.

"Aww, poor little Sammy," Ella teased and walked past them.

Sam glared at her as she walked away, then turned to face Aaron with a broad, gleeful grin – one Aaron hadn't seen in a while. "She called me Sammy."

"You hate being called Sammy," Aaron pointed out. It was partly why him and Rose called Sam that, just to rile him.

"Not by her," Sam said, turning back to gaze at Ella.

Aaron looked over at her too, watching as she filled a plate with grapes, melon and a selection of berries. His eyes widened as an idea formed in his mind.

"Come on, Sam," he said and hurried towards the table.

"What are you doing?" Sam demanded, but Aaron just waved a hand at him, gesturing for him to follow.

"Ella?" Aaron came to her side.

"What?" Ella asked, working her way down the table and filling her plate.

Aaron followed behind her. "I wanted to ask you something."

Ella snorted. "Really? What a surprise," she quipped. "What is it, Sir Asks-a-lot?"

"It's a little personal," Aaron said. "But I was wondering, what's your surname?"

Ella stopped, her serving of cherries halted mid-air. She turned to look at Aaron. "Why?" she asked with a raised eyebrow.

"Just curious," Aaron replied.

Ella silently studied him before facing the table again and depositing the cherries onto her plate. "Afton," she replied. "Ella Afton."

Aaron turned to Sam with a grin. He had been right.

"Why so curious about my name, Adams?" Ella asked.

"No reason," Aaron replied.

"You trying to figure out the Elemental generations?" she asked, turning around with a grin. "Don't look so shocked," she chastised. "You're rubbish at being sly."

"I...I wasn't..." Aaron started.

"It's alright," Ella said. "I know you're curious about this realm." She snorted at her own words. "Hell, more than curious." She picked up a grape and popped it into her mouth. Chewing slowly, she looked Aaron up and down. "How'd you find out about the Elementals?"

"Scott called me an Elemental," Aaron replied. "And there are a few books lying around about certain families."

Ella smiled. "Ah, the book store. Good for you." She picked up another two grapes and chewed them slowly, warm grey eyes fixed on Aaron. "Reading's good for you. Make sure you do plenty of it."

"I will," Aaron replied. "But there are some things you can't find in books."

"Then you're reading the wrong ones," Ella replied with a smirk. She shrugged and went back to her plate, picking up strawberries this time. "To answer you fully: yeah, I'm an Afton. I have the power of Water."

"Does that mean you can only control the element of Water?" Aaron asked. "You can't use any of the other elements?"

"Oh, I can use them, just not as well as Water." Ella smirked. "I can use Earth, Air and Fire but only the basics; but with Water, I can do anything. I can control every facet of it: its form, its temperature, its viscosity, you name it."

"Complete power," Aaron murmured. "Pretty self-explanatory," he said under his breath. "What about other mages?" he asked. "The ones who aren't Elementals? Can they use all four powers but not in depth? Just the basics?"

"Hey." Ella smiled. "You're starting to get it. Normal mages can use all four powers but only to an extent. They don't have the ability to take complete control. Elementals, however, can use all four powers but possess the ability to control and use one Elemental power to its full potential." Her gaze picked up someone beyond Aaron and it made her smile. "I'm an Afton, so my power is Water," she said. "You're an Adams so your power is Earth." She smirked. "And Skyler is an Avira, the only one, actually. You can guess his power."

"Air," Aaron answered, remembering the way Skyler had thrown him across the street, bruising his back so badly he could barely walk. "He has the power of Air."

"Good job, Captain Obvious." Skyler's gruff voice came from behind Aaron. "Now, move, before I make you fly again."

Aaron turned to face Skyler. He had seen for himself how horribly disfigured the Lycan fight had left Skyler – three deep gashes, going diagonally from Skyler's left ear across his nose and lips, down to the bottom of his right cheek. So when Aaron saw him now, he was more than surprised to find no gashes or even half-healed cuts. There wasn't a single mark, not even a faint one, anywhere on Skyler's face. He looked the same as always: perfectly unblemished skin, shocking blue eyes and platinum blond hair. Aaron was gaping at him. There was no way Skyler could have been healed this soon, and there was no way those kinds of wounds could disappear without leaving scars.

Skyler cocked his head to the side, eyes narrowed.

"What's with the intense staring?" he asked.

"You...You're healed?" Aaron said.

"Yeah?" Skyler prompted. "And?"

"I saw you...Your face," Aaron said. "It was all...cut up. How did you heal so fast?"

"It's been three days, genius," Skyler said, pushing past him to go to the table. "How long did you think it was going to take?"

"But...your wounds looked really bad," Aaron said. "I thought you would be scarred for life."

Skyler shared a look with Ella before shaking his head in annoyance. "I'm too tired for this crap." He took Ella's plate from her and walked away, back to his cottage.

"You're welcome!" Ella called after him. "Jerk."

"Did Armana heal him?" Aaron asked, turning back to Ella.

"Yeah," Ella replied distractedly, still glaring at Skyler's retreating form. She picked up another plate and started filling it.

"Wow," Aaron said. "She's really good. Really, *really* good."

"Alright, Aaron," Sam said, giving him a look. "Calm down."

"No, Sam, you didn't seen him," Aaron said. "His face was all torn up. He had these cuts right across his face." Aaron let out a breath in amazement. "But now there's nothing left behind, not even a faint scar."

"Oh for Heaven's sake!" Ella turned around. "Mages don't scar, idiot!"

Aaron stared at her. "What?"

"Mages," Ella said. "We don't scar."

"That's ridiculous," Aaron said.

"With everything you've seen so far you find *this* ridiculous?" Sam asked.

"We get hurt, like everything else in this universe," Ella said. "But when we heal, it leaves behind nothing. No marks, no scars, nothing."

Aaron couldn't wrap his mind around that. It seemed too preposterous. They might be mages, but they were still half human, and humans scarred.

"It sounds too strange to be true," he said.

"Again, *this* you're having trouble with?" Sam asked.

"Have you ever been hurt?" Ella asked Aaron. "Ever fallen off your bike? Scraped your knees, cut open your flesh? Anything?"

"Yeah," Aaron replied, "of course I have." When Matthews pushed him in the school grounds one time, he cut open his palms and knees pretty bad.

"Did it leave behind a scar?" Ella asked.

Aaron shifted from one foot to the other. "Dunno," he mumbled.

"You don't know if you have any scars, Adams?"

"I don't spend a lot of time examining my knees," Aaron replied.

Ella smirked. "Have a look now," she said. "Take a good look at yourself. Find me one, just one tiny little scar, a blemish whatsoever anywhere on your body."

Her eyes trailed his bare chest, prompting Aaron to look down at himself. His skin was smooth, not a mark of any kind in sight, and flawless – just like it always had been.

"Mages don't scar," Ella repeated slowly, but her voice had gone quieter. She looked down at her tattoo, her fingers gently traced the lily above her navel. When she looked up at Aaron, her eyes were glistening. "We choose what scars to wear."

***

After dinner that evening, Aaron and the twins stayed at the table, talking with Ava and Alan, gleaning as much information as they could about Elementals and the war between mages and demons.

Aaron saw a few of the kitchen staff carrying baskets of vegetables into the Stove while Mary stood at the door, hurrying them in.

"What's Mary doing?" he asked. "We've already had dinner."

"She's getting the soup on," Alan said.

"Soup?" Aaron asked. "At this hour?"

"It's for tomorrow," Alan replied.

Aaron thought it was strange to start preparing for soup the night before, but he didn't give it much more thought. He went back to his discussion about underage Hunters and their recovery period after a Q-Zone kill.

"It's never more than three days," Alan explained. "Usually they can recover quicker than that, but this time they were up against Lycans." He gave a little shudder. "Those things are the nastiest of all demons."

"Are Lycans really all that common?" Sam asked.

"Very common," Alan said. "You wouldn't know it. Lycans walk both realms. You never know who is a Lycan."

"Except on the nights of the full moon," Sam pointed out. "You'd know then."

"Not even then," Alan said, with a shake of his head. "Lycans aren't werewolves. They don't have to turn when it's the full moon. They can if they want to, but they're not forced to."

"Lycans aren't werewolves?" Rose asked, surprised. "I thought it was just another name for werewolves."

"Werewolves are dogs," Ava said. "Lycans..." She paused. "They're demons." There was something in her voice, a pain so bright that Aaron felt it pierce his heart.

"You've come across Lycans?" he asked, even though a part of him already knew the answer.

Ava nodded, her blue eyes glistening. "My family was killed by Lycans," she said. "I saw it, watched it happen."

"Ava," Rose gasped. "I'm so sorry."

"How did you escape from them?" Sam asked.

"I didn't," Ava replied. "I was only ten when it happened. My mum..." She choked on the word, forcing herself to go on. "She tried to fight, to keep the Lycans away from me and my brother." Her eyes glazed as she recounted the memory. "She couldn't stop the beast, not for long. It went for my brother after it...it finished with her. I still remember it, how it attacked him, tore him apart." She closed her eyes and a tear dropped down her cheek. Aaron had the unbearable urge to wipe it away. He forced himself to stay where he was, his hands clenched into fists by his side.

"I'm so sorry, Ava," Sam said.

Ava sniffed and wiped at her cheek. "It's okay," she said.

"How did you get away?" Aaron asked.

"Ella arrived with a group of Hunters," she replied. "She was only thirteen then, but she saved my life. She brought me here to Salvador, and ever since then she's been looking out for me."

Aaron understood why Ava had tied the black thread onto Ella's arm. She was the Hunter who saved Ava's life. That was their special bond.

"Ella was hunting when she was thirteen?" Sam asked incredulously.

"Most Hunters start when they're thirteen," Alan answered.

"But isn't that too young?" Rose asked.

"Maybe years ago, when Hunters had to be of age," Alan replied. "But nowadays you can start hunting the moment your core wakes up." He dropped his voice lower. "I reckon we don't have a choice any more. The way things are going…" He scrunched up his face. "It's a case of all hands on deck, and maybe, just maybe, we might make it through."

"How come you don't go hunting?" Aaron asked.

Alan looked surprised. "Me?" He shook his head. "I don't have the stomach for it. Can't handle a gun." He shrugged. "Thought about being a Lurker, like my old man, but I don't know. Maybe one day." He fished out a small ring – a simple gold band, like a wedding ring. Etched on the inside was Aric's mark and a simple circle with the letter K inside. Aaron figured it stood for 'Kings', Alan's surname.

"I use this sometimes," Alan said, his voice uncharacteristically quiet. "When I miss him too much. I use the ring to see him. To see what he was like." He puffed out his chest and smiled. "Imagine myself in his Lurker uniform. Makes me feel good. I imagine when I become a Lurker, the others will point at me and say, 'There goes Kings' little lad, looking just like his dad.'" He smiled. "It gets me through most days."

Rose was staring at the ring. "Sorry, Alan, but did you say you use the ring to see your dad?"

Alan nodded. "Yeah, I use the flesh memories."

"Flesh what?" Sam asked.

"Flesh memories," Alan repeated, then seemingly remembered their lack of knowledge for all things mage. He quickly continued, "Sorry. Flesh memories are snippets of moments, stored on items mages have touched or used. Like, this is my dad's ring." He held it up. "He used to wear it, so it's touched his flesh. Anything that my dad did while wearing the ring, a snippet of that event is stored on the ring. When I touch it, I can see the memory in my mind."

"Can all mages use flesh memories?" Aaron asked.

"As far as I know," Alan replied.

"Is it only you that can see your father's memories or can any mage see it?" Aaron asked.

"Anyone can see it," Alan said, then somewhat reluctantly, he held the ring out to him.

Aaron reached over and took it.

Nothing happened.

"Did you see anything?" Sam asked, breathless with anticipation.

Aaron shook his head.

"You have unlock it," Alan said. "It doesn't work by just touching it."

"What do I unlock?" Aaron asked.

"The memory," Alan replied.

"How?" Aaron asked.

Alan looked lost. "You...you have to pick the memory." He gestured to the ring. "Like...you have to....You imagine it and then...you..." He paused. "I don't know how to explain it. I've been doing it for years, so it's like second nature to me."

Aaron handed the ring back with disappointment sitting heavily in the pit of his stomach.

***

Aaron and the twins made their way upstairs to their rooms. Sam and Rose climbed the stairs at once, eager to get to their beds after another tiring day. Aaron was trailing behind them when Kyran walked out of the living room. Aaron turned to see Kyran lock the front door, securing the cottage for the night.

Aaron wondered if Kyran would maybe, perhaps, help him. He had seen plenty of moments in his dreams where Kyran was guiding him. But he had also seen one particular dream where Kyran blatantly refused to help him. He gave himself a mental shake. The dreams were not real, and neither were they going to be. Mages weren't seers. At least, he hoped not.

Kyran turned from the door and stopped at the sight of Aaron just standing there at the stairs, staring at him.

"What?" he asked, being rather short with him.

Aaron ignored it. He cleared his throat. "I was wondering," he said, "if you could help me with something."

Kyran's eyes widened, his eyebrows raised. "What?"

"I need to figure something out." Aaron turned away from the stairs and faced him. "But I can't work out how to do it. Could you help me?"

Kyran looked completely thrown. "What did I do that made you think this is okay?"

"Just...listen, please." Aaron came down the steps and walked forward. "I was talking to Alan and he told me about flesh memories."

"Yeah, so?"

"So, I was wondering, how do you unlock a memory?"

Kyran paused, watching him with curiosity. "What memory are you after?"

Slowly, Aaron reached into his pocket and pulled out the letter his mum had left him. It had been in his pocket when he got hit with the lake water. As a result, it was now damaged, with the ink smudged in various places. That in itself didn't upset Aaron. He had read it so many times, he knew the words by heart. He held the crinkled paper up.

"My mum and dad left this for me," he explained. "Since they obviously touched the letter, I wanted to see the memory attached to it." Aaron hoped if he could figure out how flesh memories worked, he might be able to see what happened the night his parents left. What they said and did when they wrote the letter.

Kyran stared at him. "Why would you think I would help you?" he asked.

Aaron actually had no good answer. He shrugged. "I dunno. I just reckoned you would."

Kyran breathed out a sigh and closed his eyes, shaking his head. "Alright," he said and looked at Aaron, gesturing to the letter. "Hold on to it with both hands."

Aaron grasped it tightly, his heart somersaulting with excitement.

"Take a deep breath in," Kyran instructed.

Aaron pulled in a breath and slowly let it out.

"Close your eyes."

Aaron did.

"Ready?" Kyran asked.

"Yeah." Aaron nodded.

"Now say out loud, 'Immababoonsass'."

"Imma baboons a–" Aaron stopped and opened his eyes to glare at Kyran.

Kyran grinned, winked and pushed past him, going upstairs.

"Baboon's ass," Aaron called after him

16

THE FULL MOON

The next morning Aaron awoke feeling downright miserable. His body was sore and heavy. A headache bloomed just behind his eyes. His fingertips were tingly, suffering from pins and needles. He forced his eyes open and looked around the room. Sam and Rose were still sleeping, their soft snores breaking the silence of the room. Aaron tried to sit up but his stomach rolled. He felt feverish, his skin hot and clammy. His body protested to even the thought of getting up. Aaron just lay there, groaning softly at the way his body ached. It was an hour before Rose awoke.

"What's wrong?" she asked, seeing Aaron's flushed face.

"Dunno," Aaron croaked. "Think I got the flu."

"The flu?" Rose frowned. She got out of bed and came to his side. Holding a hand against his fevered brow, she tutted. "I told you to change out of your wet clothes."

"I did," Aaron protested.

"Yeah, after you stood around chatting to Ella," Rose scolded. She seemed to feel bad almost immediately. "I'll ask Mother Mary to make some chicken broth. It's really good if you have a cold or the flu."

Aaron's stomach clenched as he remembered his mum's chicken broth. She used to make it for him, without fail, any time he was feeling poorly. It always cheered him up. The memory made his eyes burn.

"Yeah," he muttered, forcing himself to speak past the tightening of his throat. "Cool, thanks."

Rose left the room, and half an hour later Sam woke up. He went through the same routine as Rose: asking Aaron what was wrong and chastised him for staying in wet clothes too long before promising to take care of him.

"You got changed the same time as me," Aaron argued. "How come you didn't catch a cold?"

"I'm stronger than you," Sam teased. "You're just a little baby."

"Sod off." Aaron said.

Sam only laughed before heading to the door. "I'll bring you some orange juice. It'll fix you right up."

"Orange juice?" Aaron asked.

"It's really good when you're sick," Sam assured him. "I'll just run to the Stove."

Aaron was left on his own. He lay quietly, trying to ignore his thumping headache. He wondered if Armana would be able to get rid of his headache. Maybe she could take away his fever or cold or whatever it was he was suffering from too.

A gentle knock on his door made Aaron look around. He found a smirking Kyran leaning against the open door, hands tucked into his pockets.

"Morning," he said in greeting.

Aaron groaned in response.

"Feeling good I see," Kyran said.

"What do you want?" Aaron asked. He had very little patience left in him to be antagonised.

"Just wanted to see how you're coping."

Aaron looked at him with a furrowed brow and bloodshot eyes. "Coping?" he asked. "With what?"

"The full moon," Kyran replied. "It's the day of the full moon, and judging by that completely stupid look on your face, I'm guessing you have no idea what that means."

Aaron didn't say anything.

"You know what the moon is?" Kyran asked.

"Yes," Aaron hissed. "I know what the bloody moon is!"

"Good. What does it do?" Kyran asked.

"I'm not in the mood for a science test right now," Aaron said, reaching up to massage his forehead. "Leave me alone."

"Gladly," Kyran replied, "but after you answer my question." His voice steeled, making Aaron open his eyes and look over at him. "What does the moon do?" Kyran repeated.

Aaron sighed. "Lots of things," he replied. "Raises tides and affects the earth's solar orbit and rotational speed."

"Well done." Kyran grinned. "Now, wanna take a guess what the moon does to mages?"

"Dunno."

"Obviously," Kyran said. "Try and work it out. If the moon can rise the tide, what do you think it can do to mages and their power?"

Aaron's eyes narrowed as he tried to figure it out, but his fevered state didn't help his flailing concentration. "I...I don't know," he said.

"Do you know what the full moon does to humans?" Kyran asked.

"Yes," Aaron replied tersely. "Nothing! It doesn't do anything to humans."

"Wrong answer," Kyran said. "You know, it's a disgrace. You've lived your whole life with humans and you still know so little about them." He smirked at Aaron's glare. "The moon doesn't only pull on oceans," he said. "On nights of the full moon, the gravitational pull makes the blood rise to the brain, making some humans downright crazy." He looked rather happy at Aaron's stunned expression. "Now, think about that and apply it to mages."

Aaron swallowed painfully as realisation dawned on him. "The powers," he said quietly. "The moon pulls our powers."

Kyran slowly nodded. "On the day and night of the full moon, our powers are drained from us," he explained. "It makes us weak, ill, unable to fight. Never wondered how it's always on the nights of the full moon that the crime rates in the human realm are at their highest?" he asked. "It's because the mages are at their weakest on these nights. We can't be there to protect the humans and every demon in this universe knows that. They come out in full force, knowing no mage can stop them, not when the full moon is out."

"So there's going to be attacks in the human realm tonight?" Aaron asked, horrified.

"Most definitely," Kyran replied.

"We can't do anything about it?" Aaron asked.

"Can you get out of bed?" Kyran asked.

Aaron glared at him. "You seem to be doing okay," he said, his tone accusatory.

Kyran grinned. "I'm stronger than you," he said. "You're just a little baby."

Aaron gaped at him.

"The walls are very thin." Kyran said in explanation. "And mages have excellent hearing."

***

It turned out that Kyran was right. All the mages were ill today – every single one. Sam and Rose, who had gone out to get some soup and juice for Aaron, found that no one was well enough to do any chores. The Stove was unoccupied. The orchard was deserted. The farmland was left to its own devices. The only ones not in their beds, groaning and moaning about headaches and fatigue, were Sam, Rose and – strange as it was – Jason Burns.

"How come you're not ill?" Sam asked, managing to make the question sound like an accusation.

"Is only the mages tha' get ill," Jason said, setting out the table with the soup Mary had prepared the night before. "I ain't a mage now, am I?"

"You're not a mage?" Rose asked, surprised. "So what are you?"

Jason stopped to look over at them, before shaking his head, chuckling loudly. "Cannae yeh tell?" he asked. "Am a human."

"Human?" Sam was stunned. "You're a...a Shattered?"

"Aye," he said, a little quietly, his eyes dark even in the sunlight. "I came 'ere aboot twen'y years ago." He shrugged. "Ended up stayin' forever."

***

The day and night of the full moon passed. Aaron, begrudgingly, spent most of it in bed, under Rose's insistence. When he awoke the following morning, he felt light-headed but otherwise fine. His headache was gone, as were the aches and pains in his body. He emerged from his cottage feeling weary and tired, but no longer ill. He tilted his face up, warming it in the sun's bright rays. It felt good to be out in the sun again.

A bright flash signalled the opening of the Gate, and Aaron looked over to see Kyran walk down the path. Aaron hadn't seen him since yesterday morning. Aaron had figured Kyran was resting in his room, like other mages. Kyran's head was lowered, hands tucked into his pockets and he walked at a slower than normal pace. It seemed as if he was drifting along, lost in his thoughts.

"There you are!"

Ella's sharp cry snapped Kyran out of his daydream and he blinked at the enraged girl charging up to him.

"What the hell were you thinking?" Ella snapped. A hard shove accompanied her question.

Kyran looked perplexed. "Excuse me?"

"You did the same thing last month," Ella said. "You know going off on your own on the full moon is the single most *stupid* thing you could do."

Kyran screwed up his face in annoyance and waved a hand at her. "I don't need a lecture." He began to walk away.

"Agreed – you need a kick up the backside!" Ella followed after him. "You do realise going out of a safe zone on the *one* day you're vulnerable is not the brightest idea?" she asked. "Especially as all the demons on this freaking planet are out looking for idiotic mages that would do exactly that."

Kyran sighed, bowing his head in defeat. "I told you, Ella, I have to go."

"It's risky and stupid."

"It's my family," Kyran said quietly. "And I don't have a lot of it left." He met her grey eyes. "And if they want to be together on the nights we are at our weakest, then…" He shrugged. "I have to honour that."

Ella fell quiet, but her hard stare never left him. "Bring them here."

"They won't come," Kyran said. Then with a small smirk he added, "Too damn proud, not to mention stubborn."

Ella smiled a little, shaking her head at him. "No surprise. They're related to you."

Kyran grinned at her, but it was missing its usual charm. Aaron watched Kyran walk to his cottage, noting the aura of sadness about him, until he disappeared behind the blue door.

***

Salvador quickly fell back into its usual routine, with mages going off to work in the orchard or the farmland and the Hunters training in the ring, to get back into shape after spending so many days recovering from the Q-Zone hunt and the effects of the full moon.

Aaron and Sam were back in the orchard, hard at work, while Rose spent her days at the Stove. Unlike the boys, Rose wasn't progressively getting better at the chores. If anything, she seemed to be going in the opposite direction. Since she walked into the Stove this morning, nothing had gone her way. It was only midday and she had broken two plates, tipped over a bucket of milk and cracked a teapot while pouring hot water into it. All in all, a very bad start to the day.

By dinnertime, Rose had had enough. And so, it seemed, had Mary. She politely asked Rose to take a break and go to sit at the table. As Rose sat with her head in her hands, Aaron and Sam arrived, grinning in satisfaction from completing another day's work. Rose told Sam and Aaron about her horrible day.

"Why are you such a klutz?" Sam asked.

Rose glared at him.

"Way to be sensitive," Aaron whispered across the table, before turning to Rose. "Don't worry about it. Everyone has days like that."

Rose shook her head. "I can't get anything right," she said. "Everything I touch ends up either breaking or burning."

"You're just not a kitchen person," Sam said.

Rose turned to him, mouth thinned and eyes narrowed.

"What?" Sam asked. "I'm trying to help."

"Then stop," Aaron suggested. "I think you need a break, Rose. Take a few days off."

Rose shook her head. "I barely do anything in the Stove," she said, sounding miserable. "Just peel potatoes or wash vegetables." She shrugged. "How can I ask for a break when that's all I do?"

"Why don't come with us to the orchard?" Sam suggested. "There's nothing you can break or burn there."

Rose whacked him on the arm.

"You had that coming," Aaron told him.

"Damn, what's wrong with you?" Sam asked, rubbing his arm. "You need some chocolate or something. That'll cheer you up." Then added under his breath, "And weaken those violent tendencies."

"Oh, chocolate," Rose moaned. "I could kill for some chocolate."

"Happy place, Rose," Sam teased. "Go to your happy place, quick."

Rose raised a fist this time, aiming a punch, but Sam quickly pulled her hand down, smiling apologetically at her.

"I'm only teasing," he said. "What's up with you today?"

"I'm not in the mood." Rose pulled herself free from Sam's grip.

All the way through dinner, Rose's mood seemed to get darker. By the time tea and coffee was served, Aaron couldn't take any more of Rose's miserable look. He got up and hurried over to Mary's side as she handed out steaming mugs.

"Mary?"

"Yes, Aaron?"

"Do you have any chocolate?"

Mary paused, frowning. "Chocolate?" she asked. "You mean hot chocolate?"

Aaron looked back at Rose, who was watching him. Slowly, she shook her head.

"No," Aaron replied, turning back to Mary. "Chocolate. As in a bar of chocolate."

"A bar?" Mary looked really confused. "Sorry, Aaron. I've never heard of bars of chocolate," she said.

"Leave it, Aaron," Rose called, shaking her head. "It's fine."

Aaron could see it wasn't. Her shoulders were already lifted, hands balled into fists and brown eyes slowly glistening. Mary stepped towards her, realising Aaron was asking on her behalf.

"I can make you some hot cocoa." she tempted.

"I don't *want* hot cocoa," Rose said, visibly struggling to remain calm. "I don't want to *drink* chocolate. I want to *eat* it!"

"Rose?" Sam reached out to hold on to his sister. "Calm down."

"No!" Rose pulled herself free, and shot to her feet. "I'm sick of this!" she cried. "I'm sick of keeping quiet! I don't *want* to keep quiet any more. I don't want to bite back my words. I don't want to peel potatoes day in and out!"

"You don't have to," Aaron said, stepping towards her. "You don't have to work if you don't want to, Rose. You can do what you want."

"What I want?" Rose repeated angrily. "What I want? All I want is a freaking bar of chocolate!" she cried. "And I can't even get that!" She stepped back when Sam tried to hold on to her. "No! Let me go!" She pushed him back, staggering away from the table, not caring that every eye was on her. "You know what I want? I want my room, with *my* things in it," she said. "I want to eat at *my* kitchen table, not out in the street!" Tears slid out of her eyes, trickling down her cheeks. "I want to go home," she said, her voice breaking. "I just...I just want to go home."

Sam stepped forward and wrapped his arms around his sister, holding her close as she wept.

"Sam, I want to go home." Her words were muffled against his chest, but everyone heard her nonetheless. "Please, I just...I want to go home."

Aaron watched her, feeling his blood run cold with guilt. He pushed the remorse aside. He wasn't going to let self-recrimination stop him from comforting his friends. He walked over to them and Rose pulled herself out of her brother's arms, hugging Aaron tightly.

"I want to go home, Aaron," she sobbed.

"I know," Aaron whispered in her ear, at a loss of what else he could say. "I know, Rose. I know."

From the corner of his eye, he saw Kyran get up from the table and walk away.

***

"You feeling better?" Aaron asked.

Rose nodded, sitting on the floor, leaning against the wall. She sniffed and wiped her cheeks with the end of her sleeve. Sam and Aaron had taken Rose away from the table and to the closest place they could to give her some privacy – the Stove.

"What happened to you, Rose?" Sam asked, eyes crinkled in concern and face pale at the sight of his sister in tears.

"I don't know," she replied. "I just lost it." She rubbed at her cheeks again. "It all just...came pouring out."

Aaron held on to her hand. "I'm so sorry, Rose," he said, guilt thick in his voice.

Rose shook her head before leaning back to rest it against the wall. "Don't, Aaron," she said. "Don't apologise. You know none of this is your fault." She closed her eyes and breathed out a sigh. "I really made a scene out there, didn't I?"

"Don't worry about it," Sam said. "Who cares what a bunch of mages think?"

But Rose was shaking her head again, eyes tightening in a grimace. "God, I bit off Mary's head," she said, opening her eyes to look over at Sam. "And for what? Because somehow it's her fault this stupid world doesn't have chocolate?" She shook her head. "I need to apologise to her."

She made to get up, but Sam and Aaron stopped her.

"Why are you going to say sorry?" Sam asked.

"You have every right to get upset," Aaron said.

"Maybe," Rose said. "But I shouldn't be taking it out on others. It's not their fault."

Rose stood up and opened the door, walking into the warm night, Sam and Aaron following behind her. Mary and the other helpers were busy gathering the dishes and cleaning up the table.

"Mother Mary," Rose started, her voice rough and hoarse from crying. "I'm sorry I yelled at you. I...I don't know what came over me," she said honestly. "I just got so angry and I know it was a stupid, ridiculous thing to get upset over, but..." She trailed off. "I don't know. I can't explain it."

Mary smiled at her. "It's okay, Rose." She nodded. "It was bound to happen, sooner or later."

"What?" Rose asked, frowning. "What was going to happen?"

Mary's smile dropped at the corners of her mouth, but she continued staring at her with a softened gaze. "You crashed," she said. "It happens." She nodded in a placated manner. "When humans first come to this realm, they're shaken up – some in denial and others in shock. They spend a few days here in Salvador before they're taken to different cities in this realm. They are integrated into our world. Slowly, the realisation dawns on them that they are here indefinitely. There's no going back." She reached out to cup Rose's face. "It's not easy to admit that your life has changed forever. That you can never return to your former life," she said quietly. "When people eventually realise that, they have a breakdown of some sort." Her hand lowered from Rose's cheek to her shoulder. "Mages aren't all that different either. Some of us go through the same thing. We lose our family and are brought here to Salvador. Some of us stay, others move to different cities and attempt to start over." She tilted her head to the side, looking at Rose through glistening eyes. "We crash too, Rose."

Rose nodded, willing her tears to stay back. "I'm sorry," she said in a small voice.

"There's no need to be," Mary replied. Her grip on Rose's shoulder tightened. "Time is the best healer, Rose. Have faith in it." She smiled. "One day this place, this realm, will be your home and you'll be happy here. I promise."

Rose didn't say anything, but her pained expression showed her disbelief.

"Go. Rest." Mary pulled her hand away. "I'll see you bright and early tomorrow."

Rose looked to the messy table. "I should help clear up," she said. "I haven't been much help otherwise."

Mary looked surprised at her comment, but she stopped Rose. "No, it's okay," she said.

"But–"

"It's cool," Aaron said, stepping up beside her. "I'll take your shift and clean up."

Sam didn't say anything but headed towards the table. He took a tray and started loading up the dishes. Aaron sent the reluctant Rose towards their cottage and began helping clear the table.

The whole walk up to the cottage, Rose kept looking back, seeing Aaron and Sam do her job. She knew, though, if she went back they wouldn't let her do anything. With a resigned sigh, she walked into the cottage. The lamps were already on. Kyran had made a habit of leaving a few lamps on in every room – for their benefit, of course.

Rose trudged up the stairs, feeling exhausted. Her breakdown had really drained her. Who knew crying could take so much out of a person? She noticed the door to the third room was slightly ajar, but she couldn't be bothered to close it.

She walked into her room, rubbing at her eyes, but stopped at the sight of the bag on her bed. She blinked at it, surprised by its sudden appearance. There was nothing on Sam or Aaron's bed, save for a few books they had been reading, but in the middle of her bed sat a little blue plastic bag with the handles knotted.

Hesitantly, Rose approached her bed and picked up the bag. She undid the knot only to stare in surprise at the contents. She reached in and pulled out a handful of chocolate bars. The bag was filled with bars of chocolate, ones she recognised from the human realm: Mars bars, Bounty, Kit Kat, Snickers, Twix and about a dozen others. Rose stared at them in shock.

She turned at the sound of footsteps coming from the third room. Kyran, still clad in his jacket, crossed past her door. He paused, catching sight of her, the bag in her hands. Rose didn't say anything. The truth was, she couldn't find the clarity of mind to speak. She stared at Kyran, stunned that he had gone to the human realm just to get her chocolate.

Kyran smiled, and walked away without saying a word.

17

LIKE FATHER LIKE SON

Over the next few days, the individual groups of Hunters began taking their leave, having recovered from the effects of the full moon and the Q-Zone hunt. Their departure was just as loud as their arrival had been, with all the Hunters joyfully meeting everyone with promises of returning soon.

Zulf's team was the last to leave. Aaron was pleasantly surprised when Zulf took the time to bid him goodbye. No other Hunter had paid him much notice. Zulf clasped Aaron's hand in his own big, strong one and shook it.

"Stick around, kid." He grinned broadly. "Things might just get interesting with you here."

Aaron stood back to see everyone else say goodbye to Zulf. Even Skyler shook Zulf's hand. Zulf met Kyran last, embracing like brothers who didn't know if they would see each other again. Clapping a hand on Kyran's shoulder, Zulf regarded him at arm's length.

"You're not going into another Q-Zone," he said strictly. "Not without me, understand?"

Kyran smirked back.

They hugged one last time before Zulf climbed onto his green and black Kawasaki Ninja bike and led his group of Hunters out of the Gate. The door sealed for the final time that day and Salvador was left feeling rather empty.

***

Aaron was pretty sure the moment the cottages were empty, Kyran was going to kick him and his friends out. He was therefore rather surprised when he found Kyran didn't say anything to him. Wanting to make sure they wouldn't be made homeless again in the middle of the night, Aaron sought out Jason to request a cottage, only to be told that the cottages were being cleaned thoroughly before anyone could move into them.

"You really took Rose's words to heart," Aaron said.

"Aye, well." Jason scratched his head. "She ha' a point."

Aaron nodded. "How long will it take?"

"Few days, th'ee at the most," Jason assured.

Aaron nodded. "Okay."

Jason was about to walk away when he stopped and turned back to Aaron with a smile.

"I bet you jus' make yerself com'ortable with the per'ect cottage and yer folks'll come back, wantin' to leave." He walked away chuckling to himself.

Aaron's heart jolted at the thought of his parent's return. He wished with all his might that what Jason said came true. Six weeks had passed since his parents left him in Salvador. *Six weeks.* Aaron couldn't help the shiver that ran down his spine. *They should be back by now,* the voice in the back on his mind whispered over and over again, sending a spike of pain through his heart. Negotiating with Neriah couldn't possibly take six weeks, could it?

Aaron had spent every waking moment around his mum and dad. He knew his parents – knew what they were like, what they were capable of. He knew, believed with every fibre of his being, that leaving him alone in a strange place for six long weeks with no communication was something his parents were not capable of doing. The thought had been niggling at Aaron, stealing the sleep from his eyes. He had found himself clutching onto the worn, tattered letter at night, praying his parents were okay, as Sam and Rose slept soundly in the beds next to him.

Sitting at the table waiting for breakfast, Aaron couldn't hide his dejected mood. His fingers traced the edges of the letter as he told himself repeatedly that his parents were okay, that nothing ill had befallen them, that they would return soon. He felt Rose's hand close over one of his, making him look up at her.

She smiled tightly at him. "You okay?" she asked.

Aaron nodded.

Rose eyed the letter hesitantly. "Don't worry," she whispered. "They'll be back soon."

Aaron didn't say anything.

"You know what I've been thinking?" Kyran's question distracted Rose and Aaron. Both turned to look at him, but he was walking to Ella.

"What?" Ella asked.

"Why we don't interrogate demons?"

Ella raised her eyebrows, a slow grin crossed her face. "You playing?"

"No, I'm serious," Kyran said. "Think about it. We could halve our problems if we got the information out of demons rather than relying on Lurkers."

"Yeah?" Ryan asked. "And how exactly do we do that? We can't bring demons into safe zones since they can't pass the Gates."

"I know that," Kyran said, "but we can question them in their zones."

"We could," Ella said, "but just the once." She leant forward with angry lines on her brow. "Come on, Kyran! We barely have the time to get in and kill the filth and you want to hang around demanding answers from them?"

"I didn't say we had to ask them questions." Kyran replied coolly. "I'm talking about *taking* the information, not asking for it."

Ella sat back, frowning at him. "How would that work?"

"How else?" Kyran smiled. "Focus, find the flap and pull it open."

"These aren't flesh memories, Kyran," Ella said. "You can't just lift the flap on demons."

"How do you know?" Kyran asked. "I say we should try it next time."

"Fine," Ella sighed. "Next time we have a demon and we're feeling particularly suicidal, we'll test out your theory."

"Is all I'm asking." Kyran held up both hands, smiling.

Alan appeared at the head of the table, ready to lay out the dishes. "Morning, y'all," he said.

Everyone returned Alan's greeting, everyone except Aaron. He was still staring at Kyran, his mind reeling. Quite abruptly, Aaron got up and practically ran back to his cottage, the letter clutched in hand. If he had looked back, he would have found a smirking Kyran watching him.

***

Aaron closed the door and sat down on his bed. He held the folded, crumpled paper in both hands, forcing out several breaths before his heart rate slowed to an even pace. He thought about what Kyran had said. *Focus, find the flap and pull it open.*

What did that even mean? Aaron forced out another breath and closed his eyes, rolling his shoulders. Focus. He could do that. He had to focus. *On what?* came the question. Aaron felt the coarse paper between his hands and he concentrated on it. He brought up the mental image of the letter, complete with all its creases and water damage. His fingers felt every crimp in the paper, the rough sharpness of the edges.

Find the flap and pull it open.

Kyran's voice echoed in his head.

Aaron didn't have the faintest clue what that meant. He sat for long minutes, trying to find the flap. In his mind, he imagined the letter had a little overlapping corner. He tried to visualise it, so he could pull it away and reveal the memory hidden inside.

Footsteps rushed up the stairs before his door was slammed open.

"Aaron?"

Opening his eyes, he saw both Sam and Rose at the threshold, staring at him.

"What was that?" Sam asked, walking over to him. "Why'd you leave the table?"

"What happened?" Rose asked. "You ran off like a shot."

"The memories," Aaron replied, holding up the letter. "The flesh memories – the ones Alan was talking about. I know how to get to them. Well, I mean, I'm trying to get them."

Sam frowned. "What are you talking about?"

"You want to see the memory attached to the letter?" Rose asked. "Why?"

"'Cause maybe that memory will tell me what's going on." Aaron said. His brow creased and eyes clouded with worry. "It's been six weeks, Rose. They should have come back by now."

Sam stiffened, like he always did when Aaron mentioned his parents, but Rose walked over and sat next to him.

"I know it seems like a really long time," she said, "but considering they're negotiating their stay here, it's bound to take some time."

"If that's even the case," Aaron said. "Zulf only *thinks* they've gone to see this Neriah guy, but I don't know if that's true." He held up the letter. "Maybe when they were writing this, they talked about what they were going to do, where they were going, how long they were planning to be away." He held her gaze. "I need to know what's going on, Rose. It's driving me crazy."

Rose nodded in understanding. "Have you seen the...the memory thing yet?"

"No," Aaron replied. "I can't get it to work."

"What do you have to do?" Sam asked, his voice uncharacteristically quiet.

Aaron stared at the letter. "Kyran said to focus, find the flap and pull it open."

Rose and Sam frowned.

"What does that mean?" Rose asked.

"I think I have to imagine there's a flap on this." Aaron held out the folded paper. "And if I pull it open, I'm opening the lid to the memories stored in it. Alan said I had to *unlock* the memories, so I'm not sure if *pulling the flap* is unlocking them."

The twins just stared at him.

"I'm confused," Sam said, blinking like he was seeing spots. "You have to imagine a flap and then *pull it open*?"

"Yeah," Aaron replied.

"That's..." Sam grimaced. "...stupid. Where did you hear that?"

"At the table," Aaron said. "Kyran mentioned it when he was talking to Ella."

"I didn't hear him," Sam said.

"That's because you were too busy staring at Ella," Rose said. "Seriously, Sam, she's going to kick your ass one of these days if you don't stop ogling her."

"I wasn't ogling her," Sam said defensively. "I was paying her attention. It's called being a good listener."

"So why'd you not hear her talk about flesh memories?" Aaron smirked.

Sam threw him a furious look but refrained from answering.

Rose turned back to Aaron. "Why don't you ask someone what to do?" she suggested.

"I asked Alan but he doesn't know how to explain it," Aaron replied. "And I asked Kyran but he was a git about it."

"Really?" Rose said.

"Why the tone of surprise?" Aaron asked.

"No, it's just..." She shifted on the bed, dropping her gaze. "I just thought Kyran would help you, that's all."

"Why would he help Aaron?" Sam asked.

"Just...'cause." Rose was starting to blush. "You know, compared to the rest, Kyran isn't so...so...."

"Bad?" Aaron suggested with a slow smile. "You think Kyran's not bad?"

"Comparatively speaking," Rose said. Her neck, cheeks and nose were pink now as she averted her gaze. "Anyway, we better go to get breakfast before it's all gone."

"Before breakfast's gone or...Kyran's gone?" Aaron teased.

"Oh, shut up," Rose said, but her eyes flashed with amusement just the same.

"I don't like this," Sam warned, walking behind Rose, following her out of the room. "Kyran is bad news. All mages are bad news."

"Um, hello?" Aaron called, gesturing to himself.

"You're not a mage," Sam said. "You're Aaron. I'm talking about the prats out there."

"Like Ella?" Rose countered.

"She's different," Sam said defensively.

"Uh-huh," Rose mocked.

Aaron got up from his bed and pocketed the letter. He was going to try to unlock the memories later on. Preferably when his friends couldn't distract him.

***

The good thing about working in the Stove, Rose decided, was that it was so busy there wasn't much time for idle talk. For this, Rose was grateful. Ever since her breakdown, or crash as Mary put it, Rose had felt so ashamed she could barely meet Mary's eyes, let alone talk to her. So it was to Rose's great discomfort that Mary sought her out this morning.

"How are you finding things?" Mary asked with her usual gentle smile.

"Fine," Rose replied, keeping her gaze on the carrots she was peeling.

"I was thinking," Mary started, "about what you said—"

"Mother Mary." Rose turned to look at her. "I'm sorry. I said a lot of stupid things that day."

"No, no." Mary shook her head. "It wasn't stupid. Nothing about what you said that day was stupid. You got your feelings out and that's never a bad thing." She paused for a moment, staring at Rose intently. "I was just wondering if there's anything you enjoyed cooking, before coming to Salvador?"

"I wasn't in the kitchen much," Rose replied. "My...my mum..." She choked on the word a little. "She would always ask me to help with dinner and...and half the time I would just ignore her." She fell quiet, her remorse stealing her voice.

Mary watched her carefully. "But the other half of the time, you did help her. What was your favourite thing to make?" Mary pushed.

A small smile tugged at Rose's lips. "Popcorn."

Mary chuckled. "There must have been something other than popcorn."

"Not really," Rose said. "There was one thing, though. We used to make these chocolate and coconut ball things. I don't know what they're called, but they were pretty decent. We didn't make them all that often but they were fun."

"Show me." Mary said.

Rose looked over at her with surprise. "What?"

"These chocolate coconut ball things," Mary said. "Show me how you make them."

Rose started shaking her head. "They're nothing special—"

"Oh come on," Mary said. "You've got me curious."

A slow, somewhat excited smile spread across Rose's face. "Okay." She put down the carrot and knife. "We're going to need some hot chocolate powder."

Mary looked lost. "I can grind cocoa beans into powder," she suggested hopefully. "Then add some sugar, like I do to make hot chocolate?"

Rose nodded. "Should be okay," she said. "We'll also need oats, a little butter and some grated coconut."

"Not a problem," Mary said. "I'll just get some coconuts from the orchard."

"There are coconut trees in the orchard?" Rose asked with surprise. "But I thought coconuts only grow in tropical—" She stopped, seeing the confusion on Mary's face. She smiled at her and shook her head. "Never mind."

***

That night, along with all the dinner dishes, sat a plate piled with small chocolate and oats balls, covered in coconut flakes. Rose couldn't stop beaming at the sight of them. They looked positively cute, sitting amongst the dishes of roast lamb and rice. It didn't take long for the new dish to be noticed.

"What are these?" Ella asked, peering at the plate with an interested glint in her eyes.

"A special dessert." Mary beamed. "Made by Rose."

Sitting across the table, Kyran lifted his head up.

"What is it?" Zhi-Jiya asked, eyeing the balls.

Mary looked to Rose to introduce them.

"Choco-coco balls," Rose said. She and Mary had giggled endlessly when it came to naming them.

"Mmmm." Sarah stared at them. "They look...interesting."

"They're more than interesting," Sam said. "She used to make them all the time. They're delicious."

"Yep," Aaron agreed, "I can't get enough of them." As proof, he reached out and took two.

Ella picked one off the plate. She brought it close to her face and sniffed it. She took a bite of the soft, gooey chocolate and coconut goodness. Rose held her breath as Ella looked genuinely surprised. Grey eyes met hers and Ella smiled.

"What do you know?" she said. "They are delicious."

Rose's breath came out in a rush and she grinned in relief. Mages began picking up the balls, biting into them, murmuring their approval. Rose was surprised when even Skyler took one. But there was one person who hadn't tasted the dessert, and for a reason she didn't understand, Rose found herself waiting for him.

Kyran took his time, finishing his meal and draining his glass before he even looked at the dessert. He reached forward and picked up a ball. That's when he turned to look at her. Holding her gaze, he popped the whole thing into his mouth and chewed slowly. Rose watched him, waiting for his reaction. Kyran didn't say anything, but he smiled, just a small lifting at the corners of his lips. He reached out and Rose thought he was going to take another ball, but instead, Kyran pulled the plate closer, effectively hogging the dessert. He picked up another ball and bit into it.

Ryan, sitting next to him, tried to reach for one, but Kyran pulled the plate out of reach.

"Hey!" Ryan cried. "Come on, dude – share."

"No," Kyran replied simply.

"Mother Mary!" Ryan called. "Kyran's not sharing."

"Cry-baby," Zhi-Jiya teased.

"I am not," Ryan objected.

They continued arguing while Kyran sat back and steadily worked his way through the dessert, leaving the plate empty and Rose grinning.

**

The sound of soft snores broke the silence of the darkened room. Sam and Rose had fallen asleep hours ago, but Aaron was still awake. He lay on his bed, hands clutched around the letter, which was now falling to pieces. Two nights had passed but Aaron still couldn't figure out how to unlock the flesh memory.

He groaned in frustration, then quietened immediately when Sam grunted and turned over, the bed creaking under him. Aaron let out a long breath and closed his eyes, crushing the letter in his hands. He brought up a mental picture of the letter, grimacing at how tattered it had become. For a brief moment, he thought about what it must have looked like when his mum sat down to write it: clear, crisp paper with black ink dotting the words from his mum's pen. The image floated to the forefront of his mind and Aaron held it there. He imagined one of his mum's hands pressed against the paper as her other clutched a pen. As he imagined it, the image of the letter shimmered and in the bottom left-hand corner a little overlapping flap appeared. Aaron's surprise almost made him lose the image. He held it tight, focusing all his energy into keeping the picture at the front of his mind. Carefully, Aaron tugged at the flap, as Kyran's voice echoed from the back of his consciousness. *...focus. Find the flap and pull it open..."*

Aaron pulled and a translucent cover fell away from the letter. Suddenly the letter was growing, getting bigger and bigger until it was all Aaron could see in his mind's eye: a white paper with indistinguishable writing. A heartbeat later, the letter was gone, freeing his vision and Aaron found himself standing in a semi-dark room. It was lit only by a single lantern, which was floating above a small table. There upon on the threadbare sofa sat his mother.

Aaron's breath choked in his chest. He stepped forward, staring at his mum, who was leaning over the table writing furiously.

"Mum?" Aaron called.

His mum didn't react but continued to write, the pen scratching line after line.

"Mum?" Aaron called again before his rational thinking caught up with him. This was a memory. It had already happened. He wasn't really there, so his mum couldn't hear him.

Aaron watched as his mum completed the letter, feeling a strange pressure build in his heart at the sight of her. He hadn't seen his mum in six weeks. Catching her in a memory like this made Aaron realise just how badly he missed her. Aaron admitted freely that his mum was often very strict with him. She demanded a lot from him – whether it was in the shape of homework or adherence to her rules – but she was still his mother. She loved him and Aaron knew that. He could sense the underlying care and concern in her overprotective measures, which made her absence all the harder to bear.

His mum sniffed loudly but continued to write, head bowed over the letter. Aaron came closer and sunk to his knees, sitting on the carpet so that he could see his mum's face. His heart jolted at the sight of her tears, slowly trailing down her cheeks. She sniffed again and rubbed the back of her hand against one of her cheeks, drying it.

Aaron had seen his mum shout and scold. He had seen her trying to be funny and failing miserably. He had seen her smile on several occasions but he had never seen her cry. His mum wasn't the type to cry – not at sad movies, those adverts with injured dogs, not even bad news. She always had a stiff upper lip and Aaron sort of respected her for that. He had joked once to Sam that his mum was really a cyborg, which was why she never showed much emotion, other than to discipline him, of course. But today, seeing her in tears – real human tears that showed her vulnerability – it broke Aaron's heart. He felt his own eyes burn, seeing how red-rimmed her usually clear blue eyes were. She finally put down the pen, having finished the letter and brought both hands up to cradle her head. Her sobs broke the silence of the room and Aaron's heart ached anew.

"Mum?" he called again, reaching out without thinking.

His hand passed through her and Aaron snapped it back.

"Kate."

Aaron turned to peer in the darkness and found his dad at the door.

Aaron stared at him; his heart missed a beat. Chris walked in and sat down next to Kate, gathering his wife into his arms. He held her, letting her cry against his chest as he gently rubbed her back and neck.

"You don't have to do this," he said softly. "Stay with him, Kate."

She pulled away and sat up, shaking her head before wiping at her tear-stained cheeks.

"No," she croaked. "I'm not leaving you to face Neriah alone. I'm coming with you. We both made the decision. We'll both pay for it."

Aaron felt like the bottom of his stomach had dropped out. There was no denying it now. They had left to find Neriah and they were expecting a penalty from him. Aaron's fear for their safety spiked to new levels.

"Mike's refusing to stay too," Chris told her. "He wants to speak to Neriah."

Kate nodded, wiping her cheeks dry. "What did Drake say?"

"The usual," Chris replied, "but he'll look out for Aaron until we get back." He leant over and picked up the letter, silently reading it. He let out a sigh and slowly put it back onto the table. "Aaron's going to be so mad at us," he said, remorse thick in his voice.

Kate slowly nodded. "I know," she replied, "but he'll be safe here and that's all that matters."

Aaron blinked and his surroundings began to melt before his eyes, until all he could see was the dark ceiling of his room. Aaron lay on his back, his breathing fast and short, as if he had been running. Sam and Rose's snores echoed in his ears, but somewhere in his mind he could still hear his mum's soft sobs, threatening to break his resolve to stay strong.

**

Aaron didn't tell Sam and Rose that he had managed to unlock the flesh memory. Truth was that he was disappointed with what little he had learned. There was nothing in the exchange between his parents that pointed to what had happened to drive them out years ago and how long it would take them to get back to Salvador. The only conformation he'd got was that his mum, dad and uncle had indeed gone to meet Neriah. It was his mum's tone when she mentioned about paying for their decisions that worried Aaron so much that he could barely eat or sleep. There was no fear in her voice, just a defeated acceptance for whatever price they would have to pay.

After two days of quietly seething and trying to figure out a way to get his parents back to safety, Aaron realised what he had to do and who he was going to have to meet. He turned to look at Alan, as he and Ava set the table.

"Alan?"

"Yeah?" he replied, with his usual cheery grin.

"Which cottage belongs to Drake Logan?"

***

Aaron followed the track at the back of the orchard that led down to the single cottage sitting in the midst of tall trees with golden brown leaves. Aaron passed the fence and walked down the stone-slab path, which was lit to an orange hue with the setting sun. He knocked at the door and Drake answered almost immediately, wearing a look of surprise.

"Aaron?" He narrowed his eyes. "What happened? You okay?"

"Yeah," Aaron replied. "I didn't see you at the table today. Thought I'd come by."

"Why?" Drake asked, looking confused.

"Does there have to be a reason?" Aaron asked.

Drake's frown stayed but he moved aside, gesturing for Aaron to come in. The cottage seemed to have the same layout as the others: a narrow hallway, a living room with no kitchen and a small bathroom, with presumably three bedrooms and a bathroom upstairs. As Aaron walked over to the comfortable-looking sofa, he noted how much more homely Drake's cottage seemed. There was nicer furniture, a thick carpet under his feet and actual curtains hiding his windows. What Aaron had in Kyran's cottage were thin veils that barely kept the sunlight out.

Drake had a small fireplace, its mantel littered with framed pictures. On the wall above the fireplace were two swords crossing each other. Aaron wanted to go over and examine the pictures but he refrained, keeping himself tightly in place on the sofa. His gaze picked out pictures of a dark-haired woman with a beautiful smile and warm brown eyes. One framed picture was of two small boys, twins by the looks of it, holding up ice creams and grinning.

Drake sat down on the armchair next to him. They smiled at each other in awkward politeness but neither of them spoke. Minutes passed in silence before Aaron cleared his throat.

"Your place is nice."

Drake nodded. "Thank you."

They lapsed back into silence.

"Would you like something to drink?" Drake asked.

"No, thanks," Aaron replied. "I'm good."

Drake nodded and looked around, his finger slightly tapping against the armrests. "Was there something you wanted?" he finally came out and asked.

Aaron nodded and shifted in his seat, turning to face him. "Actually, yes," he said. "I want to meet Neriah."

Drake's eyes widened and he blinked at Aaron in surprise. "I beg your pardon?"

"Neriah," Aaron repeated. "I want to meet him." He held Drake's shocked stare as he continued. "I know that's who my mum and dad have gone to meet."

Drake let out a frustrated breath and shook his head. "Aaron–"

"I know you can take me to him," Aaron interrupted. "There's a reason my dad came here to speak to you before going to see Neriah. I need you to take me to him as well."

"I don't know where Neriah is," Drake said. "No one knows where he is."

"So how can my parents go to meet him then?" Aaron asked.

Drake took in steadying breath before raking a hand through his hair. "Aaron, you have to understand something." He leant forward in his seat. "Neriah is single-handedly running this entire realm, keeping it and the human realm as protected as possible. His whereabouts are kept secret for security reasons. He doesn't stay in any one place for long, so catching him is difficult, if not downright impossible." He held up a hand to stop Aaron from speaking. "But believe me, if anyone can find Neriah, it's your dad. Unfortunately, it's of vital importance that your mum and dad make contact with Neriah." He tilted his head to the side as Aaron's face fell. "I'm sorry, really I am, but I can't take you to Neriah. I don't know where he is."

Aaron nodded, his lips pressed into a line with disappointment. "Has my dad made contact with you?" he asked.

"No," Drake answered.

"That doesn't make sense," Aaron said. "It's been six weeks. They would've sent a letter, a message of some sort to say they were okay."

"I don't want to scare you, Aaron," Drake said, "but the fact is they're facing all sort of dangers trying to get to Neriah." He quickly went on at Aaron's outraged expression. "But it's nothing your mum and dad can't handle. Please trust me on that. It's difficult to send out messages when trying to stay invisible."

Aaron bit back his terror, trying with all his might to remain somewhat calm. "Can you get a message to them?" he asked.

Drake's eyes softened. "I'm sorry, Aaron."

Aaron nodded and looked away, hands balled into fists. "So I just have to wait?" Aaron asked. "Is that it?"

"Afraid so," Drake replied sadly. He stared at Aaron for a moment before getting up. "I'll get us something to drink." He walked to the door, heading to the rooms upstairs.

Bitter disappointment sat heavily in the pit of Aaron's stomach. He had come with iron intentions. He was *going* to find his parents. He wasn't going to back down until Drake gave in and took him to meet Neriah. But now he realised Drake was just as helpless as he was.

Letting out an agitated breath, Aaron got to his feet. He couldn't stay sitting, not when he had so much pent-up frustration. He walked over to the fireplace, distracting himself with the pictures on the mantel. He stared at each one, seeing the resemblance between the beautiful dark-haired woman and the twins. He didn't see any pictures of Drake with them, but Aaron knew the pictures were of his wife and kids.

Everyone here has lost someone. If they hadn't, they wouldn't be in Salvador...

Skyler's words came back to him and Aaron looked away from the smiling faces with a heavy heart. He glanced around the room. His gaze found the two sheathed swords, crossed against each other on the wall above the fireplace. Aaron moved closer, studying the hilt of the swords. He found Aric's mark, etched into the steel. He reached out to trace the insignia, to feel the carving under his fingers. He didn't know how it happened – he wasn't even looking for anything – but the moment his fingers touched the cool steel, a memory opened before his eyes.

Gone was Drake's living room, the fireplace and the swords he was currently standing in front of. Instead, Aaron was in a dark street, face to face with a big, hairy, drooling beast. Aaron gaped in horror as the fearsome dog-like creature growled, its grisly fur hanging from its emaciated frame. The beast raised its hackles and snarled at him. Its eyes were slitted, glowing red with black pupils, and staring right at him. Aaron stumbled backwards, his fear momentarily numbing him, making his legs fold under him but the dog had already pounced.

Someone stepped from behind Aaron, literally through him and faced the beast with a drawn sword. Aaron watched from the ground as a boy charged at the demonic dog. He struck out, throwing the beast back with a kick to its head. He lifted his sword and sliced it through the dog, as effortlessly as one would cut through butter with a hot knife. The dog howled and fell back but was up on its feet in an instant and charging towards him. A wave of the boy's hand and the dog froze on the spot. Life drained from its mangled body as it turned to stone. With a barely audible pop, it burst in a cloud of dust.

Aaron was still on the ground, but he wasn't gaping at the sight of a demonic dog being turned to stone and then dust. Instead, he was staring at the boy. He was a Hunter. Aaron knew that simply from what the boy was wearing – a long emerald green coat, with a silver circle on the back. It shared its elegance and design with the coat Skyler wore when he was heading to the Q-Zone, albeit with a different colour and symbol. Aaron watched as the boy turned around while wiping the back of his hand across his mouth, cleaning the splattered drops of blood from his face.

He was young, no older than early twenties. His hair was falling into his eyes – longer than Aaron had ever seen it. He grinned and Aaron felt his heart skip a beat. There was no mistaking him. Aaron was looking at his dad.

"You're welcome," the twenty-something-year-old Chris said, smirking at someone behind Aaron.

Tearing his gaze away from his dad, Aaron looked behind to see an equally young-looking Drake scowling as he limped forward. His dark brown jacket was ripped. A long scratch down his cheek was leaking blood.

"I could've handled it," he grumbled.

"Yeah? Could've fooled me." Chris threw back the sword he had used to kill the beast and Drake caught it with the hand that wasn't clutched to his side. "It looked like you were about to be its chew toy."

Drake wiped the bloodstained sword on his jeans before sheathing it. He turned to Chris, grinning at him. "We can't all be like the great and powerful Christopher Adams, now can we?" he teased.

"You could at least pretend," Chris laughed.

"No thanks," Drake said tiredly, grimacing in discomfort and pain. "I'm happy being just an average Hunter. You can wear your *Best Hunter* badge with pride."

Chris puffed out his chest, green eyes sparkling with humour. "Don't mind if I do."

Their laughs echoed in Aaron's ears as the memory melted and Aaron found himself back in the room, his hand still gripped around the hilt of the sword. He let go quickly and staggered away.

"Aaron?" Drake stood at the door holding two bottles, staring at him in alarm. "What's wrong?"

Aaron barely heard him. The roar of blood pounded in his ears as his heart raced frantically. His eyes were wide, mouth open as he panted. He turned and left, passing by Drake.

"Aaron?" Drake called again. "What happened?"

Aaron pushed the door open and raced down the path.

***

Aaron found the Hunters at the garage. Some were working on their bikes while others were in the weapons hut stocking up on new blades. The lanterns hung low, giving ample light for the boys and girls to work through the darkness of the evening. Aaron hurried past them, seeking out two mages from the gathered crowd. One of the two found him first.

"Adams." Skyler greeted him in his usual cold, domineering way. "Out at this time? Aren't you afraid of the dark?"

Aaron ignored the jibe. His fists were clenched by his sides, anger pulsing inside him, in rhythm with his heartbeat.

"I want to speak with you and Ella," he said.

From the corner of his eye, Aaron saw Kyran squatting before his bike. He slowly rose to his feet, wiping his hands clean with a towel, his vivid green eyes fixed on Aaron.

"With us?" Ella asked, looking surprised. "What about?"

Aaron gave a stiff glance to the surrounding Hunters. "Can we speak in private?"

Ella looked to Skyler, whose smirk only grew wider.

"Let me see," Skyler mocked. "I don't think I've ever enjoyed denying anyone their request as much as I'm going to enjoy this," he sneered. "Say what you have to say or sod off."

Ella looked like she was about to say something but she looked away, playing with the dagger in her hand instead.

Aaron reared his head up, squaring his shoulders as he held Skyler's gaze. "I know that you run this place," he said. "Every mage here had to get to either you or Ella before they were accepted. That's what I want: your acceptance."

"Acceptance?" Skyler's eyes were shadowed with confusion. "What exactly for?"

"To join you," Aaron replied. "To become a Hunter."

18

Hunter Training

Silence met the end of Aaron's words. The Hunters gaped at him before exchanging looks. Their surprise was easy to see. Slowly, the surprise melted and amusement took its place. Skyler started to laugh, his shoulders shaking and blue eyes lit with mirth. The others joined in, sniggering as Aaron stood stiffly with his hands still balled into fists.

"You wanna what now?" Ella asked, not looking as amused as the rest.

"I want to be a Hunter," Aaron repeated.

"Stop, stop." Skyler held out a hand, doubled over with laughter. "You're killing me."

"There's nothing funny about it," Aaron said.

"Oh it's nothing but freaking hilarious!" Skyler shot back. "You, the idiot who knows too little, want to be a Hunter?" He chuckled. "Listen here, Adams – children born yesterday have more knowledge than you."

"Maybe they do." Aaron let the insult roll off him. "But I can learn too."

"Aaron, you don't even know the basics," Ella said.

"Teach me then," Aaron replied. "I'm willing to learn."

"Good for you," Skyler drawled. "But we're not tutors."

"You teach the rest of them," Aaron argued. "I saw you training them when you had that Q-Zone hunt. If you can train them, then why not me?"

"'Cause you're an Adams," Skyler said coldly.

"Exactly, I'm an Adams," Aaron fought back. "I'm an Elemental too."

Skyler's eyebrows shot up and he spluttered a little. "An Elemental?" he repeated. "You have any idea what that even means, twerp?"

"I know that it means that I have as much right to be a Hunter as you do," Aaron replied.

Skyler fell quiet, but his piercing blue eyes cut into Aaron.

"Being a Hunter isn't easy," Ella said, sounding more worried than angry. "You have to train for years—"

"A mage's core wakes up at the age of thirteen," Aaron interrupted, remembering his dad's words. "I've only missed a year."

"The core awakens at thirteen, yes," Ella said, "but prospective Hunters start training when they're ten, eleven years old."

"Fine," Aaron said. "Okay, so I've missed a few years. But better late than never."

"Aaron–" Ella started.

"Why do want to be a Hunter?" Kyran asked from the garage.

Aaron met his gaze and was thrown by the fury in his dark green eyes. The image of his dad, dressed as a Hunter, killing a demon dog came back to Aaron. He balled his fists.

"Why not?" Aaron asked. "It's in my blood after all."

Kyran didn't say anything, but closed his mouth. A muscle twitched in his clenched jaw. He looked away, turning his back on Aaron.

"Alright," Skyler stood up. "I'll do it."

Ella turned to him with wide, disbelieving eyes. "Sky?"

"It's actually a good idea," Skyler assured her. Then, looking at Aaron, he smirked. "I need a new punching bag."

Aaron glowered at him. "I'm not taking any of your crap, Skyler."

Skyler grinned at him. "We'll see about that."

***

Aaron trudged his way up the path, heading back to the cottages. He knew Sam and Rose were probably annoyed with him for disappearing ever since dinner. His rubbed at his head, trying to figure out how he was going to explain what had happened and what he had decided to become. Sam was going to be mad at him, Aaron knew that much. Rose was going to fret over him, that too he knew. But what he couldn't understand was the cold behaviour of the boy currently walking alongside him. Kyran was mad – really, really mad. Aaron could see the fury in his green eyes, read the annoyance in the clenched jaw and the way that damn muscle kept twitching in his jaw. It was starting to annoy him. But Kyran didn't say anything, not until they reached the long line of cottages.

"You're so stupid." The words were hissed out.

Aaron turned to him. "Excuse me?"

"What were you thinking?" Kyran asked. "Asking Skyler for help? Has his animosity towards you not registered in your thick head?"

"Skyler's a git," Aaron replied. "I know that, but he's one hell of a fighter. If he can teach me that—"

"The only thing Skyler's going to teach you is how to take a hit," Kyran said, infuriated. "I just...I don't get it. Why would you go to the one person you know hates you and would love to make your life hell, and ask him for help?"

"I went to get Skyler's acceptance," Aaron said. "I know Elementals run this realm. I needed Skyler or Ella's agreement to be a Hunter. But I was asking for help from *all* of the Hunters. I want to learn how to hunt. I'm willing to learn from anyone." He glanced to Kyran. "Even you."

Kyran looked over at him angrily, clenching his teeth. "Forget it."

"You're a better fighter than Skyler," Aaron went on regardless. "If you teach me—"

"I said forget it!" Kyran snapped. "I'm not teaching you."

Aaron came to a standstill, staring after Kyran who kept on walking. The lanterns floated above their heads, casting a warm glow over them, but Aaron still shivered as the night's cool breeze washed over him.

"Why?" he asked, his voice soft and filled with honest confusion.

Kyran stopped and turned to look at him, blazing green eyes narrowed in agitation. "What do you mean, *why?*" he snarled. "Because it's up to me, that's why! It's my choice and I'm saying no."

Aaron swallowed. A painful stab of disappointment swelled in his chest. "I thought you would help me."

Kyran glared at him. "Why would you think that?"

Aaron paused. Why did he think that? Was it because he suspected Kyran had purposefully struck up the conversation with Ella about flesh memories to help him? Was it because he felt he'd somehow known Kyran longer than the rest because of his dreams?

"I don't know," Aaron admitted. "I just...I felt like you would."

"It's not my job to help anyone," Kyran replied.

Aaron nodded, his heart twisting with misery. "I get it," he said. "I have to do it myself. I'm on my own."

Kyran stared at him, the vivid green of his eyes darkened a shade. "We're all on our own, Aaron," he said quietly. "It's time you got used to it."

Kyran walked away, turning past the gate to walk up to his cottage. Aaron slowly started after him but came to a sudden stop, his eyes widening. His heart skipped several beats when he realised that the conversation he'd just had with Kyran, was the same one he had dreamt about weeks ago.

***

Aaron hit the ground with a painful thump. His shoulder took the brunt of the fall, his skin slicing open at the impact on the gritty ground.

"Come on, Adams," Skyler smirked. "I didn't even hit that hard this time. Get up."

Aaron pulled himself onto his feet. He tried to straighten up, but the burn in his side where Skyler had struck him was making it difficult. He gave himself a mental shake and took his stance again, feet parted, shoulders drawn, back curved, ready to dodge Skyler's attack.

Skyler grinned at him, flexing his fingers as he surveyed his prey. Blue eyes glinted in the sunlight as he tilted his head to the side. Before Aaron could take in a breath, Skyler sent a jolt of power straight at him, striking him in the chest, throwing Aaron back. A spasm of pain shot down Aaron's spine, making him cry out.

"Oh come on," Skyler said. "You're just embarrassing yourself. Are you made of glass, Adams? Afraid you'll break?"

Aaron rolled onto his hands and knees, breathing in great gasps of air, trying to ease himself into straightening up again. His back protested and the top of his shoulder throbbed in agony. Clutching a hand to it, Aaron staggered to his feet.

"At a boy," Skyler taunted. "Stupidity knows no bounds."

"Neither does vindictiveness," Aaron panted.

Skyler paused. "Excuse me?"

"Just saying," Aaron grunted. "Once you're done being a git, maybe you could actually teach me something." He glared at him. "Like how to block attacks?" He shrugged painfully. "Just a thought."

Skyler's eyes narrowed. "Oh, I'm teaching you something," he said, stepping closer. "A lesson."

His fingers twitched and Aaron was sent careening backwards, hitting the ground so hard all the breath was knocked out of him.

Just across the clearing in the garage, Kyran and Ryan tried to work on their bikes but their eyes were on Skyler, watching him beat Aaron. Ryan winced as Aaron was thrown back again.

"Skyler's tearing him a new one," he muttered.

Kyran watched, the wrench in his hand forgotten, as Aaron was knocked to the ground again and again by Skyler's hits. The invisible jolts were thrown without warning. There was no way Aaron could avoid them. Kyran's jaw clenched, and clear, bright green eyes darkened. Skyler's attack caught Aaron, slamming him into the ground once more. Without a word, Kyran straightened up, dropped his tools and turned to walk away. He couldn't watch Aaron take another hit.

***

Sam cursed, ugly words fell from his lips as he paced up and down the room.

"Sam." Armana's gentle voice floated to him. "Please, I can't concentrate."

"Sorry." Sam ran a hand through his hair, forcing out a breath in an effort to calm down.

Rose looked from her brother to Aaron, who was seated in the wicker chair opposite Armana. One of Armana's small, delicate hands was placed against Aaron's cut up shoulder, while the other was on his bruised chest. Armana's unseeing, pale blue eyes stared ahead, rosy pink lips pressed together as she took on Aaron's pain. Aaron was trying very hard to sit still, but Rose could see the agony he was in. The beads of perspiration glistening on his forehead and the tightness of his jaw told Rose that Aaron was biting back his cries. She looked away, feeling her eyes burn.

Armana relaxed, just as Aaron's relieved breath came out in a shaky gasp. Armana pulled back her hands and leant tiredly into her seat.

"Thank you, Armana," Aaron said before slipping back into his shirt. "All good now."

"It's *not* all good!" Sam erupted, turning to him with wide, angry eyes. "Skyler's beating the crap out of you on a daily basis and you're saying it's all good?"

"Don't start, Sammy," Aaron warned, fixing his collars. "I'm not in the mood."

"Oh? What *are* you in the mood for? Some more ass-kicking?" Sam asked. "Should I call Skyler? Or here, let me do it!"

"Sam," Rose started in a placating tone, but Sam turned to her in fury.

"It's been three days!" he shouted. "Three days of him getting kicked around like a freaking football! And *every* night he has to come to Armana to get fixed up!" He turned to Aaron. "What are you doing? Why do you keep going back to Skyler after the way he's treating you?"

"Because I want to learn," Aaron replied. "And Skyler's the only one offering to teach me."

"What's he actually taught you?" Rose asked.

Aaron looked away, buttoning up his shirt. "Nothing yet," he answered. "But once he gets out all the anger he has for my dad-"

"Skyler might never get over his anger," Rose said. "This is your problem, Aaron. You think everyone's decent. That given the chance, everyone will do the right thing eventually. You did the same thing with Matthews and what happened? He never changed, he never did the right thing and you almost got your neck broken!"

"Why are you so determined to become a Hunter?" Sam asked.

Aaron looked away, refusing to answer. Armana reached out and held on to the back of his hand.

"I know how you're feeling, Aaron," she whispered in her soft voice. "But your parents didn't betray you."

"Didn't they?" Aaron asked, his voice breaking. "My dad isn't just a mage. He didn't live in this realm, grow things from the ground and sit around the table making small talk. He was a *Hunter*. He was a big part of this world. He spent half his life fighting demons and God knows what else, and then one day he just got up and left."

"He must have had his reasons," Armana said.

"Yeah, he probably did," Aaron replied. "And right now I don't even care what they were. What I do care about is the fact that he actively went out of his way to keep me from this world. He and mum have hidden things from me – and are still hiding things from me. Dad's *specifically* warned Drake to keep me from learning too much about this realm. Why?" He looked up at Sam with angry eyes. "Why would he do that when he himself was an integral part of this community? Why keep me away if he was so involved himself?"

"So this is what?" Rose asked. "Your way to get back at your dad? He was a Hunter. He obviously doesn't want you to become one, so that's why you're fighting so hard to become just that?"

"Partly, yeah," Aaron confessed. "But it's more than that." He fell quiet for a moment, head dropped. "Mage, Hunter, Elemental...I have no clue what I am," he said. "All I know is that I couldn't be a part of the world I grew up in because of my parents." He turned his head to meet Rose's eyes. "But I'll be damned if I'm going to let them stop me from becoming a part of *this* world."

***

As soon as Aaron walked out of Armana's hut, he came face to face with a livid-looking Drake. His deep-set brown eyes were swimming with anger. His gaze scanned Aaron from head to foot.

"What happened?" he asked. Even his tone was laced with fury.

"Nothing," Aaron replied and walked past him.

Drake turned to follow. "So why are you here to see the Empaths?" he asked. "You were here last night too, and the night before that."

"No reason," Aaron replied.

Drake's hand gripped Aaron's arm and he pulled him around to face him. "I think there's a bloody damn good reason!" he hissed.

Aaron looked from the serious brown eyes down to the hand holding his arm. "Let go of me, Drake," he said calmly.

"Not until you explain to me what the *hell* you think you're doing!"

"Why?" Aaron asked, still with forced calmness. "Who are you to me? Why should I explain myself to you?"

Drake's grip slackened until his hand dropped away and he stood back, blinking in surprise. Aaron felt a stirring of guilt but he pushed it down. He wasn't being rude. He was asking a legitimate question. Drake wasn't someone he should answer to, so why should he do it?

Drake took in a breath and held Aaron's gaze. "You can't become a Hunter," he said. "I won't let you."

"Yeah?" Aaron asked. "How you gonna stop me?"

"I'll tell Skyler to stop training you."

"I'll find someone else," Aaron replied, knowing full well how difficult it would be to get another Hunter to help him.

"Why are you doing this?" Drake asked, his eyes narrowed in confusion. "Don't you understand how dangerous hunting is? You can very easily get killed! You know nothing about this realm, about the demons. How do you expect to survive a hunt?"

Next to him, Aaron felt Sam and Rose shift uncomfortably from one foot to the other, shooting him worried looks. He tried to ignore them.

"It's my life," Aaron pointed out. "If I save it, lose it, what's it got to do with you?"

"You're the son of my best friend!" Drake said. "He left you in my care."

"Then he made a mistake," Aaron said. "He should be the one caring for me, not you." He tried really hard not to let Drake's wounded expression bother him, but it did. "I can take care of myself and I can make my own decisions," Aaron stubbornly went on, ignoring his guilt. "I'm becoming a Hunter and if Dad doesn't like it, then he's going to have to come here and stop me himself."

***

As Aaron trudged up the stairs, he could barely keep his eyes open. He had forced a few bites of mashed potatoes and roast chicken at dinner tonight, fighting sleep all the time. He wasn't sore, Armana had healed him back to perfect health, but the day's activities had drained him. Who knew getting the stuffing knocked out of you could be so tiring? Aaron snorted at his own thoughts. He really needed his bed.

He walked into his room and, without closing the door, he fell face forward onto his bed. He was asleep almost instantly. It felt like he had just closed his eyes when someone was shaking him by the shoulder.

"Wha–?" A hand muffled his mouth and Aaron shot awake, all sleep draining from him as fear bubbled in its place. He blinked in the darkness, staring wide-eyed at the figure looming over him.

"Shh," the voice whispered. "Don't wake the other two."

Aaron recognised the voice and instantly calmed down. He pulled the hand away from his mouth and frowned. "Kyran?" he whispered. "What are you doing?"

"You'll see," Kyran whispered. "Come on, get up."

"What?"

"Up, from your bed. Follow me downstairs," Kyran said, sounding annoyed. "Hurry up."

Kyran slipped out of the room. As quietly as he could, Aaron padded over to the door and followed Kyran downstairs, leaving Sam and Rose still asleep. He went downstairs and saw a light glowing in the living room. Kyran was waiting for him inside.

"What is it?" Aaron asked, hurrying over to him. "What happened?"

"Nothing," Kyran replied. "Why?"

Aaron stared at him. "You woke me up at – what time is it?"

Kyran glanced at the window, studying the dark sky. "About two in the morning."

Aaron gaped at him. "What'd you wake me up at two in the morning for?" he groaned.

"To teach you a little something called self-preservation," Kyran replied.

Aaron moved to the door. "Two in the morning, Kyran. It's *two* in the morning. I don't want to learn anything right now."

The door thudded closed and a loud click rang through the room, just as Aaron reached for it. Surprised, Aaron turned to stare at Kyran.

"You wanna keep getting your ass handed to you?" Kyran asked, his eyes a blazing green. "'Cause if you've got some sort of masochistic desire to get pounded by Skyler, then I'll open that door and you can go back upstairs and sleep." He paused, holding Aaron's gaze. "But if you actually want to learn how to be a Hunter, then you can spend a few minutes learning the basics of defence."

Aaron stared at him in disbelief. "*You're* going to teach me?"

"No, the fairies are." Kyran narrowed his eyes at him. "Do you see anyone else in here, genius?"

Aaron fought to keep his smile back. "What happened to 'It's not my job to help anyone'?"

Kyran's frown melted and his lips twitched up into an almost smile. "Come on." He gestured to him. "I'm only showing you how to block. Nothing else."

Aaron smiled and walked over, taking his stand before Kyran.

***

"Ready for some world-class beating?" Skyler teased as Aaron followed him up the pathway to their usual spot – the clearing facing the garage and artillery huts.

Aaron didn't reply but noticed a small group of Hunters sitting in front of the garage. "What's with the audience?" he asked.

Skyler smirked. "I thought you'd like it," he said. "Maybe the fear of humiliation will inspire you."

Aaron didn't say anything but turned to survey the group. Ella and Zhi-Jiya were here, so was Omar and Julian. Inside the garage, squatting next to his bike, was Kyran. Ryan was standing next to him. Kyran met Aaron's gaze and a slow smirk spread across his face. Aaron returned it with his own before looking away.

Skyler led Aaron to the middle of the clearing and turned to face him, his condescending smile in place. "Alright. Ready then?" Skyler asked, cracking his knuckles.

Aaron took his stance. "Ready," he confirmed.

Had Skyler been paying attention, he would have noted right away that Aaron's stance was different. He was still standing with his feet apart but his shoulders were pulled down, back straight. He wasn't getting ready to jump out of the way. He was standing his ground. It was the first thing Kyran had corrected last night.

Don't jump out of his way. Stand with confidence. You have just as much power as Skyler. You're not going to move. Plant your feet to the ground. You're going to block him.

Skyler was smirking at him, flexing his fingers. Kyran's words flashed through Aaron's mind.

Use your senses. You can't see Skyler's attacks, but listen for them. Skyler can send a tornado at you without a twitch of his fingers, but that doesn't mean you can't hear it coming.

Aaron stared ahead but made a point of looking past Skyler, past his smirk and his cold eyes. He strained his hearing, on alert for the faintest of sounds.

Listen for it. There's a slight whistle when the air comes rushing at you. It's just like when you throw a ball across the field. You can hear it cut through the air. The powers are the same. Listen for it and you'll hear it. Faint, difficult to make out, but it's there all the same.

Skyler didn't move, except for a very slight jerk of his finger. Aaron knew it was coming. Just like last night, when Kyran had demonstrated a hit by throwing him a jolt of power. Aaron heard the faint, barely audible whoosh as something came speeding at him. Time slowed and Aaron sucked in a breath.

Stand, lift your hands and block the power. Make it ricochet off yourself.

Aaron's brow creased. His hands came up, palms out, the tips of his thumbs touching. Fingers slightly curved, just like Kyran had shown him. He felt the power hit his hands and the force was enough to have him stagger back a step. Aaron pulled both hands down and out, forcing the jolt of air to hit, gather itself into a ball under his fingers, and bounce straight back.

Skyler didn't expect Aaron to block, let alone knock back his own jolt of power. His surprise cost him as the jolt hit him smack in the chest, throwing him to the ground. Gasps were heard from the gathered crowd. Every eye was on Aaron, who was gaping at Skyler with stunned surprise himself. His hands throbbed. The skin of his palms felt like it had been burnt and a few of his knuckles had cracked when he caught the jolt of power, but Aaron couldn't hold back his grin. He had done it. He had blocked and thrown back Skyler's hit.

Skyler was on his feet in moments, platinum blond hair messy and falling into his narrowed blue eyes. His mouth twisted into a snarl and he started towards Aaron. "Where the hell did you learn that?" he spat.

Aaron didn't say anything, but smirked at the boy's anger.

Skyler turned to look at his friends, all of whom had seen him take a hit from the amateur, joke of a mage, Aaron Adams. His furious gaze found Kyran, still in the garage, wearing an amused smile that spread from ear to ear. The rest of the Hunters looked shocked. Kyran looked downright gleeful.

"Son of a demon!" Skyler growled and darted towards him. "Hey! What the hell do you think you're doing, Kyran?"

Kyran faked a perfect look of confusion. "I'm fixing my bike," he replied.

"Sod off!" Skyler raged. "You know what I'm talking about."

Kyran shrugged. "No idea what you're on about, mate."

"Come on," Skyler scoffed. "Block and throw back? That's practically your signature move!"

Kyran walked over and jumped down the few steps to be on the same level as Skyler. "That's not my signature move," he said. "Block and throw back is a basic move. One you should have taught Aaron from the word go."

Skyler's fury only grew. "You're telling *me* how to train?" he asked. "You lost your mind?"

"You're the one losing his mind," Kyran said, the mirth gone as anger flooded his eyes. "You spent days smacking him around when you should have been teaching him."

"I'll do what I bloody want!" Skyler hissed. "Who are you to tell me otherwise?"

"That's not on, Sky," Ella interrupted, coming to his side. "You said you would train Aaron, not beat him up."

"Yeah," Ryan added. "You volunteered to train him." He gestured to Aaron, who had walked over to stand behind Skyler. "No one forced you. Why are you taking your anger out on Aaron?"

Skyler looked around at the other Hunters. "Fine," he spat. He turned to Aaron. "I'm finished with you! Go and find someone else to train you."

Aaron didn't say anything, but felt his heart drop.

"I'll teach you, Aaron," Kyran said, but his eyes were on Skyler.

Skyler gave him a furious look. He turned to glower at Aaron before walking away.

Kyran shook his head, smirking at Skyler's retreating form. When he turned around, he met Aaron's eyes.

"You really mean it?" Aaron asked. "You'll teach me?"

Kyran held his gaze a moment before smiling and looking away.

"To tell you the truth," he started, "I just really wanted to piss Skyler off." He gave Aaron a head-to-toe look. "But training an Elemental might be fun in itself."

They made their way back to the cottage, working out a training schedule.

"I'm sorry, how many hours?" Aaron asked, flabbergasted.

"Sixteen hours a day is nothing," Kyran assured. "You're training to be a Hunter. It's hard work."

"Yeah, I know, but sixteen hours?"

"I've trained twenty hours a day. Trust me, you can do it," Kyran said.

"Fine, whatever," Aaron gave in. "As long as you don't get me up at two in morning."

"Get over it," Kyran said. "It served you well, didn't it?"

"Yeah." Aaron fell quiet. "I'll have to cut back my hours at the orchard, though."

"I'm sure things will continue to grow without you, like they always have since the beginning of time," Kyran said.

Aaron turned to him. "You always have to be sarcastic?"

"It's my default setting," Kyran replied.

When they neared their cottage, they found Jason Burns waiting for them.

"Ah, there yeh are." Jason gave his usual yellow-toothed smile. "I've been waitin' for yeh."

"Everything alright, Jason?" Aaron asked.

"Aye, aye." Jason waved a hand. "I hav' good news for yeh. I've got yeh yer own p'ace."

Aaron had almost forgot his stay at Kyran's cottage was only temporary. "Oh," he said. "Right, cool."

"Yeh can move in tonight." He winked at Kyran. "Bet yer glad yeh get yer p'ace back, eh?"

Kyran didn't say anything. He looked to Aaron who stared back at him.

"I'd better go and get my things," Aaron said.

"Wait." Kyran held out a hand. "Won't it be...easier if you...stay here?"

Aaron blinked at him. "What?"

"I'm just saying," Kyran replied. "We'll need to train quite a lot and if we're in the same cottage, we can work till late or get up early." He shrugged. "It's up to you. If you want your own place it's cool. I just thought it'd be simpler than going up and down the street at all odd hours of the day."

Aaron turned to Jason. "If Kyran's okay with it, then I don't mind staying at his place. I'll check with Sam and Rose, but I reckon they'd want to stay here too."

Kyran smiled and ducked his head, hiding his grin.

Jason stared at Aaron. "So, yeh dinnae wannit?"

"No." Aaron smiled. "But thank you."

"Nae bother," Jason replied. "I jus' wish I hadnae spen' t'ree days sortin' the dam' p'ace for yeh."

"I'm sorry," Aaron called as Jason walked away, shaking his head. "Sorry, Jason."

Aaron followed Kyran inside and hurried to his room to find Rose already there, sitting on the bed, head lowered over a book.

"Hey," he greeted her. "Guess what? Jason just told me he had a house ready for us to move into, but Kyran insisted we stay here. How weird is that?" He chuckled, unbuttoning his shirt, swapping it for a clean one. "I told Jason we'd stay here – figured we're settled, anyway – but if you and Sam want to move I can talk to Jason and we'll move." He looked over at Rose to see she hadn't moved or reacted to him. She was staring at the book, completely engrossed. "Rose? You heard what I said?"

Rose didn't reply.

"Rose?"

Aaron fastened his last button and walked over to sit next to her. Only when the bed dipped with his weight did Rose lift her head to look at him.

"Aaron?"

"Yeah?" Aaron replied. "What's wrong, Rose? You look like you've seen a ghost?"

Rose shook her head. "It's worse than that," she replied.

Aaron's gaze darted to the book. "What is it?"

Rose licked her lips, looking uncertain as to how to start the conversation. "You...you said you saw that...that map thing in the Hub?"

Aaron narrowed his eyes. "Yeah."

"What...what was the name of the zones? The ones without the Gates?" she asked.

"Hadrian's zones," Aaron replied.

Rose glanced down at her book before looking up at Aaron again. "I thought that's what it was," she said. "I was hoping I was wrong, but I remembered Ella mentioning the name Hadrian." She looked at Aaron. "They told you Hadrian was a demon, right?"

"Yeah," Aaron replied.

"You sure?" Rose asked. They used the actual words 'Hadrian is a demon'?"

Aaron furrowed his brow, thinking back to that day's conversation. "Scott said Hadrian was the enemy and Ella said the ones who lived in Hadrian's zones were demons," he said. "So that makes Hadrian a demon, right?"

Rose shook her head. "The ones living in his zones may be demons, Aaron, but Hadrian's not a demon."

Aaron frowned. "How do you know that?"

Rose faltered before lowering her book and reading it out loud. "*The case gathered interest from all the cities across the realm. Everyone wanted to know the fate of Giovanni, for his crime was of such a nature it divided the mage community. Some wanted Giovanni to pay, others argued he had no choice but to commit the grave act to save his loved ones. But the fate of Perves Giovanni was to rest in the hands of the Elemental council.*" She looked up at Aaron and licked her lips again. "*James Avira, Christopher Adams, Neriah Afton...*" She paused before forcing out the last name. "*...and Hadrian Aedus.*"

Aaron's eyebrows shot up, disappearing behind the stands of hair that fell across his forehead. "Hadrian Aedus?" he repeated. "Hadrian is a mage? He's...he's an Elemental?"

19

THE MAGE WHO FELL

Aaron stormed out of the cottage, the book Rose had been reading clutched in his hand. He found Ella seated at the table, chatting with Ryan and Zhi-Jiya. Aaron raced to Ella's side and slammed the book onto the table.

"Hadrian Aedus?" Aaron spat. "He's a mage?"

Ella stilled. "What?" she asked, as if she didn't understand the question.

"Hadrian," Aaron repeated. "The enemy you lot are fighting, whose name is on the zones that have demons. He's one of us?" he asked. "Hadrian's an Elemental?"

Ella didn't say anything, but her face rapidly paled.

"This fight," Aaron went on, "between Neriah and Hadrian, over the zones. It's a civil war?" He shook his head, green eyes bright with anger as well as disgust. "You lot are ripping apart your world and wreaking havoc on the human realm for what? A fight to put up Gates or a competition to see which mage is better?"

"It's not like that," Ella said. "It's not a civil war, Aaron. Hadrian isn't a mage, not any more."

"What is he then?" Aaron demanded.

Ella paused. The two mages next to her shifted in their seats, looking away from one another. Ella seemed to gather herself and lifted her gaze to meet Aaron's. "He's a vamage."

"A what?" Aaron asked.

Ella grimaced. "A vamage. A disgusting hybrid," she said, "between a mage…" She faltered before pushing on. "…and a vampire."

Aaron stilled, his narrowed eyes widened a little.

Zhi-Jiya silently got up, followed by Ryan. They left the table. Wordlessly Aaron sat down in the chair next to Ella. For long moments Ella didn't speak. She seemed to be collecting herself.

"Hadrian Aedus," she said quietly, "is known as the Mage Who Fell." She paused before looking up, soft grey eyes squinting in the sunlight. "The mages are supposed to be an example of unity. So what do you do when one of your own turns on you?"

"What happened?" Aaron asked. "How did Hadrian go from being a mage to a...a vamage?"

Ella laughed a bitter, cold laugh. "If we could have the answer to that, we'd halve our problems." She shook her head. "No one knows what happened. No one saw it coming. Hadrian was perfectly content one day, and the next he became worse than the things we hunt." Ella turned to look at Aaron, her face taut with emotion, her eyes glistening. "Stories about Hadrian say he was brilliant – smart, powerful, driven. He was passionate about mages, about Elementals. Then one day he walked away. When he came back, he was no longer a mage."

Aaron felt a prickle of fear race down his spine. "How did it happen?" he asked. "Was he attacked by a vampire?"

Ella scoffed. "Some say it was accidental, but they ignore the fact that a mage can't be *accidentally* turned into a demon. They have to willingly give up their purity. Mages weren't created to be demonic, Aaron. They don't turn like a human would. The mage has to consent. They have to want to become something other than a mage, otherwise they would simply die." She went quiet for a moment, collecting her thoughts. "Hadrian disappeared for a while. No one knew what had happened to him. When he came back, he was different. Quieter. He kept himself secluded. No one realised what had happened. No one picked up on it." She took in a shuddering breath and closed her eyes. "Until Hadrian's self resolve broke and he attacked. He killed James Avira." She looked over at Aaron and added, "Skyler's uncle."

Aaron's heart clenched in sympathy. No one deserved to have their family murdered, not even a git like Skyler. "That's horrible," he said.

"Horrible?" Ella stared at him. "Aaron, part of our bond as a mage is that we're all linked to each other. That's why we can't kill each other. We can do what we like: stab, cut, shoot, hurt each other all we want, but we can never *kill* one of our own, except of course by the ritual but–"

"Wait, ritual?" Aaron frowned. "What's the ritual?"

Ella closed her eyes and shook her head. "It's...it's disgusting. Trust me, you don't–"

"Ella?" Aaron interrupted. "Please."

Ella looked at him, holding his gaze until giving in with a resigned sigh. "You have to forge a special bullet," she started, in a tone that told how revolted she was. "You then carve the name of the mage you want to kill into the bullet. Only at dusk, if the mage is shot in the spot between their eyes with the named bullet, will they die." She shuddered. "You can imagine how many times that's happened. No one has the courage to carve the name of their brother or sister into a bullet and then shoot them like that, no matter what."

"So it's all theoretical?" Aaron asked. "It's never happened?"

Ella's expression darkened. "It's happened," she admitted. "A few mages have been executed." She shook her head. "But that's got nothing to do with Hadrian," she said. "He's no longer a pure mage. He's a vamage. His demonic power gave him the ability to kill another mage, to kill James Avira. You can't understand how devastating that one death became for the mages. For the first time in our history, a mage – if only a partial one – took the life of another in such a way. This wasn't a demon that crawled out of hell's lap. This was one of our own who turned on us."

"What happened then?" Aaron asked. "Hadrian ran?"

"No, Neriah caught him."

Aaron could hear the note of pride in her voice. "Neriah?" he asked. "Neriah Afton?" At Ella's nod, Aaron asked, "Is he your father?" He doubted it. Ella wouldn't call her dad by his name.

"Uncle," Ella replied. "Maternal." Her expression grew solemn. "The only family I have left." She paused for a moment before taking in a breath. "Neriah was too late to save James but he captured Hadrian after seeing what he had become."

Aaron didn't want to know what that discovery must have felt like. He imagined finding Sam or Rose as something else, something no longer human. He shuddered and pushed the thought out of his mind. "What did Neriah do?" he asked.

"What Hadrian deserved," Ella replied. "He bound Hadrian's powers, locked them deep within his core so he couldn't use them."

"Why didn't he just kill him?" Aaron asked. "Hadrian was part demon, it wouldn't be against the mage code to kill him."

Ella paused. "No, it wouldn't," she agreed, "but Neriah couldn't bring himself to kill Hadrian." She looked down at the table. "You have to understand, back then when all the Elementals were together, it was like one big family. Neriah, Hadrian, James, your dad." She looked over at him. "They were all like brothers. Hadrian had turned and killed James, but Neriah was still a mage and he couldn't take his brother's life."

Aaron didn't have any family other than his parents and Michael. Sam was the closest thing he had to a brother and he knew, without a shadow of a doubt, he wouldn't be able to hurt Sam, no matter what. "So what did Neriah do?" he asked.

"He imprisoned Hadrian, foolishly believing he could cure him," Ella said. "But Hadrian got away. For a few years he lay low, quietly building his own army. He lured mages to his side, turning them into this hybrid of mage and vampire. When he had enough by his side, he declared war on us."

Aaron's eyes widened in realisation. "Hadrian's zones," he murmured. "That's why they cause disasters in the human realm. It's the vamages there that are using the power of the elements," he said. "Because they're still part mage."

"Yeah, part mage and they use that part to their own disgusting advantage," Ella said.

"What do you mean?" Aaron asked.

"Vamages can use elemental power as well as the demonic power they get from being part vampire." Her lips curled in disgust. "The vamages can kill us, because their demonic power allows them to deliver a fatal blow, but their mage part protects them against our attacks."

Horrible understanding filled Aaron. "They can kill us," he said, "but we can't kill them."

"The only way is a Q-Zone," Ella said. "Something that destroys anything left inside it." A frustrated breath left her and she reached up to rub at her forehead, as if soothing a headache. "Problem is, the vamages know how a Q-Zone works. They were once mages themselves. They won't fall for any of our traps."

"So how do you destroy them?" Aaron asked.

"We don't," Ella admitted. "We drive them out of zones using our powers and, at times, outnumbering them." She sighed. "Doesn't always work, considering Hadrian's army is growing day by day." She let out a frustrated breath. "His own species of vamage is slowly taking over the world, invading zone after zone. Not to mention that Scorcher of his who's burning this realm to the ground bit by bit."

Scorcher. Aaron had heard that name before. He remembered it from the one and only Hub meeting he had attended.

"I don't get something," Aaron said with a frown. "How could Hadrian make his own army? How can he fight when Neriah bound his powers?"

"Hadrian doesn't need his powers to turn mages into vamages," Ella said. "He can do that with his charm alone. Hadrian derives his strength from his demonic part. He doesn't fight mages – he can't without his powers – but he has plenty of others to do his bidding."

"But what does he want?" Aaron asked. "Why is he after the zones? Wouldn't he be after Neriah instead?"

"Hadrian wants power," Ella said. "It's probably why he gave up his purity and became part vampire, because of the power it would reward him. But Neriah foiled his plan and took away his powers. So what does Hadrian do in return? Once he gets enough support, he starts tearing down the Gates and taking over the zones." She shook her head. "Don't you see it? He's making this realm his kingdom to gain power. Destroying the human world is just a bonus."

Aaron felt his stomach lurch with disgust. "What do the humans have to do with all this?" he asked. "Why is Hadrian involving them?"

"Because he's a demon," she said. "Demons feast on the innocent. They kill as many as they can: humans, mages – it's all the same to them." She paused, her face twisted in a mixture of anger and disgust. "But Hadrian's gone a step further than demons."

"What do you mean?" Aaron asked.

"Mages are all connected," she repeated. "But even more so when we go into a realm that isn't ours. When a mage goes to the human realm and uses their power, any other mage in the human realm will be able to feel it. They'll know exactly where the other mage is and they'll come to their aid."

Aaron sat back as it finally made sense to him. That night, when he had inadvertently cracked open the ground to stop the car, his mum, dad and uncle Mike came to him, knowing exactly where he was.

"That's how they knew," he muttered under his breath.

Then another realisation came to him and it made Aaron's breath choke in his chest. He turned to Ella with wide, fearful eyes. Ella nodded, reading the question from his expression alone.

"If a mage can feel another's presence, then so can the vamages," she said.

"Those...those men." Aaron swallowed hard, trying to speak past his frantically beating heart. "The ones that came that night and attacked Mr and Mrs Mason. They...they were vamages?"

"You used your powers to save yourself and your friends," Ella said.

"Your parents felt your power but so did the vamages. That's what they do, Aaron. They surf the human realm, just waiting for Hunters to slip up and use their powers, so they can either kill them or convert them. Humans marked by the Trace become visible to the vamages and so are found and killed." She paused, regarding Aaron closely. "Your instinctual reflux gave your location away and the vamages came for you. Sam and Rose saw you using your power, so the Trace went on them. The moment they tried to run home, the vamages – being the disgusting cowards that they are – decided to attack the vulnerable humans instead of the mages present."

Aaron already knew that the ones to kill Mr and Mrs Mason had come that night because of the power he had unleashed to stop the car. But he'd never thought he and those monsters could be connected like this. Never in his life did he think the cruel beings that killed his best friends' parents were part mage.

Aaron rubbed at his head, turning to look away. His eyes widened when he saw Rose standing to the side. She must have followed him out of the cottage. Aaron stood up, staring at her. From the look of utter devastation on her face, she had heard every word.

***

Kyran placed the last bottle on the wall and stepped back. "Alright." He rubbed his hands together. "Go for it."

"I don't know about this," Aaron said.

Kyran turned to him. "Why?"

"I don't feel comfortable."

"Why not?"

Aaron turned to glare angrily at him, squinting in the bright sunlight. "Because it's not me!"

Kyran chuckled and walked over to him.

"It is you," he said, propping himself next to Aaron against the low wall. "It's a part of who you are, deep down. You know that."

Aaron shook his head, vehemently denying it. "*This* is not me!" He held out his hand, clutched around the silver pistol.

"Deny it all you want," Kyran said. "But as it comes down to it, *this*," he pointed to the gun in Aaron's hand, "is in your blood. It's who you are. Why you were created." He smirked at Aaron. "Fighting it will only tire you. Fight *with* it, and it'll bring you nothing but success."

"The only thing this brings is death," Aaron said, feeling a horrible sense of déjà vu, but too occupied to figure out why exactly.

Kyran sighed and straightened up. "Suit yourself," he said, grabbing his pistol back from Aaron. "Good luck hunting without any weapons."

"Kyran!" Aaron called after him as he started walking away. "I want to learn how to use my powers, not guns."

"When you're hunting in the human realm you can't use your powers," Kyran said, stopping to turn and face him. "This," he held up the gun, "is your power then. Your sword, your guns, your blades – they're an extension of your hand. You have to learn to use them as such."

Aaron felt his already darkening mood take a further plunge. "Because of the vamages?" he asked bitterly. "We can't use our powers in the human realm in case vamages are lurking around."

"Pretty much," Kyran replied. "And of course to avoid putting the Trace on any spying humans."

Aaron ran a hand through his hair, exhaling deeply. "Fine!" he bit out. "Give me the gun."

Kyran smirked but held out the semi-automatic pistol.

Aaron grabbed hold of the firearm and went over Kyran's instructions again in his head. He reached out and slid the rack back. Breathing out a slow, calm breath, Aaron held up the gun, one hand underneath to steady the firearm. He took aim at the first dark brown glass bottle sitting on the wall at least three metres from him. He aimed and pulled the trigger. The shot rang loudly but nothing happened to the bottle. It sat untouched. Aaron dropped his hands with a grimace.

Kyran looked from the bottles back to Aaron. "That's amazing. You managed to get the bullet to go completely in the opposite direction. You know what to do? Aim at the other wall, you might hit the bottles."

Aaron glowered at him. "Sarcasm is the lowest form of wit."

"And pointing that out is the lowest form of cool," Kyran returned.

Aaron ignored him and took aim again. The second shot rang out and missed, leaving the bottles untouched. Aaron took the next shot, then the next and the next. Each one missed its target.

"Wow," Kyran said dryly. "You missed *every single* bottle." He gave him a mocking grin. "Nice one, Ace."

Aaron ignored him and took the last shot. It too missed.

Kyran let out a sigh, hands on his hips and head dropped. "Mages are born with good aim," he muttered.

"You're not helping!" Aaron snapped.

Kyran took the gun from him, loaded a full clip and turned to face him. With his eyes on Aaron, Kyran aimed at the bottles and blew each one off the wall until nothing was left but shattered glass.

"It's not hard," Kyran said as he handed the gun back to Aaron. He waved a hand and another dozen bottles floated up to line the top of the wall.

"Where did you get so many bottles from?" Aaron asked moodily.

"The beer fairy," Kyran replied. "Focus on shooting the damn things, will you?"

Aaron ignored him and took aim again.

"What's going on here?" Scott's voice came from behind them.

Aaron turned and lowered his gun. A sharp look from Kyran and Aaron fumbled with the little lever on its side, decocking it.

"Kyran is teaching you how to shoot?" Scott asked, as if it were the strangest thing in all the realms.

"Yeah," Aaron replied. "Apparently it's part of the requirement of becoming a Hunter."

Scott looked surprised. "A Hunter?" he asked. "You?" He eyed him for a moment before smiling. "Taking over the family business, huh?"

Aaron fought to keep his expression clear of bitter anger. "Something like that."

"It's good," Scott said. "We need more Hunters." He winked before laughing. "It'll be good for you to understand the dynamics of how to use your powers."

"Yeah, if we ever get to that part," Aaron said, throwing Kyran a look.

"You can't hit a stationary target three metres from you," Kyran said. "We'll deal with moving the earth later."

Scott chuckled, shaking his head. "Take it easy on him," he told Kyran. "I came to tell you there's a meeting in exactly thirty minutes. Get yourself down to the Hub." He looked at Aaron. "You too, Hunter." He smiled and turned to walk away.

"Half an hour," Kyran said. "Let's see how many bottles you can miss."

***

"Welcome, everyone, to another meeting." Scott smiled at the twenty or so mages. "Let's get the updates out of the way. Firstly, we got confirmation from Latan. The devastation was indeed the work of the Scorcher."

A ripple of incensed muttering spread across the room. Scott raised a hand and the mages quietened.

"Secondly, we've received information that suggests the Scorcher is moving east," Scott said. His hand hovered over the map and it changed, zooming into the mess of spidery, thin lines. "If we plan this right, we may just have a chance to get the son of a demon."

Agreement swept through the room.

"There'll be more on that in the next few meetings," Scott said. "The topic for today is the Ichadaris in Danwan. They are posing a real threat to the locals. There have been teams sent out over the last month or two but they've failed. So, it's come to us."

Ryan snorted loudly. "Of course it's come to us. We're freaking brilliant."

"There's the modesty I love." Zhi-Jiya grinned.

"Seriously, though," Omar said, "the other teams can't handle a bunch of Ichis?"

"Apparently teams have been 'lost' over these particular Ichis," Ella said.

"No, no." Scott waved a hand in dismissal, scrunching up his face. "No one's been lost. The hunts have failed, but no lives have been lost, thank Heavens."

"Alright," Skyler drawled, looking bored. "When do we move out?"

"Tomorrow," Scott replied. "Get plenty of rest tonight. You'll be going first thing in the morning." He clapped his hands. "That's it. Thank you for your attention. You can go now." He turned to the table and leant over it, examining the map.

Aaron remained seated while the rest of the mages got up and started to make their way out the doors.

"Coming?" Kyran asked, standing up.

"Yeah, in a minute," Aaron said. "I need to ask Scott something."

Scott looked up at the mention of his name. "Really?" he asked with a frown. "What do you want to ask me?"

"The Scorcher," Aaron called out. "You've mentioned him before but I don't know who he is."

Skyler and Ella were almost out the door when they stopped, turning to look at Aaron. An expression of unease blanketed Scott's face. He stepped away from the table, shaking his head.

"Of course," he mumbled. "You have no knowledge of him." He stepped forward, rubbing his hands nervously. "Now that you're training to be a Hunter, I think it's imperative that you understand the war and where the situation currently stands. Even your father can't raise an objection against that."

"Don't worry about my dad," Aaron said at once. "Or his objections."

Scott looked a little thrown by Aaron's brazen disregard for his father's wishes, but he didn't comment on it. "Okay." He looked over at Kyran and then Skyler, seemingly trying to figure out what to say. "I think it's best to start at the beginning." He walked over and sat down next to Aaron. His expression grew solemn. "To understand the war, you have to understand who Hadrian is."

"A vamage," Aaron answered.

"You know about that?" Scott asked in surprise.

Aaron glanced awkwardly at Ella. "Found out just recently."

Scott nodded, his expression darkening. "Hadrian turned about sixteen years ago," he started in a quiet voice. "When he escaped Neriah, Hadrian was the one and only vamage. A hybrid had never existed before." He looked around at Aaron. "There was nothing known about such a creature. Half mage, half vampire. What were its powers? What were its weaknesses? No one knew. Neriah bound Hadrian's power, locking it. Truth was, most of us thought Hadrian would die. Our powers are linked to our life force. If our powers are taken, so is our life."

"But Hadrian didn't die?" Aaron asked.

"No," Scott replied. "His demonic powers sustained his life force." He looked down at his hands, which had curled into balls. "He should have died," he whispered. He raised his head, his expression showed his struggle to remain composed. "For about a year, nothing happened," he managed to continue. "Neriah and the rest thought it was the last they'd seen of Hadrian, but Hadrian was slowly and quietly building an army of his own – vamages like him but with their powers unbound. They became his strength and Hadrian declared war by tearing down the first Gate."

"When did he do that?" Aaron asked.

"About fifteen years ago," Scott replied, "but it wasn't so bad. Hadrian tore down a few Gates and took over the zones but Neriah fought back. When Hadrian tore a Gate down, Neriah and his mages went in and set it back up again. They snatched the zones back from Hadrian, only for another Gate and zone to fall victim to the vamages. It went on like that for years. Even then Neriah managed to keep Hadrian back. I don't think Hadrian ever got more than three or four zones at any one time."

Aaron frowned. The map he had seen had nineteen red zones – Hadrian's zones. His confusion must have been clear to read, for Scott nodded sadly at him.

"Two years ago, we started losing the zones. One by one, the Gates fell and vamages took over. We couldn't get past their defences. The power behind their attacks had increased a hundred fold. In a matter of months, they took over twenty zones."

"How?" Aaron asked, horrified. "What happened?"

Scott held his gaze. "The Scorcher happened."

"Son of a demon popped up out of nowhere," Skyler added.

"I don't understand." Aaron looked to Scott.

"The Scorcher," Scott said, "is the reason Hadrian took twenty zones in six months. The Scorcher is the leader of the vamages. They're under his control. With Hadrian's powers still locked, it's the Scorcher's power that we're really up against."

"Why's this Scorcher so strong?" Aaron asked.

Scott paused, taking in a deep breath. "The Scorcher," he said, "is Hadrian's son."

Aaron's eyes widened with surprise. "Son?" he asked.

"Vampires can't procreate," Ella said, "and at first we thought the same would be true for vamages." She took in a long breath. "But like Scott said, not a lot is known about vamages. Their species is only sixteen years old."

"How do you know he's Hadrian's son?" Aaron asked.

"The Scorcher wields the Blade of Aedus," Scott replied. "Only Hadrian's direct descendant could do that."

"And the Scorcher is proof himself," Kyran added. "Only Hadrian's son could do the things he does."

"Hadrian didn't have any descendants when he was a mage," Scott said, "so it stands to reason that the Scorcher was born after Hadrian turned. We're assuming that vamages follow the same growth pattern as mages. At age thirteen the core awakens and powers start to come through."

"Which is why after years and years of sitting on only three zones, suddenly Hadrian's kingdom grew to twenty zones practically overnight," Ella said.

"It took six months," Kyran corrected.

"Details," Ella brushed him off.

"That's when the Scorcher turned thirteen," Aaron realised. "He started taking the zones as soon as his core awoke."

"Hadrian must have impregnated some poor woman soon after escaping Neriah," Ella said.

"Probably with the sole purpose of having a descendant do his bidding," Skyler added.

"And the Scorcher does his father's bidding well," Scott said. "He's tearing this world and the human realm to pieces at Hadrian's orders."

Aaron shook his head, trying to slow the influx of information so it all made sense. "Why do you call him the Scorcher?" he asked.

"Why do you think?" Skyler asked, in his usual, annoyed-because-you-spoke tone.

"'Cause he's hot." Ella smirked.

"He is?" Aaron asked.

"How am I supposed to know?" Ella asked. "I haven't seen him."

"The call him the Scorcher," Kyran started, "because he burns everything he touches. That's the *hot* reference." He looked over at Ella and pulled a face. "Not particularly clever."

Ella shrugged.

Of course, Aaron berated himself mentally. He should have known that. *Avira have the power of Air, Afton have the power of Water, Adams have the power of Earth so Aedus must have the power of Fire.*

"Hadrian's powers were bound by Neriah," Scott said, "but the Scorcher has his powers. He's an Elemental, so the force of his power is phenomenal. If he comes into his full power, he will destroy this realm and all the others with barely a twitch of his finger."

"Full powers?" Aaron asked. Then he realised the Scorcher had only turned thirteen two years ago, proven by the takeover of the zones at that time. Which meant that the Scorcher was only... "Fifteen," Aaron breathed. "He's...he's fifteen." The Scorcher – the one destroying this realm and wreaking absolute havoc on the human realm was a boy, only a year older than him.

"The Scorcher may be only fifteen," Scott started, "but he's got more power than most. Not only is he an Elemental but also a vamage. His power is such that in the two years since his core awakened, we've only been able to take back one zone – leaving the score nineteen to seven."

"And if this kid reaches the glorious age of nineteen before we get him," Skyler said, "he's going to be what Hadrian would have been if Neriah hadn't bound his powers: a full blown Elemental mage with all the demonic powers of a vampire."

"Which means the war will be over and all of us will be dead," Ella added.

"We'll get him," Kyran said, his voice quiet and full of promise. "We'll get him before he comes of age. We're going to win this war."

"Yes, we will," Scott agreed with a small smile. "We'll win the war, one hunt at a time."

***

Breakfast the next morning was loud and messy. The Hunters were in a great mood, clearly excited for the hunt. They were already in their 'hunting outfits': heavy boots, dark jeans, long-sleeved hooded tops which were half-zipped to show the plain vests underneath. Narrow leather bands lined with shiny metal blades criss-crossed their backs and torsos. Everyone had holsters snapped onto their belts for their firearms. Aaron noted that a few – namely Skyler, Kyran, Ryan and Zhi-Jiya – had sheaths for their swords attached to the leather strap on their back. Their rowdiness pulled even Sam and Rose out of their quiet melancholy.

"What's up with them?" Sam asked, his voice lacking its usual warmth.

"They're going on a hunt today," Aaron replied, eager to have Sam talking again. Ever since Rose overheard his conversation about vamages, both she and Sam had been awfully quiet.

"Hunt?" Sam narrowed his eyes. "You going?"

Aaron shook his head. "Scott won't let me go. Not until he deems me ready."

Sam gave a tight nod. "Good. At least someone's got their head screwed on right."

"I wish I was going," Aaron confessed. "I want to see a hunt."

"What are they hunting?" Rose asked, leaning in towards him. There was something in her tone and an odd glint in her eyes that unnerved Aaron.

"Um, it's a weird name. Icha...something." Aaron paused. "Ichadaris, I think."

Sam frowned. "Icha what now?"

"Ichadaris." Aaron shrugged. "I don't know what they are. Some weird type of demon, I guess."

Sam grunted. "Sounds like a bad rash to me."

Aaron chuckled.

"Where is it?" Rose asked. "Here or our world?"

Aaron stared at her, trying to figure out what it was that was alarming him, but he couldn't put his finger on it. "Here," he said. "Some place called Danwan."

Rose nodded and looked away, promptly losing all interest.

Aaron reached out, holding on to her hand. "You okay?"

Rose nodded. "Fine." She pulled her hand out from under his and got up, walking away.

Aaron turned to look at Sam, but the other boy dropped his head low and concentrated on his bowl of porridge. Aaron looked away, his heart clenching with a sense of dark foreboding.

***

After breakfast, the Hunters mounted their bikes and gathered in the street, like they had when they were about to go to the Q-Zone. Of course, at that time their number was a lot greater than now. This time it was only the twenty or so Salvador Hunters, grinning from ear to ear, revving their bikes in excited anticipation. Aaron saw the outfits were complete with the long coats, hiding the inventory of weapons adorned on each Hunter's body. Skyler was wearing his fancy coat again, ivory white with the spiral mark in silver. It reminded Aaron of the green coat he saw his dad wearing in the flesh memory. He shook the memory aside, not wanting to focus on it. He noted there was no sign of the cut or blood stains he had seen at the shoulder when Skyler returned from the Q-Zone hunt. The coat had been repaired to it's former glory.

Aaron stepped up to Kyran's side as he and Ryan tightened their binds and pulled on their gloves, before twisting the handlebars and making their bikes growl under them.

"How's Lexi doing?" Aaron asked with a grin.

"Not as well as Susie," Ryan answered quickly. Grinning, he patted his bike. "My baby is the fastest."

"Delusion is such a pretty thing." Kyran smirked.

"You hear him, Abigail?" Ryan turned his head to the side. "Sounds like we're gonna have to show him and his sweet Lexi by making the most hits."

"I take it Susie's your bike," Aaron said, pointing to the red Kawasaki Ninja under Ryan. "But who's Abigail?"

Ryan reached back and pulled his sword partly out of its sheath. "Aaron meet Abigail. Abigail, this is Aaron Adams." He pushed the sword back into its holder

Aaron couldn't help but laugh. "Susie?" he questioned. "Lexi? Abigail? Your bikes and blades are girls?"

"All good things in life, mate." Ryan grinned.

"There's a custom with Hunters," Kyran explained. "A Hunter's very first bike and sword is named after someone they love."

It clicked into place and Aaron turned to look at Ryan with heartfelt understanding. Ryan smiled, but this time it held sadness rather than its usual cheekiness.

"Abigail was my sister," he revealed. "And Susie was my childhood sweetheart. I lost both of them when Lycans ravaged my city."

Aaron's stomach lurched horribly. "Ryan." He felt his mouth go dry. "I'm so sorry."

Ryan smiled at him, the kind of smile that masks pain of the worst kind. "The Lycans played their hand," he said. "We'll play ours." He smirked. "Abigail here has tasted more demon blood than her fair share." He patted the hilt of his sword. "And she's gonna get more today." He revved his bike and grinned. "Let's get to this dance already!" he yelled before speeding off, going to the front.

"Ryan's in a hurry," Scott mused, walking up to stand next to Aaron.

"We all are," Kyran said, nodding to the front of the crowd. "Say your stuff, so we can go do our stuff."

Scott laughed. "Patience, Kyran. You can go as soon your apprentice climbs aboard."

Aaron turned to Scott with shocked surprise. "Sorry?"

"I heard you at the table," Scott said with a smile. "You said you wanted to see the hunt."

"You serious?" Kyran asked Scott.

"I think it's a great idea for Aaron see a hunt," Scott replied.

"Scott, it's Ichadaris," Kyran reminded.

"Ichadaris are tame compared to Lycans and vamages," Scott said. "An Ichi hunt is the safest for a Hunter-in-training to observe." He pulled a long silver chain from his pocket, just like the ones Kyran and the rest of the Hunters were wearing. This one had a silver circle dangling from it. Scott slipped the chain over Aaron's head. "So you can communicate with me and the Hunters," Scott explained.

Kyran shook his head. "This is a mistake," he argued. "He's not ready."

"*He* is standing right here," Aaron said, annoyed. "And I wanna go."

"It's too risky," Kyran said, turning to Aaron.

"That's why he's going with you," Scott replied. "I trust you'll keep Aaron safe."

Kyran glared at Scott. "Did I do something to piss you off?" he asked. "Are you punishing me?"

Scott laughed, his eyes twinkling with amusement. "Hurry up. You're leaving in two minutes." He walked past them, heading to the front.

"Wait!" Kyran called after him. "He doesn't have any weapons!"

"That's because he doesn't need them," Scott replied, pausing to look back at Aaron. "He's not hunting, only observing." His eyes flashed at Aaron. "Understood?"

Aaron nodded, barely holding back his grin. Scott nodded at him, smiled at Kyran's furious look and walked away. Kyran growled something under his breath – something Aaron was willing to bet wasn't very polite. Fierce green eyes turned to Aaron and narrowed at him.

"Get on, already!" Kyran bit out.

Aaron quickly climbed onto the bike, holding on to Kyran's shoulders.

"Don't touch me!" Kyran snapped.

Aaron didn't know where else to hold on, so he reached back and gripped the edge of the seat.

"Alright." Scott clapped his hands, getting everyone's attention. "Time for a good clean out, boys and girls." He grinned. "Send the Ichadaris back to the hell hole they slithered out of." He held out a hand in the direction of the Gate, which obediently slid open.

Aaron felt excitement explode in the pit of his stomach. Since arriving, this was the first time he was stepping out of Salvador. From somewhere in the back of his mind, his mum's voice whispered, *You are protected as long as you stay in Salvador.*

Guilt surged within him but there was no time to change his mind. Scott gave his last commanding nod, and Skyler and Ella charged towards the Gate, the rest of the Hunters roaring after them.

Kyran took off with a vehement burst of speed, almost knocking Aaron clean off the bike. Aaron latched onto Kyran, not caring about his previous warning. Kyran didn't reproach him. He was too busy racing to the front. They whipped through the Gate and along the pathway that Aaron had seen upon first arriving – the long road with the perfect trees lined along either side. A glowing ball of light sat at the end of the road, dazzling and bright.

The crowd of Hunters sped along the road, seemingly headed for the light, but quarter of a mile away, Skyler and Ella turned to the right and led them into the forest, across a thin pathway snaking its way through the trees. It was so dark here the only things Aaron could see were several bike headlights before him. A faint sliver of light beckoned them closer, far off in the distance. Aaron clutched onto the fabric of Kyran's coat; the red and black thick material scrunched under his tense fingers.

The closer they rode, the bigger and brighter the light became. It started taking shape and Aaron was stunned to see that the rays of light rearranged themselves into Aric's mark. It glowed brightly, a shimmer running through it. Skyler and Ella were the first to reach it. They rode straight through it, and disappeared.

Aaron would have gasped if the rushing wind had allowed it. The only thing Aaron could do was close his eyes as Kyran headed into the circle of light, straight through the legs of the inverted V and smack into the centre of the shimmering spiral.

20

THE ICHADARIS OF DANWAN

The bike came to a stop and Aaron opened his eyes. He unclenched his hold on Kyran and sat up, staring at his surroundings. They had passed through the glowing Aric's mark, which Aaron now understood was a portal, and entered a rural and peaceful-looking village. In the distance there were small mud huts with wide cone-shaped roofs, a fire that had long since gone out and what looked like rocks and rubble heaped in small mounds next to some of the huts.

Kyran switched off his bike and turned his head to the side. "Hey, Adams?" He still sounded mad. "Planning on getting off Lexi anytime soon?"

Aaron frowned. "That doesn't sound right," he said, but climbed off.

He caught the reluctant smile crossing Kyran's face but when the older boy swung his leg over and stood up, his expression was carefully arranged to indifference. The Hunters gathered into a tight group, scanning the area.

"Where is everyone?" asked Sarah, one of the dark-haired mages, as she squinted in the bright sunlight. "The whole place is deserted."

"Devoured more like," Julian revised.

"We should split and search," Ella said, her tone commanding than suggestive.

The twenty Hunters split into five teams, with Aaron added to Kyran's team. The groups headed out in different directions, trying to find a living being who could tell them what was going on.

Aaron walked behind Kyran, Ryan beside him. Two Hunters, both girls he had never spoken to, walked behind him. The heat beat down on them as they crossed the messy lines of huts. Their boots kicked up clouds of dirt and dust as they walked. Aaron took in his surroundings with interest. This was the first place he'd seen in the mage realm other than the City of Salvador. He had to admit as rural and village-like as Salvador was, it had its charm compared to this place.

"*Talk to me.*" Scott's sudden voice made Aaron jump. "*What do you see?*"

Kyran reached up and touched his spiral pendant to reply. "The place is deserted. The residents must be in hiding. We've split up to find what we can."

"*Good*," Scott replied in Aaron's head. "*Watch for the signs.*"

"We know," Ryan replied. "Not our first Ichi hunt, Scott."

"That was so weird." Aaron shook his head.

"What?" asked one of the girls – a blonde with a thin, pointed face.

"Scott's voice," Aaron replied. "In my head."

The girl frowned at him and looked away. The brunette by her side smiled kindly at Aaron. "That's nothing. Wait till you hear full conversations happening."

"Really?" Aaron asked.

"You'll hear anyone with the same sign as you." She pointed to his necklace. "When they talk to Scott, you'll hear their conversation."

Kyran held out a hand, gesturing for them to stop. His narrowed green eyes were staring at something in the distance. The other three Hunters went still, painfully alert. Guns in hand, they waited for Kyran's instructions. Aaron craned his neck to see past the huts but he couldn't see what had halted Kyran.

"What is it?" he whispered.

"Shut up, Aaron!" Kyran hissed. "Listen."

Aaron fell silent but he couldn't see or hear anything.

"Bloody hell," Ryan gasped, eyes widening. "You've got to be kidding me."

"What?" Aaron whispered. "What is it?"

"You don't hear that?" the blonde asked, her pointed face seemed even longer with annoyance. "The music?"

Aaron frowned. He couldn't hear anything but the whistling wind.

"Listen," the brunette instructed. "Really, listen."

"Forget it, Danielle," the blonde said. "Don't even bother with him."

"Give him a break, Jean," Ryan called over his shoulder. "It's his first hunt."

Aaron concentrated, straining his hearing, but all he could pick up was the wind. Kyran and Ryan led the way further down the road. It was another three minutes before Aaron heard the faint beat of a drum and the sound of bells ringing. They turned a corner and went into a thick cluster of trees. The sound of the drums was getting louder the further they went into the forest. Aaron could even make out clapping. When Aaron followed Kyran out of the trees, he found the strangest sight before him.

It seemed like the whole village of Danwan had gathered in this small clearing. Men, women and children alike were sitting around a fire, laughing and clapping as others played strange instruments – what looked like a cross between drums and tambourines. But Aaron's gaze quickly went from the villagers and their hybrid instruments to the dancing girls.

They were the most exotic, beautiful girls Aaron had ever seen. Tall, around six feet at least, with wild, dark hair that cascaded down to curl at the small of their backs. They had big, expressive eyes, encased by long, thick black lashes, which they fluttered unashamedly. The villagers laughed joyfully, beating the drums, making the girls sway their tiny hips. Small bells attached to the hems of their skirts gave a tiny jingle. The cropped tops bared their midriffs, exposing flawlessly smooth, tanned skin.

Ryan shook his head, chuckling. "Damn, Danwans," he muttered. "Always ready for a party."

The villagers turned to the five newcomers and smiled, nodding at them in greeting, but turned back to the dance show almost instantly. The dancing girls, all ten of them, looked around at the Hunters with bewitching smiles.

Kyran's gaze was fixed on the girl at the forefront, the one who was staring back at him with big hazel eyes.

"Jean, Dani," Kyran murmured.

That was all it took for the two Hunters to push Aaron down, forcing him to sit. They took their places on either side of him.

"What–?" Aaron exclaimed. "What are you doing?"

"Joining the party," Jean said dryly.

Ryan took a seat next to them. Kyran strode forward with a wide grin, green eyes shining with a hunger Aaron had never seen before. The girl eyed him just as intently. As soon as Kyran reached her, he wrapped a hand around the girl's tiny waist and pulled her forward into his embrace. Aaron's mouth popped open. He hadn't expected that.

"Damn, you're beautiful," Kyran said to the girl. "Where have you been hiding?"

The girl smiled back, showing her line of perfect, glistening teeth. She eased herself from Kyran's arms but didn't move far from him. She swayed her hips in time to the drumbeat, her smoky gaze fixed on Kyran the whole time.

Two girls moved towards Ryan. They took a hand each and pulled him up, leading him away to dance. One by one, the dancing girls pulled up partners from the sitting crowd. A girl moved towards Aaron, but before she could hold out a long-fingered hand, Danielle and Jean crossed their arms over Aaron.

"No!" both spat at once.

The girl stopped, big brown eyes wide with hurt. She looked at Aaron, smiled apologetically and moved away, pulling up another boy.

Aaron turned to the two girls with disappointment. "What was that for?"

"Trust us," Danielle said, glaring at the dancing girls. "You're better off here."

Aaron looked over to Kyran and Ryan's – there were no better words for it – indecent proximity to the dancing girls. Kyran was holding the girl so close their fronts were pressed together, as both swayed to the drumbeat. Aaron couldn't help but stare. It seemed so strange for Kyran to just go up to a seemingly random girl and start dancing with her. Weren't they here to hunt? Shouldn't they be looking for the Ichadaris?

Aaron glanced over at the villagers still seated around the fire, playing the drum-tambourine things. The fire was rather unnecessary. It was still daytime and the sun was scorching above them. In fact, he was already feeling the burn on the back of his neck.

Aaron's gaze studied the man playing the drums. He was sweating. His face was covered in fat droplets of perspiration, his face and neck flushed pink. Yet he didn't move away from the roaring fire. His fingers continued to beat on the drums. A closer look revealed awfully pink fingers, as if he had been playing for hours.

Aaron felt a cold prickle of dread run down his spine. He looked back over at the dancing girls, at their beautiful faces, their wild, tangled locks and the way those smiles lifted up their thin lips, almost in hidden glee.

"Danielle," Aaron whispered. "What exactly are Ichadaris?"

Danielle's hand was sneaking up into her coat, while her eyes stayed on Kyran, Ryan and their dancing partners.

"Demons," she murmured back. "They devour mages, or humans if they slither into their realm." She glowered at the dancing girls. "Disgusting things Ichadaris are." She began sliding something out of her pocket. "Time to send them back to hell."

What she brought out was the weirdest instrument Aaron had ever seen. It was small, no bigger than his hand. It looked like a flute but instead of being a long, thin stick, it was broader and had a round bulge near the top. It reminded Aaron of the flutes he'd seen in books about snake charmers in India.

Danielle paused, the strange flute thing still half hidden in her pocket. Her other hand closed around her silver spiral pendant.

"It's on," she said. "Come if you don't want to miss the party."

"*Be careful.*" Aaron heard Scott's voice.

Danielle pulled the flute out, just as Jean took an identical instrument out of her pocket. No sooner were the wooden flutes out than Danielle and Jean put them to their mouths and started playing. Their tune, a spine-tingling melody, cut through the drums and tambourines. The dancing girls came to a sudden standstill, their expressive eyes widened with horror. With an unearthly hiss, the girls pulled back and, as one, they turned to Jean and Danielle.

Before Aaron's very eyes, the dancer girls started to change. The deep brown of their eyes lightened to yellow. Their pupils slitted. The previously smooth, unblemished skin started to develop a strange rash: small brown and black boxes appeared across their cheeks, travelling down their neck to their arms, stomach and legs.

The villagers stopped playing the drums, seemingly coming out of a trance and gasping in horror at the sight of the changing girls. The boys who had been dancing with them scrambled to get away, crying out in fear. The only exception was Kyran and Ryan, who were smirking openly. The rapidly transforming girls backed away, forming a tight circle in the middle of the stunned crowd.

The girl who was dancing with Kyran tried to step away, but Kyran's firm grip on her arm pulled her back again.

"Where are *you* going?" he asked with a grin as the girl struggled. "You know, I don't understand why girls feel the need to change. Be proud and just be yourself."

The girl hissed at him – *actually* hissed. Aaron recoiled in absolute horror when the girl's eyes narrowed in rage, and she opened her mouth. Gone were the perfect, white teeth. Instead, she had fangs – two sharp, curved fangs that threatened to sink into Kyran's flesh if he didn't let go of her. Kyran's hand closed around her throat, holding her still.

"Don't get hissy with me," Kyran teased.

Jean and Danielle were still playing their strange flutes in a continuous tune – no breaks, no stops. Their cheeks were bulged out, a sign of their circular breathing.

Every single dancing girl was focusing on Jean and Danielle. Terrifying black-slitted yellow gazes were fixed on the flutes playing that tune. The girls shivered, sticking out long, black-forked tongues. Their hissing got louder, fiercer, until fangs bared, the girls came at them at once.

A sudden pandemonium broke out as the villagers leapt to their feet, screaming and crying, running in every direction to get out of the way. A wave of Danielle's hand had the girls flying backwards. The only exception was the girl in Kyran's grip.

"Sorry, Ichi," Kyran said to the girl, "it was never going to work out."

He pushed her towards her crowd of girls. Ryan held out both of his hands, palms facing up. Hovering above both hands were two small fireballs. Transfixed to the spot, Aaron watched in horrid fascination as Ryan sent the fireballs at the girls, one after the other, forcing them to stay back and huddled in a tight group.

The girls kept trying to come for Jean and Danielle in an effort to stop them from playing, as it was clear the longer they played the strange, eerie music, the more of an effect it had on them. The brown and black rash spread across their skin, forming scales. Their bodies began to get tighter, thinner and longer.

"Keep going, keep going," Ryan encouraged Jean and Danielle, as he threw more fireballs at the girls to keep them back. "Almost got 'em."

Jean and Danielle's continuous playing did its work and before Aaron's eyes, the girls changed completely. Their long, wild hair disappeared. Their faces and necks elongated until they merged with their bodies. Their long limbs fused together until, for a terrifying moment, they were no more than tall, thin poles, before they all collapsed to the ground. Gasping in utter horror, Aaron realised where the ten girls had stood there were now ten hissing snakes.

Jean and Danielle stopped playing.

"Finally." Kyran grinned, pulling out his gun. "Now we can really dance."

One of the sandy-coloured snakes leapt towards him, fangs bared. Kyran moved out of the way. Jean and Danielle rushed to their feet, guns drawn and came to Ryan and Kyran's side.

The snakes raised their heads, spitting and hissing at the Hunters. Aaron watched as the Hunters darted out of the way of the attacks. Aaron found himself watching Kyran, almost breathless with fear as he dodged the snakes' fangs. The further Kyran backed up, the closer one snake came to him. Kyran held out a hand and the snake was pushed flat against the ground. It twitched, its pointed tail flapped this way and that, trying to get free from the invisible hold. Kyran stepped forward and pinned the snake under his foot before sliding the rack on his gun back. A single resounding shot and the snake fell still, then turned to ash.

The sound of the first shot sent the other nine snakes into a panic. Their attacks increased in vigour. All four Hunters managed to avoid getting bitten by keeping low, their backs curved as they darted out of the way of deadly fangs.

Again, Aaron could only watch Kyran as he pinned the snakes to the ground with either his power or his foot, and shot each one in the head. From the sound of it, Ryan, Jean and Danielle were doing the same. The last of the ten snakes was shot by Danielle and silence fell around them. Aaron released his breath, unaware he'd been holding it. Kyran looked up at him and waved the hand that was still clutched around his gun, gesturing for him to come over.

Aaron moved forward, his legs shaky under him.

"Keep close," Kyran told him. "It's about to get messy."

Aaron turned to him with an open mouth. "What?" he asked. "Didn't you just kill all of them?"

Kyran turned to look at him incredulously. "Did you think the whole of Danwan was being terrorised by only ten Ichis?"

Cold sweat broke out over Aaron. "How many are there?" he asked.

Kyran pulled out his second gun and grinned. "Enough for all of us."

At first, Aaron didn't notice it. Then he picked up the faint hissing, which got louder with each passing moment. With a sickening lurch in his stomach, he realised what it was: the angry cries of at least a hundred snakes as they slithered out from all directions, coming right at them. The four Hunters stood in a circle, with Aaron in the middle. All four had their guns drawn and aimed.

"Where are the rest?" Jean said.

"Who cares?" Kyran grinned. "More for us."

"Too much for us." Danielle pointed out and held onto her spiral pendant. "Skyler! Get down here!"

"Relax," Kyran drawled in a perfect imitation of the blond-haired Elemental. "He'll get to the party. You know how much he loves his big entrances."

Ryan chuckled, his gaze fixed on the sea of serpents heading their way.

"That's true," he said, "but you're just as guilty of big entrances. Remember the last Lycan hunt?"

Kyran laughed, highly amused. "I choose my moments."

Ryan let out a grunt. "Yeah, but you–"

"Guys," Aaron interrupted. "Poisonous snakes, around the clock!"

The sound of the spitting and hissing snakes was terrifying in itself but to see them sit up, heads raised and fangs bared, was truly frightening. Aaron couldn't look away, even though it was all he wanted to do.

"Come on." Kyran raised both hands, guns cocked and aimed. "Time for the big finish."

His first two shots were the signal and the other three joined in. The sound of gunshots tore through the forest, reverberating throughout Danwan. Aaron covered his ears but it was hardly worth it; he was too close to the guns. His ears were ringing painfully.

The Hunters fired continuously, taking out snake after snake. Standing back to back in a circle, they managed to protect themselves and each other from the surrounding Ichadaris. When Kyran's first gun emptied, he pocketed it and held out his hand, sweeping it back. At least thirty snakes were thrown up into the air. Ryan pulled back his hand and threw out a line of fire right under them. There was nothing to stop the snakes from falling into the flames.

"That'll keep them busy for a while." Ryan grinned. He leant back to speak to Aaron. "The only way to kill an Ichadaris is to crush its head."

"Or make a hole in it," Kyran added and then did exactly that to two snakes.

"Lovely." Aaron grimaced.

"And only when they're in their true forms," Danielle said, pausing to click another magazine into her pistol. "Hence the Bean." She started shooting again.

"Bean?" Aaron asked, then realised she was talking about the strange flute she and Jean had been playing. It was obviously what forced the Ichadaris to turn back to their true snake form. "Not that I don't appreciate it," he started, "but the lesson can wait till after."

"On the field learning," Kyran laughed. "Nothing beats it, Ace."

Aaron saw a stream of snakes, still aflame, come thundering out of the fire, hissing horribly, twisting and turning on the ground. Even with their shooting, burning and using their powers, the Hunters couldn't keep the snakes back for long. A few slippery serpents found their way close enough to try to bite. Aaron understood the need for heavy boots now. Kyran and Danielle made sweeping gestures with their hands and the snakes were blasted away.

Aaron spotted one snake amongst others, coiling itself tightly, rearing back. Aaron knew what it was about to do, even though the idea seems ludicrous. But to his horror, he found the snake launched itself into the air, coming straight at them with an open mouth, its glistening fangs ready. Kyran caught it, as easily as one would catch a ball. He threw the snake down and pinned it under his shoe before shooting it in the head. Following that one snake's example, others started throwing themselves into the air, attacking the Hunters.

Ryan reached for his sword, pulling Abigail out of her sheath. He sliced the serpents that came flying towards them, swinging the sharp blade this way and that. The other three kept shooting, catching the Ichadaris with gloved hands and throwing them back down.

Aaron caught sight of one snake from the corner of his eye, cutting through the air, coming right at him. Aaron didn't turn but ducked instead. The snake landed next to him, having passed through the gap between Jean and Ryan's shoulders to get into the middle of Aaron's protective circle. Aaron could barely breathe, staring at the enraged snake as it reared its head up and looked right at him with its yellow eyes. The snake coiled tight and leapt upwards, fangs ready to sink into Aaron's flesh.

"Ky–!" was all Aaron managed to get out.

It was all that was needed.

Kyran turned and grabbed the snake, before it could get near Aaron. He turned to slam the snake back onto the ground and shot it three times.

Voices, several of them, pierced their way through the ominous hissing and Aaron looked around to see the other Hunters had finally arrived. He caught sight of Ella and Skyler, Julian, Omar and the rest as they came with their guns blazing. Skyler tore his way across the grounds, gun in one hand

and sword in the other. A mighty gust blew around him, pulling the snakes up into the air for him to shoot or slice.

"What'd I tell ya?" Kyran smiled. "Big entrances."

***

The battle didn't last long after the rest of the Hunters arrived. The Ichadaris didn't stand a chance.

"How do you know that's all of them?" Aaron asked Ryan as they walked back to their bikes in the bright sunlight. "There might be some left."

"Nah." Ryan smiled. "The Ichadaris attack together. You kill one of theirs, they'll all come as one to kill you."

"Loyalty," Aaron said. "Not something usually associated with snakes."

"These are Ichadaris," Ryan said. "Snake demons. Vengeance is inbred in these beings."

"The villagers," Aaron said, glancing at the shaken group of people sitting outside their huts. "They looked like they were under a spell."

"Enchantment of the Serpents," Ryan explained. "The Ichadaris can hypnotise and lure you anywhere. Under their trance, you'll do whatever they want. That's how they take their victims; they sit patiently in line while the Ichadaris take their time to eat their way through them."

Aaron grimaced. "That's horrible."

"That's Ichadaris," Ryan replied. "They have the power to shape-shift into pretty much anything, although they prefer to take on the form of beautiful girls." Ryan shuddered. "Such a mind mess, that."

"How come we didn't fall under their spell?" Aaron asked.

Ryan held up his silver necklace, the inverted V dangled from the end. "Aric's mark protects us, even if it's only one of the four symbols."

They reached their bikes and Aaron waited until Kyran mounted his bike first before he climbed on behind.

"So?" Kyran asked as Lexi purred to life. "What'd you think?"

"It was terrifying," Aaron replied honestly. "I don't think I've ever been more scared in my life." He smiled. "So when's the next one?"

Kyran turned to look at him, grinning broadly, a spark of pride in his eyes. He turned the bike around and sped off, following the rest back to Salvador.

***

That night there was a celebration, in honour of the success of the Ichadaris hunt. Before dinner, the Hunters and mages gathered at the table where Scott handed out beer bottles to all of them while Mary followed behind him, giving out tall glasses of fruit cocktails for the younger mages. Distracted by his talk with Mary, Scott put a bottle of beer down in front of Aaron.

Aaron lifted it up to examine the unmarked brown glass bottle. He brought it to his lips but before he could take a sip, Kyran came up behind him and took the bottle from his hand, replacing it with a glass of juice.

Aaron narrowed his eyes. "So I can use a gun but not drink beer?" he asked.

Kyran seemed to consider the question before nodding. "Yeah, pretty much."

With his and Aaron's bottle, he walked away to sit with Ella and Ryan. Aaron shook his head but sipped at his fruit juice nonetheless.

Everyone was in a cheery mood. Scott couldn't stop smiling, beaming with pride over his Hunters. The younger mages – mostly the kitchen staff – were crowded around the Hunters, listening to the recount of the hunt with awe-filled expressions. Aaron was particularly amused with Ryan's storytelling abilities.

"...then I swung round and sliced through three flying Ichis at once," he said. "They were all coming for me, hissing and spitting, fangs ready, but I sent them to hell with one strike of my sword."

"More like ten strikes," Danielle corrected. "And you still couldn't cut off their heads."

"Shut up." Ryan elbowed her.

Kyran and Ella chuckled, teasing Ryan. Through the jokes and laughter, Aaron found himself restless, waiting for his best friends. They weren't in the cottage, Rose wasn't in the Stove and Sam wasn't in the orchard. Aaron had looked everywhere before coming to sit at the table. He couldn't wait to tell them about the hunt. It had been just as exhilarating as it was terrifying. His wandering gaze saw the twins appear from the path behind the cottages. Aaron got up, eager to meet them.

"Where were you guys?" he asked, walking towards them, grinning from ear to ear. "I've been looking for–"

"Just a minute, Aaron," Sam cut him off and walked past him.

Rose followed silently after him. Aaron stared at them with surprise. Sam and Rose walked to the table, stopping before Scott.

"Scott," Sam called, getting his attention.

"Hi, Sam. Rose." Scott grinned. "Would you like a drink to celebrate the hunt?" He offered them two glasses of fruit cocktail.

"No thanks," Sam said quickly. "We wanted to speak to you."

"Oh?" Scott turned around and put the tray onto the table. "What can I do for you?"

"The vamages," Sam said, gaining the attention of everyone. "How many are in the human realm?"

Scott's pleasant smile slid away and he frowned at the question. "I'm not sure," Scott replied. "The numbers fluctuate."

"A rough estimate?" Rose asked.

Scott furrowed his brow. "Around forty, maybe fifty. Possibly more," he said. "Why?"

Sam stood to his full height. "What if I told you we have a way for you to wipe out all the vamages in the human realm?"

The Hunters at the table shifted in their seats, eyes narrowed at the twins.

Scott looked thrown. "What do you mean?"

"That Q-Zone thing you do," Sam said. "What if there was a way to gather every single vamage in the human realm and destroy them in the Q-Zone in a single attack?"

Scott's expression relaxed. A small smile curved his lips. "Sam," he said, shaking his head. "I wish it were that easy, but vamages were once mages. They know about the Q-Zone. They're well aware of our tricks. They won't fall for a trap."

"What if we made sure that they did fall for it?" Sam asked.

There was something in his voice that scared Aaron.

"What if every vamage in the human realm couldn't resist the temptation?" Rose asked.

"Temptation?" It was Skyler who asked the question. "What are you getting at?"

"The vamages roam the human realm for what?" Sam asked, his voice tight with disgust. "They look for mages to turn or kill." He looked over at Scott. "Or those who have the Trace."

Scott's eyes widened with realisation.

"If vamages pick up the Trace, they come for the kill." Sam said. He held Scott's horrified gaze before asking, "So why not use that to your advantage?"

21

PERMISSION FOR SUICIDE

Complete silence met Sam's words. Every eye was on the twins, trying to judge if they were serious or making a horrible joke. Aaron knew, though. He knew Sam meant every word. He could see it on him, thick as a coat, the sheer determination for revenge.

"I'm sorry." Scott shook his head, blinking as if to clear his vision. "Did you just offer yourself up as *bait?*"

Sam stood tall. "We have the Trace," he said quietly. "It pretty much ruined our lives, as did the vamages that killed our parents." His eyes gleamed with rage. "So why not put that Trace to a good use?"

"Sam, Rose." Aaron moved towards them. "A word?"

Without waiting for a response, he grabbed hold of Sam and Rose's arms and guided them away from the table, hoping he was far away enough to evade the mages' superior hearing. He turned to his friends with wide eyes. "What are you doing?" he asked.

"You know it's a good plan," Sam said. "Don't deny it."

"A good plan?" Aaron asked. "It's a suicidal plan."

"Vamages *killed* our parents," Sam said. "If I can figure out a way to destroy those demons, then I'm doing it – with or without anyone's help."

Aaron turned to Rose. "You're going along with this?" he asked incredulously.

"Actually, it was my idea," she replied.

Aaron gaped at her in disbelief. "Your idea?" he repeated. "Rose, what's got into you?"

"Nothing," Rose replied, "I've just decided that we're not helpless any more. We're humans, we don't have power of the elements or anything like that." She reared her head up. "But we have the Trace and I'm choosing to use that as my power, not have it as a weakness."

Aaron shook his head. "You're not going anywhere near the vamages."

Rose's brow creased as her eyes narrowed. "Excuse me?"

"You're not going," Aaron repeated.

"Aaron–" Sam started.

"No," Aaron cut him off. "It's too dangerous. I won't let you."

"You're not going to *let* us?" Rose asked. "What you gonna do?"

"This has nothing to do with you, Aaron," Sam said. "So stay out of it."

Aaron stared at them, his lips pressed tightly together as his hands curled into fists.

"Nothing to do with me?" he asked. "You're here in this mess because of me. I'm responsible, no matter what you say." He held Sam's gaze. "I'm not going to let anything happen to you – both of you." He glanced to Rose. "I'm protecting you in any way I can, and if that means you get angry with me for ruining your plans for revenge, then that's fine. I'd rather have you angry but still alive."

Sam stepped closer to Aaron and put a hand on his shoulder. "You don't have to protect us," he said. "It's always been the other way around, mate."

"Help us, Aaron," Rose said. "We're doing this, one way or another. We're not backing down. Don't fight us; stand by our side."

"Rose–" Aaron started with a shake of his head, but she stepped away, turning to walk back to the table. Aaron looked to Sam in desperation, "Sam, please."

But Sam followed his sister back to Scott and the Hunters. Aaron hurried after them.

"So?" Rose asked Scott. "What do you think? Do we have an agreement?"

Scott and the Hunters had clearly been having a discussion of their own while Sam, Rose and Aaron were having theirs.

Scott cleared his throat. "There's every possibility that your plan could work and taking out even a small fraction of Hadrian's army is a tempting offer." He closed his eyes and shook his head slowly. "But I'm sorry. The risks are too high. The Empaths don't have the ability to heal you and you both could be fatally injured."

"We understand that," Sam said. "We understand all the risks and we're okay with that."

"You're okay with putting Rose's life at risk?" Aaron asked angrily.

"*Rose* can make her own decisions," Rose said, shooting Aaron an annoyed glare. She turned to Scott. "Well?" she asked, ignoring the others.

"You maybe okay with risking your lives," Scott said, "but I'm not."

"We're sixteen years old," Rose argued. "You have Hunters that young, facing all sorts of demons."

"They're mages," Scott pointed out. "They've trained to hunt and can handle themselves."

"Just because we're human doesn't mean we're useless." Rose shot Skyler a sideways glance, as if challenging him to argue. "We can handle ourselves too."

Scott shook his head. "I'm not comfortable sending you–"

"I think they should do it."

Everyone stopped and turned to stare in absolute surprise at Skyler.

"What?" Scott asked, stunned that Skyler had agreed with a human.

"I think they should do it," Skyler repeated. "They're right. They have the Trace and we could use it against the vamages."

"Skyler–" Scott started.

"I know it's risky," Skyler cut across him, "but we can take out the vamages, actually *destroy* them. Even if it's one percent of Hadrian's army, that's better than nothing." He nodded at Sam and Rose. "If they're willingly offering themselves up, then why not?"

Scott looked back at Sam and Rose before glancing at Skyler. "We've never used humans as bait before."

"Which is why the vamages will never see it coming," Skyler pointed out.

Scott fell quiet, his eyes troubled. "You do have a point," he said.

"Oh, come on!" Kyran slammed a hand against the table; the loud thwack caught everyone off guard. Kyran shot to his feet, blazing green eyes fixed on Scott. "You're not seriously considering this?"

Scott glanced from Skyler to Kyran, looking very much in two minds. "I don't know," he said. "I can see the benefit of the plan but it's too risky–"

"Damn right it's too risky!" Kyran snapped.

"We're talking about every vamage in the human realm being wiped out in a Q-Zone kill," Skyler said.

"They're *human!*" Kyran seethed. "We don't use humans for bait. We protect them, we don't endanger them!"

"You're right," Scott said, nodding. "Of course. It would be unethical to use them."

"You're not using us," Sam argued. "We want to do this."

"Kyran's right," Aaron jumped in. "Mages protect humans. If you let them risk themselves, you're going against your own moral code."

"Scott, don't listen to them," Skyler said.

"I think Kyran and Aaron are right," Ella joined in. "It's far too dangerous."

"We're doing this, one way or another," Sam insisted.

"No, you're not!" Aaron shouted.

"Enough!" Scott's yell silenced everyone. He took in a breath and turned to look at Sam and Rose. "Give me time to consider your offer," he said.

"Scott—!" Kyran started.

Scott held out a hand to quieten Kyran, as he continued to speak to the twins. "I will decide if it's worth the risk or not. If I can come up with a way to have you there and keep you safe at all times, then and only then will you be allowed to do this."

Sam and Rose didn't say anything but nodded.

Skyler smirked. "You need permission from an Elemental and the Controller to go on any kind of a hunt," he said. "Scott will give you his decision, but I'm giving you mine right now." His eyes sparkled with excitement. "See you at the hunt, Shattereds."

***

The clang of metal hitting metal was ringing in the air. Aaron's breathing was laboured, his arms aching with the weight of the heavy steel sword that he had to hold up to block Kyran's relentless attack.

"Focus, Ace," Kyran called. "You're not paying attention."

The force of Kyran's strike had Aaron stumble backwards, his hand smarting with pain as the impact reverberated from the sword into his hand and up his arm.

"I beg to differ," he panted. "If I wasn't paying attention, I would be cut in two by now."

Kyran smirked and twirled his sword. "You're not hit because I'm not aiming to hit you, genius," he said. "You're barely defending yourself."

Another strike, and Aaron's cramping arms lifted the sword up to block it.

"Yeah..." he puffed, "...right!"

Kyran paused, his eyes narrowed. He twisted his sword once more and slashed at him. Aaron barely managed to block in time, gasping as the blows came harder and faster. He backed away, holding his sword out, doing what he could to protect himself from the furious attack. Kyran got near enough to kick Aaron's feet from under him. With a thud, Aaron fell to the hard ground, his sword knocked from his hand. The tip of Kyran's sword rested on Aaron's chest.

"What do you have to say now, Ace?" Kyran smirked.

Aaron pushed the sword away with his hand and got up. "I need a break," he said, stumbling over to the low wall to rest against it.

"This is your problem," Kyran said. "You have no stamina."

"We've been training for three hours non-stop," Aaron said, exhaustively plopping to the ground. "Give me five minutes to catch my breath."

Kyran shook his head at him, but didn't say anything. He sheathed his sword and came to sit on top of the wall.

"Kyran?" Aaron started after a few silent minutes. "Do you think Scott will give Sam and Rose permission?"

Kyran didn't answer right away. "I don't know," he replied, a tinge of annoyance lacing his voice. "Under normal circumstances it would be a definite no. But the way things are going, Scott might just be desperate enough to say yes."

Aaron twisted around to look up at Kyran, squinting against the bright sun. "He would risk their lives?"

"To take out vamages?" Kyran asked. "Yeah, I think he would."

Aaron looked to the ground, and his frantically racing heart skipped a beat. "If they go to a Q-Zone hunt, then I'm going with them," he said.

Kyran snorted. "Yeah, right." He smirked. "You don't know the first thing about hunting and you want to go to a Q-Zone hunt?"

Aaron glared up at him. "If Sam and Rose go then I'm going with them," he stated. "Skill or no skill, I'm not sitting back while my friends set off on a suicide mission."

"So you reckon it's better to assist them?" Kyran asked.

"If I can't stop them, I'll go with them and do what I can to protect them."

Kyran shook his head at him. "You can barely protect yourself."

"Doesn't matter," Aaron said.

Kyran fell quiet. His green eyes studied Aaron from top to bottom, almost as if he was considering Aaron for something. He stood up.

"Come on," he said. "I'm going to show you something."

Holding back a groan, Aaron pulled himself onto his feet. "What is it?"

"A classic move." Kyran said. "Very useful."

He held out his hands, shoulders dropped and feet planted. Taking in a deep breath, Kyran pulled back, bringing his elbows closer to his sides before extending both hands out, as if pushing an imaginary foe.

A ripple went through the ground, cracking it and marking it in a strange pattern of semicircles arranged in a straight line. The ripple reached a lone tree and blasted it out from the ground. The tree spun in the air before crashing back down.

Kyran turned to look at Aaron with a smile. "You learn this and you can make sure no one gets near you, Sam," his eyes gleamed in the sunlight, "or Rose."

***

Aaron practised all day. He worked well into the night but he couldn't get the ripple to extend out like Kyran's had. The most he could do was shake the ground under him slightly.

"I don't get it." He complained as he and Kyran made their way to the table for dinner. "I managed to crack open the ground to stop that car. Why can't I do this?"

"That was different," Kyran said. "That was an instinctual reflux action. It just happened. This is a conscious act." He smirked. "So since you actually have to *think* about it, it's no surprise you can't–"

"Alright, alright," Aaron grumbled. "Give the insults a rest."

Kyran obediently fell quiet.

Aaron walked a few steps before he suddenly froze. Turning around with wide eyes, he asked, "How do you know about my reflux? I never told anyone that."

"Your dad told Drake." Kyran shrugged. "Word gets around."

"Drake told you?" Aaron asked with disbelief. Drake hardly spoke to anyone. He didn't even seem that friendly with Kyran. The entire time Aaron had been here, he'd seen them speak once.

"Drake mentioned it to Mary," Kyran explained. "Like I said, word gets around."

They started walking again. Aaron shot Kyran a curious look. "How is it you know how to do that ground ripple thing?" he asked. "I thought your power was Air."

"It is Air," Kyran confirmed. "Just because I can use the power of Air doesn't mean I can't use the other elements to a basic extent." He elaborated for Aaron. "A mage usually has one particular power that comes easily to them. Their skill is nowhere near the complete power of an Elemental, but it's their strong point." He held a hand to his chest. "I have an affinity with Air, it's the power I'm naturally good at, but I've trained to use other elements too."

"Like Earth," Aaron said. "But that ground ripple thing doesn't look basic."

Kyran laughed. "Trust me, babies born yesterday could do it."

"Thanks," Aaron remarked as they reached the table. "You know how to make me feel better." He took his usual seat, across from Sam.

"You're welcome, Ace." Kyran grinned and sat next to Ella.

Sam frowned and leant over the table. "Ace?" he asked.

Aaron rolled his eyes. "He thinks he's being funny," he explained. "He keeps calling me Ace, to mock me because I can't do anything right – yet," he added hastily.

Sam sat back, throwing Kyran an annoyed look. "Git," he muttered.

"Annoying git," Aaron murmured back.

"An annoying git who can hear you," Kyran said, without looking in their direction.

Aaron and Sam ducked their heads, grinning at each other.

"Where's Rose?" Aaron asked, glancing to the empty seat next to Sam.

"In the Stove," Sam replied. He played with his food, glancing every so often at Aaron. Finally, he cleared his throat. "Scott came to see us," he said quietly. He met Aaron's worried eyes. "We got his permission. We're going to a Q-Zone in five days' time."

***

"Scott?"

Scott looked up from the round table, dark-circled eyes widening at Aaron.

"Aaron?" he said. "What are you doing here this late?"

"I wanted to speak with you," Aaron said. "About the Q-Zone."

Scott nodded. "I can understand your concern," he said, before sighing loudly. "Truth is, I'm more than concerned myself. I feel like I'm fighting my natural instinct by sending Sam and Rose out there—"

"I'm going too."

Scott paused, his mouth left hanging open. "I'm sorry?"

"To the Q-Zone," Aaron explained. "I get it. You need to do this to get the vamages. Sam and Rose's offer is too good to turn down. I get all of that." He paused, holding Scott's gaze. "I just wanted you to know that I'm going with them."

"I can't allow that, Aaron. You're not trained yet," Scott said.

"Are Sam and Rose trained?" Aaron asked.

"Aaron." Scott stood up from his seat and walked around the table to come to Aaron's side. "They're going to be surrounded by Hunters the whole time—"

"Good," Aaron said. "Then I'll be surrounded by them too. 'Cause wherever my friends go, I go."

"It's too dangerous and I can't risk you," Scott said.

"But you can risk Sam and Rose?" Aaron asked. "Or is it that you don't care about the lives of two humans?"

Scott's face coloured with anger, pink spots in his pale cheeks. "You know that's not true," he said. "I value the lives and well-being of humans above everything else."

"Then prove it," Aaron said. "Send me, a mage – better yet, an Elemental – where you're sending the humans."

Scott fell still. His mouth clicked closed and he straightened up, staring at Aaron intently. Aaron turned and walked to the door. "It's not going to work," Scott said. "You're not getting permission by challenging me."

Aaron paused at the door. "I'm sorry, Scott," he said, turning around. "I think you misunderstood me. I'm not challenging you, and I'm not asking for your permission, either."

Scott smiled as he slipped both his hands into his pockets. "A mage needs the permission of the Controller to go to a Q-Zone hunt," he said. "It's the rule."

"Maybe," Aaron said. He reached behind him and pulled out a thin book that had been rolled and stuffed into his back pocket. "But thanks to this, I now know that an Elemental doesn't follow the same rules as mages."

Scott eyed the book, his expression turning grim. "What is that?" he asked quietly.

"One of the books I found in the store," Aaron replied. "It's the case study for the trial of one Perves Giovanni." He noted the faint shiver the name brought to Scott. "It makes it pretty clear that the Elementals rule this realm."

Scott didn't say anything. He didn't deny it nor confirm it. He simply stared at Aaron with wide blue eyes.

"Elementals don't listen to anyone," Aaron continued. "They do what they want. They make the rules, the decisions, and they don't have to get anyone's permission. "

"Not completely," Scott replied. "The Elementals have to listen to one another."

"Good," Aaron said. "Because I've already spoken with Skyler and Ella, and they—"

"Not them." Scott shook his head. "You have to speak to the oldest Elemental, which happens to be Neriah," Scott explained. "And Neriah would never give you permission to enter a Q-Zone with next to no training."

Aaron stepped closer, staring Scott straight in the eyes. "Then unless Neriah comes in the next five days to tell me I can't do it, I'm going with my friends."

"Aaron," Scott began, desperation in his voice.

"You don't want me to go?" Aaron asked. "Then take Sam and Rose out of this plan and I won't go. But if you're sending my best friends to face demons, then I'm going with them."

***

The days slipped past in preparation for the vamage Q-Zone hunt. On the big day, Hunters arrived from all over the realm with the same enthusiasm as before. But when they learnt of Aaron's involvement in the Q-Zone hunt, along with Sam and Rose's, nervousness seemed to take the place of their excitement. None of them, it seemed, wanted to risk the humans – a notion Aaron agreed with.

In preparation for the Q-Zone, Aaron had trained endlessly over the last five days. He practised with Kyran from dawn till dusk, working until his exhaustion made his legs give out from under him. He put all his effort, his strength, his sheer determination to protect his friends into his training. He managed to make the ground shake, even crack a little, but it was barely enough to sway the targeted trees. He was left with heavy disappointment and a burning tingle in his fingertips.

"Just stick by our side," Ella told him, as Aaron stood with his arms held out, letting Ella and Zhi-Jiya fuss over him, tightening the straps across his torso and back. "You'll be fine."

"It's not me I'm worried about," Aaron said.

Ella paused to look up at Aaron before doing up the buckle at his side. "Relax," she said. "Your friends will be fine. They're going to have me, Skyler, Kyran and Zulf surrounding them – and you for that matter."

"I still can't believe Scott's letting you go," Zhi-Jiya said, buckling another holster tightly around his upper arm. "You have to jump through all sorts of hoops to get Scott's permission for a Q-Zone hunt." She studied Aaron. "What'd you do?"

"Nothing," Aaron replied. "I just told him he couldn't stop me since I'm an Elemental."

Ella whistled, sharing an amused look with Zhi-Jiya. "You used the Elemental card?" Ella asked. "Never knew you had it in you, Aaron."

"It's not like I enjoyed it," Aaron said. "Scott's always been pretty decent to me. I didn't like forcing him, but..." He trailed off before letting out a sigh. "They're my best friends. I can't let them do this on their own."

Ella and Zhi-Jiya didn't say anything but continued tightening the buckles. Aaron looked down at himself.

"I look weird," he said. He could only make out the top of his blue vest. The rest was hidden behind the criss-crossing straps of leather that had various slits and pockets for weapons.

"You look like a kid playing dress up," Zhi-Jiya said.

Ella laughed. "I think you look cute."

Aaron wrinkled his nose. "Yeah, that's what a Hunter wants: to look *cute*."

"Hey, idiot." Ella tapped him lightly on the head. "You're not a Hunter – not yet and, by the looks of it, not ever."

"Hey," Aaron protested. "I've only just started training."

"True," Zhi-Jiya mused, buckling a holster onto one of Aaron's thighs. "Just 'cause Kyran's naturally gifted doesn't mean he can work miracles." She looked up and winked at Aaron.

"You got the right tutor, though," Ella said. "Listen to Kyran and do what he tells you. You'll be thankful for it."

"He's that good, is he?" Aaron asked, already knowing the answer.

"Kyran's unbelievable," Zhi-Jiya said. "Not many can go up against an Elemental and still walk away." She smirked. "Especially an Elemental like Skyler."

"Has Kyran ever defeated Skyler?" Aaron asked.

Ella shared a look with Zhi-Jiya – one that seemed to say, 'Did he seriously just ask that?'

"No one can defeat an Elemental," Zhi-Jiya explained. "Except perhaps another Elemental."

"But Kyran's come pretty close," Ella said. "He seriously knows how to use his core."

"No wonder Skyler doesn't like him," Zhi-Jiya said, amused.

"Seriously?" Aaron asked. "Skyler feels threatened by Kyran?"

"Wouldn't you?" Zhi-Jiya asked. "If you, being the Elemental for Earth, met someone who was *almost* as gifted as you and used the power of Earth with *almost* the same natural ease, wouldn't that bother you?"

Aaron refrained from pulling a face. "I think everyone knows more about the power of Earth than I do," he grumbled. "But if Skyler is that uncomfortable with Kyran, how come he lets Kyran go to all the hunts?"

"Kyran is just that good," Ella said as she snapped his gun holster around his back. "As much as Skyler would just *love* to refuse Kyran permission for hunts, even he can't deny Kyran's got talent." She shrugged. "And if he gets too stupid, which does happen every now and again, I step in and give Kyran permission."

She tightened the last strap and moved away, giving him a look all over.

She nodded her head in satisfaction.

"Now the fun part," Zhi-Jiya said, rubbing her hands together in glee. "Pick your familiars, Aaron."

Aaron looked to the shelves lined with all sorts of weapons. He didn't have a clue what kind he should go for. He moved to the cabinet that held long, shiny swords. He reached out for the nearest one, when Ella grabbed his wrist, halting him.

"You're not strong enough for swords yet," she said, pulling him back. "How about these instead?" She nodded towards the other shelves – the ones that held a selection of firearms.

With a twisted knot in his stomach, Aaron walked over to the shelf and stared at the guns. His heart thudded and his palms became sweaty. He kept his hands by his side, not finding it within him to lift a pistol out.

"Do I really need that?" he found himself asking.

"Not at all." Kyran walked into the hut. "Only if you want to live through the hunt."

Aaron let out a strained breath, willing himself to reach out and take one. But no matter how hard he tried, he just couldn't do it. With a sigh, Kyran picked one up: a black and silver semi-automatic pistol with Aric's mark sitting proudly on both sides of the grip. Kyran picked up the loaded magazine and slid it inside with a resounding click. He reached over and slotted the pistol in the holster attached to Aaron's waist.

"Don't be afraid to use it," he warned.

Aaron couldn't find his voice, so he gave Kyran a nod. When Kyran moved away, lifting out weapons for himself, Aaron walked over to another shelf. He stared at a shiny silver dagger with a dark mahogany handle. Carefully, Aaron reached into the glass cabinet and took the blade off its hook. He held the weapon in his hand and took in a deep breath. He waited but nothing happened. He wasn't catapulted into a memory, like he had when he touched the sword on Drake's wall. Aaron frowned at the blade, shifting its slight weight in his hand.

"Nice," Zhi-Jiya commented, coming to his side. "Very good choice for your first blade."

Aaron put the dagger down. "I don't want it," he explained. "I was just looking."

Zhi-Jiya picked up the same dagger, testing its weight in her hands. "I'll take it then."

Aaron watched as she slid the blade into one of the slits on the leather band strapped across her torso.

"Can I ask you something?" he started. "Does everything have flesh memories?"

Zhi-Jiya shrugged. "Pretty much." She reached up to tug her long ponytail tighter. "Why?"

"I didn't see anything when I touched that dagger." He pointed to her pocket. "But I touched a sword and I saw a memory, even though I wasn't looking for one."

"Flesh memories are weird." Zhi-Jiya moved along the shelf picking up more blades. "They work in different ways for different things. The sword you touched had a memory that was in some way connected to you. That's why you saw it without even searching for it." She slid a dagger out of its sheath and held it up. "If it has nothing to offer you, it won't show you anything. If you want to see everything it holds, you have to open the memories yourself."

"So, theoretically, I'll see memories on items if they are connected to me?" Aaron asked. His hand crushed the letter that was resting in his pocket. "Without actively looking for them?"

"Depends," Zhi-Jiya said. "It's not the thing itself that holds the flesh memories that has to be connected to you. It's the imprint of the flesh on the item. Mages can pass memories onto one another too, like for example, you saw a memory but you want to share it with me. You would just touch my forehead and bring forward that memory and I would see it in my head."

Aaron remembered his last night in the human realm. His mum standing on the doorstep of the inn, her hand touching the elderly man's temple.

"But in the case of weapons, it's different," Zhi-Jiya was saying. "They store memories in another way."

"Can mages do that with humans?" Aaron asked.

"What – share memories?" Zhi-Jiya asked. "No. It's strictly a mage to mage deal. We can bend the will of a human, to a certain extent," Zhi-Jiya said, "but that's about it." She narrowed her eyes with curiosity. "This sword," she said. "What memory did you see when you touched it?"

"My dad," Aaron answered quietly. "Hunting."

Zhi-Jiya nodded, but Aaron could see her eyes darken and jaw clench momentarily at the mention of Christopher Adams.

"Right, so there's the connection," she said. "Your dad must have handled that sword and so left a memory on it. When you touched the sword, it opened the memory for you because the sword itself recognised your touch and linked it back to your dad."

"The *sword* recognised me?" Aaron asked. "You make it sound like the swords are alive, like they have a mind of their own."

Zhi-Jiya smiled. "Swords aren't alive, not like you or me," she said. "But they do have a mind. They do hold memories and they will show you them readily, without you even having to look."

Aaron understood it then, why he struggled for days with the letter his mum wrote but had the memory come instantly with the sword. It seemed the weapons Hunters used had stories to tell. You just have to be from the same bloodline as the person in the story to access them.

"Here." Zhi-Jiya turned to Aaron, holding at least a dozen small knives. "You're going to need these."

She slid the blades into the small slits on the leather band crossing Aaron's torso while Aaron stood still, letting her dress him for battle.

***

Fifteen minutes later, Aaron was sitting on the back of Lexi, willing his breakfast to stay put. He glanced to his left to see Rose sitting behind Ella. An uncomfortable Sam was seated behind Skyler.

Zhi-Jiya carried two helmets and handed Sam and Rose one each.

"How come we're the only ones who need these?" Sam asked.

"'Cause you're the only ones who'll break your noggins if you fall off," Zhi-Jiya replied.

Scott stepped forward, looking as if he hadn't slept in days. His worried gaze flitted from one face to the other, lingering on Sam and Rose. Aaron took in a shaky breath, trying to calm his nerves. To give Scott his due, he had come up with a plan that offered Sam and Rose the best possible protection. Ella and Skyler, the two Elementals, were going to be by Sam and Rose's side throughout the whole ordeal.

The plan was simple enough. Sam and Rose were going to walk into the human realm and stay in the protective circle of the Hunters while drawing out all the vamages. The Q-Zone would open and trap all the vamages while the Hunters led Sam and Rose out of the Q-Zone.

It sounded straightforward. Which was precisely what worried Aaron. Nothing ever went to plan, not in his experience. He couldn't even go out in the middle of the night to celebrate his birthday without all hell breaking loose.

"Ace?" Kyran's voice cut through his thoughts.

"Yeah?" he asked.

"Nervous?" he asked, seated in front of him.

"A little," Aaron admitted. "You can tell?"

"Your fingers are about to bore holes into my shoulders," Kyran replied. "Yeah, I can tell."

Aaron quickly pulled his hands away. "Sorry."

Kyran's low chuckle was the only response.

"You all know the rules," Scott's voice boomed over the grounds. "Remember, this hunt is more than just a Q-Zone kill. You have with you the very thing that we're fighting to protect." The Hunters turned to look at Sam and Rose. "You will protect them at all cost." Scott continued. "Do what you need to keep them safe." He took in a shaky breath, betraying his own nerves. "Once you have the vamages in the Q-Zone, you make sure Sam, Rose and Aaron are brought out *first*." His eyes roamed the Hunters. "And don't forget the ultimate rule: if anyone is left behind in the Q-Zone, you don't go back for them. Understood?"

A tremendous "Yes!" echoed in the air.

Scott nodded and held out his hand to the Gate.

Aaron tensed, feeling the weight of his weapons pulling him down. Subconsciously, he reached out and held on to Kyran.

"Go," Scott instructed. "May the Heavens guide you back to us."

With a rumbustious cheer, the Hunters revved their bikes and set off. Skyler took the lead with Ella behind him. Kyran took off after them, taking Aaron back to the human realm.

22

WHEN VAMAGES COME TO FEED

Aaron opened his eyes when the bike came to a stop, having passed through a glowing portal in the shape of Aric's mark. It was dark, already nightfall, but even if the street lamps hadn't been offering a dull, soft light, Aaron would have recognised where he was. The sight of the familiar street caught his breath. The shudder that went down his back had nothing to do with the icy chill of December. Aaron sat still, with a painful longing stabbing at his insides as he stared at the line of houses decorated in twinkling lights.

"Ace?" Kyran called. "You okay?"

Aaron nodded slowly. "Yeah," he whispered.

Kyran glanced around the darkened street before looking back at him. "You familiar with this place?"

A choked laugh left Aaron. "Yeah," he said. "This is where I grew up."

Aaron slid off the bike, staring into the distance at the dark shape of his house. It was one of the only two houses that were dark, compared to the rest that were dressed up for Christmas.

Kyran got off his bike and walked over to the two Elementals. "Who chose the location?" he asked.

Skyler frowned at him, annoyance in every line of his body. "What?" he snapped.

"The location," Kyran bit out. "Who chose it?"

"I did." Rose said quietly, with her brown-eyed gaze on her home. "I asked Scott if we could come here." She looked around at Kyran. "It all started here for us," she said. "It should end here too."

Sam wrapped an arm around his sister and made to walk down the street.

"Sam," Ella called behind him. "Stay beside us."

Sam and Rose halted, but their gazes stayed fixed on their abandoned house, sealed with the yellow and black police tape. Aaron walked over to them and put his arm around Rose, who immediately leant into his embrace. The trio just stood there, in the middle of the street, huddled against one another. December's wind whipped at their faces, turning their noses and cheeks pink. They stood staring at the homes they had lost because of the vamages.

Ella held up her hands, aiming at the houses lined along the street. The windows of each and every house frosted over, glazed with ice so thick it would be impossible to see anything past it. Aaron, distracted by her, looked over to see even the doors were iced, rendering them unable to open. He looked over at her as she dropped her hands, turning to do the same to the houses on the other side. She met his eyes.

"Nothing gets in, nothing gets out," she explained.

Aaron nodded. She was frosting the windows so no one could see anything if they looked outside. It was to protect the humans from getting the Trace. His gaze found the house next to his former home. The home of Rebecca Wanton, his neighbour – the girl he still dreamt about kissing.

Zulf came up to them, staring at Sam and Rose with wide eyes. "Damn that Trace," he whispered. "You two are practically glowing beacons."

"You couldn't see it before?" Aaron asked, looking at Sam and Rose carefully, but he couldn't see anything different about them.

"The Trace is only visible in the human realm," Zulf explained.

Aaron felt it very suddenly: a strange chill that spread through him, much like it had the night he saw vamages for the first time. His heart started beating faster and his stomach clenched. His fingertips buzzed and cold sweat broke out over him. His grip tightened around Rose's hand, snapping her out of her mournful daze. She looked at him with tear-filled eyes.

"Aaron?" she asked.

"They're coming," Ella said quietly. "Whatever you three do, don't leave our side."

Skyler, Kyran, Zulf, Ryan, Zhi-Jiya and Ella came to stand around them.

"*Keep your focus.*" Scott's voice echoed in Aaron's head. "*Protect them at all costs.*"

"Where are we leading the vamages?" Sam asked, looking up at the sky, waiting for the mist to appear.

"Don't you worry about that," Zulf said, gripping his sword tightly. "You just stick to our sides. Leave the rest to us."

The other Hunters hid behind the houses and bushes, so it would seem the only Hunters here were the six surrounding the trio. It took no more than two minutes for the first of the mist to appear in the sky.

Seeing it again, forming a thick, pulsing cloud against the dark night's sky, Aaron felt his breath choke in his chest. His hand tightened around Rose's, while his other gripped the gun in his holster.

The first cloud of vamages crashed onto the street, rolling in waves and coming to rest in front of the group of humans and mages. Aaron saw Ella reach for her pendant – three silver wavy lines dangling from the chain – and mutter something inaudible. As the mist cleared, Aaron saw twelve black-cloaked figures standing and grinning at them.

The six Hunters around Aaron tensed, weapons in hand. The vamage at the forefront tilted his head, his dark-eyed gaze flitting from one Hunter to the other.

"This is a surprise," he said, his voice soft and smooth. "It's not everyday we see such..." his gaze rested on Sam and Rose, and he grinned with blatant glee, "daring beings."

"They only want to visit their home," Ella said, laying the trap. "Surely you can give them that much?"

The vamage smiled, flashing dazzling white teeth. "Of course." He inclined his head. "But why settle for just a visit when we can arrange a one way ticket to hell?" He smirked, his eyes filled with malice. "Where we sent their parents."

Aaron could see Sam tense from the corner of his vision. Sam's shoulders had lifted, hands curled into fists as he glowered at the vamage. If looks could kill, that vamage would have dropped to the ground already.

"Easy Sam," Zhi-Jiya spoke from beside him. "He's only trying to get you angry so you step out of our protection and he can get to you."

The vamage chuckled. "That's cute," he said. "The puny human thinks he can take on a vamage." He stepped forward and held out both hands. "Come on then."

It happened so fast it caught Aaron by surprise. The vamages, all twelve of them, acted in the blink of an eye. A powerful blast of power came hurtling towards the mages, dragging a line of fireballs in its wake. Skyler and Kyran were at the front. Both held out their hands and Aaron saw what they were about to do.

Block and throw back, he thought to himself.

Sure enough, the boys caught the thunderous jolt of power with their curved hands and threw it back at the vamages. The fireballs dragged after the jolt, as if pulled by an unseen force. The vamages moved, avoiding the hit.

All six Hunters raised their arms and took aim, sending a stream of bullets at the vamages. It wouldn't kill them, due to their part-mage status, but judging by the looks of agony on their faces, being shot still hurt like hell.

Aaron took Sam and Rose and ducked to the ground, keeping out of the way as a blazing shoot-out started in the middle of their street. Overhead, more clouds of vamages streaked across the sky and came to land all around them. More and more vamages emerged from the fading mist until the six Hunters, Aaron and the twins were surrounded by no less than sixty vamages.

When the crowd of vamages moved in for the kill, the rest of the Hunters revealed themselves. Their element of surprise was short-lived. The vamages attacked with vigour, using their elemental powers ruthlessly. The Hunters used a mix of their weapons and powers to retaliate. Jolts of power bounced and ricocheted between the vamages and Hunters. Balls of fire flew through the air, exploding upon impact. Tiny slivers of ice, like shards of glass, rained down on the Hunters, slicing their flesh open. Every so often, Skyler used his power to blast the vamages away, or to divert the rain of fireballs and ice.

Aaron felt it – the sign that mages and vamages were using their powers. It was a strange jolt in his stomach, making his fingers tingle and his palms sweaty. This was the link all mages shared when in the human realm – one that told them another was using their powers.

Aaron watched as gunshots rang in the air, so loud Aaron was sure people four streets away could hear them, let alone the street they were standing in. Yet no one came to their windows to investigate. The frosted glass might protect the humans from seeing anything but he wondered what was stopping the sound of the battle from awakening and frightening them.

Aaron's circle of protection broke when Ryan was sent flying across the street by a vamage's attack.

"Ryan!" Aaron cried as the older boy hit the pavement with a thud.

Skyler and Ella covered Ryan's spot, shooting bullet after bullet, keeping the swarm of hybrid demons away. Aaron stood in front of Sam and Rose, his gaze darting every which way, watching out for any attacks. From the corner of his eyes, he saw a fireball coming from his left. He ducked, taking Sam and Rose with him. The ball of fire singed the tips of Sam's hair. Aaron stood up and turned, facing the vamage. The man chuckled, brushing his long hair out of his eyes before darting towards them.

A sweep of Ella's hand and the vamage was encased in a block of ice. It was only for a moment, though, as the vamage broke out of its hold and darted towards the twins again. Aaron pulled out his gun and took aim. Several shots rang out, but it was Ryan and Julian who had emptied their guns into the vamage, successfully throwing him to the ground.

"Is this it?" Kyran asked, raising his arms to gesture to the vamages. "This all you got?"

A vamage with dull yellow eyes smirked at him. "It's more than enough for you."

Kyran grinned back. "Let's lock the doors, then." He touched the spiral pendant hanging from his neck. "Curtain's up, Scott."

Four shimmering white walls that looked little more than mist towered around them, enveloping the entire street. A glittery white veil seemed to hang over the four walls, obscuring sight beyond it, so the street and houses behind were no longer visible.

The vamages stared at the walls, their eyes widening with horror. They fell still, momentarily forgetting about the battle and stared at the trap they had willingly walked into. With a loud, ominous clanging sound, three of the walls were blocked by grey bars, falling from top to bottom, criss-crossing across the whole length of the shimmering white mass. Only one wall was left unlocked, in front of which stood every single Hunter, guarding it.

Aaron gaped at the sight of the walls encasing them. They had been inside the Q-Zone the whole time. That's why the Hunters were firing their guns and fighting with no concern of being overheard by the humans in their houses. That's why no one came to their windows to check what all the commotion was – because they couldn't hear it. The Q-Zone blocked out all sight and sound, so the humans continued to sleep peacefully in their beds, unaware that a furious battle was happening outside their doors.

"What's going on?" Sam asked, staring blankly ahead. "What's happening? What are they looking at?"

"You don't see the walls?" Aaron asked incredulously.

"What wall?" Rose asked, sounding rather afraid. "What's going on?"

That's when Aaron remembered what Scott had told him. The Q-Zone was only visible to mages. Not even the demons could see it, therefore falling for the trap. But vamages – being part-mage – could see the Q-Zone, and now that Scott had locked it, the walls became visible.

"We're inside the Q-Zone," Aaron told them. "It's all around us."

"Welcome." Kyran smirked at the vamages, a sword held in one hand and a gun in the other as he stood at the forefront of the Hunters. "To your own personal hell."

With ferocious cries, the vamages lunged forward, trying to get past the Hunters that had positioned themselves along the one and only open wall. The Hunters forced the vamages back, using bullets, blades, powers – whatever it took.

"*Twenty-one minutes left*," Scott's voice echoed in Aaron's head. "*Get them out!*"

"Come on!" Ella grabbed Sam's arm.

She led them past the line of Hunters guarding the one and only exit. Ryan followed behind them, shooting back the vamages that were trying to follow them out. Ella took hold of both Sam and Rose, while Ryan grabbed Aaron and they jumped through the wall, at last coming out of the Q-Zone.

"Stay here," Ella panted.

"Where are you going?" Aaron asked.

"Back in," she said. "Gotta get the rest of the Hunters out before the zone collapses." She stepped back through the shimmering wall and disappeared.

Aaron stared at the wall, seeing only a thick cloudy mist. Nothing of the battle was visible from the outside of the Q-Zone.

"Scott," Ryan called, holding his pendant. "Sam, Rose and Aaron are out."

"*Good.*" Scott's relieved voice echoed in Aaron's head. "*Start moving out in teams.*"

"There's too many–" Ryan fell still, staring at something behind Aaron with horrified eyes.

Aaron turned, as did Sam and Rose, only to have their breath hitch in their chest. Approaching, were a crowd of vamages that had arrived late and subsequently avoided stepping into the Q-Zone. Rage that had turned to madness glinted in their eyes.

"You laid a trap?" asked the one at the front, with cold blue eyes and a twisted snarl. "For us? You worthless mages think you can get the better of *us*?" With a growl, the vamages darted towards them.

Ryan raised both hands and a line of fire erupted in front of them. Ryan clutched at his pendant as he ushered Sam, Rose and Aaron behind him.

"I'm outnumbered!" he said. "Ten vamages outside the wall. I need help!"

The vamages raised their own hands and Ryan's fire fizzled away. With a sickening smile, the vamages took aim, ready to use their powers. Hunters, a whole crowd of them, jumped out of the shimmering wall and to Ryan's side. Each and every Hunter used only their powers now, since they no longer had the walls of the Q-Zone to silence their gunshots. Aaron pulled Sam and Rose to the side, out of the way, watching as the Hunters used their powers and blades to fight the vamages, edging them closer and closer to the wall, trying to push them into the Q-Zone.

In the chaos, Rose pulled Sam's arm, moving back a few steps.

"Come on," she said. "We have to go home."

"What?" Sam asked in surprise.

"Mum and dad, they're in there – their echoes," Rose tried explaining. "They're in there, Sam. Come on, we have to go."

"Rose?" Sam pulled back, staring at her in shock. "What're you talking about? There's no one there. You know that."

"No." Rose shook her head. "Armana told me. They're there. They leave behind echoes. Come *on*."

Sam shook his head, looking at her as if she were mad.

"Rose, no," Aaron held onto her. "We have to stick together, stay next to—"

"No!" Rose yanked herself out of his grasp. "I have to see them!" She took off, running in the direction of her former house.

"Rose!" Sam darted after her.

"Sam! Rose!" As Aaron started running after them he saw a vamage break away from his fight with the Hunters and turn to look at Sam.

A heartbeat later, the vamage had torn his way across the road and leapt at Sam, knocking him to the ground. A rumbling started, shaking the ground. The vamage's sharp, claw-like nails hadn't yet dug into Sam's back when he was thrown across the road. Sam looked up, dazed and confused as to what had just happened. He saw the broken ground, a strange line of semicircles leading all the way back to Aaron, whose hands were still held out in front of him, green eyes wide with fear and panic. Sam held his gaze, swallowing heavily.

The vamage that had been thrown across the street by the ripple skidded across the ground before falling still. He got up on all fours, breathing like a wounded animal. His glowing yellow eyes rested on Aaron and he suddenly smiled, baring his fangs.

"Adams," he breathed.

Aaron held his ground, dilated eyes fixed on the vamage. His power had given away his identity. The vamages could obviously pick up the scent of Elemental power in Aaron's strike. The other nine vamages stopped and turned, hungry eyes on Aaron too. As one, they darted towards him, pushing past the Hunters.

Aaron's gun was in his trembling hand. He tried to take aim at the approaching vamages, but before Aaron even slid back the rack, Kyran stepped directly in front of him. With a pistol in each hand, Kyran fired bullet after bullet into the vamages.

Sam clambered back to his feet but before he could run down the darkened street, Ryan had grabbed him.

"No!" Sam struggled. "Let go of me. Rose!" he screamed into the night. "Rose!"

"Sam, no." Ryan shook him forcefully. "We don't know if the area's safe. There could be more vamages hiding. I can't let you go off on your own."

"My sister's there!" Sam cried, fighting to get free. "Rose!" Sam cried desperately as Ryan dragged him back. "Rose! ROSE!"

***

Rose ran, refusing to stop and look back. At this particular moment she didn't care who was yelling after her or even what was chasing her. She ignored everything and everyone. She had to get back home. She had to see her parents again.

She got to the gate of her home and swung it open, racing down the path. She ducked under the yellow tape covering the doorless entrance to the house. The moment she stepped inside the darkened house, she screamed at the top of her lungs.

"MUM!"

She ran into the middle of the hallway, panting and struggling to keep the hot tears at bay.

"DAD!" she howled.

She ran to the kitchen, swinging the doors open, searching for her parents. "MUM! DAD!" she cried over and over, running from one room to the next. "No, no, no – you have to be here!" she called as tears of pain and anguish tracked down her cheeks. "MUM?" she screamed again, her voice cracking. "No," she cried, her hands in her hair. "No, please, please be here, please!" Her whole body shook with sobs. "Mum! Dad!"

She turned and knocked into someone. Strong hands grabbed her before the collision threw her to the floor. Deep green eyes, clouded with worry as well as anger, met hers.

"What are you *doing*, Rose?" Kyran demanded, his voice raw with rage. "Didn't you hear me shouting after you?"

"Kyran," Rose gasped. "Kyran...My mum and dad..." She pointed to the stairs. "They...They're here. Their echoes – they're here!"

Understanding flooded Kyran's features and the ire in his eyes melted away. He looked up at the stairs and his jaw clenched. He looked at her.

"Rose–"

"No, they're here!" Rose insisted. "Armana told me. She...she said echoes are left behind. I have to see them. I *have* to see them, Kyran." Her hands were in the folds of his coat and she clutched at him in desperation, her vision blurred by tears. "I have to see my mum and dad again. I have to talk to them. I have to tell them I'm sorry–!"

"Rose," Kyran called a little louder. "Rose, listen. Listen." His hands cupped her face, stilling her. Slowly, he shook his head. "Rose," he breathed her name in a whisper. "Echoes don't work like that."

"No–" Rose made to struggle but Kyran's warm hold quietened her again.

"I'm sorry," he said, "but echoes are just glimpses. You can't talk to them. You can't even see them for longer than a heartbeat. Echoes don't interact with you. They *can't*." His expression was one of complete sorrow. "I'm sorry, Rose, but there's a chance you might not even see them." His thumb caressed her wet cheek. "I'm sorry."

Rose broke down. Her sorrow, bottled up for so long, came out all at once. She sagged in Kyran's arms, crying against his chest. Kyran held her close, his presence a strange warmth, melting the icy clutch of her anguish.

***

Using the force of their powers, the Hunters had managed to knock the ten vamages through the wall of the Q-Zone. Sam had his back turned to the wall, his eyes on the street, searching for any sign of Kyran bringing back his sister. Ryan hovered around him, watching him, ready to grab him if he had the slightest notion of heading into the street. Aaron was by Sam's side, but he was watching the wall as, one by one, the Hunters jumped out of the Q-Zone. They stood lined against the front of the shimmering wall, waiting for their fellow Hunters to come out. Sometimes it was a vamage that managed to escape past the crowd of Hunters still inside. That's when the mages waiting outside pushed them back in, using everything from fireballs to blasts of air.

"*Five minutes to go,*" Scott's voice echoed in Aaron's head. "*Move out! Get out of the zone!*"

Most of the Hunters were out by now, standing around the shimmering veil that was the entrance of the Q-Zone, ensuring no vamage made their escape.

"*Four minutes.*"

"Is Scott going to do the full countdown?" Aaron asked.

"Sometimes," Zhi-Jiya said, her eyes watching the wall. "But he doesn't have to. You can hear a small tick when the forty minutes are up. The zone collapses exactly ninety seconds after the tick."

"Ninety seconds?" Aaron asked. "What's the point of that?"

Zhi-Jiya grinned. "You'd be surprised with what you can do in ninety seconds." She winked at him. "As long as you know what you're doing."

Ella finally leapt out, shortly followed by Skyler. Every time a dark figure shadowed the veil, Aaron's heart jumped into his mouth as he wondered if it was a Hunter or a vamage trying to get out.

"*Two minutes left.*" Scott's worried voice sounded in Aaron's head. "*Come on, Zulf, get out!*"

Almost instantly, Zulf jumped out, landing gracefully with pistol in one hand and sword in the other.

"That was fun!" He grinned.

Now that there were no Hunters left inside the Q-Zone, there was no one left to stop the vamages from getting out. The Hunters had to keep up the blasts of power, to keep pushing back the dark shadows that were trying to escape past the wall.

"Rose was going on about echoes," Sam said quietly, making Aaron turn around. "She said Armana told her that our parents would still be there in our house. Why would she say that if it wasn't true?" A faint hope lit his eyes. "Aaron, you reckon they're really there?"

"Sam," Aaron started, but from the corner of his eye, he saw a dark figure jump out of the wall, finding a crack of space between the Hunters' jolts of power to squeeze through.

In all happened in the blink of an eye. The moment the vamage landed past the wall, he let out a guttural cry and slammed a hand to the ground. The blow cracked the ground, spreading like a ripple and threw the Hunters off their feet.

Sam, Aaron and Ryan were the only ones left standing, being at a distance from the wall of the Q-Zone. The vamage turned, his hunger evident in the dark irises of his eyes. He leapt at Sam with a growl.

"Sam!" Aaron pushed him out of the way.

The vamage growled and threw out his hand, blasting Aaron and Ryan off their feet. They hit the pavement with painful thuds. The vamage turned to Sam, who had no choice but to run. The vamage darted after him, howling with rage. Aaron pushed himself to sit up, just in time to see Sam running, head on towards the wall of the Q-Zone.

"Sam, wall!" Aaron cried.

Sam stopped and ducked, just as the Hunters sent out a simultaneous attack, catching the vamage and propelling him face forward, through the wall and into the Q-Zone.

Panting, Sam stood up, facing the wall he couldn't see before turning to look at Aaron.

"Man," he breathed, "that was clos– "

Two hands pierced out of the wall and grabbed him.

"SAM!" Aaron screamed as his best friend was pulled into the Q-Zone. "NO!"

Aaron scrambled to his feet and ran. Without a moment's pause, Aaron jumped into the Q-Zone after Sam. Just as he passed through the wall, he heard something beyond the shouts for him to stop – a small ticking sound, signalling the end of the forty minutes and the start of the collapse.

23

Saying Goodbye

The first thing to overwhelm Aaron the moment he landed in the Q-Zone was how badly the ground was shaking. The second was seeing his best friend being dragged by a vamage.

"Sam!" Aaron cried and raced towards him.

Lifting up his gun, Aaron shot three rounds. None of them hit the vamage but they distracted him long enough to stop and look up. He released his hold on Sam and straightened up before aiming a jolt of power at Aaron. At once, Aaron dropped his gun and held up his hands, catching the jolt and sending it right back at the vamage. The jolt hit the demon, throwing him across the ground to crash to the shaking floor.

"*Aaron! What are you doing?*" Scott's furious voice rang in his head. "*Get out! Now!*"

Ignoring him, Aaron ran to his friend's side. "Sam!" Aaron gasped in horror at the sight of several cuts leaking blood down his shirt.

"I'm alright," Sam groaned, looking a little dazed as he sat up. "I'm alright."

"*AARON! GET OUT!*" Scott cried in his mind.

Aaron pulled the silver chain over his head and threw it aside. He could do without the screaming in his head right now. He helped Sam to his feet.

The zone collapses exactly ninety seconds after the tick.

Zhi-Jiya's words came back to him. He had only ninety seconds. Ninety seconds to get himself and Sam out, otherwise both of them would die along with the sixty or so vamages trapped inside.

The shaking ground didn't help matters as Aaron fought to stay upright and run at the same time. His panicked, fleeting glances took in the vamages. They were ignoring them; too busy trying to claw their way past one another to get to the glowing wall. But every time they got near enough to pass through, a jolt of power caught them, throwing them back.

Aaron was almost at the exit with Sam when the ground cracked under his feet and fell away. Aaron just about managed to stagger back. The ground broke and fell into a frighteningly dark abyss. Large chunks of the street began to crumble and fall away, taking the vamages with it. The zone had started its collapse.

"Sam!" Aaron yelled, so he could be heard over the howls and cries of the vamages. "We're gonna have to jump!"

Sam nodded, looking rather pale. The ground on either side crumbled and fell away, narrowing the space so Aaron was forced to step behind Sam. Moments later, the ground before Sam fell away, pushing both boys further back. Aaron judged the distance between them and the wall. It was too far away.

"I'm sorry, Sam," he said.

Before the other boy could say a word, Aaron pushed both hands out. The ground, already greatly weakened, cracked as the ripple shot across it. The powerful jolt caught Sam and pushed him, propelling him through the air until he disappeared through the glowing wall.

Aaron breathed out in relief. He had done it. He had saved Sam. He, on the other hand, had to take a chance. Aaron knew he had no other choice: he had to jump. He took a few steps back and dropped his shoulders, ready to run and leap at the glowing wall. He gathered his power, forcing himself to concentrate. He took off, running faster than he ever had before, knowing he had perhaps fifty seconds at the most.

The ground trembled violently under him, and gave way.

Aaron fell, his cry echoing in the air. Jagged rock cut into his back as he slid down. Somehow, his flailing hands caught a rock that jutted out, just a little way under the edge. Aaron held fast, stopping his descent down into the abyss. Using the last of his strength, Aaron tried to pull himself up, struggling to climb with nothing for his feet to catch onto. The muscles in his arms screamed in protest but Aaron refused to let go. He managed to haul himself up and back over the edge. There was no time to waste. Aaron rolled back as the ground shook and crumbled away. Pushing himself onto his feet, Aaron backed away as thin cracks spread towards him, weakening the ground.

Aaron was stuck on a meagre slab of ground, barely big enough for him to take three steps. The dark abyss was slowly swallowing everything up. Blinking the sweat out of his eyes, Aaron desperately looked around him. The zone was about to collapse. There couldn't be more than twenty seconds left, if even that. The glowing wall was now even further away. He could never jump that far. The realisation hit him then like a hammer, stealing his breath. He was going to die.

A thunderous roar cut through the air. Aaron watched in disbelief as a familiar red and black bike came piercing through the glowing wall, flying through the air to land on a stretch of ground parallel to the one Aaron was trapped on. Lexi growled under Kyran as he swerved her around to face the wall again. Without a moment's pause Kyran set off, racing towards the wall – the one and only exit of the Q-Zone. Lexi lifted into the air, a heartbeat before the ground under her gave way. While airborne, Kyran reached out to Aaron, who had his hand outstretched towards him. Their hands locked and Aaron was pulled up and away from the crumbling ground.

Kyran's momentum carried them towards their exit. They had just touched the wall when the ninety seconds ended and the entire zone collapsed. The tremendous blast pushed Kyran and Aaron out with enough force to send them flying across the street, smashing painfully onto the hard tarmac. Lexi fell from under Kyran as both boys hit the road. Kyran and Aaron skidded across the ground, before finally coming to a stop.

Aaron didn't have the breath to cry out. It felt like his bones had jostled out of place before snapping back. Pain danced in every nerve of his body. When he opened his eyes, the entire street tilted. Before he could suck in a shaky breath, two hands grabbed him by the collar and pulled him up, lifting his head and shoulders clear off the ground.

"What the *hell* were you thinking?" Kyran yelled.

Aaron blinked at him, willing his vision to clear, only to see a furious Kyran.

"You almost got yourself killed!" Kyran cried. "What's *wrong* with you?"

Aaron couldn't answer. He didn't have the breath to talk. Just breathing was proving to be a difficult feat. The Hunters ran to Kyran and Aaron's side, pale-faced and wide-eyed.

"Kyran," Ella called, sounding unnerved. "Let go of him. Kyran, let go!"

Kyran's hold loosened and with a last glower, he shoved Aaron back. He moved away, anger radiating off him in thick waves. Even though Ella was kneeling beside him, asking him if he was okay, with Zhi-Jiya and Ryan at his other side, Aaron could only watch Kyran as he painfully made his way over to the broken bike lying in pieces on the road.

***

"I can't believe you!" A livid Scott paced in front of the wicker chair, hands clasped tightly behind him. He was frowning so hard, Aaron was sure the lines would never fade from his forehead. "Did you not hear me when I said, 'If anyone is left behind in the Q-Zone, no one goes back for them?' Didn't you hear me say that?"

Aaron nodded tiredly, his hand clasped in Amber's – one of the other Empaths. Armana and the rest of the Empaths were all busy dealing with the injured Hunters.

"Then explain why the *hell* you jumped into the Q-Zone *ninety seconds before it collapsed*!" Scott raged.

Aaron looked up at him. "Sam was in there," he answered simply.

"*Sam* was in there?" Scott repeated incredulously. "*Sam* was in there? That's your excuse, is it?"

"He's my best friend," Aaron replied.

"I don't care if he's your *brother*!" Scott snapped. "You don't risk your life for anyone."

"I'm sorry—"

"Sorry doesn't cut it!"

"Let me finish," Aaron said. "I'm sorry you think like that. I'm sorry if you don't have anyone in your life that you would jump into a collapsing Q-Zone for." He held Scott's gaze. "But I do. I have Sam and Rose. And I'll jump into the mouth of hell itself if it means I can save my friends."

He pulled his hand out of Amber's and walked away. His treatment was already finished, Amber was only giving him a last check. He headed to the plain white door of one of the rooms before sliding it open. He paused at the door.

"It's okay." Sam grimaced, waving a hand at him. "Come in."

Sam was sitting on a bed, topless, with Ella by his side. She was applying a yellow paste to the individual cuts on Sam's torso. She looked rather drained herself, shoulders dropped and head bowed. Her fatigue was visible in her eyes but she stood by Sam's side, attending to his injuries. Rose was sitting on the chair perched next to the bed.

Aaron stared at the tiny holes in Sam's flesh. His stomach rolled at the thought that a vamage had plunged its claw-like nails into Sam. He could feel bile rising up his throat. Stubbornly, Aaron walked in, forcing back his urge to be sick. He came to Sam's side. A strange, pungent odour that made Aaron's nose burn and eyes water was coming from the paste.

"How are you?" he asked.

"Fine." Sam hissed a little as Ella's fingers dabbed the paste onto his wounds. "Could smell better."

Ella paused, narrowing her eyes at him. "This is the only thing that can heal you," she said tightly. "The Empaths can't help. You're lucky they have knowledge of healing salves."

"Could they not have knowledge of perfumed healing salves?" Sam asked. At Ella's annoyed look, he held up a hand. "Joking, I'm joking. I'm very grateful." He held back a groan as another wound was covered.

"How are you, Aaron?" Ella asked without looking at him.

"Fine," Aaron replied. "All healed."

Sam looked over to meet Aaron's gaze. He shook his head at him. "I can't believe you did that," he said. "Really, Aaron? You used your...your power on me?"

"Had to be done," Aaron said, by way of apology. "You could never have jumped that distance, not while injured."

Sam cried out as Ella jabbed her fingers a little too harshly into a cut. "Easy there," he groaned.

"Sorry," Ella murmured.

Aaron turned to look at Rose, who was sitting silently, her head dropped and eyes shadowed. Slowly, Aaron bent down, squatting before her.

"Rose?" he called quietly.

Rose tilted her head to the side, looking away from him.

"Rose?" Aaron reached out and held on to her hand. "Talk to me, please."

Reluctantly and with great effort, Rose turned to meet Aaron's eyes with her own red-rimmed, bloodshot ones. Aaron's heart clenched. Wordlessly he moved in and wrapped both arms around her. Rose hugged him back as silent tears fell from her eyes. Aaron held Rose in his arms for a few minutes while Sam watched them silently. Finally Rose pulled away, wiping her eyes with her sleeves, sniffing.

"Why didn't you say anything?" Aaron asked. "About...about what Armana told you?"

Rose shook her head, fighting to still her quivering lips.

"You didn't even tell me," Sam said. "Why?"

Rose gave a weak, one-shouldered shrug.

Sam shook his head at her. "So was this why you planned the whole bait idea? Why you chose our street as the location?"

Rose nodded. "I just...I wanted to see—" She paused, squeezing her eyes shut, shaking her head. "I just wanted to...check, you know? See if...if Armana was right."

"You believed she was," Sam corrected. "You told me mum and dad...that they were...there," Sam said with great discomfort.

"I'm sorry," Rose said. "I wanted to tell you, Sammy. I tried so many times this past week, but every time I opened my mouth, I couldn't find the words. I knew you wouldn't believe me."

"I don't believe in ghosts," Sam said. "But two months back, I didn't believe in magic either."

"Powers," Aaron corrected.

"Fine, magical powers," Sam said. "Point is," he turned back to Rose, "you should have told me beforehand instead of springing it on me in the middle of a battle."

"I know," Rose said. "I wasn't thinking."

"That's pretty standard." Sam smiled.

Rose looked up at him, wet eyes narrowed slightly. "Shut up," she sniffed half-heartedly.

"You shut up," Sam said, still with a smile.

"Sod off, Sam," Rose said as a half-laugh, half-sob escaped her.

Ella stepped away, her fingers heavily coated in the thick paste. A heartbeat later they were clean, albeit dripping water. "There," she said. "You'll have to reapply it at least four times a day."

Sam nodded and Rose quickly stood up, wiping her cheeks dry, and took a small bag of yellow granules and the glass jar containing a white cream from Ella.

"Only mix as much as you need," Ella instructed. "Apply it liberally on the cuts and they should heal in a few days. Until then," she turned to Sam, "try to keep yourself together."

"Oh, okay," Sam said, face screwed up to show his sarcasm. "I'll try not to trip up and injure my poor self."

"It would be appreciated," Ella returned.

"Other than Sam getting injured," Aaron said, "and me almost getting lost in an oblivion, was the hunt a success?"

Ella raised an eyebrow but a tired smile came to her nonetheless. "Yes, other than two – no *three* – possible fatal casualties, the hunt was a success."

"Three?" Aaron asked.

"You, Sammy-boy here," she turned to stare Sam down before looking back at Aaron, "and Kyran."

Aaron's insides tightened at the reminder of Kyran. The mere memory of how angry the other boy had been sent shivers down his spine.

***

It was past nightfall. Dinner had been served and finished. Drinks had been toasted in Sam and Rose's names for helping execute a successful vamage hunt, and still Kyran hadn't made an appearance.

Most of the Hunters were in their beds, fatigued from exerting their powers, but Kyran wasn't one of them. He had been missing ever since returning to Salvador. Aaron had an inkling where he might be. Using the soft, glowing light of the lanterns above him, Aaron made his way down the path. Sure enough, he saw Kyran in the garage attending to Lexi, trying to repair her. Aaron came to stand as close as he dared. Kyran still looked pretty angry.

"You missed dinner," Aaron called.

Kyran straightened up, but didn't look over at him.

"Sam's fine, by the way," Aaron said. "The cuts weren't that deep. Ella gave him some herbal paste thing. Smells awful, but at least it'll heal him."

Kyran continued working, not even looking in Aaron's direction.

"Rose is still shaken up. She hardly ate anything."

Again, Kyran didn't say anything but he tensed, the wrench in his hand stilled for a moment.

"I'm sorry about Lexi," Aaron said. "Hope she's not too–"

"What do you want?" Kyran asked, cutting Aaron off and finally looking at him. His green eyes seemed fiercer against the paleness of his skin.

"To thank you," Aaron said, "for saving my life–"

"Don't even!" Kyran held up a hand, fury radiating off him in waves. He slammed the wrench down and stood up. "What were you thinking?" he asked. "You almost got yourself *killed*!"

"I had to get to Sam," Aaron said. "I knew none of you would go in to get him. Seeing as it's one of your rules not to go back into a Q-Zone–"

"Yeah, there's a *reason* for that," Kyran spat. "It's to stop idiots like you risking your life just to save someone else. That's why the rule is there. You never go back into a Q-Zone. Never. For *no one*."

Aaron nodded slowly. Keeping his eyes on Kyran, he asked, "Then why did you come for me?"

Kyran fell silent.

"If the rule's there to stop Hunters risking their lives," Aaron said, braving a few steps closer, "then why did you risk yours? Why'd you come to help me?"

Kyran didn't say anything but his eyes blazed with anger. Aaron could see the muscle twitch in his jawline. Without a word, Kyran swiped up his hooded top from the back of the single chair and walked out. He paused briefly next to Aaron.

"If you know what's good for you, you'll stay out of my way," he warned before walking away.

***

The next day tested Rose's patience, as she and Aaron attended to Sam. He was a rotten patient; he always had been.

"I can do it myself!" he snapped, when Rose tried to apply the salve to the marginally healed wounds.

"Fine!" Rose snapped back. "It's not like I enjoy having a smelly paste all over my fingers."

She handed him the prepared salve but, as Rose already knew, Sam couldn't do it himself. It was too painful. Rose snatched the bowl back, warned him to keep quiet and applied the dose. When finished, she went into the bathroom and washed her hands. Instead of returning to the room, she let Aaron keep Sam company while she headed downstairs to the living room.

Rose took a moment to be by herself, sitting on the sofa. The jar of cream and packet of granules were still lying open where she had left them on the coffee table. She capped the lid on the jar and closed the packet, tidying up. The door opened and Kyran walked in. Rose paused. This was the first time she had seen him since returning from the Q-Zone. Kyran had been dividing his time between resting in his room, recovering from the Q-Zone hunt, and spending time in the garage trying to fix his bike.

"Hey," he greeted her quietly.

"Hi," she replied.

Kyran came further into the room. His gaze flitted to the items on his coffee table. "That for Sam?"

"Yeah," Rose replied.

"How is he?"

Rose nodded. "Yeah, okay."

Kyran hesitated, the look of concern deepened as he tilted his head to the side, looking at Rose. "And you?" he asked. "How are you?"

Rose nodded, avoiding looking at him. "Yeah," she repeated. "I'm okay."

Kyran stared at her for a moment longer before nodding slightly. He walked over to the small cabinet tucked away in a corner of the room. He slid open the panel and took out a bottle with a strange green liquid. When he turned around, his gaze immediately found Rose again. He took a step towards her.

"About yesterday," he said. "I hope you didn't mind." He shifted awkwardly from one foot to the other. "I sort of yelled at you."

Rose's brow creased. "You did?" she asked. "I didn't really take it in."

Kyran looked somewhat relieved. "I panicked," he admitted. "I saw you running back to that house and there were vamages still around. They could have ..." He trailed off and fell silent.

"I know I was being stupid," Rose said. "I shouldn't have run off like that, not with those vamages there." She shook her head, closing her eyes in self-recrimination. "I'm sorry."

"You don't have to be sorry," Kyran said. "You wanted to see your parents. It's understandable."

Rose squeezed her eyes shut, her brow creased as if in pain. With a slow breath, she opened her eyes again.

"Armana spoke to me," she said. "She came to check on Sam."

Kyran walked over and sat down on the single chair next to the sofa. He settled the bottle on the table.

"What did she say?" he asked.

"She apologised," Rose replied. "Except, she has nothing to apologise for. When she told me about echoes, she explained that they were just glimpses and that I wouldn't be able to talk to them. She told me all that." Rose slowly shook her head. "But I twisted it. I made myself believe that echoes were more than that. That I could see my mum and dad and I would be able to talk to them, touch them." She paused, swallowing back the growing lump at the back of her throat before closing her eyes. "God, I'm so stupid," she whispered.

"You're not stupid," Kyran said. "You were holding out, hoping for more." He shrugged. "It's what any of us would do."

"I just…" She took in a breath. "I just wanted to see them. Just once more."

Kyran didn't say anything, but his gaze dropped to the floor and he nodded in understanding.

"You have family, Kyran?" Rose asked.

Kyran looked up at her with surprise. He slowly shook his head. "I lost my parents when I was very young."

"I'm sorry," Rose said and her sincerity showed in her eyes. "How did you…?"

"Lycans," Kyran replied, a slight growl underlined the word. He looked up at Rose and forced a smile. "It was a long time ago. I've learnt to live with it. Besides, I have some family, sort of." He shrugged. "It keeps me going."

"Does it get easier?" Rose asked. "Over time?"

Kyran looked like he didn't know how to answer that. "Truthfully, no," he replied. "Losing the ones you love, it doesn't ever get easier. Over time it becomes…bearable."

Rose nodded. At least that was something. "What do you miss the most?" she asked. "About your parents?"

Kyran shifted in his seat. His eyes were a dark forest green, full of shadows and a long-buried pain. "No one's ever asked me that."

"Sorry," Rose said, shaking her head and moving back. "If you don't want to talk about it, I understand."

"It's alright," he said. "Truth is, I miss everything about them." His lips lifted in an almost smile, his eyes bright now with the light of his memories. "My dad's strong arms lifting me to sit on his shoulders." His voice dipped. "My mum's laugh," he said quietly. "She had the most…" he searched for the right word, "…infectious laugh." A small chuckle left him and he shook his head in amusement. "It still gets me, every time I think about it."

Rose smiled too. "Do you remember the last thing you said to your parents?" she asked quietly.

Kyran looked around at her with a frown. "What do you mean?"

"The last words you spoke to your parents," Rose said. "Do you remember what they were?"

"Why?" Kyran asked.

Rose paused for a moment, before saying in a quiet voice, "I don't remember what I said to them." She shifted in her seat, staring ahead. "I remember most of that day. I remember going to school, coming back and getting ready for the Halloween dress-up at the Blaze. I remember returning late, getting changed, having dinner. I remember all of that, but I don't remember what I said to them." Her eyes fast filled with tears. "I...I was annoyed at them, at my mum for such a *stupid* reason." She squeezed her eyes shut and two drops fell down her cheeks. "I went over my minutes, so my mum took away my phone. I was so angry I stopped talking to her."

She looked over at Kyran. "I don't remember the last time I spoke to my mum. I can't remember telling her that I loved her, or telling my dad I thought his jokes were funny, or thanking my mum for putting up with my tantrums. I...I didn't even say goodbye to them." She shook her head slowly as tears continued to fall. "When I walked out of the house that day, when I went to school, when I went to the Blaze, I didn't stop once to say bye." She held Kyran's gaze. "I need to see them again, Kyran. I need to say bye. I...I need to say...so many things." She struggled to hold back the pain that was fighting its way out. "I...I thought...I thought that maybe if I saw their echoes, I could get my goodbye." Her lips quivered, but she held back, refusing to give in. "I thought, maybe I wouldn't...I wouldn't feel so guilty if I get to tell my mum how much I love her and...and tell my dad how sorry I am...and…and…that…I…I…" She gave in, finally succumbing to her grief. Holding her head in her hands, she quietly sobbed.

Kyran's warm hand rested on her shoulder and she looked up to see him standing by her side. "Come on," he said. "Get Sam too."

Rose wiped at her cheeks. "Why?" she asked.

The green of his eyes darkened. "Everyone should get to say goodbye," he replied.

***

The bike came to stop next to a set of black iron gates. Rose stared past them but she couldn't make out anything other than grass and trees. She pulled her hands away from Kyran's shoulders.

"Where are we?" she asked.

"It's the resting grounds," Kyran replied. "It's where we bring the humans who can't be laid to rest in their own realm."

Rose looked back at the graveyard, her mouth dry all of a sudden. "Is this...Are my parents in there?" she asked.

Kyran turned to look at her. "You said Aaron's uncle was left to clear things up?" he asked.

Rose nodded.

"Then your parents are definitely here," Kyran said. "This is the only place he could have brought them."

Rose slid off Kyran's borrowed bike just as Ella's came to rest alongside theirs. Sam, seated behind Ella, looked around in confusion. He got off the bike and came to stand next to Rose.

"Where are we?" he asked.

"Graveyard," Rose replied quietly.

Sam's expression morphed to one of understanding. The four of them walked past the gates and into the resting grounds. They walked past grave after grave, searching for the ones that held the Masons. Sam and Rose hurried from one tombstone to the next, reading names and, in some cases, just dates and places.

"What's this?" Sam asked, gesturing to a gravestone that read, *18/05/1996. Liverpool, England, United Kingdom.*

"It's not always possible to know the identities of the humans that are killed by demons," Ella explained. "When we don't know who the victims are, we can't put names on their graves. We put the date of their death and the place they were found."

"That's horrible," Sam said with disgust. "They don't even get names on their graves?"

"What option do we have?" Ella asked tersely. "Sometimes we get to an attack in time and we save the humans. Sometimes we're too late." It was clear how much this admission was costing Ella, as her whole being tensed and her face flushed. "We can either leave the humans to be found by their relatives, or we can take the bodies away and lay them to rest here."

"And the families are left wondering what happened to their loved ones?" Sam asked. "Isn't that worse than just letting them find their dead?"

"Trust me, if you ever saw what state a demon leaves its victim in, you wouldn't say that."

The moment the words passed her lips, Ella regretted them. Sam paled, his eyes widening with pain so intense it caused Ella to suck in a breath. Rose didn't look any better. Without saying a word, Sam turned and hurried forward, taking Rose's hand and walking ahead. Ella and Kyran followed behind them in silence.

They had to go deep into the graveyard, walking for at least twenty minutes before they found the two graves. Sam and Rose came to a stop, staring at the pair of grey stones that had *Philip Mason* and *Pamela Mason* carved into it. There was no date of birth, only the date of their untimely death. Slowly, Sam and Rose slid to the ground, sitting before the graves.

Ella lowered herself to the ground too and held out her hand. Beautiful cream and yellow lilies grew under her command, surrounding both graves.

"Sorry," she whispered. "It's the only flower I can grow."

Neither Sam or Rose said anything. Ella got up and walked over to join Kyran, giving the twins privacy to mourn. Standing under one of the tall oak trees that surrounded the graveyard, Kyran and Ella scanned the long line of gravestones, both silently asking themselves the same question: why had so many humans lost their lives at the hands of demons, when they – mages – were supposed to protect them?

"We all prepare for this," Ella said "From the moment we're old enough to understand, a part of us readies ourselves for the loss that comes with war." Her eyes found Sam who was sitting with his arm around his sister, pulling her into an embrace as both wept for their parents. Their shoulders shook as they sobbed, and even their bowed heads couldn't hide their sorrowful tears. Ella looked away. "But humans shouldn't have to lose anyone. This isn't their fight, their war." She scanned the graveyard again. "A whole cemetery full of graves of the unknown, buried here because demons got to them." She paused before forcing out, "Because we failed."

"We can't save them all, Ella," Kyran said quietly.

"Quite obviously," Ella said, nodding at the graves. "All we can to do is stand back and watch," she said bitterly. Her eyes watered at Sam's broken form. "After all, it's only another family torn apart," she whispered, as a tear rolled down her cheek.

***

Kyran closed the front door behind him. He stood and watched as Sam and Rose tiredly made their way upstairs. Both of them were exhausted, emotionally drained from visiting their parents' graves. Sam trudged up the stairs, his face still blotched red with tear tracks down his face. Rose was behind him, looking just as worn out.

Sam reached the top of the stairs and headed straight to his room, but Rose paused. She turned back to look at Kyran before walking downstairs, heading towards him. Without saying a word, Rose put her arms around Kyran, her head pressed against his strong chest. Taken aback, Kyran took a moment before gently wrapping his arms around her, holding her close.

"Thank you," she whispered.

Kyran didn't say anything, but just held her in his arms.

24

A New Hope

The days passed quickly. Before Aaron knew it, he woke up to the last day of the year.

"It's the thirty-first already?" he asked.

"Yep." Alan beamed as he set the table in his special way. "It's gonna be a real feast tonight!"

"Good, I'm starving." Ryan yawned, coming to sit at the table. "That full moon took a lot out of me."

"That was yesterday," Aaron pointed out.

"Exactly, only yesterday," Ryan said. "I need today and tomorrow to recuperate and make up for my loss of appetite."

Sitting across from him, Ella glared, shaking her head.

"Don't give me that I'm-mentally-slapping-you look," Ryan said to her. "It freaks me out."

"Good," Ella replied. "Then maybe you won't act like a baby."

"I'm not," Ryan defended. "I do have to recuperate."

"We *all* suffer because of the full moon," Ella pointed out. "You don't see us moaning about special treatment."

"That's 'cause you already get special treatment," Ryan teased. "O great Elemental one, thou hast graced us with thy presence."

"Shut it." Ella threw a grape at him.

Ryan caught it with his mouth. "Yum. Thanks." Ryan grinned as he chewed. "Any more?"

Ella wrinkled her nose. "You're disgusting."

"And you're gorgeous." Ryan winked.

"You flirting with her again?" Zhi-Jiya asked as she joined the table. "Give it up, Ryan. She's not falling for you."

"Meh, whatever." Ryan brushed a hand through his hair. "I only want her for her status as an Afton."

Ella waved her hand and Ryan was suddenly soaked with water that had just appeared out of thin air, cascading over his head. Ryan leapt from his chair, crying out in shock.

"Aaah! F-freezing!"

"That's what you get," Ella said with a smirk.

Zhi-Jiya giggled next to her.

Ryan clicked his fingers and in the blink of an eye, he was dry again. He sat down, eyeing Ella with caution now.

Kyran came to sit at the table, taking his usual seat next to Ella. He looked around, met Aaron's eye, and looked away. Kyran's threat to stay away was the last thing he had said to Aaron, and that was days ago.

"What's for breakfast?" Sam asked, coming to sit next to Aaron. "I'm starved."

"Popular expression today," Aaron muttered, then turning to Sam, he asked, "How you doing?"

"Fine," Sam breathed in a tone of irritation. "It's all healed, stop worrying."

"I still think you should get checked out, like in a hospital or something," Aaron said. "What if you need a tetanus shot?" he asked, shuddering at the memory of those sharp claw-like nails that had dug into Sam's flesh.

"I don't," Sam said. "Armana's checked me. I don't have any infections, the cuts are healed and I swear I'm gonna hit you over the head with something if you don't stop annoying me."

Rose arrived at the table, carrying a large platter of pancakes. Ava and Henry had trays with bowls of all kinds of berries. Mary arrived with her own tray, carrying more fruit and three different types of syrup. Rose sat down next to Sam, but her gaze went straight to Kyran, who returned her stare. Kyran looked pointedly at the platter of pancakes and then at her, raising his eyebrows. The look was clear to read. *Did you make them?*

With a smile, Rose nodded and reached out to stab her fork into the most browned, crispy looking pancake. She placed it onto her plate. Everyone else went for the soft, fluffy, golden-yellow pancakes. Kyran went for the brownish ones with darkened edges. He ate them with a smile – one that matched Rose's.

***

Preparations for the new year were under way. Aaron and the twins learnt that the mages celebrated New Year's Eve with a midnight feast. The kitchen staff were busy with the cooking, as were the farm and orchard workers with gathering the ingredients. Aaron helped Sam in the orchard, keeping busy so his mind didn't wander to other things. Of course, that didn't work for too long. Sooner than Aaron desired, the work was done and Drake dismissed them for the day. Sam went back to the cottage to shower and get changed.

Delivering the last of the baskets to the Stove, Aaron started walking in the opposite direction to the cottages. He walked until he reached the lake and, with a tired sigh, he sat down at the bank. But even the serene calmness of the vast, glassy pool couldn't take over Aaron today. He reached into his pocket and pulled out the withered and frail piece of paper. He held his mum's letter in his hand and the thought came to him that this was all he had left of his parents. The searing pain in his chest was so great it forced a deep, calming breath from him in effort to lessen the panic. He heard the footsteps approaching from behind and found it strange that he could tell it was Kyran. Sure enough, Kyran came to stand next to him, staring at him with a frown.

"What are you doing?" he asked.

"Sitting," Aaron replied. "Why? Is that a crime now?"

Kyran raised his eyebrows. "Aren't you in a mood?"

"Yeah, well." Aaron stared ahead of him. "Everyone gets those days."

"Even Saint Adams?" Kyran asked with a smirk, lowering himself to sit next to him.

Aaron didn't say anything. He pocketed the letter. "I thought you weren't talking to me," he said, giving Kyran a sideways glance. "What changed?"

"Nothing," Kyran said. "I'm still annoyed at you. It took me ten full hours to put Lexi right, thanks to you."

"I never asked for your help," Aaron said, irritated. "You did that on your own. Don't blame me for damaging Lexi."

"You're welcome," Kyran said dryly. "So glad I risked my neck to save your ungrateful behind."

"Who asked you to jump in after me?" Aaron bit out.

Kyran smiled a little, the green of his eyes bright and sparkling. "I jumped in after you because you're an Elemental," he said. "A stupid, rash, hot-headed Elemental that would have died and thrown the whole Elemental equilibrium into a right mess."

Aaron frowned at him. "What happens if an Elemental dies?"

"Depends," Kyran replied. "If they were good, they go to Heaven. If they were naughty, they go—"

"Not that!" Aaron snapped. "I meant the equilibrium thing."

Kyran chuckled. "Man, you're really bratty today, aren't you?"

"Forget it." Aaron glowered, turning to stare ahead again.

"No, really," Kyran said, "why are you in such a mood?"

Aaron didn't say anything. Long minutes passed but Kyran remained where he was, stubbornly staring at Aaron. Finally, Aaron gave in and sat up a little straighter, eyes crinkled against the scorching sun.

"It's the new year tomorrow," he said. "Exactly two months since I came here." His voice dropped. "Two months since my mum and dad..." He trailed off. "They should have come back by now." He looked over at Kyran to see the mirth and amusement leave him. He looked like his usual serious self, for which Aaron was grateful.

Kyran opened his mouth to speak. "Ace—"

"I know," Aaron cut him off. "I know that they've gone to find Neriah and it's an impossible task to track him down and I know two months is probably not enough time to find him but," Aaron paused, taking in a breath, "they wouldn't stay away this long without trying to contact me," he said. "I know my parents. They would have sent me a letter or...or a message somehow, to let me know everything was okay." He paused, worry and fear shadowed in his eyes. "I keep thinking, what if...what if something's happened to them? To Uncle Mike? What if they're...?" He couldn't say it. He physically couldn't form the words that suggested his parents, his uncle, his only family were no more.

"Your parents are alive, Aaron," Kyran said.

"How do you know?" Aaron asked.

"I don't," Kyran replied. "But you do." At Aaron's look of confusion, Kyran went on. "You know that mages are all connected, right?"

Aaron nodded. "Yeah."

"This connection that links all mages together becomes something more where blood is concerned." Kyran turned to stare ahead of him, choosing to look at the lake instead of Aaron. "When someone in your immediate bloodline dies, you feel it."

"Feel it?" Aaron asked with a furrowed brow. "As in?"

"As in, you feel it," Kyran repeated, keeping his eyes turned away from Aaron. "The exact moment they take their last breath, when life drains out of them, you feel it deep in your core." He paused. "The feeling is...unimaginable. It's like a part of you dies, leaving behind a hole – one that never fills up." His voice had dipped into a whisper, barely loud enough for Aaron to hear. "You feel it, the absence. The feeling of something missing within you every day from the moment you wake up to the moment you fall asleep. It never goes away." He turned to look at Aaron. "There's no mistaking it, no matter where you are, how far away you are from your family. The moment they die, you feel it, like a physical kick to your gut. You know instantly who you've lost."

Aaron stared at him, his heart racing so fast, he felt it was going to beat its way out of his chest.

"So," Kyran went on, "if you've felt anything like that since–"

"No," Aaron was quick to say. "Nothing like that."

Kyran nodded. "Well, then." He offered a weak smile. "Suffice to say your parents are alive."

Aaron let out a long breath. "That's a relief," he said. "Makes waiting for them to come back a little easier now that I know all of them are okay."

Kyran stared at him, looking like he was mentally debating something. He glanced away before sighing with resignation. "Ace," he breathed, "I really don't want to be the one to tell you this." He turned to meet Aaron's eyes. "Your parents, they're...they're not coming back."

Aaron stared at him with surprise. "Don't say that."

"Trust me, I don't want to," Kyran replied. "But that's the truth and the sooner you accept it, the easier it'll be for you to move on."

Aaron scowled at him. "You don't know what you're talking about."

"Ace, they've done this before," Kyran said. "Your parents ran out on this realm and didn't look back for fourteen years."

"Yes, but at that time they didn't leave behind their son!" Aaron snapped, so angry he was shaking. "I know they ran once before, but this is different. They're coming back for me. I know they are."

Kyran took a moment to just stare at Aaron before nodding. "Okay," he said. "We'll see if you're right."

"I *am* right," Aaron insisted angrily.

"Alright, Ace," Kyran said with smile. "Alright."

Aaron had to take in a few breaths to calm down. The mere idea of being abandoned had shaken him. It set every nerve of his on fire.

"Come on." Kyran slapped a hand on Aaron's shoulder. "Why waste a perfectly good day sitting around moping?"

"What? You mean training?" Aaron asked. He knew Kyran was changing the topic and he was partly thankful.

"It's not been that long, Ace," Kyran said, getting to his feet. "You've forgotten about training already?"

Aaron got up, dusting the back of his jeans. "I thought you gave up teaching me."

"I don't *give up*," Kyran said with a grin. "On anything." He looked Aaron up and down. "Even if you do need *so* much work that it's tempting to just quit." He flashed him a teasing smile. "But I won't. Hunter's promise." He held one hand to his chest and the other one up.

Aaron rolled his eyes. "Yeah, yeah," he muttered.

"Come on, I've got the perfect practice for you," Kyran said, leading the way towards the farm.

"I don't know if I should be excited or afraid," Aaron said truthfully.

"Both." Kyran smirked. "You should be both."

***

Aaron glanced around him before turning to Kyran. "You've *got* to be kidding me," he said. "How is this training?"

"If you have to ask," Kyran said, sitting on top of the wall, "then you obviously need a lot of work." He pointed a finger at the ground. "Come on, hurry up – before they get away."

Aaron looked down to see chickens running around, clucking and rustling their feathers. With an annoyed look at Kyran he set off, chasing after the chickens, trying to catch them and put them back in their coops.

Kyran closed his eyes and slowly shook his head. "Ace," he groaned. "Use your powers. You have powers, dammit!"

Aaron paused to look at him. "Huh?" he frowned. "How can I use *my* powers to catch chickens? It's not like I can float them back to their coops like *some* people."

Kyran raised his eyebrows. "Your powers work too. Figure it out."

Aaron chose to continue running after the chickens. He remembered the day he met Mary for the first time. He had been in a similar situation then and he had managed to catch the hen that time. Darting this way and that, crouched over, Aaron ran after the clucking birds. A familiar giggle made Aaron pause and look up. Rose was standing at the gate, smiling at him.

"What are you doing, Aaron?" she asked.

"Chasing chickens," Aaron panted as he straightened up. "Isn't it obvious?"

Rose glanced at Kyran. "I see your training's started up again," she said to Aaron.

"I'm not sure," Aaron said. "I think he's messing with me."

"Who hurt you so bad you can't trust?" Kyran called.

"You need something, Rose?" Aaron asked, ignoring Kyran.

Rose held up her basket. "Eggs," she replied. "We're making cakes for tonight."

"Give us ten minutes," Kyran said, smiling. "He'll have all the chickens rounded up and put back. He'll get the eggs for you."

Aaron groaned and immediately resumed the chase, knowing he had to stay within the ten-minute time limit now. Rose went to sit on the grass and watched Aaron as he scrambled around, trying to catch the chickens but he couldn't get a grasp on them. She tried to stop the guilty amusement that came at Aaron's loud exclamations and Kyran's sarcastic comments.

A low whistle distracted her and she turned to see Ella walking up, grinning at Aaron and Kyran.

"The old chicken routine," she mused. "Aaron's not clicked as to what he's supposed to do, has he?" she asked rhetorically. "Poor idiot."

"Just out of curiosity," Rose said, "what exactly should Aaron do?"

"Use his powers," she said. "What else?"

"Yeah, I kinda got that part," Rose said. "I meant, *how* does he use his powers to catch the chickens?"

Ella smirked and turned to face the two boys. Cupping her hands to her mouth, she yelled, "For Heaven's sake, Adams! Tilt the ground, shake it, break it, turn it to mud – *do* something!"

Aaron stopped, red-faced and breathing hard, to stare back at her.

"Hey! Stop giving him clues!" Kyran shouted back. "Let him figure it out for himself!"

Kyran had Aaron's attention back on the chickens. With a sigh, Ella sat down next to Rose.

"We'll be here till next year," she muttered.

"Which is technically only hours away," Rose replied.

"True," Ella mused. "Hey, you excited?"

"For the new year?" Rose asked. "Not particularly."

"How can you not be excited?" Ella asked. "You made it through another year. It's a cause for celebration."

Rose shrugged. "That's one way of looking at it, I suppose."

"It's the only way of looking at it," Ella corrected. "When you grow up in a world that's being ripped apart by a war, you learn to be thankful that you lived through another year."

Rose didn't know what to say. She dropped her gaze to the ground. A few minutes passed in silence before they felt the ground tremble a little.

"Finally!" Kyran's relieved voice sounded. "Ace, try to stay upright yourself, yeah?"

Ella chuckled softly. "Poor Aaron."

"So," Rose started. "Is there anything special mages do on New Year's Eve?"

"There are a few small traditions." Ella smiled. "Very different from humans."

Rose frowned. "What do you mean?"

"Don't you humans do that thing?" Ella asked. "Where you kiss the one you love at the stroke of midnight, so you're ending and starting the year with them?"

Rose looked surprised. "How do you know that?"

"Spent New Year's in the human realm once. We were hunting vampires," she explained. "Man, that was a crazy night," she said with a shake of her head.

"Did you get the vampires?" Rose asked.

"Yeah, but they weren't the scary part." She laughed, winking at Rose. "I'm only joking. Truth is, I kinda found all the kissing rather cute." She stretched out her long legs and sat back, staring ahead. "I wouldn't mind starting a new year like that, locked in a kiss." Her eyes stared at something in the distance. "I even have someone in mind."

Rose followed her look to the two boys next to the coops. She felt her heart drop. "Do you mean...Aaron?" she asked, hopefully.

Ella turned to look at her with a half-disgusted, half-horrified expression. "What?" she asked. "Are you mad? No, not baby Adams!"

"Baby? He's only three years younger," Rose pointed out.

"He's a lot younger mentally," Ella said. "I can't believe you would think...me and...and Aaron?" She shuddered.

Rose felt her mouth go dry. With great effort she spoke, keeping her eyes lowered to the grass. "So, you meant Kyran?"

"What?" Ella shook her head vehemently. "I'm not talking about *Kyran*! You know what? Just forget I said anything." She scrunched up her nose and shook her head. "Seriously, you thought I was talking about Aaron or Kyran?"

"You were staring in their direction," Rose said.

"I was just looking ahead," Ella said. "I didn't mean Aaron, and *definitely* not Kyran. Jeez!"

"Oh, okay." Rose smiled. Then, inexplicably, she was annoyed. "What do you mean?" she turned back to Ella. "What's wrong with Kyran?" she asked defensively.

"Nothing." Ella shrugged. "Kyran's nice and all, but he's not my type."

Rose snorted. "Right," she muttered, picking at the grass. "Perfect's not your type."

Ella turned to look at Rose with a slow smile. "Oh?" She grinned. "The P-word?" She moved a little closer. "Have a little crush on our Kyran there, have we?"

Rose frowned at her. "What? No, no." She waved a hand, a little too forcefully for it to be believable. "I just...I mean, come on." She gestured to Kyran, who was explaining something to Aaron. "You can't say he's not good-looking."

"Oh, I can say that," Ella replied. "Kyran's not good-looking. Kyran is freaking *gorgeous*." She moved behind Rose, staring at Kyran over her shoulder. "Look at him," she prompted. "With his dark hair and those mesmerising green eyes," she said in a purposefully low and seductive voice. "Bet he makes you melt with just a look." She grinned. "And what about that beautifully sculptured face? Those lips – perfectly kissable, no?"

Rose couldn't help but stare at Kyran. She agreed with Ella, wholeheartedly, but didn't say anything.

"Those broad shoulders," Ella continued, teasing Rose. "You could rest your head against those, no problem. Those strong arms could hold you, keep you safe. Not to mention those killer abs..."

"Stop it." Rose smiled, blushing.

"You know what? You're right." Ella grinned, moving to sit facing Rose. "Kyran is strong, talented and very, *very* hot. He's perfect, as you put it, but take a word of warning." She craned her head back to glance at Kyran. "When a boy's *that* perfect," she smirked, meeting Rose's eyes, "there's gotta be something wrong with him."

***

Night had fallen. Lanterns were lit and floated in the air, rocked by the gentle breeze. The table was currently being set with dish after dish of hot, sizzling food. Mostly everyone was gathered around the table, chatting and laughing. The mood was so great, Aaron forgot all about his disastrous training session with Kyran and those blasted chickens. He sat with Sam, grinning at Ryan's funny story about his first hunt.

Rose placed the last dish of roasted lamb and glanced around the table. She didn't find who she was looking for.

"Where's Kyran?" she asked Aaron, who was almost bent over, laughing at something Ryan had said. Rose had to shake his shoulder. "Aaron? Where's Kyran?"

Wiping the tears from his eyes, Aaron looked up at her. "Dunno," he said. "He might still be home." He turned back to Ryan at once, dissolving into fits of laughter again.

Rose headed to the cottage they shared with Kyran. Sure enough, she saw the soft light coming from the living room window. She walked into the hallway but knocked once on the living room door before opening it. She found Kyran sitting on the sofa, an array of weapons laid out on the coffee table before him. She paused, staring at the blades and the dismantled pistol that Kyran was in the process of putting back together.

"Hey," she greeted him. "What're you doing?"

"It's for Genius out there." Kyran nodded at the window, but Rose understood he was referring to Aaron. "I'm going to drag him out of bed at the crack of dawn tomorrow and continue his training." He shook his head. "He's probably forgotten all the weapons training I gave him."

Rose smiled. "Give him a break," she said. "He's trying."

"He needs to try harder," Kyran said. "A *lot* harder. The easy stuff ends with this year. It's a new year – time for a new, super tough training regime."

Rose slipped into the chair next to the sofa. "The end of the year," she said. "Have to say, I never imagined it would end like this."

Kyran paused, before slowly lowering the gun onto the table. "It's also the start of another year," he said. "A new year, a new hope."

"Yeah." Rose smiled. "A new hope. I like that." She looked over at Kyran, studying him. "Do mages have new year resolutions?"

"Sure." Kyran slid a short dagger into its sheath. "Resolutions are aspirations. Why wouldn't mages have them?"

Rose leant forward slightly. "What's your new year resolution?"

"That's easy." Kyran slid a magazine into the pistol, and slid back the rack with a resounding click. "Win the war. What's yours?"

Rose grinned. "Just as important as yours," she said. "Cook something that's fairly edible."

Kyran smiled. "Give yourself some credit," he said. "You're not as bad as you think."

Rose could feel the blush heat her cheeks. "What about you?" she asked. "Anything you're not good at that you want to improve this year?"

Kyran looked caught off guard. He narrowed his eyes at her. "You mean, like a fault?"

Rose's heart skipped a beat. "Yeah," she uttered softly. "What are your faults, Kyran?"

There was a spark of amusement in Kyran's eyes. "I have too many to list."

Rose was surprised. "I thought you were going to insist you didn't have any flaws."

Kyran shrugged. "What can I say? I'm brutally honest." He raised an eyebrow. "Can that be termed as a fault?"

"No," Rose said. "Honesty can't be a fault."

Kyran thought for a moment. "I don't know when to quit and walk away," he said. "If I think I'm right, I'll fight to the death to prove it."

"I have to say," Rose said, smiling, "that doesn't sound much like a fault to me."

"No?" Kyran asked.

"No," Rose replied.

Kyran smiled. "I'm a mean snorer too."

"What?" Rose barely held back her laughter. "You snore?"

"Like a bucklebearer."

"What's a bucklebearer?" Rose asked.

"You don't have bucklebearers in your world?" Kyran looked surprised.

Rose shook her head, laughing. "No, but they sound like fun."

"They are the nosiest little buggers," Kyran said.

"And you snore like them?" Rose asked.

"You probably snore just as loud," Kyran said with a grin.

"Hey!" Rose stopped laughing. "*I* don't snore."

"How do you know?" Kyran teased. "You're asleep. Maybe you do."

"I know I don't snore," Rose insisted. "Trust me, Sam would never let me live it down."

"Sam probably snores too," Kyran said.

"Why are you so obsessed with snoring?" Rose asked, grinning.

"What? It's true," Kyran said. "If you're asleep, how do you know that you don't snore?"

"How do you know that you do?" Rose asked. "You're asleep too."

"I don't know," Kyran replied.

"What?" Rose frowned. "You just said you were a mean snorer?"

"I'm assuming I am," Kyran replied, "but I'm asleep so I don't know if I do or don't. I'm just going with the fact that I probably do."

Rose dissolved into a fit of giggles. "That's the craziest assumption I've ever heard."

Kyran watched her for a moment before smiling. "You have a great laugh," he said. "You should do it more often."

A tingle ran through Rose.

"You need to have a reason to laugh," she said.

"Not necessarily," Kyran said.

"You do know what people call others who laugh for no reason?" Rose asked.

"Happy?" Kyran offered.

Rose giggled, shaking her head.

Voices were heard outside, doing the countdown.

"Five...four...three...two...one..."

Several loud bangs went off, accompanied by loud cheery voices shouting, "Happy New Year!"

Rose didn't even flinch at the sound of gunshots. She was too caught up by the vivid green eyes that were staring at her. At the back of her mind, Ella's voice echoed, *Don't you humans do that thing? Where you kiss the one you love at the stroke of midnight, so you're ending and starting the year with them?*

Rose took in a breath and moved forward, towards Kyran.

"Happy New Year," she said against his ear, so he could hear past the gunshots.

Kyran smiled back. "Happy New Year, Rose."

***

Most of the mages were still firing shots into the air when Rose and Kyran walked out of the cottage together. A few were at the table, clinking their glasses and laughing. Ryan and Julian waved Kyran over, grinning from ear to ear.

"Come on, Kyran!" Ryan yelled. "Where's your greeting?"

Kyran raised his arm, pistol clutched in hand, and fired three shots in the air.

"Drinks for everyone!" Alan laughed, hovering three full trays in front of the mages. Everyone took a beer bottle, including Aaron.

He had just brought it to his mouth when Kyran appeared by his side, smoothly swiping the bottle from his hand. At Aaron's scowl, Kyran only grinned.

"Aww, come on, Kyran," Ryan laughed. "It's the new year. Let him have one."

"The last thing his aim needs is the influence of alcohol," Kyran said.

"I'm not training right now," Aaron protested.

"Not yet, you're not," Kyran said. "But you will be in three hours' time."

Aaron groaned.

"Be careful, Aaron," Ryan smirked. "He won't rest until he makes a Hunter out of you."

Kyran smiled and swung his arm around Aaron's shoulders. "You can bet on that."

Aaron rolled his eyes but couldn't hold back his laugh.

Soon, it was time for the New Year feast. For the first time since arriving in Salvador, Aaron saw Mary sit at the table to eat. Before anyone could take a single bite, though, a jolt of light shot across the sky. It exploded into Aric's mark – a bright white symbol glistening against the night sky.

"Cool." Sam grinned, staring up at it. "You guys do fireworks too?"

No one answered. They were too busy staring at the mark, their expressions morphing to looks of horror. The joyful atmosphere from only moments before changed, making a chill run down everyone's spine. At once, the sound of chairs scraping against the ground echoed in the air as everyone rushed to their feet. Aaron and the twins followed after them as the mages ran towards the path leading to the Hub. That's when Aaron understood that the mark in the sky wasn't in celebration of the new year – it was a distress signal sent by Scott. Sam and Rose stopped outside the Hub, knowing humans couldn't enter the circular building. Leaving them there, Aaron ran inside and headed to the main room, only to see everyone crowded around the white table. Pushing his way to the front, Aaron saw Scott standing with his head lowered, hands clutched around the edge of the table. Kyran, Skyler, Ella and the rest of the Hunters were at his side. Every eye was fixed on the map, their expressions one of utter terror.

At first, Aaron couldn't figure out what they were looking at. All he could see was the map of the human world. Then, he saw it, the strange cloud covering what he recognised as Canada. He moved closer, staring at the wisps of mist swirling around that one particular location. He felt his heart miss several beats.

"What is that?" he asked.

"That," Scott said in a broken voice, "is a tsunami."

25

Losing Faith

There was a sense of urgency in the air as the mages ran from the Hub to the buildings next to the garage. The shutters to three of the workshops were lifted to reveal towering stacks of boxes, piled high to the ceiling. One by one, the mages began lifting the boxes out and stacking them in the street. Four pairs of headlights cut their way through the dark forest, pulling up in front of the garage. The drivers of the SUVs stayed in their seats while the rest of the mages loaded the boxes into the back of the vehicles.

Aaron, Sam and Rose quickly stepped forward to help, packing the heavy boxes into the back of the cars. The moment the SUVs were loaded, they took off, disappearing down the dark path. Hunters strapped the leftover boxes to the back of their bikes and set off after the cars.

The mages left behind slowly made their way back to their cottages. The midnight feast to welcome the new year was forgotten. Dishes of untouched food were left to go cold on the table. Where the atmosphere had been one of joy and jubilation a few minutes before, now it was forlorn and heavy with despair. Aaron, along with Sam and Rose, headed back to their cottage. They got into their beds, but none of them slept that night, each wondering what this new year would bring after a start like this.

It was well into the afternoon when the Hunters returned, wearing weary and mournful expressions. Tiredly, they came to sit at the table as Mary hurried to serve them hot drinks and food.

"Doesn't matter how many times you see it," Zhi-Jiya said quietly, shaking her head. "It never fails to shock you."

"The day you become numb to suffering is the day you stop being a mage," Mary said.

"Another hit," Ella said. "That's another one the human realm took because of Hadrian's zones."

"That's what, the fourth disaster in six months?" Ryan asked.

"It just keeps getting worse," Ella murmured, closing her eyes.

Mary took in a deep breath. "Come on. Get cleaned up, all of you. I'll get some food out."

The Hunters listened to their Mother Mary and got up from the table. "Aaron," Mary called. "Could you go and get Scott? He hasn't eaten all day."

Aaron nodded and set off to the Hub, where he knew Scott would be. He found Scott sitting on his chair next to the round table, staring at it.

"Scott?" Aaron called.

Scott looked over at him and lowered his clasped hands, straightening up. "Aaron?" he looked confused at his appearance. "What is it?"

"Mary's asking for you," Aaron replied. "She wants you to come and eat."

Scott managed a weak smile. "I'm not hungry, Aaron, but thank you."

Aaron stepped closer. "You really should eat something."

Scott nodded but made no move to get up. Aaron shifted from one foot to the other, not sure if Scott was coming or not.

"Okay." Aaron turned to go. "I'll just...leave you to your thoughts then." He opened the door but couldn't make himself walk out. He couldn't leave Scott when he looked so miserable. He closed the door and turned back to him. "It's not your fault, you know," he said quietly.

Scott looked up at Aaron. "I never said it was."

"You don't have to," Aaron replied. "It's written all over you."

Scott sagged a little, as if the guilt were in fact a physical weight pressing down on him. He shook his head slowly, staring at the map.

"Two years ago, this map looked so different," he said. "Hadrian had three zones." He looked up at Aaron with tired, bloodshot eyes. "Three zones," he repeated. "And now, in two years, he's got nineteen." He closed his eyes. "He's ripping apart our realm, piece by piece, and he's taking the human realm down with it."

"Scott..." Aaron stepped closer, struggling to find something to say, anything that would bring comfort. "It's only a matter of time," he said. "Sooner or later, the Hunters will find Hadrian and the Scorcher and—"

"Sooner or later," Scott repeated, nodding his head but his tone was bitter. "Yes, sooner or later. That's what I keep telling myself. It'll be over soon. We'll catch Scorcher soon. Without him, Hadrian's strength will be gone. We just have to wait for the right opportunity." His gaze snapped up to Aaron, full of anger and frustration. "We've been chasing after the Scorcher for *two* years now and got nowhere. All that's happened is that we've lost zone after zone and the human realm is paying for our failures." He shook his head and leant over in his seat, elbows resting on his knees. A minute passed in strained silence as Scott fought to compose himself. He let out a shaky breath. "We're losing, Aaron," he said quietly. "This war, this fight...We're losing it every day. Neriah's not enough, not any more, not since Hadrian's Scorcher arrived."

"Don't say that," Aaron pleaded. "There must be a way. The Hunters are really good and they've won every hunt so far—"

"We might be winning the hunts, but Hadrian's winning the war, despite having his powers locked," Scott said. "His son, the Scorcher, is devastating this world and, by proxy, the human realm." He pointed to the table as he stood up. "That tsunami that hit the human realm only happened because of the sheer amount of power rushing out of the tears. It's because that part of the human realm happens to lie under one of Hadrian's zones. With no Gate to utilise the power flow, it seeped out and resulted in *hundreds* of humans being killed and injured. Thousands of homes lost, families torn apart and all because we couldn't safeguard that zone!" Scott shook his head as angry tears escaped his eyes. His chest heaved with quick breaths as he stared at Aaron. "If we don't do something, if we don't stop the Scorcher, soon there'll be nothing left to fight for." He looked down at the map of the human realm before meeting Aaron's eyes again. "There'll be nothing left to protect."

***

The sky was slowly turning to glorious hues of pink and orange with the setting sun. The mood around Salvador stayed the same, though: grey, drab and depressed. The mages busied themselves in their work, not talking much. Scott kept himself locked in his Hub. The Hunters were uncharacteristically subdued too, staying at or around the table, talking in low tones.

Rose finished her day's work and left the Stove. Instead of retiring to her cottage, she headed in the opposite direction, to the lake. She sat down at the bank, watching the setting sun reflect in the still, calm water. It was so strange to think that something so tranquil and soothing could wreak havoc and destroy homes and lives. She had seen footage of tsunamis before, on the news channels. She'd even watched a movie or two re-enacting the disaster. But until now, she had never really thought about it.

Footsteps approached from behind her. Rose turned and smiled at Kyran.

"Hey," he said, taking a seat next to her. "What are you doing here?"

Rose took a moment to answer. She stared at him, taking in the tired and defeated look he shared with the rest of the Hunters today.

"Nothing," she replied. "Just didn't want to go inside yet."

They sat in silence, staring ahead at the glistening water of the lake.

"Was it really bad?" Rose asked after a few minutes.

Kyran paused before nodding. "Yeah," he replied. "It was bad."

Rose didn't know why she was asking. It wasn't going to make her feel any better, but she couldn't stop herself. "Any idea how many casualties?"

"Too many," he replied.

Rose felt the uncomfortable churn in her stomach get worse. "That was aid in those boxes, wasn't it?" she asked.

Kyran smiled a bitter, grim smile. "Salt on their wounds," he muttered. "We couldn't stop the energy flow from spilling out and destroying their world, so we take aid to them whenever a disaster strikes." He turned to look at Rose with fierce anger lurking in his eyes. "So we can tell ourselves we're doing *something*. So maybe we might be able to get some sleep tonight." He shook his head in disgust. "Truth is, the only way we can help them is to prevent the disasters, not offer insufficient help afterwards."

"The Gates," Rose said. "That's the only way to stop the power from spilling out?"

"The only way," Kyran confirmed. "But until we clear out the demons from those zones, we can't set up the Gates."

They lapsed into silence.

"When I was younger, I used to wonder about natural disasters," Rose said. "I guess everyone does at some point. You see the aftermath of earthquakes and tsunamis and you think, why does this happen? Why is Mother Nature so brutal?" She shook her head, looking down at the ground. "It turns out the reason lies in another world, another realm altogether."

"It wasn't always like this," Kyran said. "Once upon a time, when all the Gates were up, the human realm was safe. And once this war is over and we defeat the demons, the Gates will be back up and the human realm will be safe again."

Rose looked over at Kyran. "Tell me something," she said in a quiet voice. "Why is it in the fight between mages and demons, it's the humans who get hurt?"

Kyran was taken aback by the simple question. He held her gaze for long minutes but finally looked away, not having an answer.

***

The loud bangs rang in the air. One by one the flying bottles were smashed by the pellets. Aaron lowered his hand after his last target exploded in an impressive shower of glass. He smiled, immensely pleased with himself. It took endless hours of training but now he could hit moving targets with ease. His teacher, though, wasn't as happy.

"What did I say?" Kyran snapped.

Aaron clicked the small lever on the side of the gun. "Sorry," he said quickly.

Kyran glared at him, giving him one of his slow you're-an-idiot head shakes.

"Decock your gun or I'll decock you, got it?" he warned. Distractedly, he waved a hand to sweep the shards of glass to one side of the clearing. "Right." He turned back, surveying Aaron. "Your aim is improving but you're still taking far too long to take the shots."

"Aiming does take a bit of concentration," Aaron quipped back.

"It has to be quick," Kyran said. "You have to go from one target to the other without taking so much as a breath in between."

"I'll get there," Aaron said.

"So you keep saying," Kyran replied. He waved a hand at Aaron. "Come on, I wanna try something else."

Aaron put the pistol into its holster and followed Kyran to stand in the middle of the clearing, facing him.

"Your weapons are important," Kyran said, "but your true weapon is your power."

Aaron tensed. His aim was improving, as was his footwork when dodging attacks, but when it came to using his Elemental power, the only thing he could do was the ripple. According to Kyran, it wasn't enough.

"When you're in Gated zones," Kyran continued, "your powers will clear an area faster than any sword or gun."

"I don't get it," Aaron grumbled. "I thought the whole point of a Gated zone was that it was a demon-free area?"

"Demons are like viruses," Kyran said. "Nasty viruses that come back, even if they've been defeated and thrown out in the past."

"So it's just a circle?" Aaron asked. "We just keep on fighting? It never ends?"

"Hey, you're the one who wanted to be a Hunter," Kyran said. "One of the neatest tricks to fight demons is to turn the ground itself into a trap." He pointed to the ground between them. "Turn this area into a sinkhole."

Aaron gaped at him. "Excuse me?"

"A sinkhole," Kyran repeated. He drew a circle with his finger, mapping out the ground between them.

"Okay," Aaron started, licking his dry lips. "How exactly do I do that?"

"You're the Elemental," Kyran replied. "Figure it out."

Aaron drew out a slow breath and raised his hands, staring at the ground, willing it to give way and sink into itself. He stayed like that for about a minute. Nothing happened. "Am I supposed to say something?" he asked, glancing up at Kyran.

"Yes," Kyran replied. "You're supposed to admit out loud that you're an idiot."

Aaron dropped his hands. "You're not helping."

"You're not listening," Kyran said. "You're an Elemental, Ace. You can use the power of Earth as you see fit."

Aaron breathed out and tried once again. He stared at the ground, begging it to cave in and form a sinkhole. Again, nothing happened.

"Okay." Kyran sighed. "Maybe we should start with something a little simpler." He surveyed the area. "Alright, bend that tree."

"Bend what?" Aaron frowned. "What good would that do?"

"Just do what I'm saying," Kyran said. "Bend that tree over there." He pointed to a small, thin one.

Aaron turned around and focused on it, bringing up his hands again. No matter how hard he tried, he couldn't make even a single leaf move.

"Take control, Ace," Kyran encouraged. "Anything and everything that's connected to the ground is under your power. You can twist it to your will. You just have to want it badly enough."

Aaron pushed harder, willing his power to rush through him and escape past his fingers. He wanted to bend that tree in front of him. He felt a slight tingle in his fingertips and the leaves on the branches ruffled a little, but that was the extent of it.

"Damn it!" Aaron ran both hands through his hair.

"Come on, Ace," Kyran said. "Keep trying."

"What's the point?" Aaron spat. "I'm obviously *never* going to get this!"

"You've done it before," Kyran said. "You split the ground to stop a car from running over you. That's pretty intense. If you can do that as an instinctual reflux, you can do pretty much anything."

Aaron exhaled slowly and raised his hand, aiming at the tree.

"Don't think about it too much," Kyran instructed. "Free your mind from the constraints of *how* to do something. Focus instead on what you want. You want to change the ground. You want that tree to bow before you. Make it so. Command the ground to do as you say, Aaron, don't ask it."

Aaron tried to do what Kyran said. The result was – nothing.

"It's not working," Aaron groaned.

"You're not focusing, Ace."

"I am!" Aaron snapped. "I'm trying! I don't know how to *command* the stupid tree!"

"Obviously." Kyran smirked. "Otherwise it would be doubled over by now."

Aaron's hands curled into fists. "Either help me, or stop talking."

"I am helping," Kyran said. "I can't demonstrate this power. The element of Earth is your power, Ace."

Aaron forced out a breath. He pumped and shook his hands, trying to get rid of the pins and needles sensation in his fingers. He aimed again and this time, he put every last bit of his concentration into it.

Still nothing happened.

"Come on, Ace," Kyran said, irritation seeping into his voice. "Strip away everything: the guns, the blades. Take it all away and you're still left with your power. No one can take that away from you," he said. "Use it, Ace. It's yours. Command it."

Aaron tried; he forced all of his energy forward and tried to bend the tree in half. The leaves swayed in response.

"Come on, Ace," Kyran groaned. "It's not that difficult."

"You do it then!" Aaron snapped.

"I would if I were the Elemental for Earth," Kyran replied. "But it happens to be you. So drop the attitude and get on with it."

Aaron tried again. The branches moved a little more, swaying from side to side.

"Is that it?" Kyran asked. "That all you got, Ace?"

"Stop calling me that!" Aaron dropped his hands and turned to face Kyran. "I get it, okay! I get that I'm rubbish at this. You don't have to rub it in *every single time*!" he shouted. "My name is Aaron! Call me Aaron, or call me Adams if you have to, but quit this *Ace* business, alright!"

Kyran stared at him with something akin to amusement. "You think that's why I call you Ace?" he asked. "To make fun of you?"

Aaron glared at him. "Don't you?"

"Yeah," Kyran admitted, "but not for the reason you're thinking."

"Then what is it?" Aaron bit out.

Kyran grinned but shook his head. "It's not important," he said, "but if you tried a little harder, or had any confidence in yourself, you wouldn't be so paranoid as to think everyone's making fun of you."

"Shut up!" Aaron growled. "I *am* trying hard! And how am I supposed to be confident about something I don't know how to control?"

Kyran raised his eyebrows. "Don't you?" he asked.

Aaron paused. Kyran tilted his head, gesturing for Aaron to look behind him. When Aaron turned, he saw a whole cluster of trees had bent in half. Their trunks bowed in arcs and full heads of green leaves touched the ground. Ironically, the one thin tree he had been aiming for was still standing tall and proud in the middle of the bowing trees. No sooner had disbelief clouded Aaron's mind than the trees snapped back up, violently swaying, their branches shaking countless leaves free.

With wide eyes, Aaron turned back to Kyran.

"Anger and rage are like speeding," Kyran said. "It propels you to go further, faster than you thought possible, carrying you with its momentum, but if you don't know when to let go, you'll inevitably crash." He moved forward and clapped a hand on Aaron's shoulder. "Use your anger if you have to, until you gain the confidence you need, but don't let it overtake you. You do that, and you'll fail."

Aaron nodded.

Kyran smiled and stepped back. "You perform under stress," he stated. "You split the ground on instinct because there was a car coming at you. You did a perfect ripple but only to throw a vamage away from Sam." He tilted his head to the side, observing Aaron. "You need to learn to do the same under calmer situations." He gestured to the trees. "Again, but this time, get the tree you were targeting." With a slow grin, he added, "Alright, Ace?"

***

It wasn't long before Aaron found himself accompanying the Hunters on another trip out of Salvador. This time it wasn't a hunt. It was a trip to the City of Balt, to meet with someone named Mandara, who had asked Scott for help on a 'missing-mages' case in Zone L-26.

Aaron felt jittery as Lexi passed through the glowing portal shaped like Aric's mark. Kyran swerved the bike around and paused, waiting for the rest of the Hunters to pass through the portal and arrive at his side.

Aaron took in his surroundings. They were at one end of another long road, similar to the one they had just passed outside the Gate of Salvador. But where that path was lined with tall green trees and a clear blue sky, this one had acres of flat land stretching out on either side of it. Far off in the distance, Aaron could see rocky mountains tinted white with frost. The sky was like a snapshot taken at the point of sunset: a beautiful array of orange and red, with the golden sun giving out its last rays.

One after the other, the Hunters arrived, passing through the portal. When the twentieth and last Hunter arrived, Skyler and Ella led the way onwards, racing along the glittering white stone pathway.

They arrived at the Gate, which was the exact replica of the towering mass of white that guarded the entrance to the City of Salvador. Skyler and Ella got off their bikes and walked over, slipping off their gloves. Each placed a palm on the door and spoke.

"Skyler Avira."

"Ella Afton."

The symbols on the door brightened before fading. Aric's mark was the only one left before it too slowly melted into the door. Ella and Skyler climbed back onto their bikes and led the rest into the City of Balt.

The place wasn't all that different from Salvador. There even was a long table planted in the middle of the street. Tall buildings lined both sides of the road. Some were houses, others were shops – or what was commonly referred to as stores in the mage realm. A few mages were crowded outside a partially open door, through which Aaron could smell freshly baked bread.

The Hunters parked their bikes and climbed off. They huddled in a circle, scanning the area, ignoring the mages of Balt.

"Scott said to speak to Mandara," Skyler said to the rest of the Hunters. "He's the one who requested our help. Don't bother with anyone else."

He turned around and met a fist. It was mostly the surprise, rather than the blow, that made Skyler stagger back. Aaron stared at the punch-thrower. A familiar red-haired girl stood, seething at Skyler.

"You son of a demon!" she cursed.

"Is that how we're greeting Skyler now?" Kyran asked. "'Cause I like that."

Skyler stared back at the girl with wide eyes, a hand over his nose.

"Bloody hell, Bella!" He recovered, pulling his hand away. There was no blood. The punch wasn't hard enough.

"You let *humans* into a Q-Zone?" Bella cried. "*Humans,* Skyler! You let humans into a Q-Zone when you refused *us*!" she came forward, prompting Skyler to step back.

"Now hold up." Skyler held up a hand. "You failed the ring."

"Humans!" Bella shrieked. "Did you have humans win the ring?"

"No, obviously–" Skyler started.

"Exactly, no!" Bella glared at him. "What the hell–!"

"Bella." A deep, rumbling voice interrupted from behind her. "Give the boy a chance to speak."

Everyone turned to see a tall, dark-skinned man with black tufts of hair flecked with grey. He was dressed in long robes and sandals. He stood with his arms behind him, staring at Skyler with serious brown eyes.

"I'm sure Elemental Avira has a fascinating explanation as to why he allowed two humans to enter a place he went out of his way to prove the Hunters of Balt couldn't handle."

Skyler, Aaron noted, wasn't looking too good. His face was pink, his nose a little red. The usually icy blue eyes were now burning with humiliation and anger. With his fists clenched into tight balls, he stepped out of the Hunters' circle to meet the man.

"Mandara, I presume?" he asked in a clipped tone.

"Your assumption is correct." The man inclined his head and held out a hand. "I've heard a lot about you, Elemental Avira."

Skyler shook the man's hand. "I wish I could say it was a pleasure to be here." He threw a sideways look to Bella. "But I'm afraid that would be an outright lie."

The man – Mandara – smiled, but it didn't reach his solemn eyes. "You must forgive Bella," he said. "She is a little...high spirited."

"With a mean right hook," Skyler said, rubbing at his nose.

Bella glowered at him.

"I believe Scott has already briefed you?" Mandara asked, getting to the point of business.

"Yes," Scott replied.

"Come." Mandara said. "Rest and have some refreshments before we discuss the situation."

Skyler followed after him, leading the others. Kyran paused to grin and wink at Bella. She smiled back at him.

Mandara led them all to the table, where a great selection of food was prepared for them. Skyler and Ella had a quick bite and left the table with Mandara, disappearing into one of the cottages for the meeting. As Aaron enjoyed his second helping of chicken fried noodles, he struck up a conversation with two Hunters of Balt – Andrew and Mark – seated opposite him.

"So what exactly is the problem in L-26?" Aaron asked.

"There've been a number of disappearances," Andrew replied. "There are another three sub-zones that have to be conquered before a Gate can be set up for the L-Zone."

"Which means that although we chased out the demonic forces from L-26 a year ago, they tend to sneak back," Mark added.

"We don't know what's terrorising the locals." Andrew said. "Mandara wouldn't let us go, not without Salvador's Hunters backing us up. The Lurkers have failed to find anything."

"Lurkers?" Aaron frowned.

"Lurkers, Ace." Kyran leant sideways, joining the conversation. "Hunters make up one part of the fight, Lurkers make up the other. Most hunts wouldn't be possible without them. The groundwork is done by the Lurkers; the killing is done by the Hunters."

"Do we have Lurkers?" Aaron asked.

"Lurkers don't belong to any one city. They work for everyone," Kyran explained.

"What do Lurkers do?" Aaron asked.

Kyran smirked. "Lurk."

Aaron narrowed his eyes at him. "You think you're funny, but you're really not."

Kyran chuckled before going back to his food, his attention diverted by something Zhi-Jiya was saying.

Aaron turned to Mark and Andrew. "So is Mandara the Controller for Balt?" he asked.

Andrew and Mark looked at each other in surprise.

"There's only one Hub," Mark said. "And only one Controller."

"Scott is not Salvador's controller," Andrew said. "He's the Controller for this realm."

Aaron's eyebrows shot upwards and he spluttered on his mouthful of noodles. No wonder Scott was always so stressed out. He had to take care of all the Hunters of this realm.

"So who is Mandara then?" Aaron asked.

"He's like our chief," Andrew said. "He took over less than six months ago."

"What happened to your last chief?" Aaron asked.

Andrew pulled a face. "You don't want to know."

The doors on the far right of the hallway opened, and Skyler and Ella appeared, followed by Mandara. Skyler walked over to where Ryan and Julian were seated and crouched between them, talking in a low voice. Ella came to Zhi-Jiya and Kyran.

"So?" Zhi-Jiya asked. "We have any clues?"

"Not much to go on," Ella sighed. "Pretty much what Scott said – there've been disappearances. Boys and girls are being abducted without a trace. No tracks left, no blood or evidence of any kind of a struggle. It's like mages are just vanishing into thin air."

"What's the plan?" Kyran asked.

"We go out in two hours," Ella said. "Do a preliminary check, talk to the locals and get more info. You never know. We might hit it lucky and catch a trail."

"Here's hoping," Zhi-Jiya said. "Otherwise we'll have nothing to show Aaron." She winked at him.

"Hey, I'm still in shock that Scott let me come on this trip." Aaron shook his head. "I thought after the Q-Zone thing he wouldn't let me go on any hunts."

"This isn't a hunt," Kyran said. "Which is why you're here. We're only looking for a trail."

"And if we find it?" Aaron asked.

"Then you stay out of the way while we take care of it," Kyran replied.

***

As soon as lunch was over, the group assembled at the door. The hunters of Balt and Salvador made a team of forty-eight, including Aaron. Mandara stood to the side, his dark eyes scanning the crowd. He didn't say a word, just nodded to Skyler, gesturing for him to take over while wearing a tight smile.

"Alright," Skyler called out, commanding a hush over the rest. "We go out in teams. You must wear your mark and use it to converse with the others." He held up his own silver spiral pendant. "You all know this, but I have to stress it once again." His cold blue eyes scanned every individual mage, stopping on Aaron. "L-26 is an open zone. There is no Gate. You cannot under *any* circumstance use your powers." He said the words slowly and clearly, watching Aaron for confirmation that he understood. "Should the need arise, our guns and blades are our only weapons today. Is that understood?"

"Understood," everyone chimed.

Aaron turned to look at Kyran. "What if someone acts on reflex?" he asked nervously.

"Then they contribute to the flow of energy that'll spill out and damage the human realm," Kyran replied.

Aaron swallowed. "Okay," he said, nodding to himself. "Hold back the instinct to survive. Can't be that hard."

Kyran chuckled. "Relax, Ace. You'll be fine. I'm going to be right there with you. We all are. Besides, we're only going to gather more information about the disappearances. There'll be no need to use our weapons."

Aaron felt a little better. His hand reached up and he fingered one of the sharp blades strapped across his torso. He could feel the weight of his black and silver pistol resting in its holster at his waist. If he needed them, he had plenty of weapons. Feeling a bit more confident, Aaron followed Kyran out the door.

***

Zone L-26 was accessed via another portal, one set up just past the Gate of Balt. As Aaron blinked the white spots from his vision left by the blinding glow of the portal, he saw his surroundings were little more than vegetation. Tall, leafy plants grew from the moss-covered ground. Incredibly high trees swayed in the wind, their branches full of green, gold and brown leaves. As far as he could see, all that met his eyes were trees, bushes and big, leafy plants.

The Hunters got off their bikes, abandoning them for the time being, and trekked a way through the forest. Aaron walked alongside Kyran, trying not to slip on the mossy ground, or get his foot trapped in the thick vines.

They pushed their way through the forest for at least twenty solid minutes before they reached a clearing. The crowd of Hunters split up into eight groups of six. Aaron was with Kyran, Julian, Andrew and two other Hunters of Balt. They walked in silence, each one busy searching the area for clues that would lead them to the local mages. Aaron couldn't imagine anyone living here, except for wild animals maybe. They reached a high cliff top and stopped, taking a moment to catch their breaths. The heat, coupled with their heavy attire, only served to make them sticky with perspiration. Aaron pulled at the uncomfortably warm leather belts that were crossed over his chest.

"What now?" Julian asked.

Kyran stood with his hands on his hips, eyes narrowed as he scanned the area. He caught sight of something in the distance and stopped, eyes narrowing further. His expression hardened suddenly. He looked down into the mess of vegetation before looking back up. A look of surprise blanketed his features.

"Did you see that?" he asked.

"See what?" Julian asked.

"The Lurker," Kyran said.

"Lurker?" Andrew frowned. "Really? Where?"

Kyran looked back at the spot in the distance where he'd been staring. Something flickered in his eyes before he shook his head. "Nothing," he said quietly. "Forget about it." He pointed to the ground below them. "We need to get down there. There's a pathway just here."

"How'd you notice that?" Julian asked, sounding impressed with Kyran's sharp eyesight.

"I think we could climb down from here," Andrew said, moving to the left.

Kyran held out a hand, stopping him. "Wait," he whispered, staring below.

This time, they all saw what Kyran had. Something had moved behind the bushes. Without a word, Kyran and the others crouched to the ground, hidden from view. Aaron quickly followed their example, pressing his front to the soft grass. He peered over the edge of the cliff to the ground below. The rustling of leaves and bushes got louder, until something emerged from them into Aaron's view. The breath Aaron wasn't aware of holding rushed out of him with relief. It was only a man. A filthy-looking man with long, matted hair that reached to his waist. Most of his face was hidden behind a wild beard that trailed to his chest. His exposed arms and torso were caked with dirt. A loincloth was his only clothing. His legs were abnormally long, covered in downy hair – or maybe it was filth, Aaron couldn't be sure. But it was when Aaron saw the man's feet that he realised the man was in fact not a man at all. His feet were pointing backwards. Completely backwards. His toenails had grown into claws, which ripped parts of the soft grass out with every step he took. The nails on his hands were just as long and curved, and looked just as sharp.

Kyran cursed. "Abarimons!" he hissed furiously. "Dammit! What are they doing here?"

"Abarimons don't have a valley near here," Andrew protested in a whisper.

"They must have," Julian argued. "Abarimons don't venture too far from home."

"They probably set up a valley near here," Kyran said. "Which is why mages have started going missing."

"Why's that?" Aaron asked.

"Abarimons gotta eat," Kyran replied.

Aaron forced back bile.

"What do we do?" asked one of the other Hunters, a brown-haired girl.

"We call for back-up," Julian said and reached for his pendant. Holding onto it, Julian began relying his message.

"We need to track it," Kyran said. "If we can find their valley, we can take out all of them."

"What?" Andrew asked. "Are you insane? You breathe in the air of an Abarimon's valley, you'll never leave it!"

"I know that!" Kyran snapped. "I didn't say anything about going *into* their valley. We stay outside and take out each one of those back-footed freaks."

Aaron saw the Abarimon stop near a tree and bend down behind it to pick something up. Aaron never imagined that when the savage-looking beast straightened up it would have a little girl thrown over its shoulder.

Aaron could feel the Hunters around him tense while his own heart jumped horribly at the sight.

"Come on," Kyran whispered urgently. "We can't wait. We gotta take him out – now."

In the blink of an eye, weapons were out and clutched in everyone's hands. Aaron held on to his pistol and racked back the slide. His gaze was on the girl. She was unconscious, thrown unceremoniously over the Abarimon's shoulder. She couldn't be more than nine, maybe ten years old. Andrew held onto his pendant and repeated Julian's request for back-up.

"Don't do anything yet," Scott's voice echoed in all the Hunter's heads. *"Wait for back-up."*

"We can't wait, Scott" Kyran argued. "It's one Abarimon. We can handle it." He turned to Andrew. "We take the Abarimon, you get the girl out."

They pulled themselves up and began sneaking their way closer to the oblivious Abarimon, that was making its way through the forest with its victim. Climbing down the steep hill proved to be a feat in itself, never mind doing it stealthily. A small slip and the brown-haired girl's foot knocked into a rock, which tumbled down and landed with a thump on the soft ground. The Abarimon froze mid-step.

There was nothing they could do. The Hunters held up their weapons – ready. The Abarimon turned around to face them. Closer to the demon, Aaron could see the face was as creepy as the backwards feet. The Abarimon's high forehead hung over dark eyes. Its cheekbones were too prominent, widening the face. The dry lips, just visible through the overgrown hair of its moustache, parted to show a mouthful of sharp, pointed teeth.

A heartbeat later, a single bullet from Julian's gun was sent towards the Abarimon's chest. The demon twisted out of the way, dodging the bullet. Its speed was surprising for a being with backward feet. The demon threw the unconscious girl and ran off. Thankfully the mossy ground softened the child's fall. Andrew and the other two Hunters were by her side in an instant. Aaron followed after Kyran and Julian. The three raced after the Abarimon, firing bullet after bullet at it. But the overgrown bushes and trees blocked their view and soon they had lost sight of the demon. They came to a stop, catching their breath.

"Where'd it go?" Julian asked.

The sound of rushing air made Aaron turn around – just in time to see a branch thicker than Aaron's leg come hurtling towards them. It hit Julian on the back of his head, throwing him face forward to the ground.

"Julian!" Aaron rushed to him, pulling him onto his back. The boy was knocked out cold.

Kyran raced after the Abarimon, disappearing into the thick forest. Aaron, not sure if he should leave Julian or go to help Kyran, grabbed onto his circle pendant.

"We need help!" he cried. "Julian's out and it's just me and Kyran left with the Abarimon."

"*Don't worry, Adams,*" Sarah's soft voice said, flooding his mind. "*We're coming.*"

Aaron got up and ran after Kyran. He couldn't leave him alone to face the demon. He followed the sound of the gunshots and raced deeper into the forest, his pistol clutched in his hand. He caught sight of Kyran running down a steep hill and, a little ahead of him, a fleeting glimpse of the back-footed demon as it threw itself off the edge of a cliff.

Kyran came to a skidding stop. Aaron was already running down the hill, the sharp incline making it impossible to stop or slow down. His foot slipped and Aaron yelped as he tumbled forward, rolling down the hill. He knocked into Kyran and both fell over the edge.

They were lucky the fall wasn't too high. Kyran and Aaron rolled all the way down another hill until they hit the ground. Aaron lay dazed, all his breath knocked out of him.

"Aww, Ace!" Kyran groaned. "Now you've done it!"

"What?" Aaron asked breathlessly, picking himself up onto his hands and knees. "What'd I do?"

Several shadows fell over them. Looking up, Aaron found a whole crowd of Abarimons surrounding him and Kyran. It suddenly occurred to Aaron that Kyran had stopped running for a reason other than it being the edge of a cliff.

Aaron glanced at his pistol, lying ten steps away, knocked out of his grip when they had fallen straight into the valley of the Abarimons.

26

THE VALLEY

The itch was driving Aaron crazy. No matter how hard he tried, how much he struggled, he couldn't loosen the scratchy fibre from around his wrists. All his efforts got him was more pain spiking through his already aching shoulders. He tried turning, as much as he could in his position, but he couldn't see Kyran, though he knew the other boy was in the same predicament. Both of them had been dragged here by the Abarimons after being relieved of their weapons. The demons had then used what Aaron could only presume was rope made from some natural fibre to bind their wrists tightly behind them, securing them against the trees. Then they had left.

Aaron tried once again to reach up and find the knots. He could just about touch them but he couldn't tug them open. Aaron groaned in frustration.

"Kyran," he called. "What you thinking?"

He heard Kyran sigh. "I'm thinking...what do I want for dinner," Kyran replied.

"What?" Aaron asked frowning.

"For dinner," Kyran said. "I can't decide between lamb and beef."

Aaron strained to look over at Kyran, glaring at him. "I meant, what are you planning for our escape?"

"Oh, that." Aaron could hear the grin in Kyran's voice. "We're not escaping."

"What?" Aaron asked.

"We're in their valley," Kyran replied. "And breathing their enchanted air. For now, anyway." He paused for a moment. "Which means we can't leave their valley. No one can leave an Abarimon's valley once they enter it, except for Abarimons of course."

Aaron struggled with increased vigour, managing to twist around enough to see Kyran.

"That's it?" Aaron asked. "We just...stay here?"

"Pretty much," Kyran replied, looking perfectly calm. "Well, until they get hungry enough. Then *we're* for dinner."

"Why aren't you freaking out?" Aaron exclaimed.

"What's the point?" Kyran asked. "Besides, I'm too cool to freak."

"Kyran!" Aaron shouted. "I swear to God, if you don't help me think of a way to escape, I'll–"

"Relax, Ace," Kyran said, with a chuckle. "You'll give yourself an aneurysm."

Aaron struggled even harder. The rope was cutting into his skin now but Aaron couldn't stop. His weapons may have been taken but he still had the silver pendant hanging from his neck. He could hear Scott's panicked voice calling out his and Kyran's name in his head. If he could just free his hands, he could hold on to the circle and ask for help and....Aaron paused. Would the Hunters come to help them? Would Scott let them enter the valley of Abarimons?

He stopped struggling. The other Hunters wouldn't risk themselves by coming into the valley. It would only serve to trap them too. Scott wouldn't put all his Hunters into danger just to rescue two, would he? Aaron sagged against the tree, falling limp in his restraints.

"Oh good," Kyran said dryly. "Here they come."

Looking up, Aaron saw at least fifteen Abarimons heading towards them. Aaron found himself tensing at their feral appearance. Their wild untamed hair hid most of their lower face, leaving their cold black eyes to strike fear in Aaron's heart. The strange way they walked, with their feet pointing in the opposite direction, made a shiver run down Aaron's spine.

"Whatever you do, Ace," Kyran said in an urgent whisper, "don't stare at their feet."

"What? Why?" Aaron asked, panicked because that was all he could focus on. "Do your feet turn like theirs if you stare at them?"

"What? No," Kyran replied. "It's just impolite to stare."

Aaron threw him a frustrated look.

The Abarimon at the front came to rest before Aaron. Aaron noted that this one was slightly less dirty-looking than the others. Its hair was just as long and tangled but its chest and arms were clean. Aaron couldn't help but stare at the backward feet, despite Kyran's warning.

The Abarimon moved past him, coming to stand in front of Kyran.

Even though a part of him was relieved the demon had moved away from him, Aaron felt a new bout of panic for Kyran.

The Abarimon easily dwarfed Kyran's six-foot frame. The demon leant down, its crooked nose only inches away from Kyran's face, and took a great big sniff before pulling away. When it smiled, it revealed sharp, pointed teeth.

"Hunter," it said, its accent heavy and clumsy, giving away its unease with the English language.

Kyran smirked. "The name's Kyran."

The Abarimon regarded Kyran before a deep, throaty laugh escaped it. "Hunter," it growled again. "No come here."

"It wasn't intentional," Kyran replied. "I was sort of pushed into coming."

The Abarimon leant in, sniffing at Kyran again. It reached out with one of its claws and parted Kyran's coat. The silver spiral caught the sun's ray, shining proudly. Kyran tensed as the Abarimon trailed its filthy, curved nail down his chest and looped the chain. With a sharp tug, the Abarimon yanked at the chain, snapping it, and pulled it away. It held it up, as if to show to Kyran what it had done.

"No Hunter more," it growled and threw the chain aside.

Kyran glared after it as his pendant cut through the air before plopping into the nearby stream. Another Abarimon strode towards Aaron and did the same, snatching the chain from his neck with such vigour that it left long scratches down Aaron's neck. The Abarimon paused, staring at the fine red lines. Aaron recoiled as much as he could when the Abarimon leant into him, sniffing at his neck, growling low in its throat. Its black as coal eyes glinted with hunger.

"Hey! Easy there," Kyran called, getting its attention. "You're gonna ruin your appetite if you keep smelling him like that."

The Abarimon pulled away from Aaron, turning to look at Kyran with its nostrils flared and teeth bared.

"Don't you know that smelling your food fills you up?" Kyran asked with a smirk.

The Abarimon standing by him growled and grabbed Kyran's face with its clawed hand, yanking it back around to face him. The Abarimon said something that sounded like nothing more than guttural groans. The Abarimon's native tongue wasn't intelligible but Aaron could tell from the tone alone that it was grunting threats to Kyran. The Abarimon finished by jerking Kyran's face to the side, leaving small scratches on his cheek. Kyran turned back to the Abarimon with narrowed green eyes but his smirk was still in place.

"I didn't get any of that," he said. "But please don't repeat it. I can't take any more of your breath."

For a terrible moment, Aaron was sure the Abarimon was going to lash out, but the demon only growled at him and moved back. It turned and left, the crowd following after it. They disappeared from sight behind the tall trees.

Aaron let out the breath he had been holding, sagging with relief. He turned to look at Kyran.

"Are you mad?" he asked. "Why were you mouthing off to him?"

"Why not?"ABauldbmbmbmb Kyran asked, tensing, pulling at his hands. "They're gonna kill us anyway. And it's not like they can understand everything we say."

"Yeah, but–" Aaron stopped, his mouth falling open when Kyran pulled his hands forward, freed but with loops of rope still around each wrist. "How'd you do that?" he asked.

"Magic." Kyran grinned, holding up a small blade.

"Where were you hiding that?" Aaron asked. The Abarimons had been thorough in snatching the weapons from them.

"Always keep at least one blade in the lining of your sleeve," Kyran instructed, pulling the loops off each wrist before walking over to him.

Aaron felt himself smile. "You had that all along?" he asked. "You couldn't have told me?"

"And ruin the fun?" Kyran asked before cutting through the rope tying Aaron's hands. "You have any idea how hilarious you look when panicked?"

The moment the rope parted, Aaron pulled his hands forward, holding back his groan of relief. He reached up with stiff arms to rub at his sore shoulders before turning to face Kyran. "Now what?" he asked, pulling the scratchy loops off his wrists.

"Now we get out of here," Kyran said.

"You said we couldn't leave the valley."

"We can't," Kyran confirmed, "unless we take the valley from the Abarimons."

Aaron nodded. "And how do we do that?"

"Simple," Kyran replied, meeting Aaron's eyes. "The valley is ours after we kill all the Abarimons."

***

Keeping to the shadows, Kyran and Aaron made their way deeper into the forest. When the trees finally thinned to a large clearing, Aaron saw a cluster of small huts. The Abarimons bustled in front of them: some carrying wood, others dragged what looked like the carcasses of wild animals to one side. A few Abarimons scratched and sniffed each other, their claws poking at each other's flesh. The female Abarimons were just as wild-looking as their male counterparts, with long, straggly hair and clawed nails on their hands and backward feet. They too wore loincloths to protect their modesty and their long hair covered their naked fronts.

Sitting in the middle of the village was a wooden cage – a square monstrosity. Crammed inside were children.

Aaron's stomach turned so violently it was a miracle he didn't retch. Around thirty young boys and girls were trapped inside, forced to kneel in the small cage. It wasn't tall enough for any of them to stand up in. Their tears tracked paths down their dirt-streaked faces; small hands pressed against the wooden bars, begging to be let out. Aaron felt sick.

"My God!" he breathed.

Kyran didn't say anything, but his eyes had darkened as he stared from one small face to the other.

"They're mages," Aaron whispered. "Why don't they use their powers?" He knew the place was an open zone – an area without a Gate – but surely the instinct to survive would have taken over.

"Take a closer look, Ace," Kyran said, a slight growl underlined his words.

Aaron didn't know what he was supposed to be looking for, but after a moment or two of staring from one sobbing child to another, it clicked. The mages, all of them, were children. None of them looked even close to the age of thirteen, when their core would awaken and give them their powers. They were just kids; completely vulnerable and unable to protect themselves.

"Come on," Kyran said and turned towards the hut that was adjacent to the caged children. "Our weapons must be in there."

"What makes you say that?" Aaron asked.

"It's the only decent-looking one, which makes it the chief Abarimon's hut," Kyran said. "I swear, if he's touched my sword with those filthy claws of his I'm gonna split him in two!"

"Focus, Kyran," Aaron said. "We have bigger problems." He stared at the caged children. It was one thing to kill all the Abarimons and take their valley so they could escape, but a whole other situation when they had to do it with thirty panicked, sobbing children at risk of getting caught in the crossfire.

Aaron followed behind Kyran, going from one tree to another, hiding behind each. The Abarimons seemed distracted; between scraping the last bits of meat off the carcasses and dragging wood into a large pile, none of them noticed who was moving in the shadows. It took Kyran and Aaron almost eight minutes to time their stealthy, short sprints from one tree to the next. They had almost reached the hut when two Abarimons walked out of it. One was the marginally clean-looking Abarimon – the one who had stood in front of Kyran. The other, Aaron realised, was the demon they had chased into this valley.

"He must be the chief," Aaron whispered, staring at the slightly cleaner-looking Abarimon.

Kyran didn't say anything. He simply watched, waiting for the two demons to walk away. Unfortunately, only the chief walked away, leaving the other Abarimon to guard the doorless hut.

"Now what?" Aaron urged.

Kyran gave the hut and the demon pacing before it a final look before gesturing Aaron to follow. Using the cover of the trees and the shadows from the setting sun, both boys made their way to the back of the hut. Leaving Aaron to stay behind, Kyran inched around to one side of the hut. Staying pressed up against the wall, Kyran leant around the edge to see the Abarimon still pacing and growling, staring at the caged children with barely hidden hunger. Kyran shifted from the side of the hut, just enough so the frightened children could see him. Looks of surprise and desperate hope flitted across the faces of the children, alerting the Abarimon. The demon turned to look behind, following the childrens' stares. It didn't see anything.

Grunting with suspicion, the Abarimon moved forward, the curved nails of its backward feet scratching against the dry ground as it headed to investigate behind the hut. As soon as the Abarimon turned the corner, Kyran leapt at it. His hands grabbed the Abarimon's head, his feet on the demon's chest. Without missing a beat, Kyran twisted his hands and the Abarimon fell to the ground, taking Kyran with it. As the dead demon hit the ground, Kyran simply stepped off. Straightening his coat, Kyran turned to look at the body at his feet. Glancing up, he found Aaron staring at him with horror.

"What?" Kyran asked. "At least it can see its toes now."

Aaron gaped at him, rapidly turning pale.

"Don't go squeamish on me, Ace," Kyran warned and gestured for him to follow.

Aaron carefully stepped around the collapsed body of the Abarimon, trying not to look too closely at it or its broken neck. He hurried after Kyran, who was standing at the edge of the hut, scanning the area, waiting for the right moment to slip indoors. He met the stares of the frightened children again and quickly held a finger to his lips, winking at them. The children nodded, taking in deep gulps of air in effort to calm down and stem their tears. Taking their chance, Kyran and Aaron slipped inside with only the children watching them.

The hut was small and dark but pleasantly cool. Aaron wiped a shaky hand across his sweaty brow, breathing out in relief. Kyran had already moved towards the single table in the far corner, upon which rested their familiars.

Kyran picked up his sword with a grin. "Hurry up, Ace," he said. "Get your stuff."

Aaron picked up his pistol. A blissful feeling of calm overtook him as soon as his fingers touched the cold metal. He picked up the holster and quickly clicked it around his waist before sliding his pistol safely inside. Kyran did the same for his twin pistols. They worked quickly, snapping and clicking their leather bands and straps back onto their sweat-drenched bodies.

"What's the plan?" Aaron asked, slipping the last of his daggers into his pocket.

"We go out. We kill," Kyran replied. "What more you looking for?"

"Bullets will...will kill them?" Aaron asked, his voice shaking a little.

"The bullets have Aric's mark carved on them," Kyran said, slotting the last dagger into his pocket. "As do our blades. One shot, doesn't matter where, will bring the demons down. You just have to make a hit."

Aaron paled but gave a jerky nod.

Kyran looked at him and narrowed his eyes. "Ace?" He moved closer. "What is it?"

"Nothing," Aaron said. "It's just..." He swallowed heavily before looking up to meet the intense green gaze. "I've never...killed...before."

"Aaron," Kyran started, reaching out to hold him by the shoulder. "I need you to focus." His grip tightened. "I know you haven't had enough training. I get that you're nervous, but we don't have a choice here. It's just you and me, Ace. We're the only Hunters in this valley. There are kids out there who need our help." He shook his head. "I can't take out a whole valley on my own. I need your help."

Aaron's mind went back to the crying children, trapped in a cage, waiting to be killed. He steadied his resolve, his hand gripping the gun at his waist before he gave a slow nod.

***

Aaron took in a steadying breath and stepped out of the hut. He stood at the threshold, watching and waiting for the Abarimons to notice him. The demons went about their business, taking no notice of him, until one Abarimon turned its head and caught sight of him. Its eyes widened and mouth dropped open, showing glistening, sharp teeth. A hand came up and a clawed finger pointed at him before a shrieking sound left the demon. It was as if Aaron was watching it happen in slow motion, as every demon head turned in his direction. The Abarimons growled. Almost at once, the back-footed beings came at him, dropping what they were doing. Aaron waited, forcing himself to stay at the threshold, watching the demons race closer. He counted down in his head.

The countdown wasn't even complete when Kyran attacked. His bullets rained down on the distracted Abarimons. Standing on the roof with a pistol in each hand, Kyran fired bullet after bullet into the demons. Aaron watched as the wounded Abarimons dropped to the ground, their flesh turning grey as life evaporated out of them and their bodies turned to dust. The others scampered away, fleeing from Aaron, eyes turned upwards to the roof – to Kyran.

One Abarimon took the risk, dodging the bullets as it came for Aaron. Aaron's trembling hand gripped the pistol and he raised it, willing himself to pull the trigger. He found he didn't have to. In a heartbeat, Kyran had jumped down, standing directly before the door, shielding Aaron. Holding up both guns, Kyran fired two bullets into the approaching Abarimon. The rest of the demons had hurried back, growling and grunting to one another.

"Oh come on!" Kyran called after them. "We were just starting to have fun." He darted after them, chasing them into the dark forest.

Aaron raced out of the hut, straight to the wooden cage with the frantic children inside. He found a thick stake slotted through two loops, holding the lid down on the cage. Aaron pulled at it, trying to get it out but the thing wouldn't budge. It was jammed right in. Aaron didn't waste time fighting it. He pulled back and pointed his gun at it.

"Move back!" he told the kids.

The children did, as much as their limited space allowed. Aaron fired two bullets, splintering the wood so the stake weakened. It slid out easily and Aaron quickly threw back the lid. The children scrambled to get out, lifting themselves off their aching knees. Aaron helped the younger ones out of the cage.

"Come on, quickly," he said, leading the panicked children to the chief's hut. All thirty children ran out from under the scorching sun into the cool shade of the hut. "You have to stay here," Aaron said as he grabbed the table that had minutes before held his weapons. "Just until the Abarimons are gone." He pulled the table towards the door before stepping out. He tilted the table to stand on its side. "We'll come back for you," he promised before wedging the table into the doorway, successfully blocking it. There was only a tiny gap at the top, enough to give the children some light in the dark hut. Aaron eyed the mark Kyran had carved on the underside of the wooden table. Aric's mark would keep the children safe. No Abarimon could touch the table now.

Aaron turned, pistol in hand, searching for Kyran. He saw him in the far distance, fighting the Abarimons with a combination of guns, blades and kicks. Aaron raced forward to Kyran's side.

Kyran swerved out of the way of the vicious claws aiming to tear his chest open. He retaliated with a point blank shot. Turning around, even before the dead Abarimon could hit the ground, Kyran fired another bullet into the nearest Abarimon.

The demons seemed to be in two minds: fight or flee. Some had already torn down the murky path, running deeper into the forest. Others were trying to get to the Kyran, to take him out before he killed all of them. In the midst of the growling demons, Kyran spotted the furious chief. Kyran smirked at him and beat his hand, still clutched around his gun, to his chest.

"Hunter!" he introduced, mimicking the chief's rough accent. "Gonna kick your ass!"

The chief growled but backed away, joining the frantic crowd running away. Kyran fired shot after shot, dropping Abarimons to the ground, where they turned to dust. One of the demons approached from behind, claws out and teeth bared, as it prepared to rip into Kyran. A shot just missed the Abarimon, hitting the tree next to its head. The Abarimon fell back and turned to see Aaron racing towards him, his pistol still aimed. Before Aaron could aim a better shot, Kyran took care of the Abarimon, delivering a bullet to its chest.

As soon as Aaron reached Kyran, both boys darted behind the large tree, taking refuge for a moment. Kyran slid out the empty magazines from both guns, dropping them to the ground. He pulled out his last full magazine. He gave it a long look before slotting it into one of his pistols.

"How many bullets you got?" he asked.

"Two in here," Aaron panted and held up his pistol, "and this." He pulled out his one and only magazine from his pocket.

Kyran stared at it, green eyes narrowed and his glistening brow furrowed. Aaron met his troubled eyes with a sinking heart. They didn't have enough bullets. There were still at least thirty or forty Abarimons left. Maybe even more hiding throughout the valley.

"What do we do?" Aaron asked.

Kyran pocketed his empty pistol and pulled out his sword. "Close combat," he said. "Stick close and don't waste the bullets."

Kyran took in a breath, pushed himself out from behind the cover of the tree, and paused.

The Abarimons were gone.

Kyran looked around, his fierce gaze darting this way and that, searching for demons.

"What now?" Aaron asked.

"We have to get every last Abarimon," Kyran said. "We can't leave this valley otherwise."

They hurried down the dark path, searching for the demons. With every step, Aaron's heart pounded, expecting an Abarimon to jump out from behind a tree. He kept a firm grip on his gun, aimed it before him, but feared he might not react fast enough. The only thing keeping him somewhat calm was Kyran's presence by his side.

"Maybe they left?" Aaron suggested, hoping that was the case. "If all of them run away, that makes the valley ours. Then the enchantment in the air ends and we can leave too, right?"

Kyran nodded, his eyes scanning the area. "Yeah, but...but Abarimons don't do that," he said. "They don't abandon their valley, not that easily."

"You call that easy?" Aaron asked.

Kyran stopped and turned to give Aaron a look, shaking his head at him. "Come on," he said. "They're here...somewhere."

They crossed the clearing. They searched for what felt like hours, but there was no sign of the Abarimons. They came to another clearing, a bigger one, marked in a perfect circle by the surrounding trees.

"Kyran, they've left," Aaron said. "I say we get the kids and get out of here."

"Abarimons are territorial creatures," Kyran replied, still scanning the empty grounds. "They wouldn't leave, not because of two Hunters."

"Maybe they got scared?" Aaron suggested.

"Fear?" a voice growled from behind him.

Both Kyran and Aaron whipped around, guns aimed. The chief Abarimon, looking no more than a deranged beast, walked out from behind the tree. Its darkened gaze stayed on Kyran, glaring at him with fierce hatred.

"Fear not my feel," it said in strained English. "Fear you be."

From behind the trees Abarimons appeared, holding their own weapons. Long wooden spears with sharp-pointed ends were clutched in almost every Abarimon's clawed hands. Kyran and Aaron looked around to see they were completely surrounded. Aaron's back pressed against Kyran's as both boys held out their weapons, targeting one Abarimon, then another, but both of them knew it was useless. There were at least seventy Abarimons closing in on them. They didn't have enough bullets and there was only so much close combat Kyran could do on his own.

"Kyran?" Aaron called.

"Stay by my side, Ace," Kyran said. "Shoot till your last bullet. Leave the rest to me."

Aaron swallowed heavily and gripped his pistol tightly, steadying it with his other hand. He took aim at the closest Abarimon. He sucked in a breath and held it, willing himself to fire the first shot and start his first, and probably last, battle.

Shots rang out, deafeningly loud, but they were from neither Aaron's nor Kyran's gun. Startled, Aaron turned to see a whole group of teenagers clad in long coats and boots come spilling out from the darkness of the forest. They fired at the Abarimons, dropping the demons to the ground. The Abarimons turned, momentarily forgetting about Kyran and Aaron and focusing on this new threat.

From the crowd of boys and girls in dark coats came a flash of ivory white with a glint of studded silver. Aaron's breath rushed out of him in surprise. Skyler was here. The sight brought a reassuring comfort that confused Aaron. Never did he imagine he would be glad to see Skyler. With a closer look, Aaron realised it wasn't just Skyler; the rest of the Hunters were here too. Ryan, Julian, Ella, Zhi-Jiya – the whole lot of Salvador's Hunters were here but so were the Hunters of Balt. A glimpse of Bella slicing off the head of an Abarimon confirmed that. It was only when Aaron felt Kyran's firm grip under his elbow that he snapped out of his shock. Kyran pulled him quickly to the side, practically throwing him behind a tree.

"Stay here," he instructed. "Any demon comes near you, shoot it."

With that, Kyran sprinted forward to join the battle. This time it was the Abarimons that were surrounded, having no place to run from the Hunters. They fought back with their sharp spears, trying to impale their attackers. Aaron's blood ran cold when he saw one of the Abarimons plunge the spear into Zhi-Jiya. Without a moment's thought, Aaron was running towards her. Ella shot the demon before Aaron could get near enough to aim. With a sharp tug, Ella pulled the spear out of Zhi-Jiya's torso and threw it aside. Zhi-Jiya staggered forward, bending over, with both hands clutched around her stomach.

"Zhi-Jiya!" Aaron came to her side. "Oh God! You okay?"

Zhi-Jiya was breathing heavily, head lowered as she stayed doubled over.

"Give me a...a minute," she managed to say.

Slowly, she straightened up, panting past the obvious pain. Her face was covered in a fine sheen of perspiration. Her hands were stained with blood, but she simply brushed them down her legs and pulled out another magazine from her pocket.

"Get my gun, will ya?" she asked breathlessly.

Aaron picked her black and red pistol up from the ground. "You okay?" he asked again, as he held her gun with one hand and steadied her with the other.

Zhi-Jiya grinned, even though her eyes with bright with pain. "Please," she scoffed, but Aaron could hear it lacked her usual charisma. "It takes more than a flimsy stick to get the best of Zhi-Jiya Hau."

She slid the magazine into her pistol, cocked her gun and aimed at the Abarimons, taking out four of them in a matter of seconds. Aaron stayed by her side but Zhi-Jiya continued the fight, paying little attention to her wounds.

On the other side of the clearing, Kyran turned to the Abarimons with his sword, having used up all his bullets. He swung the blade, slicing through the demons. He blocked another spear attack and knocked the stick out of the demon's hand before plunging his sword into the Abarimon's stomach. Just as Kyran pulled the sword out and turned, another demon leapt at him, successfully throwing him to the ground. Kyran was pinned under the filthy Abarimon, who had dug his claws into Kyran's sword-wielding arm, piercing through his flesh. With its other hand, the Abarimon viciously back-handed Kyran, whipping his head to the side. With teeth bared and claws ready, the Abarimon went for Kyran's throat, wanting to rip it out. Kyran caught his hand, struggling to keep the demon back. A shot rang out and the Abarimon stilled, eyes wide open but lifeless. It turned to dust, coating Kyran's front. Grimacing in disgust, Kyran looked up to find a smirking Skyler standing over him.

"Don't look so surprised," Skyler said. "You know *I'm* the only one who gets to kick your ass." He extended a hand, which Kyran took to get pulled back to his feet.

Kyran's arm was bleeding badly – four punctures where the demon's claws had cut into him were weeping blood down his arm. Kyran hugged his injured arm to his chest and picked up his sword with the other hand. A growl brought his and Skyler's attention to the chief Abarimon who was staring at them with wide, mad eyes. Its demons had fallen. There were perhaps five or six left. Kyran and Skyler shared a look before smiling. They rushed towards the chief with their swords and guns raised.

***

After the last demon had fallen, the Hunters made their way back to the huts. Aaron and Ella lifted the table away from the chief's hut to get the scared children out. For the first few minutes, they simply sat in front of the hut, calming the children. Other Hunters gathered around, each talking to the distraught kids, assuring them they were going to take them back home to their families.

Aaron watched as Zhi-Jiya stood to the side, her eyes on the huts. He got up and walked over to her.

"I can't believe they had a valley here," she said quietly. "How could we not know what was going on?"

"You know what I can't believe?" Aaron asked. "That all of you came to help us."

Zhi-Jiya turned to him with a frown. "Why wouldn't we?" she asked. "We're Hunters, Aaron. We don't leave one of our own behind."

"Unless it's a Q-Zone," Aaron said.

Zhi-Jiya smiled. "Even that's been challenged now, what with Kyran jumping in after you and all."

Aaron turned to see Kyran, who was talking with Ryan and Julian, his injured arm held to his chest. A moment later, Ryan and Julian walked away, heading to where Skyler was deep in conversation with Bella. The four talked for a minute before pulling out their guns, loading them with more magazines and spreading out. Other Hunters followed their example by loading their weapons and walking after them.

"What are they doing?" Aaron asked, watching the crowd head to different corners.

"We have to take out every last Abarimon," Zhi-Jiya said. "It's the only way we can leave and take those kids home."

Aaron turned back to her with wide eyes. "You mean...?"

Zhi-Jiya nodded. "Every last Abarimon," she repeated. "Old..." She paused for a brief moment, "...and young."

27

Changing Tactics

Aaron couldn't sleep. Sam and Rose were snoring softly in their beds, but Aaron was wide awake. Eventually he got up. There was no hope for any sleep tonight. He headed downstairs, pausing briefly at Kyran's door. He wasn't back yet. As soon as Aaron and the Hunters had returned to Salvador, Zhi-Jiya and Kyran were rushed to the Empaths to be healed.

Aaron went to the living room and sat down in the semi-darkness. The soft glow from the lanterns outside shone into the room, giving just enough light for Aaron to see the outline of his hands before him. A few minutes later, the front door clicked open and Aaron saw Kyran's silhouette in the hallway.

"Hey," Aaron called, and Kyran turned towards him at once.

A wave of Kyran's hand and the lamps in the hallway and living room glowed. "Ace?" Kyran looked surprised, as well as exhausted and a bit pale. "What you doing still up?" he asked, walking into the room.

"Couldn't sleep," Aaron replied. His gaze rested on the torn sleeve of Kyran's coat. "How's the arm?"

"Fine," Kyran said and sat down, his narrowed eyes fixed on Aaron. "Why can't you sleep?"

Aaron shrugged, but didn't say anything.

"Ace?"

Aaron looked up at him before sighing. "I keep thinking...about today."

"What about it?" Kyran asked.

"Those demons, the Abarimons," Aaron said. "I can't get them out of my head."

"Don't worry about it." Kyran said, leaning back in his seat. "They're gone; their valley's wiped out."

"Exactly," Aaron replied.

Kyran's brow creased, vivid green eyes narrowed in confusion. "Ace," he said, "they were demons."

"I know," Aaron said. "I know they were demons and they were savage, flesh-eating monsters. I know that killing them was the only way of protecting ourselves as well as those kids they had captured, but...but we still wiped out an entire population today."

"Of demons," Kyran repeated. "That's what we do. We're Hunters."

"And that's the thing," Aaron said. "I don't know if I have what it takes to be a Hunter."

Kyran stilled, staring at Aaron.

Aaron dropped his gaze to the floor before continuing. "I know that Skyler and the others hunted down the Abarimon young and killed them. That's the only way we could leave the valley. I know that, but I also know that I could never do that." He looked back up at Kyran. "I couldn't even shoot an adult Abarimon when they were attacking us! My hand shook every time I had to take aim." He paused to take in a breath and he slowly shook his head. "You asked for my help and I did nothing. I couldn't take down a single demon."

"So?" Kyran's question threw Aaron. He looked up at him with surprise. "So what if you didn't make a hit?" Kyran asked. "What matters is that you were there. You stood by my side, like a true Hunter. A true mage." He leant forward. "As for taking down demons, killing isn't easy, Ace. *No one likes doing it.*"

"You were breaking necks and making jokes," Aaron said.

"That's because I've been hunting since I was thirteen," Kyran said. "I've accepted that even if I don't want to kill, I have to, 'cause mages were only brought into existence to kill demons."

"What about mages like Alan and Mary and all the others that don't go hunting?" Aaron asked. "They're still mages, but they don't kill."

Kyran laughed. "Don't be so sure. Mother Mary can behead a demon faster than she can cut a turnip. Alan, son of Thomas Kings, could kick demonic ass with about the same ease as he lays the table. If it comes down to it, every mage in this realm could take down a demon." He paused for a moment. When he next spoke, he was quieter but there was a fierceness in his words. "You have to have the hunger to kill, Ace. A hunger that only comes after you've lost something that meant anything to you." He held Aaron's gaze with darkened green eyes. "Because that's when you understand that being a Hunter isn't about what you're killing, but what you're protecting."

***

Rose passed basket upon basket of overflowing fruit, each settled next to the tall trees.

"Aaron? Sam?" she called again.

She wandered down the orchard path for almost forty minutes before giving up. With a sigh, she sat under the shade of a huge tree. She leant against the wide trunk, her legs stretched out before her. The warm breeze flitted over her, freeing a few strands from her bun to fall across her face. Pushing them behind her ear, Rose closed her eyes and let out another tired sigh. Her eyes slipped closed and she stayed like that for a few moments, silently relishing the feel of the warm breeze across her face and the sweet smell of mangos in the air.

"Don't fall asleep."

Rose opened her eyes with a start, only to stare up at Kyran. She relaxed and smiled. "I was just resting my eyes."

"Yeah, yeah." Kyran came closer. "You seen Ace?"

Rose frowned. "Ace?"

"Just a demeaning nickname to annoy Aaron into working harder," Kyran explained with a grin.

Rose clicked her tongue while shaking her head. "Positive motivation is still a thing, you know," she said. "You should try it sometime."

"Humiliation seems to be the only thing that works," Kyran replied. "You seen him?"

Rose shook her head. "I was looking for Aaron and Sam myself."

Kyran let out a sigh before sitting down on the ground opposite Rose. "He's hiding from me, I know it. He can't handle the tough training."

Rose chuckled. Her gaze moved from Kyran's face down his shoulder to his arm. Last night, when the Hunters had returned, she had learnt from Aaron that Kyran had been injured.

"How's the arm?" she asked.

Kyran lifted up his hand and pulled back his sleeve, examining the flawless smooth skin. "Good as new," he said.

Rose noted the way the four silver lines, tattooed across the back of Kyran's hand, gleamed in the sunlight. "It's just as well mages don't scar," she said. "Can you imagine what you'd look like if you got to keep reminders of all your battles?"

"Not all scars are bad," Kyran said. "Sometimes it's good to keep a reminder of your battles. That way, you'll never forget what you lost."

"Isn't the loss itself a reminder?" Rose asked. "You don't really need a physical mark, do you?"

Kyran smiled up at her and the green of his eyes stole Rose's breath. The intensity of his gaze was such, Rose found herself completely lost. She only realised she was staring when Kyran shifted, as if uncomfortable under her gaze. Rose quickly looked away. She glanced up at the branches of the tree she was sitting under and spotted the small green mangos clumped together in bunches. It would be a few more hours before the mangos would be ripe enough to eat. Of course, in her world it would take days, not hours, for fruit to grow and ripen, but Rose found herself wishing the mangos were ready. Their sweet smell was making her mouth water. When she looked down, she found this time it was Kyran staring at her.

"What?" she asked.

Kyran didn't say anything. With a smile, he leant forward. For a moment, Rose thought he was about to touch her shoulder, but Kyran's hand went past her and rested on the trunk. No more than a heartbeat later, the fruit started to grow; the mangos got bigger and heavier, weighing down the branches. The green of the mangos changed to a sun-kissed yellow and the sweet aroma only got stronger. Kyran kept his hand on the trunk until the branches lowered to offer the ripe and ready to eat fruit. Kyran lifted his hand from the trunk and plucked off a single mango. The branches slowly lifted upwards and settled, the mangos dangling from them. Without a word, Kyran held out the fruit to Rose. Astonished, Rose took the offering.

"How...how did you do that?" she asked.

Kyran grinned. "I know a trick or two to speed things up," he said.

Rose didn't say anything. She held the mango in her hands and smiled. Her heart gave a little skip at the thought that Kyran knew exactly what she wanted, without her having to say a single word.

***

Sam and Aaron were at the far side of the lake, watching the strange way mages went fishing, from a safe, dry distance. This time, both boys rather enjoyed the sight of the towering wall of water and the way the silvery fish were scooped out by the floating net.

Ahead of them, walking along the bank of the lake, were two people Aaron never thought he would see together – Skyler and Armana.

"Where are they going?" Sam frowned, looking at the unlikely pair.

"No idea," Aaron replied.

Skyler and Armana seemed to be deep in conversation. Armana must have said something to annoy Skyler, as he suddenly stopped and pulled Armana by the arm to face him.

"Oh, hell no!" Sam started angrily. "What does he think he's doing?" He stepped forward, ready to march up to Armana's rescue.

Before Sam or Aaron could climb up the bank, they saw Armana gently pulled her arm out of Skyler's grip, smiling the entire time. She rested both hands on Skyler's chest and tilted her face up, her lips moving as she said something. Surprisingly, Skyler smiled and leant forward. He rested one hand on her cheek, and wrapped the other around her waist as he pulled her closer and kissed her.

Sam and Aaron stopped in their tracks, mouths dropped open, eyes wide and unblinking.

"What the–?" Sam uttered.

"Skyler and Armana?" Aaron choked.

Sam turned to gape at Aaron. "That's why she was all, 'Skyler's not bad, he's got a good heart'," he said. "It's 'cause she was with him!"

"Skyler and *Armana*?" Aaron repeated. "How? He's so...so... and she's so...you know?"

"Yeah, exactly!" Sam agreed.

The mages that were fishing must not have seen Skyler and Armana, as they raised their hands, building the water once again. The huge wave climbed high into the air, heading straight at the kissing couple.

"Oh – hey! Watch out!" Aaron shouted in panic, not wanting Armana hit by the water.

Without breaking their kiss, Skyler raised a hand towards the approaching wave. The water spun around him and Armana, making it look like they were encased in a waterproof bubble. The water crashed to the ground all around them, before dragging its way back into the lake.

A flash went through the city, finally pulling the kissing couple apart. Sam and Aaron looked around at the sound of a truck hooting. With a last look of stunned surprise at Skyler and Armana, the two boys climbed the bank and made their way towards the Gate. They arrived to see a huge truck parked in front of the Stove. Mages had already gathered around it. At the front was Jason, instructing the mages to float one item after another from the truck. Sam and Aaron reached the crowd and watched as everything from furniture to sealed boxes were hovered through the air and stacked onto the cobbled street.

"What's going on?" Aaron asked Ryan. "What's all this?"

"Rations," Ryan replied. "And about time too."

Some of the mages started taking several boxes to the Stove, while other boxes were hovered to the path that led to the stores that held everything from clothing to books. Beds and wardrobes were taken away under Jason's instruction.

Aaron walked over to see the word *LAMONT* in bold letters across the side of the truck. "What's Lamont?" he asked.

"You mean who," Ella said, coming to his side. "Fredrick Lamont, the most successful mage of this realm."

"By successful you mean wealthy?" Aaron asked.

"Yeah." She smiled. "Ever since the war started, Lamont's been sending whatever Salvador needs – beds, clothing – pretty much everything a sanctuary requires."

Aaron glanced at the truck before looking back at Ella. "Why? What does he get out of it?"

Ella turned to look at him with a frown. "Why so cynical?" she asked. "He doesn't get anything. He owed Neriah, so he chose to look after Salvador's needs." She turned to look at the truck. "He did his duty all his life. After his death, his family decided to carry on the commitment."

Aaron and Sam followed her to help carry boxes from the truck to the side of the street, where Mary and Jason were opening them to sort what went where.

"There you are." Rose's voice interrupted Aaron, just as he pulled out a heavy box. "I've been looking for you."

"What's up?" Aaron puffed.

"I'm finished for the day," Rose said. "I wanted to hang."

"Well, Rose, *we're* not done," Sam said. "As you can see, we're helping empty out this massive truck."

Rose just gave Sam a look before turning back to Aaron. "And Kyran's looking for you."

"For me?" Aaron asked. "Why?"

"Something about training," Rose replied.

Aaron turned around to see Kyran talking to Ryan and Julian, who were opening some boxes, checking them before handing them to other mages to carry to various stores. Aaron was about to climb off the truck when he saw something lying in the corner. It was a small, rectangular box, ten times smaller than the other boxes. He picked it up as Sam walked over to peer at it. Rose climbed up too, coming to Aaron's other side. Aaron clicked the small latch open. Lifting the lid, Aaron found what looked like thick bits of carved wood piled inside. He frowned at the sight.

"What is it?" Rose asked.

"God knows," Sam replied, promptly losing interest.

"Look," Rose called. "It's a stage." She held up two pieces.

Under the planks of wood was another rectangular box, even smaller this time. Rose pulled it out and clicked it open. Inside was a wooden puppet: a little monkey with big brown eyes and a long curved tail. It wore a sleeveless red and gold jacket with matching shorts. A plaster was on its forehead and a bandage on the very tip of its tail.

"Aww, cute," Rose said, picking up the puppet, running her fingers over the bandage.

"Seems to be missing something," Sam chuckled. "What's a puppet without its strings?"

"I don't think mages need strings to make their puppets dance," Rose said. She looked into the box and pulled out a small, colourful book. "*Adventures of Ace*," she read. "*The hapless monkey who...can't get anything...right.*" She looked up at Aaron, trying her best not to laugh at his gob-smacked expression.

Aaron pulled the book out of her hand. It was a script for the puppet show. On the cover was a drawing of the little monkey, sitting under a tree, holding its head and seeing stars while bananas lay scattered around him. Aaron put the book down and picked up the puppet. Turning around, Aaron glared at Kyran, who was still talking to Julian. When Kyran met his eye, Aaron held up the puppet with an incredulous look.

Kyran grinned, showing all his teeth. He raised both thumbs at him, snickering.

Aaron muttered under his breath and dropped the puppet back into the box, not at all amused with Rose and Sam's stifled giggles.

***

"Time's running out," Scott said, pacing before the seated Hunters. "Our attempts to end this war have fallen flat." His gaze went from one Hunter to the next, resting on Aaron. There was something in Scott's eyes, in his clouded gaze, that unnerved Aaron. He shifted uncomfortably and Scott looked away. "There was another attack last night. It left the City of Jharna burnt to the ground."

The Hunters grew restless at the news, shifting in their seats, leaning forward with blazing eyes and clenched jaws.

"Let me guess." Ella glowered. "Work of the Scorcher?"

"No one else," Scott said. "We *need* to take the Scorcher out, but so far we haven't found anything on him. We're no closer to apprehending him now than we were two years ago." Scott reached into the hollow of the table and touched its surface. "So we need to change tactics. We focus on the next best thing."

Scott's touch caused ripples in the map, distorting the image only to replace it with another. A snapshot of a man with dark hair and strange, glittering blue eyes stared out from the table.

"Daniel Machado," Scott said slowly. "Once the right-hand vamage of Hadrian, he is now at the side of the Scorcher." Scott tapped a finger on the image. "Wherever Machado is, the Scorcher won't be too far away. We get *this* son of a demon, we get to the Scorcher."

Aaron was staring at the image with disbelief. "I know him," he said. "I...I know him."

Scott and the rest of the Hub's attention, shifted to Aaron at once.

"What?" Kyran frowned beside Aaron.

"He was...he was there," Aaron said. "That night, when I did the...the instinctual reflux thing and the vamages attacked. He...he was standing in front of Sam and Rose's house. He fought with my dad."

A ripple of surprise spread around the circular room, with the Hunters turning to one another, their muttering incomprehensible.

Scott hurried towards Aaron. "Christopher Adams engaged in battle with him?" he asked.

"That vamage – Machado – he sent the other vamages at my dad," Aaron recalled, shuddering at the memory of the crowd of men descending onto his dad, surrounding him completely. "My dad and Uncle Mike, they fought them off but...it was too late. Mr and Mrs Mason, they had already..." Aaron couldn't finish. He turned to see most of the Hunters looked solemn, even Skyler looked troubled. Kyran was sitting with his head bowed, looking rather pensive.

Scott cleared his throat, taking a moment to speak. "I wasn't aware that Daniel Machado was the vamage that led the attack on you," he said. "When you performed your reflux action, the vamages must have sensed that the power came from an Adams, from an Elemental. That's why Machado got involved. He wouldn't go for just any mage," he deduced. Lines furrowed his brow and he dropped his head in thought. "That means there's a possibility...*he* could've been there too," Scott said. He looked up, wide hopeful eyes fixed on Aaron. "Think back to that night, Aaron, recall everything you saw," he said. "In the midst of the vamages, did you see a boy? Anyone around your own age?"

Aaron shook his head. "No."

"Take a minute to think about it," Scott prompted. "Really think, Aaron. Anyone around the area? Anyone young near the house, going in or out?"

Aaron shook his head. "I didn't see anyone other than the vamages," he said. "And none of them were young. But I wasn't around for long. My mum drove us out of there pretty fast."

Scott looked disappointed. He fell back, nodding. "Of course, you had to get to safety." He gave a tight smile. "I just thought, maybe if you had seen the Scorcher..." He trailed off. With a sigh, he moved back to stand in the middle of the room again. "From what we have gathered so far, every bit of information suggests that Daniel Machado stays close to the Scorcher. There's every possibility the Scorcher was there when the vamages came to attack Aaron."

Aaron tried his best not to shudder at the thought. He had seen Machado; he could never forget those cold blue eyes and that cruel smirk on his face. But as far as the Scorcher was concerned, there had been no boy in the crowd of men – that he knew for sure.

"We find Machado, we'll find the Scorcher," Scott continued.

"Fair enough, but how do we do that?" Ella asked. "As Hadrian's right hand, Machado is as difficult to get to as Hadrian and his Scorcher."

"I know who can get us to Machado," Scott said, "but we need help to get to them first." He stepped towards the doors. "I ask that all of you keep an open mind and hear me out before raising any objections." He swung the doors open and stuck his head out. "You can come in now."

Aaron's breath evaporated, leaving him breathless with shock as Sam and Rose walked into the Hub.

28

THE PECOSAS

In the entire history of the mage realm, never had a human set foot in the Hub and taken part in a meeting. At least, that's what Aaron had been led to believe. Yet here stood both Sam and Rose, looking nervously at the Hunters. It took a moment for the sight to sink in before the Hunters went up in arms.

"What the hell?" Skyler shot to his feet. "What are *they* doing here?"

"They can't come in!" Zhi-Jiya cried. "Scott, what are you doing?"

"Is this a joke?" Ryan asked. "It is, isn't it? It's a joke."

Aaron didn't bother shouting. He got up and raced to his friends' side instead. "What's going on?" he asked.

Sam and Rose didn't say anything but turned to look at Scott, who held up a hand, quietening everyone.

"We need Sam and Rose's help to get to Daniel Machado," he said.

"Have you lost it?" Skyler seethed.

"You forgotten what happened the last time we used them as bait?" Ella asked.

"No," Scott replied. "But even then, that hunt was a success. We took out a number of vamages in that Q-Zone." He straightened up, holding his head high. "However, that was the first and last time I would ever consider using them as bait."

The Hunters looked confused.

"So what exactly are you planning?" Kyran asked. There was an edge to his voice, one that made every eye turn to him. Kyran's piercing gaze was fixed on Scott. His expression seemed calm, but Aaron could see the anger in his clenched fists and furious green eyes.

Scott moved away from Aaron and the twins, coming to stand directly in the middle of the room.

"Machado is the key to getting to the Scorcher," he repeated. "And the only ones we know for certain that are in contact with Machado are the Pecosas."

Kyran's expression clouded with annoyance. He hissed in a breath.

"Scott." He shook his head. "We've already tried this route. We wasted ten days with them and we got nothing."

"You're right." Scott said. "We got nowhere and the reason is simple: the Pecosas blame us." Scott turned to look at the rest of the Hunters. "They claim this war is between us and the vamages but they're the ones affected. Their people have been killed. They've lost their homes, been driven out of their zones by Hadrian and forced to take refuge in our zones. They hold us responsible just as much as the vamages, and maybe they're right." Scott nodded. "Maybe it is our fault, but even that admission won't pacify the Pecosas. They won't help us. They don't trust us. But you know who they might trust?" He turned to look at Sam and Rose. "Humans." He uttered the word quietly, staring at the twins. "Humans who had nothing to do with this war but are suffering because of it. Humans who have lost their families, their homes. Humans that have had to leave everything behind and relocate in a place they don't feel they belong." He turned to face his Hunters. "Just like the Pecosas."

Sam and Rose didn't say anything but just stood in silence.

Scott stepped forward. "We couldn't gain the Pecosas' trust," he continued, "but maybe where we failed, Sam and Rose will succeed. The similarity of their situation, their loss, their pain – it might make the Pecosas reveal what they're hiding." He looked around the room. "There is something Machado is holding over them, something that keeps the Pecosas unwillingly tied to the vamages, to the Scorcher. We need to find what that is and use it to get to Machado and the Scorcher."

"What can Sam and Rose offer the Pecosas?" Julian asked.

"Hope," Scott said. "They can show the Pecosas that they're affected as well, that they've suffered but are fighting back. Sam and Rose risked their lives to get to the vamages and helped us destroy some of them. Maybe if the Pecosas see that the humans are fighting too, they may find the strength to do the same."

***

The days sped by, and as Aaron recovered from another draining day and night of the full moon, arrangements were made for Sam and Rose's trip to Harban – a small village in Zone G-15 where the Pecosas resided. There were only six Hunters going with Sam and Rose, not including Aaron, who planned to travel via a portal into G-14 before making their way into G-15.

"Why can't Scott set up the portal directly into G-15?" Aaron asked.

"Because he thinks we need the exercise," Kyran said as he pulled on his jacket. He turned from the weapons cabinet to smirk at Aaron. "The Pecosas banned us. If Scott puts up a portal in their zone, they'll be pretty mad about it. Seeing as we're trying to get the Pecosas to help us, angering them beforehand isn't a great strategy."

Aaron rolled his eyes. "You could have just said, 'No, Scott can't set up the portal there.'"

Kyran chuckled and turned to pull out his blades.

"I thought this was a low-risk assignment," Aaron said, uneasy at the sight of the weapons.

"It is low risk," Kyran replied, "but you never leave the house without your familiars." He held out Aaron's pistol.

Aaron took it. "Would I need to surrender it to the Pecosas?" he asked.

Kyran sighed, dropping his head.

"Ace, I told you. Scott doesn't want any mages going in with Sam and Rose," he said.

"And I told you, I don't care. I'm going in with my friends," Aaron replied.

Kyran threw him a look and slid his twin pistols into their holsters. "The whole point of this is to have the Pecosas speak only to the humans."

"They don't have to know that I'm a mage," Aaron said.

"They can tell the difference, Ace."

"How?"

Kyran shrugged, sliding a sheathed knife into his inner jacket pocket. "No idea, but they can tell."

Aaron shrugged as well. "Well then, that's too bad," he said. "I'm going wherever Sam and Rose go."

Kyran turned to look at Aaron again, staring at him silently for a moment before sighing. He reached into the back of the cabinet and pulled out a small wooden box. Clicking it open, Kyran picked out a spiral pendant.

"Here," he said, holding it out.

"What's this for?" Aaron asked, taking the silver chain. The spiral hung from it, swaying back and forth. "I've already got my own." He zipped open his top, showing Kyran the small circle pendant resting on his chest.

"If you're really planning on going into Harban, then I want you to wear my mark," Kyran said. "That way, if anything happens – the Pecosas get riled up with your presence or they get too close for comfort – you just call for me."

Aaron looked at the necklace before glancing at the matching one around Kyran's neck. He slipped the chain over his head. The spiral came to rest on top of his circle pendant.

"So this is for us to talk to each other?" Aaron asked.

"Yeah," Kyran said, closing his cabinet and locking it with a wave of his hand. He turned to face Aaron with serious eyes. "You need me, you hold on to that mark and call me with one breath, I'll be there by the next."

***

The Hunters parked their bikes soon after passing through the portal. Aaron rode on Lexi with Kyran, while Sam was with Skyler and Rose with Ella. Zhi-Jiya, Ryan and Julian made up the team of six Hunters. Skyler and Ella led the way. Tall trees lined both sides of the wide brick road. When they had left Salvador, it was the middle of the day, but here it seemed the sun had already set.

Sam, Rose and Aaron stuck together, staying within the protective circle of the Hunters. They walked in silence, bracing themselves against the gusty wind.

"This is a Gated zone, right?" Aaron asked.

"Yeah," Kyran replied.

"So there's no danger here?"

"Danger is everywhere, Ace," Kyran replied. "Gated or not, demons find their way in."

Aaron glanced behind him at Ryan and Zhi-Jiya. They seemed calm, walking leisurely, as if taking a stroll in the park. On Aaron's other side was Julian – tense and focused, as usual. In front, Skyler and Ella led the way. They walked in silence. Quite suddenly, something occurred to Aaron.

"Kyran?" he said quietly. "What exactly are Pecosas?"

"What do you mean?" Kyran asked.

"They're obviously not a type of mage, like the Empaths," Aaron said. "They can't be demonic, so what are they?"

"They're Pecosas," Kyran answered with a smirk. "Nothing more, nothing less."

Aaron opened his mouth to tell Kyran exactly how unhelpful he was, but decided not to. It would only encourage Kyran to annoy him.

It took almost forty minutes of walking down the empty road to reach the Gate – another towering mass of shimmering white. This time, however, no mage touched it. Skyler turned and motioned to Sam and Rose to step forward. Aaron walked with them, refusing to leave their side.

"Put your hand on the Gate," Skyler instructed the twins. "Ask for permission to enter." He shot an icy look at Aaron, warning him not to touch the Gate. "Once you get in, ask to speak with Grandor."

Sam and Rose nodded. After a moment's hesitation, they extended their hands and rested them on the gleaming surface. With a faint tremble in their voice, both spoke out loud.

"We seek permission to enter."

The Gate glowed, then all sorts of symbols flashed over it. Aaron watched, recognising some of the marks now. He had seen similar symbols tattooed on the Hunters. Other marks he recognised from the books he had read, and knew to represent different demonic beings. He could see the personification of particular demons in the sharp lines – the curved fangs in the circular mark for vampires; the image of a beast standing on two legs, with knees bent and its pointed head turned upwards in the Lycan mark.

All the symbols faded, leaving Aric's mark pulsing against the Gate before it too melted away. The Gate slid open, revealing Zone G-15.

"Go on," Ella encouraged Sam. "We'll be right here."

Gripping Rose's hand, Sam stepped through the doorway and into the quiet street. Aaron held on to Rose's other hand. He looked back at Kyran one last time. Kyran nodded at him, intense green eyes fixed on him. The Gate slid closed, blocking all sight of the Hunters.

Aaron turned to face his surroundings. He saw a brick road with small cottages lined along both sides. There was a cluster of trees in the middle of the street, and under their shade, sitting on large, square stools, were the Pecosas.

In the last four months, Aaron had seen all sorts of creatures: beautiful, exotic girls that changed into snakes; savage-looking men and women with backward feet; he'd even seen strange dogs with glowing eyes in a memory. The Pecosas, Aaron imagined, were going to be just as strange a creation. What he saw, however, were perfectly normal-looking people. There was nothing strange about them. They were fair-skinned – although rather heavily freckled – light-eyed people dressed in long robes. Aaron frowned.

So were the Pecosas human? No, that couldn't be it. Then everyone would just refer to them as human, or Shattered, as their preferred term.

The seated Pecosas got up as Aaron and the twins approached. Creases of confusion morphed into lines of anger on the Pecosas' brows as they focused on Aaron. The man at the front, dressed in a pale blue robe, held out his hand.

"That's close enough," he said, looking at Aaron. "I thought I had made it clear: your kind isn't welcome here."

Aaron tightened his grip on Rose's hand. "I've only come to be at the side of my friends," he said. "They're here to speak with Grandor."

The Pecosa looked at Sam and Rose with narrowed grey eyes. "I am Grandor," he said. "And I don't want to talk to anyone." He turned back to Aaron. "I've already told your Controller that we can't help you. Leave now!"

"Grandor," Aaron called. "If you would just listen—"

"We've been *listening*!" the Pecosa – Grandor – said with a hiss. "That's all we've been doing! It's what got us neck deep in this pit of *misery* and if you were kind, you'd leave us alone instead of pushing our heads further down and drowning us!" He glared at Aaron, a tinge of pink colouring his pale cheeks. "I will ask you once, and *only* once, Elemental," he said in a dangerously quiet voice. "Leave and never return."

"Please," Rose bravely raised her voice. "We'll only take a minute of your time."

Grandor straightened to his full height, grey eyes shadowed with anger. A gesture of his hand and the crowd of Pecosas behind him moved towards Aaron and the twins. Their hard expressions and threatening stance had Aaron reach for the spiral pendant around his neck.

"Hey, hey! Hold on," Sam started, holding up his hands. "We only want to talk."

The Pecosas continued walking towards them.

"Kyran," Aaron breathed, one hand on the spiral, the other on his gun.

At once the Gate slid open and Kyran came striding in, Skyler by his side and the other Hunters behind them. The Pecosas halted in their tracks, staring in surprise at the six Hunters. Grandor's wide-eyed gaze was on Kyran, who came to stand by Aaron's side. Slowly, Grandor looked at each Hunter, before resting his gaze on Kyran again. He smirked, nodding at him.

"So this is what it comes down to?" he asked. "You ask first, then demand answers by force?"

"You're mistaken," Kyran replied calmly. "We're not here to force you. We want to help."

"Help?" Grandor growled the word, his rage visible in his straight back and clenched jaw. "I've heard enough about help from you, *mages*." He spat the word as if it were cursed. "All you're interested in is winning your war. You come to us offering help, but all you want is information."

"Great," Skyler smirked. "Now that *that's* out in the open, how about you start sharing?"

Grandor seemed to grow taller in fury. He pointed a finger at the Gate. "Leave, or I won't be responsible for what happens next!"

"You're honestly threatening us?" Skyler sneered. "There's wishful thinking and then there's just being plain dumb."

"Sky!" Ella hissed.

"He's being unreasonable," Skyler said. "We're trying to help and he's mouthing off to us!"

"We don't need your *help*," Grandor spat.

"Like hell you don't!" Skyler snapped back.

The Pecosas behind Grandor let out angry yells and moved forward.

"Whoa, whoa. Wait! Wait!" Sam called, holding up his hands as he stepped forward to stand between the mages and the Pecosas. "You're right, you're right," he said to Grandor.

At Grandor's command, his crowd of men stopped, eyeing Sam and the Hunters warily. Sam took another step forward, his gaze fixed on Grandor.

"About the mages," Sam continued. "You're absolutely right. They are only here to use you."

"What are you doing?" Skyler asked, incensed. "You're supposed to be on our side!"

"Oh?" Sam turned to look at Skyler. "So now I'm worthy enough to be on your side, am I?" he asked. "What happened to humans being worthless and stupid and weak, huh?" he asked. "You treat us like crap and then all of a sudden, when you see a use for us, we're good enough to be part of your team."

Skyler glared at him.

Sam turned to face Grandor, who was staring at Sam with careful scrutiny. "The only reason the mages have come here today is because *they* need help," Sam said. "It isn't about you or your people, not really. It's about them and what they can do to win this war. And you know what? The fact that they're doing all this – using and manipulating people so they can beat the demons, beat the vamages – *that's* what makes it acceptable."

The Hunters stared at Sam in stunned surprise. They hadn't anticipated him twisting his words to their favour like that.

"At least, it does for me," Sam continued. Taking in a breath, Sam stepped closer, staring straight at Grandor. "Four months ago, vamages came into my world, into my home and killed my parents." A suffocating silence fell over the street, all eyes on Sam as he stood before the leader of the Pecosas. "I want answers too," Sam said. "I want to know why my parents had to die? We're not a part of this war, so why did we suffer?" He paused for a moment. "The only ones who can answer my questions are the ones responsible, and that's not the mages."

Grandor's eyes softened and his jaw slackened a little.

"I know that you feel the same way," Sam said. "You don't want to be a part of this war. It's not our fight. This is between the mages and the vamages, so why should we pay the price?"

Grandor's head moved a bare fraction, nodding to Sam's words.

"But just because we don't want to be a part of it, doesn't mean we get to stay out of it," Sam said. "We're already involved. I lost my parents and you're losing your people. Sitting back and refusing to fight, isn't going to help–"

Grandor held up a hand to quieten Sam. "My kind is not affiliated with war," he said quietly. "We are passive by nature. We do not fight."

"I get that," Sam said, "but surely you have a sense of self-preservation. You're not extinct. That proves you must be fighting in some sense to have survived this long."

"Our survival is done by keeping out of danger," Grandor replied.

"What about your people who have fallen?" Rose asked, drawing the Pecosa's attention. "Don't you have any loyalty to them? Do they not deserve to be avenged?"

Grandor smiled. "Vengeance is just another name for self-destruction," he said. "It may be associated with humans but it doesn't have any place in our kind." His grey-eyed gaze moved past Rose to all the Hunters, looking at each and every one. "You're wasting your time. I cannot help you."

He turned his back to walk away, and Sam called out, "What's the Scorcher got over you?"

Grandor stopped. Tension stifled the very air, making it hard to breathe. Grandor turned around with narrowed eyes, looking straight at Sam. "The Scorcher?" he asked. "I have told the mages before: I have not met the Scorcher."

"You've met Daniel Machado, though, right?" Rose asked.

At the name of Hadrian's right-hand vamage, the Pecosas flinched, looking to their leader. Grandor didn't speak. He just stared at Rose.

"Machado is using something to hold your silence," Rose said, braving a few steps closer. Kyran moved right behind her, staying close, his eyes on the Pecosa leader. "Please, tell us how to get to Machado," Rose said. "If the mages get him, they'll get to the Scorcher and then all of this will be over."

Grandor stared at her before a slow smile spread over his face. He started to laugh, surprising everyone. He shook his head, reaching up to pinch the bridge of his nose. It took several moments for the bitter laughter to die down. When he looked back at Rose, he had pity for her naivety in every line of his face.

"No one can get to the Scorcher," he said quietly. "Not through Machado, not through anyone else. Machado doesn't come to us. He sends us messages, using our own people." His face shadowed with misery, while his eyes burnt with anger. "He corrupts my people and then sends them back to us to deliver his messages. We do as he asks so that one day, when the vamages' purpose is over, we'll have our people back."

"He's blackmailing you?" Ella asked, aghast.

It seemed the interruption from a mage was all it took for Grandor to come to his senses. His head snapped around in Ella's direction and he stared at her, as if only just realising that she, along with the rest of the Hunters, were still here. Grandor straightened up, running a hand down his robes.

"There is nothing that I can do for you," he said. "I can't get you to Machado, even if I were willing to risk my people by helping you." He looked straight at Sam. "I feel for your loss. You, much like us, have been dragged into this war." He glared at the Hunters behind Sam, "But stay out of their fight. Don't let them destroy you too."

"Sorry." Sam shook his head. "I want answers. I want the vamages defeated. If that means I have to help the mages, then that's what I'll do."

Grandor didn't say anything. He looked at Sam with something akin to pity welling in his eyes. "Do as you see fit," he said quietly. He turned away, gesturing to his people to leave.

Slowly the Pecosas began to move away, still glancing at the mages and two humans left standing.

"Come on," Kyran said quietly, his hand on Rose's back. "This was a waste of time."

"You did good," Ella whispered to Sam. She threw a hard look at the retreating Pecosas. "They're just not willing to listen."

The Hunters began leading Aaron and the twins back to the Gate when Grandor called to them.

"The sun is about to set," he said, halting the Hunters. "If you wish, you may rest here tonight and leave in the morning."

The mages looked to each other, surprised at the Pecosa's hospitality. Sam looked to Ella and, at her approval, turned back to Grandor, nodding.

"Thank you," he said.

Grandor smiled, but his eyes hardened when he turned to the Hunters. "It is not in our nature to wish harm on any being," he started. "So take what I have to say with the utmost sincerity." His gaze moved to rest on Kyran. "Forget about the Scorcher. He's too powerful to fall into your grasp."

"Don't you worry about that," Ella said. "Just point us in the right direction."

"It'll do you no good," Grandor said. "If by a stroke of luck you do get to him, you won't survive the encounter. The Scorcher is like nothing you've seen before. He can bleed you out with nothing more than a touch."

"You know an awful lot about a person you claim to have not met," Skyler accused.

Grandor smiled bitterly. "You don't have to be burnt to know what fire is capable of."

***

The evening was surprisingly pleasant. The Pecosas set out a variety of dishes for dinner. The previous ire was gone and all the Pecosas seemed rather happy to have visitors staying the night – although their warmth and charm was reserved only for Sam and Rose. With the mages, they still seemed rather closed off.

After dinner, a large group of Pecosas gathered around a fire, inviting Sam and Rose to join them. Aaron, refusing to leave his friends' side, sat with them. Kyran followed after him, with Ella, Zhi-Jiya and Ryan trailing after. The Pecosas shot uncomfortable looks at one another but still offered the mages drinks before sitting on the other side of the fire.

"You're very brave," a young Pecosa girl said to Sam. "No one has said such things to Grandor before."

"Like what?" Sam asked, looking confused. "I didn't say anything rude."

"You told him he should fight." She shook her head. "No one tells Grandor what to do."

"Other than Machado, of course," Ryan said. At the hostile looks he got, he quickly held up his hands. "Okay, okay, no talking about the war and our impending doom if we don't find a way to defeat the vamages." He smiled with exaggerated sweetness. "What shall we talk about instead?"

Silence met his words.

"Hey," Ella started, looking at the fair-haired crowd. "I've heard Pecosas are really good storytellers." She grinned excitedly. "You got any good stories?"

The crowd looked to one another with humble smiles.

"Keena is our storyteller," one Pecosa said, nodding at the wavy-haired girl sitting to Ella's right.

Keena smiled before looking over at Ella. "Well," she started, "what kind of a story would you like?"

"I don't know about everyone else," Zhi-Jiya cut in, "but I'm a sucker for a good love story."

"It's one thing in stories," Ryan said, "but love in real life is—" He stopped as Zhi-Jiya turned to him.

"Yes?" she prompted. "Please, do go on."

Ryan grinned and fell quiet, making the surrounding Pecosas reluctantly giggle.

"I don't agree," Ella said. "I think love in real life can be just as exciting as in stories." She smiled. "Just imagine being caught up in an epic love story with the only person you can't be with." She looked to the others. "Thrilling, no?"

"Sounds like the recipe for non-stop heartbreak," Rose said. "Pass, thank you."

"You're telling me you wouldn't want an epic love story of your own?" Ella asked.

Rose couldn't help but chuckle. "I didn't peg you as a hopeless romantic, Ella."

"What, you don't think mages fall in love?" Ella asked.

"No, of course they do," Rose replied. "But epic tragic love?"

"Is any other love worth the trouble?" Ella asked with a grin.

"Each to their own, I guess," Rose replied. "But I wouldn't want an epic love story of my own. I'd be happy with just a simple romance."

"Come on," Ryan said. "You're telling me you would rather have a boring romantic relationship than a truly meaningful, deep-seated, soul-shattering, eternal bond of love? Like what I have with Zhi-Jiya?"

"Nice save," Zhi-Jiya smirked.

"No, I'm not saying I don't want a deep relationship." Rose shrugged. "I'm just saying that I don't see the allure of falling for someone I can never be with. I mean, what's the point in that?"

"That's exactly the point," Kyran said, joining the discussion. "The attraction lies in the temptation to have what's forbidden."

Rose paused for a moment, before smiling. "True, but that's just infatuation. We were talking about love."

Kyran smiled. "What if you fall in love with the very person you can't be with?" he asked.

"I won't," Rose replied. "I'll make sure I go for someone that is suited to me."

"You can't choose who you're going to fall in love with," Keena said. "Love just happens."

"See, this is exactly the notion I despise," Rose said. "Why can't I choose who I'm going to fall in love with? Why is it that love makes the choice for me? It's my life but somehow I can't choose who I'm going to spend it with? How messed up is that?"

"The fates decide who your partner is," Keena said. "It's always been that way."

"Not for me," Rose said. "The fates can decide what they want. *I'll* decide who I'm falling in love with."

Kyran straightened up a little.

"Alright," he said. "So if you were to choose, what kind of a love story would you want?"

Rose paused for a moment, thinking. A slow smile came to her face and she dropped her gaze to the fire. "Just a simple romance," she said. "I meet someone. I like him. He likes me. We fall in love. Get married. Have a sweet little house somewhere. Have kids. Grow old together." She lifted her gaze to look at Kyran. "Make our own family. Our own world."

"That sounds so...boring," Ella said. "Where's the thrill? The drama? The heartache?"

"I would take boring over heartache any day," Rose said.

"If there's no heartache," Kyran said, "there's no heart. Where's the love if there's no heart?"

Rose smiled. "You do know people love with their brains, not their hearts, right?"

Kyran laughed, his eyes sparkling with amusement.

"Okay," Ella said. "On that unbelievably unromantic note," she gestured to Keena, "start an epic, tragic love story."

"There's always the favourite, *The Tale of the Waiting Bloom*?" Keena suggested.

"No, I know that one," Ella said. "How about one from the human realm?" she asked. "In honour of your guests." She grinned at Sam and Rose.

Keena smiled as she turned to Rose. "Humans have great love stories," she said. "How about the retelling of the greatest love story of the human realm – *Romeo and Juliet*?"

"Please." Rose pulled a face. "*Romeo and Juliet* is the worse example of love you could give."

Ella turned to her with wide eyes. "Rose!"

"I'm sorry, it is," Rose said. "I studied *Romeo and Juliet* for my English class at school, and the more I read, the more I realised it isn't a love story. It's a story about a rash little boy who can't decide what he wants. First he's so in love with Rosalyn, then he falls for Juliet, marries her, kills her cousin, flees the city and commits suicide, without even waiting to see if she's *actually* dead or not – and all this happens in the space of five days." She turned to look at Ella. "Five days. You don't kill yourself over a girl, or a boy for that matter, who you've only known for *five* days!"

"Yeah," Aaron said. "You have to wait *at least* ten days before you off yourself."

Rose bowed her head. "Correction: you don't kill yourself for anyone, at all, ever," she said.

"Yes, but they were in love," a young Pecosa said.

"They were infatuated with each other," Rose corrected. "You can't be in love with someone you don't know."

"Okay," Keena started, brow creased in thought. "How about *Antony and Cleopatra*?"

"Ah, yes, I know that one." Ella nodded. "Great love demands great sacrifices," she quoted.

"Oh, please," Rose said. "Love demands sacrifices? That's not right. Love should be about acceptance and...and the bliss you find in one another."

"Sacrifice is the purest form of love," Zhi-Jiya recited. "Neriah says it all the time."

"Fantastic," Kyran groaned. "Love stories and Neriah. There's two images I want in my head."

"Have you heard the story of *Pyramus and Thisbe*?" Keena asked.

"No." Ella settled down with a grin. "Go for it."

Rose let out a sigh.

"What? What's wrong this time?" Zhi-Jiya asked.

"Nothing," Rose said. "It's just...well, it's sorta silly, isn't it? Pyramus and Thisbe both stab themselves over a misunderstanding and their blood changes the colour of mulberries forever. What's the message in that story? Don't eat mulberries?"

Ella gaped at her with an open mouth. "I can't believe you just gave away the ending."

"Okay," Zhi-Jiya said. "How about a story Rose hasn't heard?" she said to Keena.

"Yeah," Ella said. "She can't ruin it then."

"You asked for an epic, tragic love story," Rose defended. "All epic, tragic love stories end with one or both lovers stabbing themselves and dying. What major spoiler did I give away?"

"I have a story that's different." Keena said. "It's a story from the human realm, so you may have heard it before," she said to Rose, "but it doesn't end like most love stories. In fact, there is no other love story quite like it." She looked around at the Pecosas before meeting Rose's eyes. "The tale of *Mirza Sahiba*."

Rose frowned. She hadn't heard of that one. She looked around at Sam and Aaron who shrugged at her.

"I'm still trying to figure out what a mulberry is," Sam said.

"Mirza Sahiba," Keena started in a soft voice. "Childhood playmates, they grew up in each other's company. Sahiba was the daughter of the chief; Mirza, the son of the tribe's leader. The blossoming love of Mirza and Sahiba raised concerns, for their parents disapproved of the union. Sahiba's father decided to forcibly wed her to another man."

Ella gritted her teeth. "I *hate* it when that happens!"

"The night before her wedding, Sahiba sent a message to Mirza," Keena continued. "She taunted him, saying that if he was as brave as he claimed, then he should come and take her away, or join in with the festivities of her marriage to another man. Mirza, a truly fearless man, arrived on his horse and carried Sahiba away in front of her family."

Ryan and Kyran let out approving whistles, smirking at one another.

"Sahiba's brothers, humiliated by Mirza's bold actions, set out to follow him," Keena continued. "But Mirza was already far ahead, out of their reach. Eventually, there came a time when Mirza and Sahiba had to stop to rest. As Mirza lay under the shade of a tree, exhausted from the day's events, he fell asleep. Sahiba rested with him. She awoke to find her brothers in the distance, racing on their horses, trying to catch up with them. Sahiba knew that Mirza was an accomplished archer. He would not miss his target. If he shot at her brothers, they would die. So before waking Mirza up, Sahiba took Mirza's arrows and broke each one in half."

The mages sucked in a breath. Their shock rang in the air.

"What was she thinking?" Ella asked.

"She wanted to protect her brothers," Keena replied. "Sahiba thought she could get through to her brothers. She thought that maybe, if she begged and pleaded, her brothers might change their minds. She thought her brothers would understand her love." Keena shook her head. "But her brothers didn't understand. They didn't listen. They charged at the defenceless Mirza with their swords drawn. Although Mirza fought with all his might, he was one against several. He was killed."

The mood around the fire dropped. The Hunters sat deep in thought, wondering what it would be like to be caught by the enemy while defenceless.

"What happened to Sahiba?" Rose asked quietly.

"Some versions of the story say she killed herself that day," Keena said. "Others say that her brothers forced her back home, but Sahiba never did marry anyone else. Legend has it that for years, an old women dressed in black, her face hidden behind a veil, used to sit next to Mirza's grave. The old women called out to anyone who passed by and told them the story of Mirza Sahiba. She told anyone who listened how Mirza had turned to her, in shocked denial upon seeing his broken arrows. She would weep and say Mirza had asked only one question: 'Why?' When Sahiba replied that she feared for her brother's lives, Mirza, heartbroken, had replied, 'I would never hurt your family. Did you not know that?' The women in black cried day and night at Mirza's grave and warned all to never do what she did: never betray the one you love."

Keena finished the story and looked around at the saddened faces. "What did I say?" She asked. "No love story quite like it."

29

Hearing Silent Calls

The Hunters walked along the brick road in Zone G-14, heading back to the portal that Scott was waiting to open for them. They walked in silence, each lost in their own thoughts. Aaron couldn't help but feel the entire trip was pointless. They got nothing from the Pecosas. They still weren't willing to help the mages fight against the vamages.

The wind ruffled the leaves of the trees on both sides of the road and Aaron bristled at the howl of an animal somewhere in the distance. Or was that just the wind? A prickling sensation ran down his back. Even though G-14 was one of Neriah's zones, and therefore a safe zone, Aaron couldn't help but feel a dark sense of foreboding growing within him.

The wind battered its way through the trees, swaying branches this way and that. Quite suddenly, everyone halted, ears strained and eyes narrowed. Hands were already on familiars, ready to pull them out.

"Did you guys feel that?" Ella asked quietly.

"Yeah," Julian replied. "Something's not right."

"You can feel it too?" Aaron asked. "I thought it was just me."

"Hunter instincts," Kyran said quietly, his gaze searching the area. "Learn to trust and listen to them."

The six Hunters stayed where they were, weapons held out in front of them, eyes scanning their surroundings. Then they heard the growling. As one they turned, weapons aimed at the dark shape that was slowly approaching them. When it stepped out of the shadows, Aaron got his first look at the beast.

It was a dog – a gruesome, ugly dog. Its fur was matted, singed in places. It had a strange, narrow head with tiny ears, raised up at the moment. It was big, almost as tall as Aaron but its form was thin, skeletal. Its most terrifying feature by far was its eyes: red, glowing eyes with black-slitted pupils. Its fangs were bared, and thick globs of saliva dropped from the corner of its mouth.

Aaron recognised it. It was just like the dog he had seen his dad fight in the memory he found at Drake's house.

The dog growled again, its echo ringing around them, or that's what Aaron thought at first. A muttered curse from Zhi-Jiya made Aaron and the others look behind them, only to see two other dog-like beasts inching closer. Aaron found to his mounting horror, another six beasts approaching from behind the trees – their red eyes glowing and long, sharp fangs bared. The dogs raised their hackles and barked at them.

"Great," Ryan said. "Devil dogs."

"Devil dogs?" Sam asked, sounding just as panicked as Aaron was feeling.

"Hell hounds," Skyler replied, not taking his eyes off the dog. "Demonic beasts."

"Alright, just take it slowly," Ella spoke to Sam, Rose and Aaron. "No sudden moves, no yelling and screaming." She inched backwards, eyes still on the dog in front. "These things are vicious but they can be killed. Just stay next to us and you'll be fine."

The hell hound before Ella lifted its head, sniffing the air before a low chuckle sounded. It took Aaron a moment to realise it was the dog that was laughing.

The next moment, pandemonium broke out as the hell hounds, all nine of them, charged at once. They attacked the group from all sides. Gunshots rang loudly as the Hunters fended off the beasts. Swords were drawn, guns were aimed and silver daggers were already cutting through the air, stabbing through the grisly fur of the beasts.

Aaron, Sam and Rose tried their best to stay in the middle, to keep close to the Hunters, but it was next to impossible. The attack had torn the group apart, forcing Aaron and the twins to jump out of the way of rabid fangs and claws.

"Ace!" Kyran yelled. "Run!"

Aaron didn't need telling twice. He grabbed Rose's hand, who had clutched onto Sam, and the three of them ran. Aaron reached for his silver necklace, closing his hand over both marks.

"Hell hounds! Open the portal!" he yelled as he bolted down the road, all too aware of the snarling dogs chasing behind him.

Scott's voice flooded his mind. *"It's open,"* he said. *"Hurry, Aaron!"*

Aaron let go of the pendants and pulled out his gun. Still running, he turned, stretching back to fire at the dogs chasing him.

"Weapons will only slow them down," Kyran's voice echoed in Aaron's mind,

thanks to the spiral pendant around his neck. *"Only your power can kill them!"*

Aaron remembered how a simple wave of his dad's hand had turned the dog to stone. The problem was that Aaron knew performing the wave was anything but simple. Pocketing his gun, Aaron ran blindly down the path, Sam and Rose beside him. The sound of gunshots and growls, gasps and whimpers filled the air, but Aaron didn't dare slow down to look back.

Aric's mark suddenly glowed before him a short distance away; a beautiful white insignia that brought a rush of relief to Aaron. All he had to do was get Sam and Rose there. If they jumped through the portal, they would land in the deep forest just outside the Gate of Salvador. Seeing the portal so close made Aaron and the twins run faster, pushing their muscles past their dull ache. Just as they approached the six bikes parked to the left of the mark, Aaron let go of Rose's hand and turned around, facing the beasts that were chasing them. Two hell hounds came at him, frothing at the mouth, snarling and gnashing their teeth.

"Aaron!" Rose screamed.

Aaron forced out a rushed breath, held out both hands and with a cry of his own, he pushed his hands to either side. The ground trembled and split in two, the large crack swallowing whatever came its way. It took one hell hound down, but the other one jumped over the opening, and continued racing towards Aaron. A perfect ripple caught the dog, blasting him back.

"Aaron! Come on!" Sam yelled.

Aaron turned and ran, hoping he had slowed the beast down enough so that it wouldn't chase them through the portal. He grabbed Rose's outstretched hand and the three of them raced towards Aric's mark. Sam had almost stepped into the glow when Aaron felt the air shift and change. The tiny hairs on the back of his neck prickled, as if in anticipation of something horrible, moments before he felt the sharp claws cut into his back. With a grunt, Aaron let go of Rose's hand and fell, the hell hound on his back.

Sam and Rose's screams faded into the background as the blood pounded in Aaron's ears, followed by the racing heartbeat thudding at his insides. Aaron rolled over, forcing the dog to move. But with Aaron now on his back, the hell hound pounced onto Aaron's torso, trying to rip him open. Its claws slashed at Aaron's chest, ripping three lines down his jacket and top. With its fangs bared, the beast went for Aaron's neck.

Aaron's hand found one of his blades and before he could think clearly, he dug the knife into the beast's side. With a choked growl, the dog fell limp, its fangs just barely away from Aaron's flesh. With a revolted groan,

Aaron pushed the dog off, letting the whimpering creature fall to the ground. Sam hurried to help Aaron up, looking horribly pale.

"Oh God! You alright? You okay?" he asked, wide-eyed and shaking.

Aaron didn't have the time or the breath to answer. The hell hound was only injured, not dead. They had to get out before it recovered. From the corner of his eye, Aaron saw another dark shape scurrying towards them.

Aaron grabbed Sam and pushed him towards the glowing mark. Sam held on to Rose's hand and all three jumped into the portal, falling onto soft, cool grass on the other end. They all scrambled to sit up, chests heaving and eyes wide, fixed on the glowing symbol. They watched, just in case something other than the Hunters came out after them. Nothing happened.

"You okay, Aaron?" Rose asked in a shaky voice.

"Yeah," Aaron breathed. He reached up to feel the tears across his chest. "It didn't get me – too many layers." When he got to his feet, he felt pain shoot down his back.

"Come on," Sam said, coming to Aaron's side. "We should go. You need an Emapth for those cuts on your back."

They turned and started walking. The forest was so dense they could barely see where they were going.

"It's this way, I think," Aaron said, following the track marks left by the bikes.

"There's a path up this way," Rose pointed in another direction.

"Reckon both lead to Salvador?" Sam asked.

"Probab–" Before Aaron could finish, a hell hound darted from behind a shadowed tree, coming straight for Sam. Rearing onto its hind legs, the beast shoved Sam using its front paws, with enough force to knock him against a tree.

"Sam!" Rose cried.

Aaron pulled out his gun and fired three shots, but the hell hound dodged them before running towards Sam. Aaron dropped his gun and raised his hands, aiming another powerful ripple at it. Rose reacted at the same time.

"Get away from him!" she screamed, when she saw the beast running at her brother.

She picked up a stone and threw it. It hit the tree, distracting the hell hound, which stopped and turned towards her with its fangs bared. It was all the pause Aaron needed. His ripple thundered across the forest ground, catching the hell hound and throwing it away from both Sam and Rose. The beast hit a tree with a sickening thud and fell to the ground.

Aaron and Rose both let out gasps of relief, leaning on the closest trees to take in shaky breaths.

"That was too close," Aaron said, straightening up. He saw Sam huddled at the foot of the tree he had been knocked into. He hadn't moved. "Sam? Sam, you okay?" Aaron called, moving towards him.

"Sammy?" Rose hurried forward.

The second hell hound came out from nowhere. It headed straight for Rose, its teeth bared and ready. Aaron saw it before Rose. His ripple caught the hell hound, pushing it away from Rose, but not before its wild swipe caught her. Rose staggered back, a hand clutched to her side. The hell hound hit the ground and scampered off, running into the darkness, disappearing from view. Aaron lowered his hand, breathing heavily and started towards Rose.

"Rose, you–?"

He paused in his tracks, his eyes slowly widening at the crimson trickle spilling out over Rose's hand. Very slowly, Rose lifted her bloodstained hand and held it up, staring at it in disbelief. She looked at Aaron, shock and surprise in her eyes. She took a step towards him and stumbled.

"Rose!" Aaron darted forward as his friend collapsed to the ground.

He picked her up, cradling her in his arms. Rose took fast, short breaths, both hands clutched to the cut in her side.

"A-Aaron!" she gasped.

"It's okay, Rose, it's okay," Aaron said, his voice trembling just as badly as his hands. "You're gonna be okay. You'll be okay." He raised his head, his vision fast blurring with tears. He had no idea how far the Gate was. "Hang on, Rose, hang on," he told her. "You're gonna be okay. You're gonna be okay." He reached for his pendants, for the two marks that would connect him straight to Scott. His hand fumbled at his neck but all he could feel was his ripped top and shirt. Aaron pulled at his clothes, searching desperately for the silver necklaces. There was nothing there.

His hands trailed down to the three cuts in his clothes and, with a sickening lurch, Aaron realised he must have lost his pendants in the hell hound attack. The razor sharp claws must have sliced through the chains. His two marks were gone, left behind in G-14.

Rose let out a choked cry of agony. Her breathing was becoming increasingly strained. Her hands were covered in blood. Aaron pulled off his jacket and then practically tore off his zipped jumper. He scrunched it up and held it against the cut, trying to slow the bleeding. Rose gasped in great, heaving breaths.

Aaron desperately looked around. The hell hound could come back at any time. He couldn't leave Rose here and run for help, and he couldn't carry her either. Something at the back of his mind told him not to move her. She was bleeding badly. He could do more damage than good by dragging her out of here. If only he knew of some way to get to Armana...Aaron paused, rooted in sheer terror when he remembered Armana could do nothing for Rose. Empaths could heal mages, not humans. Aaron gathered Rose in his arms, one hand still pressed down on the cut, willing the bleeding to stop. Rose groaned, breathless with pain.

"Stay with me, Rose. Just...just stay with me," Aaron said, trying to figure out a plan, a way to save his best friend.

He looked down at her. Beads of perspiration had gathered on her brow, pain evident in every tight line of her face as she struggled to take in a deep breath. Her panting became faster, growing shallower.

Aaron looked up in sheer desperation. "Kyran!" he screamed, knowing perfectly well Kyran was still in the other zone and couldn't hear him, but in his moment of utter panic, Kyran was the only one he could think of calling out to. "Help me! Please! Help me!"

"A-Aaron," Rose gasped. "Aaron...S-Sam...Sam!"

Aaron turned his head, his gaze darting to the slumped figure lying at the foot of the tree.

"Sam!" he yelled, his voice breaking. "Sammy! Sam!"

Sam didn't move. Aaron wanted to put Rose down and to run to Sam, to shake him awake. Maybe Sam would know how to help, would know some kind of first aid that Aaron was clueless about. But Aaron couldn't put Rose down. His arms refused to uncurl from around her. He could feel her body tensing. She sucked in a breath, trying desperately to hold herself together, but tears were already leaking from behind her tightly shut eyes. Her moans were getting louder, the agony making her writhe in his arms. Her blood had spilt past her hands and pooled on the forest ground.

"Aaron," she moaned, choking her words out. "Help me...p-please!"

Aaron gripped her tighter, his heart racing as tears rolled down his cheeks.

"You're gonna be okay. You're gonna be okay," Aaron comforted. "I'm not gonna let anything happen to you," he promised. "You're gonna be okay." His eyes closed and in his mind, he screamed for help again – for Kyran, for anyone.

The sound of pounding footsteps behind him made Aaron snap around quickly. He reached for his gun and aimed, but even though tears had blurred his vision, he still made out Kyran's form racing towards him.

"Rose!" Kyran yelled, falling to his knees at her side, opposite Aaron. His wide green eyes met Aaron's with so much panic and worry it hit Aaron like a physical blow. He had never thought he would see Kyran – too-cool-to-panic Kyran – look so terrified.

"Rose? Hey? Hey, look at me," Kyran called, reaching out to her. As soon as his hands touched her cheek, Rose opened her eyes, her gaze unfocused and bright with pain. Kyran looked to the bloodied jumper at Rose's side. He reached out, pushing it away. "Let me see."

Pulling the top away, Aaron got a proper look at the wound too – a large cut, just under her ribs. It was horribly deep, and still oozing blood. Aaron wasn't sure, but he though he saw a glimpse of her rib bone. Aaron quickly covered the cut again, applying pressure to it, trying to stem the blood flow. Rose gasped and groaned, coming out of her shock at the sensation of pain.

"S-Sam..." she called out again.

"It's okay," Kyran said, his worried gaze darting to her face. "Just lie still, Rose. Don't move."

Rose gripped at her side, desperate whimpers escaping her.

"K-Kyran." She held out a bloodstained hand, which Kyran took at once. "H-help me, please," she begged. "I-I don't w-want to...to die–"

"You're not going to die," Kyran said. "I promise you, Rose. You're going to be fine." He leant down, one hand gripped in hers while the other caressed her cheek. "Rose, hey? Look at me. Look at me, Rose," he said, as she squeezed her eyes shut. Rose painfully met his gaze, and he moved closer, his hand still on her cheek. "I'm not going to let anything happen to you," he repeated, looking her straight in the eyes. "Believe me, Rose," he whispered. "Believe me." He leant down and captured her lips in a kiss.

Aaron was taken by complete surprise. By the kiss and the sudden sound of several hurrying footsteps heading their way. He saw Scott, looking pale with worry, running towards him with a group of mages. From the shouts behind Aaron, he figured the other Hunters had passed through the portal and were running this way too.

Kyran pulled away from the kiss with a groan and fell back. Scott managed to catch him, just before Kyran could hit the ground. Rose sat up suddenly, gasping. Her eyes were wide and fixed on Kyran who had paled to the hue of a ghost. A sheen of sweat gleamed on his face and his eyes were clouding with pain.

"Are you okay?" Mary asked, coming to Rose's side. "Rose? Rose, you okay?"

Rose looked down at her side, at her ripped top. Her clothes and skin were still stained with blood but the hideous cut was gone. There was no sign of it – as if it had never happened. She looked over at Kyran, at his hands which were pressed against his side, just below his ribs, where a dark stain had started to appear.

***

It was half an hour later when Aaron got to fully understand what had happened. After the Empaths had healed the small cuts on Aaron's back, they left to attend to the other Hunters' minor injuries and, of course, Kyran's pretty serious condition. Aaron paced the bright hallway, outside the Empath's rooms, waiting for news on Kyran. Sam, still a little groggy from his head injury, was sitting on the sofa, Rose by his side. Ella appeared, coming out of one of the private rooms.

"How you feeling?" she asked Aaron.

"Fine," Aaron replied quickly. "Where's Kyran? Is he okay?"

Rose got up from Sam's side and hurried towards Ella, anxious and worried.

"He's fine," Ella said.

Aaron felt an immense weight lift from his chest, making it easier to breathe again. "What was that?" he asked. "What did Kyran do?"

Ella glanced to Rose, before looking back at Aaron.

"It's called a transfer," she said. "Empaths can't cure humans, but mages can sometimes take the injury of a human onto themselves," she explained. "It doesn't work all the time. I think the basis is that as long as the injury doesn't prove fatal to the mage, they can transfer it onto themselves."

"Fatal?" Aaron asked. "It looked pretty bad to me." He glanced to Rose. He had honestly thought he was going to lose his friend today.

"Mages are different, Aaron," Ella reminded. "What proves fatal to humans isn't so for mages. That cut could have killed Rose. She would have bled out in a matter of hours. But for Kyran, it's different. He took on her injury because he was strong enough." She smiled and shook her head. "I can't believe Kyran did a transfer. No one likes doing those things."

"I still can't believe he kissed you," Aaron said, turning to Rose.

"What?" Sam stirred out of his headache-induced silence. His eyes narrowed at Aaron. "What'd you say? Kyran kissed Rose?"

"Glad you weren't awake to see that, eh Sammy?" Ella teased with a small smile.

Sam wasn't amused. He tried to get up and then groaned. He had hit his head against a tree, he had to be gentle with his movements. "He kissed you?" he asked Rose.

Rose shook her head, closing her eyes. "Obviously he did it for that…transfer thing," she mumbled. She looked over at Ella to see her confused expression. "What?" She narrowed her eyes. "What is it?"

"Nothing," Ella said. "It's just…" She paused. "You don't need to kiss for the transfer to work," she explained. "As long as you have flesh-to-flesh contact, the transfer will work. You could hold hands, touch the face, neck – any exposed area," she said, "but you don't have to necessarily kiss."

Rose stared at her, first in disbelief, and then with a small, embarrassed smile.

***

Aaron knocked on the door of the Empath private room, before pushing it open. Kyran was inside, in the process of pulling on his shirt. Aaron paused in the doorway, his gaze darting to Kyran's stomach and sides. There was no mark on him. The transfer hadn't left any scars, just like any other injury for a mage.

Aaron found the four silver lines on the back of Kyran's hand wasn't the only tattoo he sported. He had a black circle inked on the left side of his chest. Aaron wasn't sure if the slight red tinge around it was part of the tattoo or just a skin reaction. Regardless, it was the simplest tattoo he had seen around here, perhaps that's why he found he liked it.

"Nice tat," he remarked.

Kyran only smiled and buttoned up his shirt, which was still stained. "Empaths had a look at you?" he asked.

"Yeah," Aaron replied. "All healed."

"Good."

Aaron paused, before stepping into the room. "Kyran," he started, "I don't even know what to say—"

"Then don't say anything," Kyran said.

"I need to," Aaron said. "I owe you, for saving Rose's life."

Kyran gave him a look. "You don't owe me anything."

"You don't know what you did today, how much it means to me," Aaron said. "Rose and Sam, they're my best friends. I've known them all my life. They stuck by me when no one else would." His voice dipped and Aaron had to force himself to go on. "Because of me, they're stuck here in this realm. My friendship cost them everything and not once have they taken their anger out on me." He met Kyran's eyes. "What happened today, when Rose was..." He couldn't repeat it, those awful few minutes when he had held his bleeding friend in his arms, fearing that there was nothing he could do to help her. "I thought I was going to lose her," he admitted. "I didn't know what to do, how to help her. If you hadn't come—"

"Ace," Kyran interrupted, turning to face him. "As long as I'm around, nothing's gonna happen to Rose," he said. "Or Sam." He paused. "Or you."

Aaron stared at him, lost as to what he could say to that. Kyran simply moved towards the bed and picked up his jacket, slipping it on.

"Where you going?" Aaron asked, surprised and a little nervous. Kyran had fought a pack of hell hounds, literally just recovered from a horrible injury, and was now heading back out again.

"To get Lexi," Kyran replied. "She's still in G-14. I can't leave her out there all night."

He moved past Aaron and came into the hallway but stopped at the sight of Rose, who was helping Sam stand up so they could leave the Empaths building. Both paused, staring at the other. Rose opened her mouth to speak but Kyran shook his head, smiling at her.

"You alright, Sam?" he asked instead.

Sam groaned, holding his head. "Define alright."

Kyran chuckled and stepped past them.

"Hey," Aaron called, halting Kyran. "I meant to ask – how did you know where we were?"

Kyran frowned. "What d'you mean?"

"How did you know we had jumped back through the portal?" Aaron asked.

Kyran looked at him as if he were mad. "What are you talking about?" he asked. "You're wearing my mark. I could hear you calling me."

Aaron stilled for a moment before nodding at him. "Right, yeah, sorry. Forgot about that."

Kyran shook his head at him and turned, heading out the door. Aaron watched him go, waiting for the door to close before meeting Sam and Rose's eyes. Without a word, Aaron reached for his top and tugged it down, revealing his bare chest.

"Your pendants?" Rose asked with surprise. "Where'd they go?"

"I lost them," Aaron said. "When that hell hound attacked me, its claws ripped my clothes. It must have caught the chains too and snapped them."

Sam and Rose stared at him.

"But that hell hound attacked you *before* you jumped into the portal," Rose said. "So how did Kyran know where you were, or that you needed help?"

"Exactly," Aaron replied, feeling his heart leap uncomfortably. How did Kyran hear his cries for help when he didn't have the pendant acting as a link between them?

30

Epic Love

That night, even though they were beyond tired, Aaron, Rose and Sam couldn't sleep. They lay on their beds, talking to each other. Kyran still wasn't back with Lexi yet, so Aaron could talk without the fear of being overheard.

"Tell me I'm crazy," he said, "but isn't it weird that Kyran heard me calling for him without the necklace?"

"You are crazy," Sam replied, "but you're also right. It doesn't make sense how Kyran knew where we were without having the pendant to guide him."

"I heard Ella talking to Armana," Rose said. "She said Kyran called for Scott before jumping through the portal, telling him to come to the forest. So he definitely heard Aaron when he was in that other zone, but I don't get how that's possible without the pendants."

"Kyran said he heard you calling for him." Sam faltered for a moment. "Did you call for him?"

"Yeah," Aaron replied.

"Why?" asked Sam.

Aaron paused, thrown by the question. "What d'you mean?"

"Why did you call to Kyran when you knew he wasn't there?" Sam asked.

"To be honest, I don't know," Aaron replied. "I panicked. I didn't really think about it. Kyran's name just sort of popped into my head and I called for him."

Rose and Sam were quiet for a moment.

"So it was, like, an instinct to call to Kyran for help?" Rose asked.

"Yeah, sort off," Aaron replied.

"What is it about him?" Sam asked. "You had dreams about him before you even met him. You listen to him more than any other mage. You take his crap–"

"Hey, hey," Aaron interrupted. "What're you talking about? What crap?"

"Come on, Aaron," Sam said and his tone had a bite to it. "Kyran ridicules you, teases you, hell, even threatens you and you shrug it off with a grin."

"It's not like that," Aaron argued. "I know Kyran doesn't mean it."

"How? How do you know what he means?" Sam asked, sounding annoyed. "You've known him what, a few months? How is it you know him so well that you know what he means?"

"You can tell," Aaron replied. "When Skyler makes fun, he's malicious and mean about it. Kyran's more playful."

"Yeah, when compared to Skyler, Kyran's a freaking saint," Sam said. "But when you look at how he treats you on its own, it's a different story."

"I think you're just overprotective," Rose chided Sam. "Kyran's not mean. He's just a strict teacher, that's all."

Aaron found himself grinning. "A little biased there, Rose?"

"He just saved my life today," Rose said. "Forgive me for being a little defensive of him."

"Yeah, that's it," Aaron teased. "It's because he saved your life that you're defending him. It's not because you like him or anything."

Rose didn't say anything.

"At least you know one thing," Aaron started, propping himself up on one arm, facing her in the dark. "Kyran likes you."

"Please," Rose dismissed, but Aaron could hear the smile in her voice.

"Come on," Aaron said. "He kissed you when he didn't have to."

"Can we not talk about that?" Sam said, disgust thick in his voice. "I'm pretending that didn't happen. That it's just something my concussed mind came up with."

Aaron and Rose ignored him.

"You like him too, Rose," Aaron said.

"What makes you say that?" she asked.

"I have eyes." Aaron grinned. "I can see the way you look at him."

"What d'you mean?" Sam asked. "I've not seen anything."

"That's because you're too busy gawking at Ella," Aaron replied.

Sam grunted. "I don't gawk."

Aaron rolled his eyes. "Fine. You stare at her without blinking," he revised. "Why don't you just ask her out?"

"Yeah, I'll get right on that," Sam said dryly. "First thing in the morning, right after the unicorns fly overheard, shooting rainbows out of their backsides."

"Sam," Aaron chided. "Why won't you ask her out?"

"You lost your mind?" Sam asked. "If she was a girl at Westbridge, I'd ask her out in a heartbeat, but this is Ella – the mage, the *freaking* Elemental," he said. "She could probably drown me with nothing more than a blink."

"Yeah," Aaron agreed, "she probably could. So you're just going to harbour feelings for her but not ever ask her out?"

"Pretty much," Sam sighed.

"Good," Rose said. "'Cause Ella's *way* out of your league."

"Hey!" Sam exclaimed. "You're my sister! Your loyalty should be in *this* direction."

Rose giggled.

"Me and Ella could happen," Sam defended. "Ella's got that whole, love-someone-who-is-a-challenge thing going on," he pointed out. "A mage and a human, what's more challenging than that?" He fell quiet for a moment. "Sam and Ella," he muttered, his voice dreamy and soft. "It's got a ring to it, don't you think?"

Aaron wrinkled his nose. "I don't know, mate," he said. "Sounds like Salmonella."

"Yeah, you definitely don't want any of that," Rose added.

They snickered as Sam huffed.

"You're really not funny," he said, moodily.

"What about you, Aaron?" Rose asked with amusement in her voice. "You ever gonna ask Ava out?"

"What?" Aaron was surprised. "No. Why would you say that?"

"Oh come on," Rose said. "I have eyes too. I see the way you *both* look at each other."

A slow grin spread over Aaron's face. "I do like Ava," he said, "but honestly? I still find myself thinking about Rebecca."

"Aww, Aaron," Rose cooed. "No one forgets their first love, particularly their first unrequited love."

"Yeah, like I haven't forgotten Jessie McGuire," Sam said.

"Sammy," Rose sighed. "That's different."

"How?" Sam asked.

"She has to know you exist for it to count as a romance," Rose said.

"She knew about me," Sam protested.

"Keep telling yourself that," Rose teased.

The front door closed, followed by a resounding click. Sam and Rose fell quiet, listening as Kyran's footsteps trudged up the stairs. The conversation ended, as all three knew Kyran would be able to hear the whole thing from his room next door.

Aaron felt an odd sense of comfort spread over him now that Kyran was safely back home. Up until now, he wasn't even aware that a part of him was tense and waiting for Kyran's return. He closed his eyes and, almost instantly, fell asleep.

***

The days got cooler as March rolled in. The sun continued to beat down on the City of Salvador, but the cool breeze made it a little more bearable. Aaron continued his training with Kyran, honing his power and learning how to manipulate his core. He attended all the meetings at the Hub, realising with each one just how much trouble their realm was in.

"The Q-Zone will be ready in three days," Scott was saying, standing before his Hunters once again. "According to the reports, Raoul and his Lycans have taken up residence in Zone T-26. There's a substantial number that we could take out in one–"

"How did that happen?" Aaron asked.

Scott turned to him, surprised at the interruption. "What?" he asked.

"Sorry," Aaron quickly apologised, "but you just said Raoul's taken over T-26. Isn't Zone T one of Hadrian's zones?"

"It is," Scott replied.

"So how did the Lycans take over a part of it? Or did Hadrian give it to the Lycans himself?" Aaron asked.

A ripple of surprise went around the room. Hunters turned in their seats to give Aaron incredulous looks. Scott looked like he didn't know whether to laugh or frown. He dropped his head and shook it slowly from side to side.

"Aaron," he started, "Hadrian is a vamage, and vamages don't work with anyone. Least of all the Lycans."

"Why?" Aaron asked. "Lycans and vamages are both enemies of mages, right?"

"They are," Scott confirmed.

"Then isn't it possible they could join together to fight us?"

Scott paused and Aaron could see fear cloud his eyes at the thought. With great conviction, he shook his head. "Lycans and vamages are enemies – not just of mages, but of each other. They could never join together." He nodded at the map on the table. "Raoul took Zone T-26 by force. Raoul will be expecting an attack from Hadrian, but not us. We can use that."

Aaron stared at the map, his brow furrowed in thought. "Can you choose where to put the Q-Zone?" he asked.

"Yes," Scott replied.

"You can make it as big or small as you like?"

"Pretty much," Scott replied.

"Then why don't you make a Q-Zone big enough to cover the whole of T-26, and destroy all the Lycans without sending in any Hunters?" Aaron asked.

Scott stared at Aaron, as if he couldn't believe what he had just heard.

"Better yet," Aaron continued, "turn all of Hadrian's zones into Q-Zones, and eradicate the whole lot of them without risking a single Hun–"

Kyran grabbed hold of his hand, shaking his head from side to side with a grave look. Aaron glanced around the room to see everyone staring at him in a mix of surprise and, strange as it was, sympathy.

"I wish it were as simple as that," Scott said quietly. "But if I turn Hadrian's zones into death traps, I would not only be killing the demons living there, I would be murdering the hundreds of thousands of mages trapped in those zones."

Aaron stilled, eyes widening with horror.

"There are mages stuck in the same zones as demons," Scott explained with a heavy heart. "Families, children, thousands upon thousands of them. They're terrorised every day by the demons, by the vamages that came and took over their homes. Sometimes, a mage gets lucky and manages to escape. They come here to Salvador and we help them settle in one of our zones, one of Neriah's zones." He sighed deeply. "But not everyone can escape. Their only hope is for us to help them, to kill the demons and give them back their homes, their zones." Scott met Aaron's eyes. "This...this option, to use the Q-Zone and kill everything...It's been considered in the past." He took in a shuddering breath. "But I can't do it. I can't eradicate my own people. They're the ones we're fighting for. If we lose them then we lose the war, regardless of how many demons we manage to kill or how many zones we take over."

"The way to think about it," Ella said, "is to believe that we only have one option: taking one sub-zone at a time, cleaning it out and setting up Gates before moving to the next zone." She held Aaron's gaze. "There is no other way."

Aaron nodded at her.

"The vamages have been terrorising Zone T-26 for far too long," Scott said. "Now the Lycans have taken it over and Heaven only knows what they're doing to the mages trapped there." Scott's eyes darkened as he looked around the room. "Provided the Lurkers have done their job, the Q-Zone will be in a mage-free area. It'll be your job to get the Lycans into the Q-Zone. We're taking this zone back," he said, "from vamages, from Lycans," his fists clenched, "from Hadrian."

He nodded at the Hunters, gesturing to the door, signalling the end of the meeting. As the Hunters got up to leave, Scott called Aaron over.

Aaron approached the table, his apology already on his lips. "I'm sorry, I didn't mean—"

"That's okay." Scott smiled tiredly. "I sometimes forget there's so much you still don't know." He folded his arms. "I wanted to speak to you about the Q-Zone hunt. I know you're more than aware that I can't stop you from going," he said, "seeing as you went to the last Q-Zone hunt against my wishes."

Aaron felt slightly guilty at defying Scott, but he held his head up and replied, "You were sending my friends into a Q-Zone. I wasn't going to sit back and let them go in alone."

"They weren't alone," Scott said. "They had Hunters with them." He waved a hand. "Anyway, I hope you understand Lycans are a different game altogether. You're not ready to face them, not by a long stretch—"

"I know," Aaron said quickly, "but Sam and Rose aren't going on this hunt so, if you want, I'll stay back too."

"I didn't say you had to stay back," Scott said. "I don't want you going to the Q-Zone but I would like your help on this hunt."

Aaron frowned. "How does that work?"

Scott smiled and turned to the table. He waved his hand and the image flickered to life again, dissolving the red and blue zones into intricate patterns of wispy lines that criss-crossed the zones, to make it look like each zone had its own web.

"Zone T is one of Hadrian's zones," Scott started. "I explained before that each zone is divided into sub-zones." He pointed to the small blob that was T-26. "We take each sub-zone and clear it out. Once we have all the sub-zones we set up a Gate, to protect not only the human realm but also to stop that zone from being taken over again." He paused and looked over at Aaron. "T-26 is the last sub-zone for Zone T. The Gate can only be set up by Elementals. Neriah used to set them up, but in his absence Skyler and Ella have taken that responsibility." He met Aaron's eyes. "A Gate set up by two Elementals is powerful, but one set up by *three* Elementals will be pretty much invincible."

Aaron's eyes widened with understanding. "You want me to help set up the Gate?" he asked in disbelief. "Scott, I don't know the first thing—"

"You don't have to," Scott interrupted. "Ella and Skyler will set it up. You just need to touch the Gate, that's all."

"That's all?" Aaron asked.

"Trust me." Scott smiled.

Aaron didn't say anything. He looked down at the map. "The very first Gates," he said, "the ones Hadrian tore down – they were set up by Aric, weren't they?"

"Yes," Scott replied.

"Aric was pretty much the strongest mage, wasn't he?" Aaron asked.

"Where you going with this?" Scott asked.

"I'm just wondering how, if Aric was so powerful, did Hadrian manage to tear his Gates down?"

Scott didn't speak right away. He looked pained, as if giving the answer was digging into half-healed wounds. "He corrupted them," he said quietly. "The Gates of Resistance were set up by Aric to protect the human realm.

That was their primary purpose," he explained. "Hadrian corrupted the Gates, used his demonic power to weaken them and tear them down." He shook his head in barely concealed disgust. "It was Hadrian's way to declare war against the mages, against Neriah. The human realm was, and probably still is, of very little importance to Hadrian. He tore down the Gates only to defy Neriah and, of course, to give the proverbial finger to Aric."

"So Neriah set up the Gates again on his own?" Aaron asked.

"He had to," Scott replied. "He was the only Elemental left. Hadrian had become the enemy, James Avira and his brother, Joseph, were dead and Christopher..." He paused. "Your dad had left the realm."

Aaron could feel the burn of humiliation seep up his neck and ears. Hearing it like that, learning how fragile the mage realm was when his dad left, Aaron could almost understand the cold behaviour he had endured from most mages.

Aaron thought about Neriah, momentarily placing himself in Neriah's shoes. If his best friend – someone he regarded like a brother – turned into his worst enemy, his other friend was killed and the only other person that could help him had fled to another realm, what would he do? A bout of panic erupt in the pit of his stomach. Neriah would be beyond furious with his dad, with his parents. Would he forgive them? Or would he punish them?

Aaron had to forcefully stop that train of thought before it unsettled him completely. He looked over at the map again, trying to pull himself back into the conversation.

"So, let me get this straight," Aaron said. "Aric had set up the Gates. Hadrian corrupted them and pulled them down. Neriah waged war and set up the Gates again. But two years ago, Hadrian pulled them back down–"

"No," Scott interrupted. "Hadrian didn't pull them down. He couldn't, not this time." At Aaron's frown, he explained. "I told you that when Aric had set up the Gates, they were solely to protect the human realm – to stop the elemental energy from leaking out. After Hadrian pulled them down, Neriah knew that if he were to set up the Gates again, Hadrian would just do the same thing. So Neriah changed the Gates. He encrypted them with Glyphs – specific ones that repelled the touch of demons such as Lycans, vampires and of course, vamages." Scott smiled with something akin to pride for his leader. "It was ingenious. The Gates protected not only the human realm but ours too. For years the vamages couldn't get past our Gates, nor could they touch them. One by one, Neriah went through all the zones, locking them with Gate after Gate. Hadrian was left with only three zones; ones so heavily protected they became untouchable. But it was a loss we could live with. He had three zones, we had the rest." His face fell, eyes becoming shadowed. "That was until two years ago, when Hadrian's Scorcher started pulling down the Gates and taking over."

Aaron frowned. "I don't get it. If Neriah made the Gates immune to vamages, then how did the Scorcher manage to get to them?"

"The Gates were immune to vamages like Hadrian and the rest," Scott said, "ones that were born mages, but who turned into vamages. The Scorcher is a *born* vamage. His blood is different. Since Glyphs are created with the blood of the species that the Gates have to repel, they can't block out the Scorcher. We only had the blood of three of our worst enemies: the Lycans, the vampires and the vamages." Scott shook his head. "We never anticipated we'd have to deal with something stronger."

***

The day of the Q-Zone hunt came on a fresh summer day. Hunters began arriving from the moment of daybreak. Long after breakfast had been served, Aaron, Sam and a few of Salvador's mages stayed at the table, just watching the visitors stream in through the open Gate. Aaron grinned at the sight of Zulf leading his group in.

"Where's he going?" Aaron asked, seeing Zulf ride past the cottages.

"Probably looking for Kyran," Ryan said. "For Zulf, coming to Salvador only means one thing: Kyran."

The Gate opened again with a bright flash, drawing Aaron's attention. This time, though, there were no bikes, just three men oddly dressed in long white tunics with their hoods pulled up to cover their heads and shadow their faces. The one at the front lowered his hood, scanning their surroundings. His gaze rested on the table and he began walking towards it, with the other two men following him.

"About time," Ryan muttered, his tone starkly dark compared to only moments before. "I was wondering when they'd show up."

"Who are they?" Aaron asked.

"Lurkers," Ryan replied. "Here to answer to Scott."

"About what?" Sam asked.

"Why they didn't pick up the fact that Zone G-14 had hell hounds," he said. "Not to mention why they didn't notice an entire Abarimon valley in Zone L-26."

Aaron watched with interest as the three men neared the table. Four months ago, Aaron would have only seen the white-hooded tunics the men wore, but his stay in the mage realm had taught him to notice what lay beyond the surface. The passing breeze pressed their clothes against them so Aaron could see the faint outline of leather bands criss-crossing the men's torsos. Their sleeves were long, but Aaron saw a flash of silver slotted in leather pockets at their wrist when their arms swung in time with their steps. The Lurkers carried weapons, just like Hunters did.

When they got close enough, Aaron got a good look at the one Lurker who had lowered his hood. He was surprised to see a mature face. Aaron had only met young Hunters, aged anything from sixteen to early twenties. This Lurker was likely in his late forties. His short, dark hair had a splattering of grey; his sharp brown eyes were lined. It was only when Aaron finished his private analysis of the Lurker did he realise that the man was staring at Aaron just as intently.

"Patrick," Ryan greeted him, drawing the Lurker's attention away from Aaron. "It's been a while."

The Lurker – Patrick – smiled tightly and nodded. "More than a year, by my count," he said, extending a hand to shake Ryan's. He turned back to Aaron, almost immediately. "You...you can't be...Are you related to Christopher Adams?"

"You could say that," Aaron replied. "I'm his son."

Patrick's eyes widened with surprise. "Chris? Chris is here?" He looked back at Ryan. "When did this happen? When did the Adams return?"

"About four months ago," Ryan replied. "Don't get too excited. Christopher Adams isn't here. He's tracking down Neriah."

A look of grim understanding crossed Patrick's face. He turned back to Aaron and smiled, holding out his hand. "Patrick Sweeney," he said, introducing himself.

Aaron shook his hand. "Aaron," he returned.

"It's a pleasure, Aaron," Patrick said.

The two men behind him lowered their hoods and introduced themselves as Bryce and Harvey. Aaron noted they were younger than Patrick, but not by much.

"I figured I wouldn't be seeing any of the Adams again," Patrick said.

"So did we," Ryan added, with a wink at Aaron.

"You look very much like your father," Patrick said, gazing at Aaron with a wide grin. "It's almost like Chris is sitting here."

Aaron didn't say anything. It wasn't the first time someone had commented on his likeness to his father, but it was the first that didn't fill him with pride. "Did you know my dad well?" he asked.

Patrick laughed. "I knew him really well. I was friends with your father and uncle, worked with both of them on a number of hunts back in the day." His smile broadened. "It'll be great to see Chris again."

"Patrick?" a voice called.

Aaron turned to see it was Drake, with a crowd of orchard workers behind him, all carrying baskets to the Stove. It was no doubt for the feast Mary was preparing in anticipation of the victorious return of the Hunters tonight.

Drake's brow furrowed as he walked over to the table. "What are you doing here?" he asked Patrick.

"I have to speak to Scott," Patrick replied, reaching out to shake Drake's hand. "You're looking well, Drake," he said.

A look of great unease flickered over Drake. He shot a look at Aaron. "Times are changing," he said. "It gives a little hope."

"All the Elementals back in one realm," Patrick said with a chuckle. "Times are changing indeed."

"Ace!"

Aaron turned at Kyran's yell, to see him standing with Zulf, at the foot of the path that led towards the orchard.

"Yeah?" he called back.

"Get over here and show Zulf your ground split," Kyran said.

Zulf continued to shake his head in denial.

Aaron turned back around with a grin. "He can't stop showing off that he taught me that," he said.

"Proud teacher," Sam smirked.

"I'll see you later," Aaron told Sam, and started getting up from the table. He caught the look on Patrick's face and paused. Patrick was gaping at Kyran with wide eyes. His mouth had dropped open and the colour was slowly draining from his face.

"Patrick?" Aaron said. "You okay?"

"How?" Patrick gasped, staring unblinkingly at Kyran. "How can...He...he can't—"

"It's not what you think," Drake said quietly at his side, staring at Kyran too. "He just looks like him."

"Like him?" Aaron frowned. "Who are you talking about?"

Drake shook his head. "It's nothing," he said. "Just one of life's strange coincidences." He turned to look at Sam. "I believe Henry was looking for your assistance."

Sam's brow knitted. "Really? For what?"

"You'll have to ask him," Drake replied. He turned to Patrick and the other two Lurkers. "Come, I'll accompany you to Scott. I have to speak to him too."

Patrick looked like he was barely listening as Drake pulled him away. His gaze was still on Kyran, his mouth opening and closing, but no sound left him.

***

The time for the Q-Zone hunt had come. The street was lined with Hunters. Sam and Rose stood in their midst, Aaron by their side. The residents of Salvador gathered to give the Hunters encouragement and good wishes. The Hunters had already straddled their bikes, grinning and soaking up the attention.

"They seem excited," Sam commented.

"They're always excited," Aaron replied.

"How come you're not going with them?" Sam asked.

"Scott wants me there only when the Gate's ready to go up."

Sam nodded. "Nervous?" he asked.

"Very," Aaron admitted. "I still have no idea what I'm supposed to do with the Gate. Scott keeps telling me all I have to do is touch it."

"You don't believe him?" Sam asked.

Aaron paused. "It can't be that easy."

"Let's hope it is," Sam said. "Right, Rose?"

There was no answer. Sam and Aaron looked around, only to see Rose wasn't by their side any more.

"Where'd she go?" Sam asked.

They didn't see her making her way through the crowd, inching closer to the red and black bike that held a grinning Kyran, lost in his conversation with Zulf. But as soon as her shadow fell across Kyran's bike, he looked up at her. His dazzling green eyes somehow looked brighter as they met hers.

Zulf moved away, smiling, nodding once at Rose in greeting. He revved his bike and moved forward, going to the front and leaving Kyran alone with Rose. For the first few moments, neither of them said anything. Things had been a little awkward between them ever since their kiss.

Rose cleared her throat, forcing herself to look up at him. "I...I wanted to wish you luck," she said. "For the hunt today."

Kyran nodded but didn't speak.

Rose reached in and pulled something out of her pocket. Kyran stilled at the sight of the thin black thread in her hand. He looked up at her.

"That's not for luck," he said.

Rose smiled. "I know what it's for," she replied quietly.

"You know what it means if you tie that around my wrist?" Kyran asked.

Rose looked down at the thread she had got from Ava. Her thumb caressed the strong, coiled thread. "I know that it'll make you a little less reckless," she replied. "After seeing you in battle, I know you could do with being more careful."

"Is that right?" Kyran asked.

Rose shrugged. "What can I say? I like having you around."

Kyran tilted his head to the side, his eyes narrowed a little. "Why's that exactly?"

Rose stilled as her heart skipped a beat. She shrugged again, trying to act nonchalant. "You're teaching Aaron," she said. "He needs his tutor."

Kyran raised his eyebrows, surprised at her answer. "Really?" he asked. "Nothing else?"

Rose took a step closer. "Well, we are living in your house," she said. "It'd be awful to be there but not have you around."

Kyran smiled. "And?"

Rose stepped closer. "And watching you fight it out with Skyler is my only source of entertainment. I'd be so bored otherwise."

Kyran chuckled. "And?" he asked.

Rose stepped forward, standing right next to his wheel. "And you get me chocolates when I need them." She grinned as Kyran dropped his head, clearly fighting back a laugh. When he looked up at her, his eyes smouldered, making Rose's breath catch in her chest.

"And?" His voice was deeper.

Rose took in a breath and moved closer still. "And the thought of not seeing you again..." She faltered. "It hurts in a way that I can't explain."

Kyran held her gaze, smiling in silent triumph, as if he'd finally got the answer he was waiting for. "You remember what you said?" Kyran asked. "About wanting to choose a simple romance?"

Rose nodded. "I do."

Kyran straightened up. "Before you make that choice, keep in mind that, for some of us, simple romances aren't possible." He tugged up the sleeve of his coat and held out his right hand. "Epic love is the only kind we can offer."

Rose stared at him, locked in his intense gaze. She took a last step, standing as close to him as she could. "Well," she said quietly, wrapping the thread around his wrist, knotting it securely. "I guess I'll just have to settle for epic then." She smiled and leant closer, whispering, "'Cause you're the one I choose, Kyran." She closed the small gap between them just as Kyran tilted his head up so their lips met in a kiss.

Rose didn't care about the crowd around her. Nor was she aware of the stares. All Rose could focus on at that precise moment was Kyran and Kyran alone. His lips on hers, one of his hands on the back of her neck, gently pulling her closer. The feeling of being so close to him held a comforting familiarity, as if she had always belonged in his arms, locked in his kiss.

A slow cheer was starting around her, but Rose was still blissfully unaware. It was only when a round of clapping started that Rose pulled away. The surrounding Hunters were whistling as they applauded, grinning at her and Kyran. Amongst them, staring at her with wide eyes, were Sam and Aaron. Rose bit her lip to stop herself from smiling and just shrugged at them.

"Finally!" Ella rolled her eyes. "I was beginning to get worried about you two."

Rose laughed and looked back at Kyran who was grinning too, running a hand through his hair.

Standing amongst the crowd was a silent Drake. His gaze was on Kyran, watching as he pulled Rose close once more, this time to whisper something to her. Rose headed through the cheering crowd, making her way towards the Stove with her head lowered, but a beaming smile on her face.

"I know what you said," Patrick said, appearing at Drake's side. "But I still can't believe it."

Without looking over at him, Drake asked, "Would I have a reason to lie?"

"I'm not saying you're lying," Patrick said. "It's just...he looks too much like Alex for it just to be a coincidence."

Drake turned to face Patrick. "Some things are strange but that doesn't mean they're not true," he said. He looked back over at Kyran, watching as the boy tried to ignore the teasing crowd. "Kyran may look like him, but he's got nothing to do with Alex."

Drake watched as Kyran swung a leg off the bike, sitting on it with both legs to one side, before beckoning Aaron to come closer. As soon as Aaron got near him, Kyran reached for the leather bands crossed at Aaron's torso. He began adjusting them, all the while giving the younger boy his green-eyed glare.

Patrick smiled at the sight. "Seeing the two of them together like that, who do they remind you of?" he asked with a small chuckle. "It's like having Chris and Alex back again, only this time, the roles are revers–"

"Don't you have a zone to secure?" Drake snarled, turning to glare at him.

Patrick was momentarily thrown, before his eyes widened in realisation. "I'm sorry," he said. "You were close with Chris and Alex, I–"

"You should go," Drake dismissed with a glower.

Patrick closed his mouth, giving Drake a look filled with sympathy before leaving. Drake watched him go with angry eyes before his gaze settled back on Kyran and Aaron. He watched them for another minute before turning and walking away, with curled fists and a clenched jaw.

31

SELF-RIGHTEOUS SUICIDE

The blinding brightness only lasted for a few seconds before Aaron walked out of the portal and straight onto a dusty, dry road. The heat was the first thing he registered, and it sweltered down on him. The hot breeze choked him, with speckles of dirt stinging his eyes. Aaron rubbed at them, blinking and squinting against the glare of the sun.

"Aaron? You there?"

He reached up to hold the circle pendant Scott had given him. "Yeah, Scott. I'm here," he replied.

It had taken two hours for the Hunters to corner and lure the Lycans into the designated area where the Q-Zone was set up. Dark clouds had gathered in Salvador's skies, with thunder clapping ominously overhead the moment the Q-Zone opened. Scott had given Aaron the go ahead, and Aaron left immediately to use the portal set up in the forest outside Salvador's Gate.

Aaron spotted Skyler and Ella at the top of the hill. Both were squatting, studying something on the ground. Aaron quickly began climbing his way up.

"Ah, Adams," Skyler drawled, throwing him a sideways glance when he reached the top. "About time."

There was a rip in one of the sleeves of Skyler's coat, the ivory material stained crimson from a bleeding cut. Ella looked physically unhurt, but Aaron could see her exhaustion. Aaron stepped closer to where both were crouched. All he found was a long, rectangular stump protruding from the ground. Moving closer, Aaron spotted a small cloth bag resting next to it. Ella was taking out thin glass vials from it and setting them on the ground.

"Come on," Ella said, getting to her feet. "The sooner we have the Gate set up, the sooner we can get back to hunting."

Standing at the top of the hill, Aaron could clearly see the square bubble of the Q-Zone in the valley below. Its transparent walls showed the Hunters inside, engrossed in a fierce battle. That meant the Q-Zone was still open, it hadn't been locked yet.

Aaron could see the silver flashes of blades as they glinted in the sunlight. He couldn't hear the shots, as the Q-Zone muted all sound, but he could see the guns in many Hunters' hands.

The sight of the Lycans, however, momentarily wiped everything else from Aaron's mind. When he'd first heard about Lycans, he had imagined wolf-type creatures, maybe a little bigger than the average wolf. Seeing them now, Aaron realised how badly he had underestimated them. They were big, fearsome beasts, the dark fur on their back so thick it sat like a coat. The Lycans weren't on all fours like Aaron had imagined, but standing on two legs, towering a good eight foot high at least. Even from a distance, Aaron could see the sinewy muscles of their legs and arms tensing as they leapt at the Hunters with their fangs bared and claws ready.

"Sometime today, Adams," Skyler called from behind.

Aaron came to stand between Ella and Skyler. Ella held out her hands over the top of the jagged rock stump. Skyler did the same. Following their example, Aaron held out his hands too, palms facing down. Not a single world was spoken. Skyler and Ella closed their eyes. Half a minute ticked by and nothing happened. Then, a gradual tingle started in Aaron's fingers, the sensation running from the tips all the way up to his hand and wrist.

There was a moment of complete silence before a tremendous outburst of power erupted from the stump: a gush of brilliant white fluid rose up, shaking the ground as it came from deep within the earth's core. Aaron lost his footing and fell, but still watched the liquid wall as it continued to rise upwards, aiming to touch the sky. Ella bent low and picked up half a dozen vials; Skyler picked up the rest. Methodically, they uncapped each small glass bottle and spilt the crimson contents onto the wall. The red droplets spotted against the white canvas for no more than ten seconds before disappearing. The wall continued to swallow every vial Ella and Skyler poured onto it. After the last one, Skyler and Ella pushed up their sleeves and held out both hands. That's when they noticed Aaron wasn't standing next to them. Ella looked around before spotting Aaron sitting on the ground, gaping at them.

"What are you doing?" she snapped.

"No time to sit around, Adams," Skyler said dryly.

Aaron snapped out of his shock and quickly got to his feet, hurrying forward.

"Just hold your hands against the Gate," Ella instructed.

Aaron did as she asked, so all three of them were standing with their hands up, palms almost touching the wall.

"On the count of three," Ella said, "push your hands onto the Gate."

At Ella's countdown, Aaron prepared himself. He had no idea what was going to happen when he touched the Gate and the uncertainty was making his heart hammer at his insides. A trickle of sweat ran from his temple down the side of his face. At Ella's prompt, he took in a breath and pushed both hands onto the white wall.

Aaron was expecting the Gate to feel somewhat solid, as it was standing free, but his fingers met a cold pool of water instead. Six sets of ripples spread across the surface as the three Elementals touched the Gate at the same time. Aaron felt his fingers tingle again. Deep in his belly, he felt a strange pulling sensation. His heart began beating even faster. His hands felt cold but the rest of his body started to heat up, until it was uncomfortably hot. Sweat trickled from his brow into his eyes but Aaron blinked it away. He glanced to either side to see the perspiration on Skyler and Ella as well.

Aaron looked to his hands in time to see thin white lines appear under the skin of his exposed arms. Frozen in shock, Aaron watched as the white lines ran down both his arms, branching off into multiple little lines, like pale nerves. They ran to his wrists and across his hands, reaching all the way up to his nails. Ten glowing white lines snaked out and onto the surface of the Gate. The same was happening to Skyler and Ella. The Gate shimmered as the thirty lines swam all the way up the length of the wall. A moment later, the entire Gate lit up, its glow so bright that Aaron had to squeeze his eyes shut and turn his head away. The glow faded, and the surface under Aaron's hands solidified.

Opening his eyes, Aaron saw the Gate, just as tall and magnificent as the one guarding the entrance to Salvador. Aaron didn't pull his hands away, not until Ella and Skyler dropped theirs first. Aaron felt a little nauseous; his stomach quivered and his hands wouldn't stop shaking. He could see Skyler and Ella were the same. They looked paler, their hands trembling as they reached for their guns and swords, pulling them out. Ella's sharp grey eyes met Aaron's and she smiled tightly at him.

"Stay here," she instructed, before reaching up to her pendant. "It's done; the Gate's up." She turned to look at the Q-Zone. "Drop the veil."

Before Aaron's eyes, the transparent walls of the Q-Zone clouded, until nothing was visible inside. The Q-Zone was now locked.

Aaron had to watch from the top of the hill as Skyler and Ella raced back to the Q Zone and leapt inside using the one and only open wall. It was increasingly unnerving to sit by himself, watching the clouded bubble, unable to see what was going in inside. The only source of knowledge he had was Scott's voice, giving out instructions to the Hunters. When it came to Scott's explicit commands for him, though, Aaron disregarded him.

"*Aaron, get back to the portal.*"

"I told you, Scott, no," Aaron replied tiredly. "Not until the hunt's over."

"*Just stay next to the portal, then,*" Scott's voice pounded inside Aaron's head. "*Out of the way. I don't want you anywhere near the Q-Zone. You understand?*"

"Yeah," Aaron replied. "Don't worry. I've seen the Lycans. I don't wanna be anywhere near them."

Aaron kept a note of the time, of how much longer the Hunters had in the Q-Zone before it collapsed. When they only had ten minutes left, unlike with the previous Q-Zones, Scott didn't tell any of the Hunters to move out. Instead, they guarded the one and only unlocked wall, preventing the Lycans from escaping.

"*Seven minutes to go!*" Scott informed them. "*Start inching towards the exit. Keep it tight, keep the Lycans back. Step out when I give the command.*"

Aaron paced on shaky legs, unable to sit still. His gaze was locked on the Q-Zone bubble, waiting impatiently for the Hunters to step out. The very idea of all of the Hunters being inside the Q-Zone when it came so close to collapsing was panicking him. He told himself things had been worse. He himself had been inside the Q-Zone when there were only ninety seconds left. Compared to that, the Hunters had plenty of time to get out.

"*Five minutes!*" Scott called.

The fog clouding the walls of the Q-Zone suddenly lifted, halting Aaron in his steps. He stared at the transparent bubble with wide eyes. He could see the line of Hunters against one wall, with the wounded, bloodstained Lycans before them. The criss-crossing bars that usually locked the three walls of the Q-Zone were slowly receding upwards.

Aaron grabbed his pendant. "What are you *doing*, Scott?" he cried.

"*I'm not doing anything!*" Scott's panicked voice returned. "*What's–? How is this–? I don't understand!*"

Aaron watched as the bars almost reached the top, before suddenly stopping. They slammed down again, locking the three walls of the Q-Zone.

"Oh thank God," Aaron breathed.

The grey bars were back but the veil that usually covered the Q-Zone was still missing, allowing Aaron to see everything that was happening. The

Lycans were ferociously trying to attack the Hunters, who were guarding the one and only exit.

Skyler was pushing the Lycans back, using his power to throw the beasts against the walls and hold them there. But somehow the Lycans were fighting back, managing to claw, rip and tear their way closer to the line of Hunters. Bullets, blades, powers – everything was being thrown at the Lycans but they were still getting closer to the exit by the second.

Two Lycans, their fur stained with blood and daggers still embedded in their legs, managed to get past the rain of bullets and jolts of power. They went straight for Ryan and Sarah, sinking their fangs into both Hunters. In a heartbeat, Aaron was racing down the hill towards the Q-Zone. He was almost there when the two Lycans leapt past the wall, successfully escaping the Q-Zone and leaving Ryan and Sarah's convulsing bodies behind them.

Aaron came to a stop, wide eyes fixed on the pair of bloodstained beasts as they licked their jowls and stared at him with slitted yellow eyes. Snarling at him, they went down on all fours, tensing their muscles and getting ready to pounce. Aaron gathered up as much of his concentration as he could, fighting back the crippling fear that was trying to overwhelm him. He cupped both hands and held them ready. The Lycans let out twin growls and came at him, fangs and claws bared. Aaron threw out his hands and the ground under him shook before cracking. Two simultaneous ripples tore across the ground and caught the Lycans, hitting them with enough force to throw them back into the Q-Zone. Through the clear wall, Aaron saw Skyler and Julian empty their guns into the beasts before they could get up. Skyler looked around at Aaron with just a hint of a smile crossing his lips. He nodded at Aaron in silent praise and turned, focusing on the rest of the Lycans.

Without hesitation, Aaron ran into the Q-Zone, coming to Ryan and Sarah's side as they lay bleeding, writhing on the ground. The Lycans closed in, dodging the bullets and blades. Aaron stood up and threw out his hands again – but this time the ripple didn't work. The ground shook, small cracks formed, but no mighty jolt of power threw back the crowd of beasts. He saw Ella and Skyler sending their own powers at the Lycans but they didn't amount to much either.

Aaron didn't have the time to wonder what was happening, why their powers were failing. All he could focus on were the snarling beasts, trying to get near enough to rip them apart. Seeing the Lycans this close made Aaron's knees weak with fear. Their hideous faces were distinctly dog-like. They had overbearing foreheads, and yellow eyes with slitted black pupils. They had snouts and their wide lips pulled back to show sharp fangs.

Before Aaron could take out his guns, Kyran and Zhi-Jiya reached him. Kyran pushed Aaron back, towards the exit.

"Out, Ace!" he instructed before leaning down and picking Sarah up in his arms.

Despite Kyran's command, Aaron hurried forward to help Zhi-Jiya pull Ryan to his feet.

"*I've lost control of the zone!*" Scott's voice, twisted by panic, was barely recognisable as it echoed in Aaron's head. "*I can't get the locks to stay in place!*" There was a moment's pause before he cried, "*Get out. Everyone get out! Abort the hunt!*"

"No!" Ella yelled. "Not when we're *this* close!"

She aimed her hands at the walls. A thick block of ice, almost as tall as the walls themselves, encased the three walls. There was no way anyone was getting through that. But as soon as she lowered her hands, the ice melted and disappeared.

"What?" Ella gasped. "*What's* going on?" she shrieked.

"*Abort the hunt!*" Scott instructed. "*You have less than three minutes. Get out of there!*"

"Come on!" Zhi-Jiya yelled and stepped past the glowing wall, supporting Ryan. Kyran followed after her with Sarah in his arms. "Ace!" he stopped to yell. "Out! Now!" He ran past the wall with a convulsing Sarah in his arms.

Aaron neared the exit, but didn't step out of the Q-Zone, not until the rest of the Hunters had joined him. The Hunters began moving back, still keeping the Lycans pushed against the locked walls with their bullets, blades and weakening jolts of power. All the Hunters reached the exit, except for Zulf.

"Come on!" Ella yelled at him, while firing more bullets into the struggling Lycans.

"Go!" Zulf yelled, both arms extended to either side of him. "I'll keep them in!"

"Zulf!" Ella cried, her eyes widening with shocked horror. "No!"

"I'm not letting these dogs out again!" Zulf yelled, twisting back to look at Ella, his eyes dark with determination. "Go! I'll keep the locks down. Get out, Ella!"

"*Two minutes!*" Scott counted down. "*What are you doing? I said abort the hunt! Get out of there!"*

Aaron looked back at the bars and then at Zulf – at his stance, with both arms extended outwards. *He* was the one who was holding down the locks. Scott had lost control; it was Zulf who was keeping the three walls of the Q-Zone under lockdown so that the Lycans couldn't escape. That meant if Zulf dropped his arms or stepped out of the Q-Zone, the bars would lift and the Lycans would be free again. The realisation of what Zulf was planning to do stole Aaron's very breath.

"Zulf!" he choked out. "Zulf, no!"

"Go!" Zulf snarled.

"Time's up!" Scott's voice thundered in their heads. *"What are you doing? Get out! Ninety seconds! Get OUT!"*

The ground started to tremble.

"Zulf!" Skyler snapped, throwing jolts of power at the Lycans that were trying frantically to get to the Hunters. "Enough! Get back now!"

"I'm not losing this hunt," Zulf said. "We're *not* losing another zone. This one, we're getting back!" He twisted around to look at Ella. "Eight months," he hissed. "It took us eight months to get here. It's not going to be for nothing!"

The ground under their feet began to shake as the Q-Zone started its collapse. Ella threw out her hands, encasing the Lycans in ice, but it didn't last. They broke out of their frozen cage almost immediately. Skyler tried again and again to hold the Lycans back with his power, but it didn't last long either.

"Sixty seconds!" Scott counted down. *"Everyone out! Now!"*

"Go!" Zulf urged.

Ella and the rest stepped towards the edge of the wall, every eye on Zulf, every bullet, blade and power aimed at keeping the Lycans away from Zulf. They hesitated to step out and leave their fellow Hunter, for he would be torn apart by the raging Lycans as soon as they did.

"Twenty seconds!" Scott was screaming in their heads. *"Why aren't you getting out? What's the problem? Talk to me!"*

No one had held onto their pendant to tell him what Zulf was planning on doing. Scott didn't know he was about to lose one of his Hunters.

"Ten seconds!"

The Hunters moved as one, inching backwards, eyes still on Zulf who was holding the bars down in place.

"*Five seconds!*"

Firing their last shots at the Lycans, the Hunters forced themselves past the wall and stepped out, Aaron along with them. The moment he was out, Aaron turned to see Kyran and Zhi-Jiya running full pelt at them. They had obviously taken Ryan and Sarah to the Empaths and only just returned.

Kyran came to a stop, breathing heavily. His narrowed eyes moved from Aaron, and down the line of Hunters before glancing behind them, at the transparent wall. His eyes widened when he saw Zulf, standing alone in the deteriorating Q-Zone, surrounded by furious Lycans.

"ZULF!" he yelled and darted forward, only to be grabbed by Skyler and Julian. "NO!"

In a tremendous blast, the Q-Zone collapsed and vanished, taking the Lycans – and Zulf – with it.

***

"What the hell happened, Scott?" Skyler raged, pacing the spot where the Q-Zone had been moments ago.

"*I don't know,*" Scott's broken voice replied in all the Hunter's minds. "*I've...I've heard of this but...I never thought it was possible.*"

Most of the Hunters had sunk to the ground, devastated with the death of one of their own. A few remained upright, but only because they were too angry to sit. Aaron turned to look at Kyran, who hadn't moved from the spot where Zulf had been standing last.

"What?" Skyler asked, anger visible in every line of his face. "What's not possible?"

"*The Zone was warded,*" Scott replied after a pause.

"What?" Zhi-Jiya asked. "That's insane!"

"*It's the only thing that makes sense,*" Scott said. "*I lost control of the Q-Zone because it was taken from me.*"

"By who?" Aaron asked, holding on to his pendant.

"*Hadrian,*" Scott replied. "*Hadrian's protecting his zones. He's using the Scorcher's power to ward them. It was the Scorcher's power that sabotaged the Q-Zone.*"

Kyran suddenly wrenched his pendant from his neck, snapping the chain. He threw it aside furiously and turned to walk away, heading to the newly set up Gate.

"Kyran." Ella went after him, but Skyler held on to her arm, stopping her.

"Let him go," he said quietly. "He needs to deal, his own way."

Aaron watched as Kyran strode past Lexi and walked out of the Gate, disappearing behind the bright flash of light.

***

It was dark when the Hunters returned to Salvador. Lanterns lit the night sky but even their glow wasn't enough to pierce through the melancholy that hung like a thick curtain over the city. As usual, everyone was gathered in the street when Hunters returned from the Q-Zone hunt, but this time when the Gate opened and the Hunters rode in, there was no rejoicing. No one cheered. No one slapped their hands on the Hunters' backs in praise of a job well done. Truth was, although the hunt had ended with the Lycans destroyed and a Gate in place, it was not a victory. The mages had gained another zone but had lost one of their own.

The Hunters parked their bikes in the street and got off, their movements slow and drained. With tired steps they made their way towards the table where the residents were crowded.

Aaron pulled himself off Zhi-Jiya's bike. He was exhausted, drained with all he had witnessed today. Every time he closed his eyes, he could see Zulf standing in the Q-Zone, alone and ready to die. He couldn't erase that last look Zulf had given them. The determination was visible in every line of his body. He was willing and ready to sacrifice himself, that much was clear to see, but there had also been a hint of fear on Zulf. Aaron had seen it in his grim expression and at the very centre of his fierce eyes: the regret of cutting his life short. Zulf was only nineteen; it was hardly an age to die.

Aaron's thoughts went to Kyran. He was hurting, having lost his best friend. It wasn't just Kyran, though – everyone was genuinely upset at Zulf's demise. Even Skyler, who seemed not the type to care about anything beside himself, seemed down and depressed.

Aaron started making his way to the table. He saw Sam and Rose hurrying towards him. He must have looked as awful as he was feeling, for Sam and Rose raced to his side with worried looks on their faces.

"Aaron," Rose called, somewhat nervously.

Aaron shook his head at her, signalling he was okay as he made his way down the cobbled street. He glanced at the crowd behind the twins and stopped dead in his tracks. Sitting at the table, staring at him in shocked horror, were his parents.

32

VISITORS

It must have been a full minute where no one said anything. All eyes were on the three Adams. Aaron was vaguely aware of Sam and Rose's presence somewhere beside him. Slowly, Chris and Kate stood up, staring at Aaron in stunned surprise. Their gaze travelled down Aaron's attire, stopping at his belt, where Aaron had his pistol sitting in its holster.

"What is this?" Chris asked, looking back up at Aaron.

Aaron didn't answer. Chris took a step closer, his green eyes narrowed with anger.

"Aaron? *What* is this?"

"What does it look like?" Skyler replied for him. He cocked his head and smirked, his tired eyes sharpened back to their usual ice blue. "You should be proud," he said. "Your son's a Hunter now, just like us."

"*Hunter?*" Chris asked incredulously, his eyes widening. His gaze darted from Aaron to the crowd behind. He took in the Hunter outfit on all of them, before he turned to look at Drake, who was standing quietly next to the table. "Since when did *children* start hunting?" he asked, shaking with rage.

"About the time adults went into hiding," Skyler replied.

Chris turned to him with a dangerous look in his eyes, his jaw clenched so tightly that a muscle twitched. "Save it!" he snarled. "Another word from you and I'll forget you're Joseph's kid!"

Skyler's demeanour shifted. He went from cocky to enraged in a heartbeat.

"Sky," Ella whispered from beside him, holding onto his arm. "Sky? Sky, come on. *Come* on!" Ella managed to drag Skyler away.

Chris watched him go with furious eyes, before turning back to Aaron. "We need to talk," he said, striding up to him. He took Aaron by the arm but stopped. Aaron had dug his feet into the ground, refusing to move. Keeping his eyes locked with his dad's, Aaron pulled his arm out of the strong grip.

"Four months," he said quietly. "You come back after *four* months and *you're* angry at *me?*"

Chris was staring at Aaron, shock and disbelief written all over him. "Aaron—" he started, shaking his head.

"Four months," Aaron repeated, his voice a little louder. "Four *months*, Dad. You disappeared on me—"

"No." Chris shook his head, wide-eyed. "No, we didn't. We left you a letter. Your mum—"

"What good was the letter?" Aaron asked. He dug a hand into his pocket and pulled out the withered folded piece of paper. "What did you actually tell me in this?" he asked, holding it up. "That you were leaving? Yeah, I kind of figured that out, since you weren't here!"

"Aaron!" Kate stepped forward, her face taut with anger. "That's enough!"

"No!" Aaron shouted, for the very first time at his mum. "It's not enough. It's nowhere *near* enough!"

Kate gaped at him, completely taken aback.

"We'll talk inside," Chris said with forced calm. He reached out for Aaron's shoulder, so he could guide him towards the nearest cottage.

"No." Aaron stepped out of his reach. "Is this it, huh? You wanna talk so we'll talk? When I want to talk, when I want answers, it's too bad. I just have to shut up and wait until you're good and ready." He shook his head. "I don't think so, Dad. Now *I* don't want to talk to *you*."

"It's not like that," Chris said. "We weren't keeping things from you because we wanted to. It's...it's difficult to explain."

"I don't care!" Aaron spat, so angry he could feel his whole body tense and his fingertips tingle. "I don't care how difficult it is. You should still tell me! You *should've* told me, about a *lot* of things, a long time ago!"

"Aaron." Chris looked exasperated, close to his wit's end. "Please, just...just come inside so we can talk in private." He cast a pointed look at the crowd behind Aaron.

But Aaron shook his head resolutely. "I don't want to talk to you, not any more."

"Aaron," Kate tried, her voice calmer, gentler.

"You had your chance," Aaron cut her off. "You could have answered my questions but you didn't. You left me." His words choked in his throat but Aaron kept going, using his anger as momentum. "You left me here, *alone*, and went off to do God knows what! You didn't tell me a single thing about this realm, or anything that could've helped me. You disappear on me for *months* and don't even think to send me a note or a message of some sort to tell me you're okay, or how long—"

"Wait, wait." Chris held up a hand, his eyes narrowed. "You didn't get our letters?"

Aaron stilled, staring at him. "Other than the one you left for me, no."

Chris turned to look at Drake with surprise. "You didn't pass my letters on to Aaron?"

All eyes turned to Drake, who stood next to the table, staring back at Chris. "I would have," he replied, "if I had received any."

Chris stared at him. "I must've sent you twenty letters," he said. "You didn't receive any of them?"

Drake shook his head. "No, I didn't," he said. "I had thought you wouldn't risk sending messages, so I didn't think much of their absence."

"I had left my son here," Chris said, a quiet fury in his voice. "Of *course* I would have sent word back." He turned back to Aaron, his expression one of remorse. "Aaron," he started. "I…I'm sorry. I thought you were receiving my letters. I explained in them what was going on…" He trailed off, looking uncomfortable. "I don't know what happened. My letters should have reached you."

"But they didn't," Aaron said. "I've not heard from you ever since the day you left me here."

"Aaron—" Kate stepped towards him.

"No," Aaron cut her off. "You can't just disappear on me and return after months and expect—"

"I'm afraid that's my fault," a deep, baritone voice interrupted.

Aaron looked around to see a man approaching from the path behind the cottages, with Scott trailing behind him. The man was tall and muscular with wide shoulders. His brown hair was pulled back, neatly arranged into a small ponytail. A short goatee beard adorned his handsome face. His eyes, Aaron noticed, were the strangest shade of blue and violet he had ever seen.

"I think your parents didn't realise how long it would take to find me," he said with a small smile.

There was something about him, about his overwhelming presence that commanded a hush over everyone. The Hunters and residents of Salvador seemed overjoyed at the sight of the man, judging by their wide smiles, but not a single person spoke. Aaron realised who the man was. It could only be Neriah Afton, the oldest Elemental and leader of the mages.

Neriah came to rest before Aaron with a smile. His violet eyes gleamed with delight as he held out a strong hand. "Neriah Afton," he said, introducing himself. "I've been waiting to meet you, Aaron."

Aaron slowly reached out and shook hands with the Elemental. He noted the dark tattoo on Neriah's inner wrist: three wavy lines.

"I understand your annoyance with your parents," Neriah continued, looking up at Chris. His gaze cooled considerably. "But I think these matters should be discussed indoors." He held out a hand, gesturing to the cottages.

Aaron turned to look around at his dad, before his gaze went to his mum. "I don't have anything to say to them." He turned and walked away.

***

When Aaron awoke the next morning, he lay still for a moment, recalling last night's events. The memory of his parents' shock and surprise made his heart skip a beat. Stubbornly, he refused to feel sorry for them. He had only spoken his mind. He had taken their wishes as commands for so long and what did he get? A life full of secrets. His parents had hidden so much from him: his true identity, his real world, his bloodline that was a part of the Elemental history, and God knew what else.

Aaron let out a sigh and rolled over, only to see Sam and Rose awake.

"Morning," Sam said in greeting.

"Morning," Aaron mumbled and pulled himself to sit up.

"How'd you sleep?" Rose asked, tilting her head to study him.

"Fine," Aaron replied, pushing the covers aside.

Aaron looked to the other side of his bed, where he had dumped his weapons. He cringed, thinking what Kyran would do to him for not safely storing his familiars. At the thought of Kyran, he turned to the twins. "Did you hear Kyran come in?"

"No," Rose replied. "I don't think he's back yet." Her expression alone told of how worried she was. "Aaron, about last night–"

"No," Aaron cut her off.

"Aaron–"

"Drop it, Rose." Aaron picked up the discarded weapons from the floor and began piling them onto his bed.

"For what it's worth," Sam started, "I thought you did great yesterday. Told them what they needed to hear."

"Sam," Rose admonished, turning to look at him.

"What?" Sam asked, lifting his shoulders.

Rose turned back to Aaron before shifting to sit at the edge of her bed. "I know you're mad at them—"

"Shouldn't I be?" Aaron asked with quiet anger.

"Of course you should," Rose said. "You have every right to be mad at them. Even a part of me is congratulating you for telling them all you did last night." She paused for a moment. "But a bigger part of me thinks you should give them the opportunity to speak, to say their part."

"Say their part?" Aaron frowned. "What are they gonna say? What's a valid excuse to dump me here and disappear for months?"

"At least they came back," Rose said.

Aaron stilled, staring at her.

"No matter what they did or didn't say," Rose said. "No matter how much or little they told you, the point is they're still your mum and dad. You've got parents, Aaron, and take it from me, fighting with them for something big or small is just not worth it." She nodded to the window. "You've seen the kind of world this is. Who knows what can happen? Who's going to come back after walking out that Gate?"

Aaron's mind went straight to Zulf.

"Talk to them, Aaron," Rose said softly. "You never know, they might just give you a valid reason."

***

When Aaron walked outside, he didn't find his mum or dad at the table. A moment of panic seized him. Had they left? Were they perhaps so disappointed that they decided to leave him again? Ava must have read his quiet distress, for she told him his mum was talking with Neriah and his dad had gone to see Scott.

Leaving Sam and Rose at the table, Aaron hurried to the Hub. He had a suspicion his dad might be berating Scott for allowing him to hunt. He practically ran down the path that twisted behind the cottages, but as he emerged from the forest, he saw something that momentarily wiped Scott, his dad and the Hub from his mind.

There, in the middle of the ring, was Kyran. He had taken off his heavy Hunter's coat and rolled up his sleeves. Gripping his sword, he twisted out of the way of the blades that were spinning in the air, coming at him from all directions.

Aaron hurried to him, coming to rest outside the ring, just at the rocks encircling it.

"Kyran," he called. "What are you doing?"

Kyran swung his sword, deflecting three spinning knives. Perspiration glistened on his face as he dodged another onslaught of blades that the ring spat at him.

"What's it look like?" he puffed. "I'm training."

Aaron stared at the drenched form of his friend. "Kyran," he called again. "Can you stop? Just for a minute."

But Kyran continued knocking back the blades, hitting them with vigour. His jaw was clenched, green eyes burning.

"Go away, Aaron," he growled.

"Kyran–" Aaron stopped, seeing the door of the Hub opening in the distance.

Giving Kyran a last look, Aaron hurried to the steps of the circular building, just as Chris walked out.

Seeing him in the light of day, Aaron could tell how tough these last few months had been on his dad. He looked haggard – his skin pale and tight over his face, his hair showing more glints of grey than before, and his eyes seemed dull and troubled. The closer Aaron approached, the guiltier he felt for yelling at him.

Chris stopped at the door, his gaze on Aaron. A look of surprise flickered over him before he smiled tiredly at him. "Hey," he said.

"Hey," Aaron replied quietly. "What were you doing in the Hub?"

Chris turned back to look at the door. "I had to speak to the Controller, Scott," he said. "I needed to know what the hell's been going on. This...this hunting...*Kids* hunting." He shook his head. "It's not right. You start to hunt when you come of age. That's the way it's always been."

"Fourteen years is a long time," Aaron said. "A lot can change."

"Basic principles shouldn't," Chris said.

Aaron paused, trying his best to push down his rising annoyance. "Where's Uncle Mike?" he asked.

"He had to hold back," Chris replied. "He'll be here in a few days." He looked at Aaron and took in a deep breath. "Aaron," he started. "I owe you an apology. I know I asked a lot from you." His whole expression showed regret, from his troubled eyes to the lines on his brow. "You had to be on your own for months and...and I'm sorry, I really am." He walked closer, putting both hands on Aaron's shoulders. "I'll explain everything to you, from the absolute start. I promise. I'm going to make this up to you. I'm..." He stopped, eyes narrowed at something past Aaron.

Aaron turned to see what had caught his dad's eye. He found Kyran, still training in the ring, his sword swinging this way and that. Turning back around, Aaron caught the look on his dad's face, and it made his heart skip a beat.

Chris was staring at Kyran without blinking, his mouth open, his body frozen stiff, the colour drained from his face.

"Dad?" Aaron called. "Dad? Dad?" Aaron gave him a little shake.

Slowly, Chris looked over at Aaron, his eyes wide and filled with disbelief. He opened and closed his mouth several times, but his voice seemed to have failed him. He turned to look at Kyran again. "Who...who is he?"

"That's Kyran," Aaron said. "He's a friend."

"Kyran?" Chris said. "Kyran what?" he asked, a note of desperation in his voice. "What's his family name, his surname?"

"I don't know," Aaron replied. "I've never asked. Why? What is it, Dad?"

Chris didn't answer. He stood staring at Kyran, gaping at him in such a way it unnerved Aaron. He turned to look at Kyran too.

As if feeling the weight of their stares, Kyran's gaze – that had been watching the blades – shifted to them. The moment Kyran's eyes met Chris's, he stopped, his sword forgotten in hand. A look of disbelief clouded Kyran's expression before something shifted in his intense green eyes. It sent a shiver down Aaron's back.

A spinning blade grazed Kyran's arm, snapping him and Chris out of their locked stare. Kyran threw down his sword and grabbed his bleeding arm. Raising his other hand, he commanded the blades to stop and fall to the ground.

Without a word to Aaron, Chris hurried down the steps, heading towards the ring. Aaron followed after him. Kyran raised the stone archway and exited the ring. He had just reached down to pick up his coat when Chris and Aaron reached him.

Kyran slowly straightened up, his eyes on Chris. "Look who's back," he said, a little tightly. He looked to Aaron. "I guess you were right. You win."

The way Kyran said it, with so much bitterness, it made Aaron's stomach twist into knots. Regardless, Aaron stepped forward.

"Kyran, meet my dad," he said, introducing them. "Dad, this is Kyran."

Chris's gaze roamed over Kyran, taking in everything. "I'm sorry," he said. "Forgive me for asking, but what's your family name?"

Kyran's eyes darkened a shade. "Who needs family names?" he asked. "We're all individuals."

"Yes, but it's still your name," Chris said, moving closer, his desperation evident. "What's your father's name?"

Kyran's persona shifted, growing visibly darker, so dark in fact that his eyes were almost a different shade of green now. He smirked and tilted his head, observing Chris. "Why?" he asked. "Think you knew him?"

Chris didn't say anything, but his face blanched, losing more colour than Aaron thought possible.

"If you'll excuse me," Kyran said, his poison-green eyes fixed on Chris, "I have to get cleaned up."

He turned and walked away, leaving Chris to stare after him and Aaron to wonder what was going on.

***

"He had a son," Chris muttered. "How could he not tell me he had a son?"

"Chris, you have to listen to me," Drake said. "Sit down."

Chris paced the room like a caged animal, his hands running through his hair and down his face, brow knitted and eyes clouded in confusion.

"It doesn't make any sense," he continued to mutter. "He can't be...but he looks *just* like him."

"Chris, listen." Drake had to step in and hold on to Chris's shoulders to still him. "He's not Alex's son."

"He must be." Chris shook himself out of Drake's hold, moving back a step. "Have you seen him?"

"Yes, I've seen him," Drake replied, exasperated. "I've been living in the same city as Kyran for the last year now. I see him every day."

"Then explain this," Chris said. "Explain how he can be the exact replica of Alex without somehow being related to him. How can he be so similar? The hair, the face, the way he talks, walks, everything!"

"Kyran doesn't talk like Alex," Drake objected. "I don't think Alex could ever be that mean."

"Drake!" Chris yelled. "Look at him! Go outside and *look* at Kyran." He pointed a finger at Drake's window.

Drake didn't move. Instead, he asked Chris a question very calmly, "Can you feel him?"

Chris paused, wide eyes fixed on Drake. "What?"

"Kyran," Drake asked quietly. "Does he feel like family?"

Chris swallowed heavily. "No," he admitted, with great pain.

"Then how can he be Alex's son?" Drake asked.

Chris sagged into a chair, hands in his hair. "I don't...I don't understand. How can he be so similar if he's not....?" he trailed off, his eyes clouded with confusion and heartache.

Drake knelt next to Chris's chair. "Alright, listen to me, Chris, and listen well," he said. "Kyran is not Alex's son. He's the son of Fredrick Lamont."

Chris looked up at him in surprise. "Lamont?" he asked. "But...but Lamont only had daughters."

"From his marriage, yes," Drake said. "Kyran is Lamont's other child, one out of wedlock. No one knew about him until Lamont was on his deathbed. Kyran's mother and step-father died in a Lycan attack when he was very young. Lamont knew that since he was about to die, Kyran would feel the connection break and would come looking for answers. He told his daughters and wife about Kyran, so that when he came, they would give him his right."

"Did they?" Chris asked.

"Like hell," Drake scoffed. "The girls aren't so bad. They keep in contact with Kyran and he watches over them, goes to protect them every full moon. It's the mother who can't get over her husband's infidelity, of which Kyran is a living, breathing reminder."

Chris narrowed his eyes. "How do you know this?"

"I investigated him." Drake smiled sadly at Chris. "When Kyran walked through Salvador's Gate for the first time a year ago, I reacted like you did. I was certain he was Alex's son. I pestered him but he wouldn't tell me what his family name was. After a few months, I noted he left every full moon. I followed him at the next one and saw him go into Lamont's mansion. When I confronted him, he told me the whole story. I swore to keep Kyran's secret." He gave a pointed look to Chris. "I'm only telling you so you know the truth. Kyran's understandably touchy about his family name, so don't ask him. He can't say he's a Lamont for the shame it'll bring on his sisters, something that he's reminded of almost every time he meets Mrs Lamont. The only ones who know about his family are myself and Neriah's niece, Ella."

Chris sat in silence, processing all the facts. He shook his head, reaching up to rub at his eyes. "But why does he look so much like Alex then?"

"I don't know," Drake replied. "Sometimes there's no blood connection, but there's a resemblance nevertheless." He looked into Chris's tortured eyes. "Kyran has a likeness to Alex, but that's all it is. Kyran's not your family, Chris, no matter how much you'd like him to be."

**

Kyran walked into his room after taking a shower to find Aaron waiting for him.

"What was that?" Aaron demanded.

"What was what?" Kyran asked.

"That thing with my dad?" Aaron said. "Why were you staring at him?"

Kyran pulled a face. "I think it was the other way around." He combed his fingers through his damp hair as he walked over to the dresser.

"You were staring at him too," Aaron said. "Don't lie, Kyran. You stopped in your tracks at the sight of him."

"I was surprised," Kyran admitted. "It's not every day you find the Adams have returned to Salvador." He pulled open a drawer to take out a hooded top to wear over his vest.

"That's not it," Aaron said. "You were staring at him as if...as if you knew him."

Kyran turned to give him a look. "How could I know him? I've not met him before today."

"My dad looked like he had seen a ghost when he saw you," Aaron said. He paused for a moment, frowning. "Why was he so interested in your family name?"

"You tell me," Kyran said.

Aaron shook his head, failing to work out why his dad seemed so interested in Kyran. He looked up at him. "Come to think of it, what *is* your family name?"

A slow smile crossed Kyran's face as he zipped up his top. "Trust me, Ace. You wouldn't believe me if I told you."

***

Aaron and Kyran walked out of the cottage together. Aaron took a seat next to Sam at the table, while Kyran went to sit with Ella.

"How'd it go?" Sam asked.

"It didn't," Aaron said. "My dad got...distracted and I've yet to see my mum."

"They still haven't spoken to you properly?" Sam asked with surprise. "That's just messed up," he said. "I get what Rose was saying but your folks aren't exactly making it easy to forgive them."

Aaron didn't know what to say. He looked down at the table, idly tracing the wood markings with his finger.

"Fine. Don't ask how I am."

Looking up, Aaron was surprised to find Ryan sitting across from him. His shoulder was heavily bandaged, his face pale and pinched. The dark circles under his eyes told of his sleepless night.

"Ryan?" Aaron blinked. "I didn't expect to see you so soon. You okay?"

Ryan gave a one-shouldered shrug. "Still healing," he said. "Which in itself is an accomplishment. If Zhi-Jiya and Kyran hadn't got me and Sarah to the Empaths when they did, we'd be dead."

"How's that?" Sam asked. "I thought mages didn't die easily?"

Ryan snorted. "You call getting chewed on by a Lycan easy?" He shook his head. "Even if Lycanthropy wasn't fatal, being ripped apart by fangs is a tough way to go."

"Lycanthropy?" Aaron raised an eyebrow. "You make it sound like it's a disease."

"It *is* a disease," Ryan replied.

Aaron shared a look with Sam.

"Demons are one thing," Ryan began, "Lycans and vampires are another. Don't get me wrong, they're still demonic, but they didn't come from hell itself. Lycans and vampires were created over time."

"You mean, they're an evolved condition?" Aaron asked.

"Lycanthropy and Vampirism are two strains of a virus," Ryan said. "If infected, the virus takes over the body, mind and soul. It gives the body certain advantages to help its survival: super speed, super hearing, immense strength–"

"Immortality," Aaron added.

Ryan shook his head. "They're not immortal. Lycans, vampires and, of course, vamages are powerful but they're not immortal. They can die, just not very easily. Mages can survive a demon attack but Vampirism and Lycanthropy are viruses that get into our system and kill us."

Aaron frowned. "But...but what about Hadrian?"

Ryan's expression darkened. "He chose to forsake his purity," he said. "He consented to change. It's what made all the difference. He wanted to become a demon." He straightened up, looking like he was making an effort to keep calm. "For normal mages, though, it's pretty straight forward. You get bitten by a Lycan or a vampire, you're going to die – unless you have a friend like Kyran and a girlfriend like Zhi-Jiya who'll get you to an Empath in time."

"How do they help?" Sam asked. "I mean, do the Empaths have, like...like, an antibiotic to fight the virus?"

It was Ryan's turn to look confused. "Antibio-what?"

"He means like an antidote," Aaron explained. "Something that kills the virus."

"Oh." Ryan smiled wryly. "Yeah, I wish." He took a sip from his mug. "Nah, it's the old painful way of flushing the virus out."

"Drinking lots of water?" Sam asked.

Ryan frowned at him. "That's painful for you, is it?" he asked. With an annoyed shake of his head, he continued, "The virus has to be drained out of you." He grimaced. "Trust me, it feels a whole lot less fun that it sounds."

Aaron didn't want to even imagine how a virus would be flushed out of a body. "Sorry, Ryan," he said.

"It's fine." Ryan smiled back. "It's not the first or last time that I'll be having deadly viruses pulled out of me." He winked at Aaron. "Occupational hazard."

Aaron smiled, until he caught sight of his mum, standing talking with his dad and Drake. They seemed engrossed in their discussion. Aaron stared at his mum, watching as the lines deepened on her brow and the corners of her mouth dropped. He couldn't hear what was being said, and lip reading was never a strong suit of his, but Aaron could tell the conversation was a sour one. His mum held up a hand, objecting to whatever it was Drake had said. Drake, Aaron noticed, kept going regardless. With clear agitation, Kate looked away, rolling her eyes and pressing her lips together to bite back her words. Her gaze caught something and, in an instant, her expression changed. Her eyes widened and slowly the colour drained from her face. Her mouth opened in a breathless gasp. Aaron followed his mum's gaze, to find it on Kyran as he sat talking quietly with Ella. Aaron turned back to his mum, to see her gaping at Kyran with disbelief. She even shook her head a little, as if in denial.

"What's wrong with your mum?" Sam asked.

"No idea," Aaron replied.

He looked back at Kyran, to see him nod to whatever it was Ella was saying. Kyran turned his head and that's when he saw Kate. For the second time that day, Aaron saw that strange, unnamed emotion flicker in Kyran's eyes. Slowly, Kate began walking towards the table, her eyes on Kyran the whole time. Chris and Drake followed behind her.

Time seemed to have slowed down, for it took Kate *ages* to get to the table. Kyran, Aaron noted, kept his attention on the approaching trio, his eyes growing fiercer with every passing minute. They finally came to sit, taking seats across from Kyran, ignoring Aaron completely. When Kate spoke, her voice trembled – something Aaron had never before witnessed. "You...you must be...Kyran," she said.

"Kate Adams," Kyran said and she bristled, as if his voice had pricked her skin with needles. "You couldn't possibly be anyone else." Kyran smiled but, to Aaron, it seemed like an awfully empty one.

"My husband mentioned..." Kate paused before shaking her head, her brows knitted. "You seem...very familiar."

Kyran raised his eyebrows but the smile that twisted his lips was an ugly one. "Oh? How's that?"

Kate didn't answer right away. She took her time, studying every inch of Kyran's face. "You remind me of...of someone."

"I would have to agree," a deep voice said. Everyone turned to see Neriah approach the table but the leader of the mages had eyes only for Kyran. "The resemblance is uncanny," he said. He pulled out a chair and sat down. "I believe we've not met," he said to Kyran. "Neriah Afton," he introduced with a nod.

Kyran smiled too, but his eyes remained cold. "An introduction is hardly necessary," he said. "I don't think there's a being in this realm who doesn't know who you are." He held a hand to his chest. "Kyran."

"I've heard a lot about you, Kyran," Neriah said, unfolding the napkin to lift out the cutlery. "Scott speaks very highly of you. He's told me about some of your impressive hunts."

"They're nothing compared to the legends of Neriah," Kyran replied. "I think it's safe to say you still wear the crown."

It was the tone with which Kyran spoke that made his words sound more like a jibe than praise. Neriah didn't miss it either.

"A thirst to prove yourself?" He nodded. "It's good – makes you work harder."

"Isn't it fools who waste time working harder?" Kyran asked. "I thought it was the ones who worked differently that secured success?"

Aaron heard his dad's choked gasp but he kept his eyes on Neriah, watching as his expression stayed the same but something flickered in his violet eyes. He tilted his head a fraction and pointed his fork at Kyran.

"What did you say your surname was?"

"I didn't," Kyran replied.

"And why is that?" Neriah asked calmly. "Are you not proud to bear the name of your father?"

Kyran's expression grew colder. "Pride has nothing to do with it."

"Quite the contrary," Neriah replied. "It's always about pride."

"It's a personal decision," Kyran bit out, visibly angry now. "One that I would appreciate you respect."

"Respect comes with understanding," Neriah said, "and right now, I don't understand your need for secrecy."

"No secrecy," Kyran insisted. "I just don't see the point of telling you. You wouldn't have known my father anyway."

"There isn't a face or name that I don't know," Neriah said. He sat back in his chair, staring at Kyran. "And your face reminds me of someone, but your demeanour is of another entirely. So, I ask you once again." His eyes cooled. "What is your family name?"

"My name is mine to divulge," Kyran said with quiet fury. "And I'll do that when I see fit." Aaron could see the tension in Kyran's shoulders and the muscle twitch in his jawline as he leant across the table to look Neriah in the eyes. "And if that's not okay with you, just say the word and I'll walk out that Gate."

"Kyran?" Ella gasped.

Neriah didn't say anything but continued to stare at Kyran. With a last glower, Kyran got up and walked away from the table.

33

Regrets

Lunch wasn't even finished when Chris and Kate left, looking too distracted to eat. Aaron watched, waiting for the moment they would beckon him over, so he could have the promised talk. But his parents got up and walked to one of the sanctuary cottages, closing the door behind them, not sparing him a single glance.

Aaron remained seated as the others steadily went through their lunch, whispering about Kyran's open defiance. Aaron stubbornly kept his eyes on his plate, which he had hardly touched, but it was no use. Eventually, his anger won and Aaron got to his feet. Sam looked up at him with surprise, opening his mouth to speak, to ask where he was going. Aaron's expression must have given him the answer, because he didn't say a word and just nodded at Aaron with silent encouragement.

Aaron hurried towards the green-doored cottage. He didn't knock on the door, but pushed it open, heading straight into the living room. He stopped at the sight of his mum sitting inside alone.

"Where's Dad?" Aaron asked.

"Upstairs," Kate replied, looking slightly thrown by Aaron's sudden appearance. She straightened up in her seat. "He won't be long. He's taking a shower."

Aaron wanted answers, but he wanted them from his dad. He was the one that promised him an explanation. He glanced at his mum, but knew she wouldn't give him anything other than instructions. He was about to leave when Kate called to him. "Aaron?"

He stopped, turning to look at her. Last night's discussion came back to him, but unlike with his dad, Aaron didn't feel guilty for yelling at her. Kate stared at him, her gaze raking him from head to foot before she smiled.

"You look very different," she said. "With your hair that long, you look like your dad when he was your age."

Aaron nodded. "And Kyran? Who does he look like?"

Kate's smile vanished. Her face blanched and she quickly looked away. "It's...it's a long story, Aaron—"

"Oh really? A long story?" Aaron cut her off, so angry his hands were shaking. "How long is it, Mum? Is it that long that you can't take time out of your *busy* day to explain what the hell is going on?"

"Aaron." Kate's voice cooled at once. "Watch your language. This isn't how I raised you."

"No, no you didn't," Aaron said. "You raised me to keep quiet and not ask questions. You raised me to do what you asked, and I always did. I've always listened to you, did as I was told, and what did that get me?"

Kate looked shocked. She raised a hand to quieten him, swallowing heavily. "You're upset right now," she said. "We'll talk when you're calmer."

"We'll *never* talk!" Aaron yelled. "Never! You and dad will just keep pushing me back, promising answers when you know you won't give them!"

"That's not true," Kate objected.

"The first day we came here, Dad told me he would sit me down and explain everything," Aaron said. "I wake up the next day and he was gone. You and Uncle Mike – gone. What happened to that promise?"

"You don't understand," Kate started. "We had to go. We had to–"

"Find Neriah and explain to him, yeah, I get it," Aaron interrupted. "I get all that and right now, I don't even want to know what your reasons were for running away all those years ago. I don't want to know why you left your friends. Why Dad, while being a Hunter, left the rest of the mages to their fate and ran out on them. That explanation can wait. Right now, I want you to explain why you left *me* behind."

Kate was staring at him in shock, stunned speechless.

"Tell me, Mum!" Aaron demanded, stepping towards her. "Explain why you left? Why you didn't take me with you?"

"It was too dangerous," Kate said. "We needed you to be safe." She shook her head and her eyes sharpened at once. "But you? You didn't listen, did you? What were you thinking going out of Salvador, to go hunting no less?" She stepped towards him. "Didn't I tell you specifically that as long as you stayed in Salvador you were safe?"

"Yeah. Safe but totally clueless, right?" Aaron said.

"What's got into you?" she asked. "This isn't you, Aaron. You would never speak to me like this."

"'Cause I was scared of you, Mum," Aaron admitted. "I've always been afraid of you. But that was before you showed me what fear really was. That was before you left me alone in a world that I had just walked into the *night* before. You walked away without even telling me why."

"That's not true," Kate objected, her eyes filled with pain. "I left you a letter–"

"A letter. A *letter*, mum?" Aaron shouted. "You couldn't have told me in person?"

"You were sleeping."

"You could've woken me up!" Aaron raged. "I was asleep, not dead!"

Kate's mouth dropped open and her face drained of colour. For a moment, Aaron thought she was going to faint. Reaching out to the back of the sofa, Kate steadied herself. A trembling finger was lifted in warning. "Don't," she warned, her voice barely above a whisper. "Don't you ever, *ever* say that again."

Aaron stared at her. "You don't want me even suggesting it?" he said. "But you don't care if I thought the same about you?" He stepped closer. "I spent almost every night imagining the worst. I watched that Gate every day, waiting, just waiting for you, Dad and Uncle Mike to come back and when you didn't, what do you think I imagined had happened to you?"

Kate's face crumpled. Her eyes welled up and she let out a pained gasp. "Oh, Aaron." She stepped forward, her arms stretched out for him but Aaron stepped back, out of her reach. Kate stopped, staring wide-eyed at him, hurt with his rejection.

"I've spent every moment, hoping and wishing that you were okay," Aaron said. "Do you have any idea what that feels like?" he asked. "I spent months worrying about you, praying every damn night that you were still alive! Asking myself again and again why you hadn't returned. Why you hadn't made any contact if you were okay."

"We sent you letters–" she started.

"That I never got," Aaron said. "Just take a moment and think about that, Mum. I never got any of your letters. I waited months without knowing if you were okay. I had given up hope that you would even come back."

"That's impossible," Kate said, hurrying forward. She held on to Aaron's shoulders. "We'd always come back for you, you should know that."

Aaron pulled away from her. "I thought I did know you," he said. "I thought I knew exactly what my parents were like. I thought my mum wasn't the type to ever leave me alone in a strange place. I thought my dad was brave and courageous and he would always fight to protect–"

"He is," Kate interrupted. "Your dad has always fought to help others."

"Then why did he run?" Aaron asked. "Why did he leave his realm?"

Kate went very quiet. Her eyes shadowed and she looked away, pressing her lips together to fight back tears.

"It's not what you think," she started.

"Doesn't matter," Aaron said. "It's what every mage here thinks. Everyone I've met has told me you and Dad ran, leaving the rest to their fate."

"Aaron." Kate looked at him. "I...I can't...this is not how I wanted to tell you–"

"Did you even want to tell me?" Aaron asked. "If that car accident had never happened, if we were still in the human realm, would you have told me what I really was?"

Kate didn't give an answer but Aaron wasn't expecting one. He already knew. He slowly shook his head. "Admit it, Mum. You hid this from me because you didn't want me to know what I was. You were happy to keep lying to me."

"Yes, I was lying to you!" Kate snapped. "I lied to you! I would have lied to you *every* day for the *rest* of your life if it kept you safe!"

"Safe from what?" Aaron shouted. "From demons? Lycans? Vamages? What, Mum? What are you trying to protect me from?" he yelled. "Or is this just a way to keep me under control?"

Kate's mouth fell open in shocked disgust. "Aaron!" she yelled.

"That's all this is," Aaron cried, lost in his anger. "You don't want me here doing my own thing, choosing what to be, because you want to keep making my choices for me! It's not about keeping me safe. You just don't want to lose your control!"

"Aaron!" Kate raised her hand but stopped, her tear-filled blue eyes widening with horror.

Aaron stared at her, at the hand she had lifted but not struck him with. His angry green eyes moved to stare at his mum's shocked expression. She lowered her hand.

"A-Aaron," she gasped. "I...I didn't...I...I'm sorry–"

Aaron tore his gaze away, turning to wrench open the door and walk out.

Kate chased after him. "Aaron! Aaron, wait!"

Aaron pushed her hands away and continued down the street.

"Please, I...I didn't mean...Listen to me." Kate tried to stop him, but Aaron pulled himself out of her grip and stormed down the path. "Aaron! Aaron, please, stop!"

Aaron spotted Kyran sitting on his bike. The Gate was sliding open, Ella and Skyler already racing towards it. Aaron bolted towards Lexi, ignoring his mum's calls from behind. He climbed on after Kyran.

"Ace?" Kyran turned to him with a frown. "What–?"

"Just drive," Aaron bit out.

"Aaron!" Kate yelled, running after him.

Kyran looked over at Kate before glancing back at Aaron. Without another word or question, he kicked Lexi into gear and rode out through the Gate, leaving Kate to yell after them.

***

Aaron had no clue where they were, just that it was another one of Neriah's zones accessed via the portal in the forest. Kyran had parked Lexi next to a tree and sat down at the bank of a wide river next to Aaron. Ella and Skyler had ridden on, going off to complete one of the Hub's assignments.

"You don't need to go with them?" Aaron asked quietly.

"It's not a biggie," Kyran said. "Just a pick up. Ella and Skyler can handle it." He fixed Aaron to the spot with an intense look. "What's going on with you?"

Aaron shook his head but gave up on resisting halfway. For the next hour or so, Aaron talked and Kyran listened. Aaron let out every thought, accusation and blame against his parents. He told Kyran everything, from the first argument he had at the age of six to the fight with his mum today. He talked until his throat was hoarse, but somehow, even that didn't extinguish the fiery rage in him.

"She thinks I'm just stupid. That I'll sit around and not ask questions." He shook his head in a mixture of anger and hurt. "She doesn't care how I feel, neither does Dad. They only care about what they have to go through."

"That what you really think?" Kyran asked.

Aaron snorted. "It's what it looks like," he said. "Did they care they were leaving me in Salvador? They must have known the others would ask me questions. Did they care I didn't have the answers? It didn't bother them that I knew *nothing* about mages. They didn't care that I would get laughed at and ridiculed for not knowing anything. I didn't even know who Aric was and that's a bedtime story for young mages!"

Kyran ducked his head to hide his smile. "Yeah, that was kinda pathetic."

Aaron let out a frustrated sigh, staring at the water glistening under the sun. "They didn't want me to know about the mage realm," he said. "Drake let it slip that my dad wanted it like that 'cause he didn't know if we would be allowed to stay here." He paused for a moment. "I lived my whole life in the human realm, but I didn't really *live* there. My mum and dad didn't let me be a part of it. I went to school until I was eleven, then they pulled me out and kept me in the house. I didn't go out. I didn't get involved in anything. My friendship with Sam and Rose was the only thing that saved me from going insane." He closed his eyes, pushing all the bitterness down. "My parents stopped me from being a part of the human realm and now they're gonna do the same here." He opened his eyes and looked over at Kyran. "Which world do I get to live in – really live in, and be a part of?"

"You're a mage, Aaron – an Elemental," Kyran replied. "Your place has always been here. This realm belongs to you. And you're a Hunter now, that's a big part of this world."

"Yeah, lets see how long that lasts now that Dad's back," Aaron scoffed.

Kyran fell silent for a moment, staring at Aaron before he straightened up. "Forget them," he said. "Don't let them live your life for you. Do what you want, regardless of what they say."

"Easier said than done," Aaron replied, rubbing at his head to ward off the headache that was just blooming behind his eyes. He sighed deeply. "I wish I had, though. I wish I had done what I wanted."

Kyran watched him carefully before asking, "What's your biggest regret?"

"That's easy," Aaron replied in a quiet voice. "Sneaking out with Sam and Rose that night, doing the reflux and causing the vamage attack." He shook his head sadly. "If I was ever given the chance to go back and change things, I would – even if it meant I had to give up Sam and Rose's friendship. I would rather they were with their parents, living in their own world, than stuck here with me."

"Other than that?" Kyran asked. "Anything else you would do if given the chance?"

Aaron went quiet for a moment before a slow smile spread across his lips. "Other than that," he said, "I would kiss Rebecca."

"Rebecca?" Kyran raised his eyebrows.

"She was my neighbour," Aaron explained.

Kyran gave a low whistle. "You've been crushing on your neighbour?"

"Look who's talking?" Aaron retorted. "At least I had an entire house between me and Rebecca. You and Rose had a wall."

Kyran chuckled. "Did she like you?" he asked.

"Dunno." Aaron shrugged. "I think she did. It's hard to tell with girls."

"Did you ask her out?"

"Yeah, right," Aaron said. "I was lucky when I was able to talk to her from my back garden." He went quiet for a moment. "If there's anything I regret other than what happened to Sam and Rose and their parents, it's that I never got a chance to tell Rebecca how much I liked her. I never got to kiss her." He looked up at the clear sky, letting out a deep breath. "I didn't get to say goodbye."

Kyran stared at him for a moment longer before getting to his feet. "Come on."

"Where we going?" Aaron asked.

Kyran smirked. "To get your goodbye."

***

Kyran parked his bike in front of the gates. The square building of Westbridge Secondary sat proudly beyond the black railings. It must have been lunchtime, for every student was outside. Aaron stared at them with wide eyes, his heart hammering at his insides. He couldn't believe he was here, back in the human realm, in front of Westbridge Secondary School.

"This isn't a good idea," Aaron fretted.

"You said you wanted to kiss her," Kyran reminded him. "Now's your chance. Go get your kiss."

"I didn't think you would actually bring me here," Aaron said. "We were just talking hypothetically."

"No, we were talking practically," Kyran replied. "Now go."

Feeling like his legs were made out of jelly, Aaron climbed off the back of the bike. "Okay, so what do I do again?" he asked.

"You walk in, find your girl and kiss her," Kyran said. "It's not complicated, Ace."

Aaron let out a deep breath. "Okay." He took a step forward before turning back. "What if she doesn't want to kiss me?" he asked. "What if she, like, slaps me or something?"

Kyran paused. "Then I'll go kiss her."

"What?" Aaron frowned. "How does that help anything?"

"It doesn't," Kyran said. "But girls like kissing me."

"Kyran!" Aaron snapped.

"Either you go kiss Rebecca," Kyran said, "or I'll do it for you."

"Do it for me?" Aaron scoffed. "This isn't a test you can sit on my behalf."

"Are you going, Ace?" Kyran asked.

"I am," Aaron said, "I just wanna make sure she wants to kiss me too, you know? I can't just go in and...and walk up to her and—"

Kyran started getting up.

"Okay! Okay! I'm going," Aaron said, hurrying to the gates, shooting Kyran dirty looks.

Kyran settled back on his bike, smirking at the younger boy.

Aaron paused at the gates, staring at the school he had so desperately wanted to attend. He never thought this would be the circumstance that would bring him here. Taking in a deep breath, Aaron crossed the threshold and walked in.

It didn't take long for Aaron to spot the girl he still dreamt about. It was almost as if his eyes were drawn to her, seeking her out from the crowd. She was standing near the double-door entrance to the school, a group of girls around her. Aaron stared at her. She looked even more beautiful than he remembered.

Aaron started walking towards her. It was one of Rebecca's friends that noticed him first. She pointed him out, making Rebecca turn to face him. Her eyes narrowed at him, a frown on her face. Then recognition settled in and Rebecca's features pulled into one of surprise.

"Aaron?" she called with disbelief.

Aaron knew her astonishment wasn't only because he had been missing from this world for the last four months; it was also because he didn't look like he used to. His skin had tanned from spending time out in the scorching sun. Working in the orchard and then training with Kyran had toned his body, giving his lithe physique a bit more muscle. His hair was longer, almost falling into his eyes since he hadn't had a haircut in months.

"Oh my God, Aaron! It is you!" Rebecca exclaimed. "What–? Where have you been?" she stepped towards him.

Aaron didn't say anything, but continued walking towards her.

"Everyone's been looking for you," Rebecca continued. "The police came asking questions. The Masons are missing too. The whole neighbourhood's been asking questions."

Aaron didn't say a word. He reached out to touch her cheek before leaning in and kissing her softly. Time seemed to have stopped for Aaron, allowing him to relish the feel of her lips on his. She didn't pull away. Instead, her hand came up to rest on his shoulder. When the kiss ended and Aaron stepped back, he saw the surprised, yet dreamy, smile on her lips. He smiled too, staring into her eyes.

"Bye, Rebecca."

She stirred from her daze, narrowing her eyes in confusion. "Bye?" she frowned. "Aaron? What–?"

But Aaron had already turned to walk away.

"Aaron?" Rebecca called after him.

Aaron didn't look back at her until he climbed onto the bike behind a grinning Kyran. He smiled at Rebecca one last time, as Kyran started Lexi up, before speeding away. Rebecca stared after them, looking surprised and confused, but with that stunned smile still on her lips.

***

Aaron was on a high. He could barely sit still long enough for Kyran to enter Salvador.

"If you fall off, it'll be your own fault," Kyran admonished, as Aaron kept pulling himself into an almost standing position, pumping his fist and letting out all kinds of hoots.

"Oh man!" Aaron grinned. "That was…that was…something!"

Kyran came to a stop just past the entrance, afraid Aaron was going to fall if he kept going. "All right, get off Lexi right now," he instructed.

Aaron jumped off, practically bouncing with delight. Kyran parked Lexi in the street and climbed off. "You need to calm down," he said.

"I just kissed Rebecca Wanton," Aaron said. "*Rebecca* Wanton!"

Aaron had walked two steps when he saw the large crowd gathered at the table, turning to stare at them with surprise, probably because of the grin on his face. Aaron tried to stop smiling but couldn't quite manage the task, not while the memory of Rebecca's kiss was still on his mind. He saw his mum and dad quickly get to their feet, immense worry etched on their faces as they stared at him with wide eyes. Aaron's euphoria started to die down. He had almost forgotten he had a mess to sort out with his parents.

Skyler emerged from the crowd wearing a smile, both hands tucked behind him as he walked forward.

"You're back quickly," Kyran said. "Assignment over already?"

"Yeah," Skyler replied, looking at Kyran with gleaming blue eyes. "And it was an enlightening experience."

He unfolded his arms from behind him, raised the hand clutched around his gun and fired a single shot straight into Kyran's chest. The force of it knocked Kyran onto his back.

"What the–!" Aaron turned to face Skyler with a snarl. "What are you *doing*?"

"What does it look like?" Skyler replied calmly. "I'm neutralising the threat." A slow smirk spread across his face as he looked at Kyran. "Isn't that right, Scorcher?"

34

SHATTERED TRUST

Aaron gaped at Skyler, whose cold, blue-eyed gaze was fixed on Kyran. The crowd at the table had suddenly moved, coming to stand behind Skyler. Every Hunter had a gun in hand – aimed at Kyran.

Aaron turned to see Kyran slowly pick himself up from the ground, one hand clutched around the bloody wound in his chest. He straightened up, breathing heavily, pain in his expression, but his eyes were blazing.

"Have you lost your mind?" he snarled at Skyler.

"Not at all," Skyler replied calmly. "But you must have lost yours to come to Salvador, Scorcher."

"You've gone insane," Aaron said, shaking his head at Skyler.

"Aaron!" Kate called, hurrying out from the crowd. "Get away from him!"

Aaron stood where he was.

"Aaron!" Chris called sharply. "Come here!"

Aaron in response took two steps closer to Kyran.

"Move, Adams," Skyler drawled, still holding Kyran at gunpoint. "I have no qualms about shooting you as well."

Chris and Kate both hurried forward to physically drag Aaron away from Kyran's side but Aaron halted them with a shout.

"No!" He turned back to the crowd, seeking out Ella, Zhi-Jiya and the rest of the Hunters. "What are you doing?" he asked. "You're listening to *him*?" He pointed at Skyler. "He's always hated Kyran. How can you believe him?"

"They didn't have to," Skyler smirked. "They saw proof."

"Proof?" Aaron scowled. "And what's that?"

"Why don't you ask the Scorcher himself?" Skyler said, gesturing to Kyran with his gun. "He's the one who came up with the brilliant plan." He chuckled as he took a step closer. "It's life's little ironies that make you laugh sometimes, no?" he asked. "I bet when you made that off-hand comment about forcing memories from demons, you didn't think it could actually be done, did you?"

The lines on Kyran's brow eased a little, as if he finally understood. Aaron remembered that day – they'd been at the table having breakfast when Kyran had dropped heavy hints about how to access flesh memories, by suggesting they take memories from demons.

"What does that have to do with anything?" Aaron spat.

"It has everything to do with it." Skyler grinned, turning back to Kyran. "That assignment you were supposed to be a part of today? That was to pick up the first successful memory snatch done on a demon." He chuckled as he shook his head. "You missed the one assignment that could have kept your cover."

Kyran didn't say anything. He stood where he was, listening to Skyler. Aaron, however, was fast losing it.

"What are you *talking* about?" he yelled.

"Proof," Skyler said. "I'm talking about proof, Adams, from a vamage named Don Kamara." He turned to look at Kyran. "Know him, Scorcher? He's the one Machado keeps by his side. Well, *used* to, anyway."

"So a vamage told you crap and you bought it?" Aaron asked. "He's obviously trying to turn the mages against each other. Didn't it occur to you that he might be lying?"

"And has it occurred to you, Adams," Skyler started, "that the entire time you've stood here fighting Kyran's corner, he's not said a word in his defence?"

Aaron stilled.

That's when the low chuckle started behind him. Slowly, Aaron turned to see Kyran laughing. His green eyes were bright with amusement. His demeanour had changed, going from angry to relaxed. He shook his head before looking up, locking his gaze with Skyler. Kyran cocked his head to the side and grinned.

"I've got to say, you sure took your sweet time putting it together," he said. "I've been here for how long? A year now? And you still needed a *demon* to help you figure it out."

It was as if the ground had been snatched from under Aaron's feet. "Kyran?" he choked.

Kyran looked over at him and smiled. "Sorry, Aaron," he said. "I hate admitting Skyler's right, but," he shrugged, "what can you do? When it's the truth, it's the truth."

From the folds of the crowd, Rose staggered out, staring wide-eyed at Kyran. But Kyran didn't look at her. His fierce green-eyed gaze was sweeping through the crowd of armed Hunters. "You can lower your weapons. I'm not going to attack you," he said. "I mean, if I wanted to kill any of you, I could have at any point this last year. It would only have been too easy." He smirked. "But you've been so entertaining, I couldn't bring myself to end any of you. Watching you bumbling idiots put together a profile of the Scorcher, only to get it *completely* wrong, was particularly amusing." His gaze darted to Scott and he grinned at him. "The best detail to botch up? *The Scorcher can't be older than fifteen.*" He laughed loudly. "Really, Scott? You thought I was only fifteen?"

Scott didn't say anything. The look of betrayal on his face was heartbreaking.

"How did you get in here?" Ella asked the question, her words barely making it past her clenched teeth. "The Gate blocks all vamages."

Kyran held out both arms. "Who says I'm a vamage?" he asked. "Or maybe the Gate didn't refuse me entry because I'm a...What did you say it was, Scott? A true-born vamage?" He shrugged. "Or maybe I'm just a mage. Who knows?"

Scott didn't speak but gestured to the Hunters, who moved to surround Kyran.

Kyran didn't fight them. He simply held up his hands while Zhi-Jiya, Omar and Julian stripped him of his familiars. Kyran seemed not to mind. He continued to smirk and hold Skyler's gaze the entire time. Ella handed Julian a pair of manacles – thick silver bracelets with dark engravings etched along them. Julian took them and pulled Kyran's hands behind him, locking them in place. Kyran still wasn't fazed.

"To think," Kyran spoke only to Skyler, "you owe this victory to a demon."

"You're right," Skyler said, pulling back his gun. "I do owe this to Kamara. Without his memories we'd probably never know who you were." He started a slow walk towards Kyran. "There was one memory I saw, a partial one, but it was by far the most interesting." He walked closer. "It looked like a recent attack. It was in the dead of the night. Kamara and filth like him were in a house with two bodies on the floor." Kyran's grin started to fall as a slow smile started on Skyler. "Their victims were human, a man and a woman," Skyler continued. "Outside, the sound of an attack was getting louder while you stood with the dying humans at your feet." He came to stand right before Kyran, smirking at his growing discomfort. Skyler turned his head to look directly at Rose before turning back to Kyran. "She has her mother's eyes, doesn't she, Scorcher?"

It was as if someone had poured ice-cold water over Aaron. His entire body seized up in shocked horror.

"Kyran?" Rose's voice echoed in the street. She took a step forward, staring at Kyran with disbelief. "Why...why aren't you saying anything?"

Kyran remained silent. His arrogance from moments before had vanished. His mouth thinned, eyes clouded before he dropped his gaze.

"Kyran?" Rose called, a little louder now. She hurried over to him, passing the Hunters, who let her through at Skyler's command. "Say something. Tell him he's lying!"

"He can't," Skyler said, "He can't deny it. When it's the truth, it's the truth." he repeated Kyran's words.

Kyran looked up at him with a glare, but still didn't speak.

Rose's breath was beginning to quicken. "No." She shook her head. "No, Kyran, no." Her voice cracked as she reached out to touch his chest, her hands trembling. " You...you weren't there."

"Oh, but he was," Skyler said. "Not only was he there when your parents were murdered, he didn't do a thing to stop the vamages – who obey his every command."

"Shut up!" Kyran snarled, and for the first time he struggled in the Hunters' hold, trying to get free.

"Kyran?" Rose called to him, halting him instantly. "When...when they were...attacking my parents," her voice had dropped to a pained whisper, her eyes brimming with tears, "were you there?"

"Rose." Kyran heaved out her name, like it was the most difficult thing, as he looked over at her.

Rose stared into his eyes and the first tear rolled down her cheek. "Kyran," she whispered. "Tell me. Were you there?"

There was a strained pause before Kyran finally answered, "Yes."

Rose pulled back, staring at him in abject horror.

"It's not what you think, Rose," Kyran started.

"Yeah, Rose, listen to him," Skyler said. "He's only been lying to you since he met you."

Kyran swore at him, fighting to get free. Skyler drew his gun once more, aiming another shot at Kyran's chest, this time at point blank range.

"Enough!" a booming voice commanded and everyone fell still. All eyes turned to Neriah, who stood at the side glaring at Kyran and Skyler. "Take him away," he instructed, and at once the Hunters began pulling and dragging a resisting Kyran.

"Rose! Rose, listen to me!" Kyran yelled, struggling wildly. "It's not what you think! There was nothing I could do! Rose! Rose!"

His shouts grew fainter as the Hunters forced him away. Rose stood where she was, watching him go with tears sliding down her face.

***

The street was slowly emptying. Neriah, Ella and Skyler had left with Scott, heading to the Hub. Chris had followed after them. Kate and Drake had gone into the Stove with Mary. Sam had taken Rose into the cottage but Aaron remained outside with a handful of Hunters. His mind was on Kyran and the events that unfolded over an hour ago. No matter what he had heard, even from Kyran himself, Aaron didn't believe it. It wasn't possible. *Kyran* couldn't be the Scorcher.

"What'd you think Neriah'll do to him?" Ryan asked morosely, seated a few chairs down.

"Execution, most likely," Zhi-Jiya replied in a quiet, broken voice.

That snapped Aaron out of his thoughts. He looked over at her. "What?"

Zhi-Jiya glanced to him, her eyes void of their usual sparkle. "It's what the plan was," she said. "Catch the Scorcher and execute him."

Aaron felt his body numb with terror. "No," he gasped, shaking his head. "You can't do that."

A few heads turned his way. Zhi-Jiya frowned at him. "He's the Scorcher," she repeated.

"So what?" Aaron said, quickly. "You just gonna kill him?"

"Aaron," Alan called to him, shaking his head. "Don't– "

"No," Aaron cut him off. "You can't kill Kyran, even if he's the Scorcher. What about all the other things he did?" Aaron asked. "He jumped into a collapsing Q-Zone to save my life. He saved Rose by doing that transfer–"

"He also stood back and let his vamages kill her parents," Zhi-Jiya interrupted.

Aaron stopped, his words dying on his tongue. Fighting past the pain, he forced himself to speak, refusing to give up. "It doesn't make sense," he said. "Why would Kyran stay in Salvador for a year, helping all of you if he's the enemy? Why would he help you fight against the vamages?" he asked. "Kyran was there when the Q-Zone was set up in my street. If he's the Scorcher, why did he kill his own vamages?"

"He didn't have a choice," Ryan said. "He had to keep his cover."

"I remember Kyran fighting to stop that Q-Zone hunt from happening," Omar said. "He made it look like he cared for Sam and Rose's safety, but now we know the real reason."

"He disappeared every full moon," Julian said. "He probably went back to Hadrian those nights, to give him monthly updates."

"And set up the attacks that happened while he was in Salvador," Omar added. "He made damn sure he was around us when the attacks happened, so we couldn't – even in our wildest theories – think he was the Scorcher."

"He pretended to be our friend," Ryan said, his eyes blazing with the anger of betrayal. "He came to all the hunts with us, killed demons by our side and sat around the table, laughing with us." His hands curled into fists. "Laughing *at* us," he corrected.

"He's smart, you gotta give him that," Omar said. "He was a part of every trip made to the Pecosas. If they really did know who the Scorcher was, like Scott suspected, there was no way they would open their mouths with the Scorcher standing right there."

Zhi-Jiya watched Aaron closely before putting her hand over his, startling him. "You're in denial," she said. "I can see it in your eyes." She paused for a moment before meeting his gaze. "You need to see what we've seen. Then you'll believe who Kyran really is."

Without giving Aaron a chance to object, Zhi-Jiya reached over the table and touched his temple. Aaron's surroundings melted and he found himself in a village that was burning to the ground. Everywhere Aaron looked, there were houses aflame, bright flickers of orange flames against the dark. Thick black smoke was billowing upwards, joining the night sky. The sound of screams and cries filled the air and Aaron shivered. He turned to see a cliff, on top of which stood two men. They were just standing there, watching the destruction and mayhem with ease. Aaron recognised one as Daniel Machado. His glittering blue eyes gave him away. The man next to him seemed familiar too but Aaron couldn't place him.

"What do you say, Scorcher?" Machado asked, turning his head to look at someone out with Aaron's sight. "Have they had enough?" If it wasn't to do with the fact that he was watching a memory, Aaron would've never heard him. There was no way Machado's voice could have carried down here.

A third person, dressed in a long red coat, appeared at the edge of the cliff, standing between the two vamages. Even at a distance, in the dark, there was no doubt who he was. The dark hair ruffled in the wind. Piercing green eyes seemed to glow, and that smirk – one Aaron had only ever seen playfully – held a sinister undertone. There was no denying it now – it was Kyran.

With a lazy step forward, Kyran jumped to the ground, landing gracefully on his feet. In mere moments, Machado and the other vamage – who had to be Kamara – appeared at Kyran's side. Aaron watched in numbed disbelief, as Kyran sauntered forward, smirking at the devastation around him. In his hand he held a sword, one unlike any Aaron had ever seen. It radiated power, every inch of it menacing with strange engravings running down the length of the blade.

When Kyran turned to face the vamages, Aaron saw the silver-studded inverted V on the back of his red coat.

"I think they can stand the heat a little longer," Kyran said. Turning, he looked straight through Aaron. "In fact, I think it needs to be turned up a notch."

He raised his sword and swung it. A wave of fire erupted outwards, rushing like a tidal wave, crashing down on the village. It passed through Aaron, but of course he didn't feel anything. Aaron still reacted though, stepping backwards, arms thrown up to protect himself. The screams ended abruptly and even through closed eyes, Aaron could tell the darkness was gone and daylight was back. When he opened his eyes, the memory had ended and he was back in Salvador, sitting at the table with a tearful Zhi-Jiya facing him.

***

"What are we going to do?" Scott asked, his eyes shadowed and brow furrowed, as he stood in front of the round table. "Where do we go from here?"

"It's obvious," Skyler drawled. He leant back, his elbows resting on the bench behind him. "Execution."

Chris looked at him with surprise. "No. You can't execute him."

"Did anyone ask you?" Skyler asked with a raised eyebrow. "You shouldn't even be a part of this discussion."

Chris ignored him, turning towards the one man that had the authority to sentence Kyran to death.

"Neriah, don't do this," Chris pleaded.

"Why not?" Skyler interrupted. "Isn't this what we've been working towards for the last two years now?" he asked, turning to Scott. "Find the Scorcher. We must get to the Scorcher. We get the Scorcher, we get rid of Hadrian's power." He sat up, holding out his arms. "We have the Scorcher. We've had him for almost a year." He snorted. "What do we do now? Let him live and run the risk of him escaping? Or do we put a personalised bullet between his eyes and end Hadrian's legacy?"

"Neriah, please," Chris continued. "Don't execute him. We need–"

"You need to stay out of this," Skyler said irritably.

"Shut up, Sky!" Ella bit out.

"What? You're taking his side?" Skyler asked, nodding at Chris.

"Yeah, I am," Ella replied. "Because I'm not eager to *kill!*"

"That's enough," Neriah said, commanding an instant hush. He turned around to face the gathered Elementals.

"Neriah," Chris started again only for Neriah to hold up a hand, silencing him.

"I don't need your opinion," he said coldly to Chris. "You may be an Elemental, but you've given up the right to stand council."

Skyler was practically glowing with glee. "Great." He smiled, getting to his feet. "I'll just get the bullet ready then."

"No one's executing anyone," Neriah said.

"But–?" Skyler stared at him in confusion. "Neriah, he's the *Scorcher.*"

"I'm aware of that," Neriah replied, "but until I find out why he spent a year here undercover, I'm not sentencing him to death."

"He was obviously sent by his father to spy on us," Skyler said.

"Yes, but that's not enough of an explanation," Neriah said. "Hadrian wouldn't deliver his son straight into our hands just to spy. He's got plenty of others for that job. Besides, the Scorcher's death will bring us nothing. Alive, he has memories that can be very useful in tracking Hadrian's whereabouts." He furrowed his brow, his eyes narrowed in thought. "Until I find out exactly what Hadrian's after, nothing will happen to his son." He looked straight at Skyler. "Is that understood?"

Skyler's hands curled into fists. "Yes, sir," he replied stiffly. Without another word, Skyler turned and walked out of the Hub.

Chris looked to Neriah and let out a relieved breath. "Thank you," he said. "I thought...I was certain you were going to agree with Skyler."

"I have my reasons to keep Kyran alive," Neriah replied, his tone still cold, "but I don't understand your desire to save the Scorcher from execution."

Chris bristled. "You know why," he said. "You don't need me to say it."

Neriah walked slowly over to Chris. "Ella shared the memory with you, did she not?" he asked.

Chris nodded. "Yes."

"Did you see the sword in his hand?"

Chris swallowed heavily. "Yes."

Neriah came to rest before him. "Has being away from this realm affected you so much that you can't recognise one of Aric's Blades?"

Chris dropped his gaze to the floor. "I know." His voice was almost a whisper. "I know but...but he looks—"

"He wields the Blade of Aedus!" Neriah said angrily. "Aedus, Chris. You know the *only* one who can do that? A direct descendant of Aedus! The legacy holder for Aedus! *Kyran* is the son of *Hadrian*!"

"I know that!" Chris argued. "I know what I saw but Neriah, Hadrian turned sixteen years ago. Kyran's obviously older than that. Kyran's a mage, he has to be. There's no way he could pass that Gate if he wasn't. So Hadrian had to have had him when he was still a mage. But we both know Hadrian didn't have any kids—"

"You know *nothing* about Hadrian," Neriah said. "None of us did."

"Neriah, just consider this," Chris started. "Maybe Alex—"

"No!" Neriah yelled, holding up a hand, silencing Chris. The violet eyes filled with unadulterated anger. "Don't Chris. Don't you *dare* say his name!"

Chris fell quiet.

"You walked away," Neriah accused. "You *left*. You left them, both of them! You don't have the right to speak their names!" He stood to his full height, towering over Chris. "Understand this and understand it well. Kyran may look like Alex, but it doesn't mean what you're thinking. That sword you saw in Kyran's hand, the one he used to *massacre* an entire village, proves he's Hadrian's heir." He held Chris's gaze. "Don't delude yourself with foolish fantasies. It's what got us into this mess in the first place."

***

The sun blazed overhead, the heat was insufferable, but Kyran couldn't do much about that. The iron cage he was locked in was heating up, the individual bars fast becoming too hot to bear. But the confinements were such that at least one wall was pressed into him, no matter how he positioned himself. His hands were still chained behind him, the metal cuffs taking in their own heat, driving an agonising burn into the flesh of his wrists. Kyran tried shifting again, pulling his back away from the scalding heat of the bars.

The sound of amused chuckling made Kyran look up, squinting into the sun's glare, blinking the sweat out of his eyes. He made out Skyler's grinning face.

"How's the Scorcher doing in this heat?" Skyler asked, coming to stand before him.

Kyran smirked up at him. "You do know my power is Fire, right?" he asked. "You think I can't handle a bit of the sun's heat?"

"You can say what you want but your condition begs to differ," Skyler said. He made a show of stepping back, examining Kyran's drenched form – hair flattened on his head, face and neck covered in beads of perspiration. "You don't look so good, mate."

Kyran snorted. "Trust me, I'll be fine," he said. "You should worry about yourself. By the time I'm finished with you, even your girlfriend won't be able to piece you back together again."

"Oh, yeah?" Skyler asked, leaning forward but not touching the blisteringly hot bars. "I've put the great and feared Scorcher on his ass many times." He cocked his head to one side. "I knew you were more hype than substance."

Kyran chuckled. "That's what you think," he said. "But consider something, Skyler. If I can pretend to be a Hunter, live in Salvador for a year, spend all my time with you lot, all to keep my cover – don't you think I could hold back from burying your pathetic, untalented ass?" He grinned as Skyler lost his smile. "That's right, Avira, I've been *letting* you win."

The taunt had Skyler's face tinge pink, his eyes a cold furious blue. With great effort, Skyler forced a smirk.

"If only you weren't wearing those inhibitors," he said. "I would've tested that theory of yours."

"You mean these?" Kyran pulled a hand from behind him, holding up the shackles.

Skyler's eyes went wide. Before he could do anything, Kyran pushed out his hands, sending the entire front side of the cage smashing into Skyler. The impact threw him to the ground. Kyran stepped out of the cage, tossing the cuffs aside.

Skyler gaped up at him in shock. "How did you do that?" he asked. "No one can take them off."

"I just did," Kyran replied.

Skyler jumped back onto his feet, his hands already twisting to form a powerful jolt, but Kyran beat him to it. With a swipe of his hand, Skyler went careening backwards, hitting the ground with a thump. The force of the power that hit Skyler left him completely winded. Skyler turned to Kyran in shock.

"You have no idea how badly I've wanted to do that," Kyran said, rubbing at his wrist before extending both hands to lift Skyler up and throw him back. "The hardest part of staying undercover," Kyran said as he moved forward, "was pretending to lose to you. It would have been just so easy to defeat you, but I had to hold back – until now."

His jolt picked Skyler up, and raised him high before smacking him down again. It was a move Kyran had done against Skyler plenty of times, but this time it had Kyran's full power behind it, leaving Skyler with broken bones. Groaning in pain, Skyler tried to move out of the way but Kyran's last sweeping gesture threw him across the grounds, like a discarded toy. Skyler rolled to a stop and fell still.

Kyran smirked at the prone form before walking away.

***

"When should we transfer him?" Scott asked.

"As soon as possible," Neriah replied. "The sooner I have him out of Salvador, the better."

"If you permit it," Chris said, after a strained pause, "I'd like to join you."

Neriah looked over at him, staring at him for a long moment. "I only allow those I trust to accompany me," he replied. "And I don't trust you any more."

A look of heartbreak crossed Chris's face. "Neriah–"

An almighty explosion shook the Hub, smashing each and every window. Shards of glass rained down on the four mages crowded around the table. By the time Scott, Chris and Ella pulled their hands away from their heads and looked up, Neriah was already at the door, throwing it open. The other three rushed after him. Stepping outside the Hub, they saw the culprit.

Kyran was standing in the middle of the grounds, his hands tucked into his pockets. "You know what they say, Neriah," he called. "Those who live in glass houses...should really move into better buildings."

Neriah walked down the steps, his face taut with anger. "How did you get out?"

Kyran smirked. "You can't hold fire in cages."

"If you got out, why didn't you run?" Neriah asked, making his slow way towards him. Ella followed after him, and so did Chris, but Scott was inching backwards into the Hub.

"What? Leave? Just like that?" Kyran chuckled, shaking his head. "That's rather rude, Neriah. I had to say a proper goodbye."

"Such manners," Neriah said. "Who'd have thought?" He came to a stop, keeping his distance from the boy. "But I'm curious," he said. "You got out of the inhibitors, proving you're in fact not a mage. You can't be a vamage since the Gate permitted you entry." His gaze narrowed. "What are you?"

Kyran held out his arms. "I'm the Scorcher," he said with great pride. "Maybe I'm a mage, maybe a vamage, or maybe I'm neither." He smiled. "There is one way to find out. All I have to do is kill a mage. If they survive, then I'm a mage. If they don't, well – that's just too bad."

He threw his hand up but the jolt of power didn't touch Neriah. It went behind him and surrounded Ella. In the blink of an eye, Ella was pulled from behind Neriah, straight into Kyran's arms. Before Ella could use the gun still in her hand, Kyran snapped her neck.

Ella's limp body fell to the ground with a thump.

35

FIGHTING FIRE

Neriah took one look at Ella's unmoving form at Kyran's feet and in the blink of an eye, he had tore his way across the grounds towards Kyran. Chris ran after him and Scott threw himself past the doorway of the Hub, racing inside to send the distress signal and gather his Hunters.

A powerful blast shook the ground, sending Chris flying backwards. Flames shot up from the ground, encircling Kyran and Neriah, keeping them inside a ring. Several rocks lifted from the ground and flew into the fire. Wincing, Chris stood up, staring at the ring of flames.

Neriah didn't seem to notice that he was trapped. His rage was such, all he could see was the boy before him. A twist of Neriah's hand had propelled a thousand sharp shards of ice at Kyran – to rip him apart. Kyran held up his hands and the shards melted before reaching him. Neriah stopped in his tracks, eyeing the boy – another Elemental who could match his power. Neriah cast a single glance to the flames surrounding them before turning to glare murderously at Kyran.

"Learnt that at your father's knee, boy?" he snarled.

"You can't deny my father's talent," Kyran answered. "He managed to train me, despite having his powers locked by you."

"Such a waste since you're going to die at my hands today," Neriah glowered.

Kyran chuckled. "Die? Yes," he agreed, "but not at your hands and definitely not today."

Kyran had to leap out of the way as Neriah threw icicles, sharper than swords, at him. He retaliated by sending out a stream of fire, which failed to hit the oldest Elemental as he deftly moved out of the way. They fought each other, their attacks escalating in ferocity with every jolt blocked and dodged.

***

A ball of light streaked through the sky, exploding into Aric's mark, directly above the table. The Hunters turned to look upwards, staring in surprise at the distress signal. Aaron's heart sunk – what had happened?

As one, the Hunters leapt to their feet, racing to the path behind the cottages to get to the Hub. Aaron ran after them. The Hunters had their guns in hand by the time they reached the clearing in front of the Hub. Aaron came to a shocked standstill, staring at the sight before him. A ring of fire encircled Kyran and Neriah, both locked in a furious battle. Behind them, Aaron spotted Scott running down the steps of the shattered Hub, racing to Chris's side – who was trying his best to extinguish the flames. But no matter what Chris did, the fire continued to burn. The Hunters ran to Chris and Scott's side. All of them tried to fight the fire, but nothing worked.

"Why can't we get past this thing?" Zhi-Jiya cried.

"Look!" Julian pointed at something in the fire.

It was a stone lying in the flames. A little distance away there was another stone and further away another one, and another and another. The Hunters looked around and saw that the entire ring of fire was mapped out with rocks – the same ones used for the fights in the ring.

Realisation dawned on Aaron. Kyran had used the rocks to safeguard his fire. Nothing could get past the flames now.

Scott hurried to the front and raised a hand. Aaron remembered once seeing Scott lift the rocks that Skyler had put down. Being the Controller, it seemed Scott had the power to lift the rocks once another had placed them down. Scott pulled his hand up but the rocks remained in place.

"What–?" Scott raised both hands, but nothing happened. "What's going on?" he cried. "I can't lift them." He looked at Kyran with wide, fearful eyes. "How's he doing this?"

Aaron looked at Kyran too, watching as he ducked and dived, throwing Neriah's jolts back at him. Neriah raised both arms and a wave of water towered behind him, seemingly formed from thin air. It grew until it was three times Neriah's height. With a swipe of his hand, Neriah sent the wave at Kyran. The water bypassed Neriah's form to crash over Kyran. For a blinding moment, Kyran disappeared from view, engulfed by the wave. Then a tremendous blast sent the water to all sides of the ring. It hit the wall of flames and Aaron thought the fire would finally be put out, but instead the water disappeared, leaving the fire burning. Kyran stood with his arms pushed out to either sides, dripping wet but that smirk was still on his face.

Neriah sent a stream of water which wrapped itself around Kyran, turning to ice as it raced up his body, attempting to encase him. Before it could reach his waist, Kyran closed his eyes and flames leapt up his body, evaporating the ice and water. Kyran straightened up, still aflame from head to foot. The flames disappeared, leaving Kyran untouched. Opening his poison-green eyes, Kyran smirked before pulling back a hand and sending out a long line of fire, which curled like a serpent before leaping at Neriah. The oldest Elemental pushed the attack aside by his own jolt of power. It hit the ground, singeing it.

It was then that Aaron and the others spotted the third person in the ring, lying on the ground. The long dark hair with streaks of electric blue gave away Ella's identity, as she lay face forward, unmoving as the battle happened around her.

"Ella?" Aaron called. "Ella!"

"No!" Zhi-Jiya gasped, her eyes impossibly wide. "Ella!" she cried.

"She's dead," Scott said in a tight voice. "Kyran killed her."

Aaron's gasp got caught in his chest, sparking a sharp pain in his heart.

Every eye, filled with tears of rage and pain, turned from Ella's body to Kyran, in time to see him dodge the five spear-shaped icicles Neriah was throwing at him. Kyran caught the sixth one and swung it around, turning with it and sliced it across Neriah's front. Neriah jumped back, looking down at the cut in his clothes. He looked back up and raised a hand, aiming another strike at Kyran when he suddenly stopped, his violet eyes widening slowly.

A triumphant smile spread across Kyran's face. He held up his hand, showing Neriah the chain with a strange purple gem dangling from it.

Neriah's hand shot to his own chest. He raised both hands, the jolt working its way up past his knuckles, but before it could leave his fingertips, Kyran had turned and waved a hand, making a doorway in the wall of fire.

"NO!" Neriah raged and the jolt came thundering out of his hand, rushing as a tidal wave towards Kyran.

Kyran leapt through the doorway and the wave crashed onto the walls of fire, but failed to put the flames out once again. The moment Kyran stepped out of the ring, the Hunters reacted, throwing everything from bullets, blades and jolts of power at him. Kyran raced out of the way, ducking and diving. A flick of his wrist and lines of fire erupted behind him, stopping those chasing him in their tracks. Neriah followed Kyran out of the ring, just in time to see Kyran run to the edge of the cliff and, without a moment's pause, throw himself over it.

Aaron and the Hunters ran over to the edge of the cliff, staring in shock at Kyran who was surely falling to his death. They watched as Kyran waved a hand and a familiar bike floated upwards from the ground. Still in mid-air, Kyran mounted his trusted Lexi moments before hitting the ground and taking off, zipping over the rocky ground.

Neriah reached them and jumped off the cliff too.

"Neriah!" Scott yelled after him.

As he fell, Neriah formed a pool of water that expanded outwards. It was deep enough to take his fall. The Hunters shared a look before rearing back and throwing themselves over the edge, following their leader. Aaron was about to do the same when his dad grabbed his arm.

"No!" he commanded.

Aaron pulled himself away and turned, running back along the path, behind a handful of Hunters. Chris watched him before leaping over the edge, after Neriah and the rest of the Hunters.

***

Kyran swerved to avoid the jutting rocks, racing his way forward, staying a step ahead of the thunderous wave that Neriah had sent after him. He turned a corner and found himself next to the orchard. Kyran sped his way through it as the water chased him, sweeping the baskets of fruit away.

Kyran drove out of the orchard and towards the lake. The wave spilt over the bank and flooded the lake, scattering the fruit to float on the surface. Kyran changed direction, heading for the Gate – the one and only exit from the city. His way was blocked by a few Hunters who had ran back through the forest and not over the edge of the cliff after him. They raised their guns and shot at Kyran, who was forced to manoeuvre out of the way by tilting the entire bike onto its side. As he dragged across the ground, Kyran sent a single jolt of fire at the Hunters, forcing them to cease attack and leap out of the way.

Kyran came to a stop and straightened his bike. He looked down both sides of the street, at the Hunters and mages who had gathered with weapons in hand. Even Mary and her kitchen staff had come out of the Stove. Drake and Kate stood to one side, staring at him. Kyran was completely surrounded. His gaze found Aaron, seeing him standing in front of Jason's cottage, staring at him with shock.

Kyran smirked and looked ahead, at the firmly closed Gate. Without warning, a great blast of fire erupted, lining both sides of the street. The mages cried out, leaping out of the way. Aaron ducked as the cottage behind him lit up in flames. Kyran bolted forward on his bike, racing towards the Gate, which was sliding slowly open.

The Gate suddenly stopped and started to ice over. Throwing a look behind him, Kyran saw Neriah had caught up with him. The leader of the the mages was ignoring the towering flames devastating the city, focusing on stopping him instead. Raising his hand, Kyran threw a ball of fire behind him to stop Neriah, and blew a cloud of fire at the doorway, melting the ice mere seconds before he drove through it.

Neriah and the Hunters followed Kyran out the Gate. Aaron picked himself up and raced after them, ignoring his mum's cry for him to stop. The Hunters were chasing Kyran along the brick road, firing bullet after bullet at him. Kyran ducked and dived, but he couldn't avoid the attack forever. Two bullets caught him, one in the shoulder blade and one in his side. They didn't slow him down. He kept going, turning into the forest to race towards the portal.

Kyran drove towards the glowing portal. He raised a hand upwards, just as he passed through it, and touched the tip of the inverted V. As soon as the end of Kyran's bike disappeared through the portal, the entire mark lit up in flames. It hovered in the air for a moment, a blazing version of Aric's mark, before it fell to the ground, reduced to nothing but ash. Neriah came to a stop before it. The Hunters gathered around him, panting and sweating, looking unnerved at what they had witnessed. Aaron came to stop next to them. Not a moment after, his mum caught up with him. They all stared at the remains of the portal with wide eyes.

"He's gone," Neriah whispered, his voice tinged with fear. "He's gone. He's taken it."

"Taken what?" Chris asked by his side. "That stone? The one you wore around your neck?"

Neriah shook his head. "That wasn't a stone," he said, turning to look at him. "That was the key," he breathed. "The key to unlock Hadrian's powers."

***

"Neriah, what happened?" Mary asked, running over to him the moment the Elemental walked back through the Gate with the Hunters following in after him.

Everyone had gathered around him, their eyes on Neriah. The fire Kyran had started had been put out, thankfully before too much damage was done. Aaron noted Sam standing at the fence, watching them with narrowed eyes.

Neriah raised his head and looked around at the people of Salvador. "The Scorcher got what he came for," he said, addressing them. His fingers traced the cut in his clothes. "He took the key that will unlock Hadrian's powers."

Fear spiked through the crowd. They turned to look at each other in panic.

"It seems the Scorcher's purpose to infiltrate Salvador was to acquire the key," Neriah continued. "My frequent visits to Salvador made it the perfect place to wait for me." He closed his eyes, shaking his head in self-recrimination. "How he came to learn about the key, I don't know," Neriah continued, "but the time is not to solve puzzles, but to act."

Scott stepped forward. "What do you need us to do?" he asked.

Neriah took a weary step towards him and reached out to pat his shoulder. "Alert the rest," he said. "It's time to gather our forces. Get every Hunter here. Pull the Lurkers together. We need to be prepared."

"Prepared for what?" Aaron couldn't stop himself from asking.

Neriah turned to him, his violet eyes darkening. "For Hadrian's return."

Look out for Book Two, *Playing With Fire*, in the Power of Four Series by SF Mazhar

Printed in Great Britain
by Amazon.co.uk, Ltd.,
Marston Gate.